The Working Men Series

The Firefighter
The Cop
The Paramedic

RAMONA GRAY

Published by
EK Publishing Inc.

ISBN-13: 978-1-988826-86-8

This book is a work of fiction and any resemblance to persons, living or dead, or places, events or locales is purely coincidental. The characters are productions of the author's imagination and used fictitiously.

Adult Reading Material

Cover Art by
The Final Wrap

Edited by
L. Nunn Editing

The Firefighter
(Book Seven)

Ramona Gray

Chapter One

Mia

"Maybe we should talk about what happened."

"Nope. No way. Not gonna happen." I shook my head emphatically to really hammer home my refusal. "You promised me, Matt."

"I know, but," Matt gave me an uneasy look, "it's starting to affect our working relationship."

"It isn't," I said. "You only think it is because normally something like this *would* affect our working relationship. But it isn't, and it won't, and you promised you'd never bring it up. So, stop breaking that promise." I dusted the sandwich crumbs off my pants and held out my hand. "Give me your trash, I'll throw it away."

"I didn't know, Mia, I swear. I wasn't trying to lead you on or anything like that," Matt said quickly. "I feel terrible that you thought it was something more, and I know it's my fault for -"

"It isn't your fault," I said. "You didn't flirt with me any more than you flirt with other women. I took a chance and it didn't work out. No big deal."

"Mia -"

"Mattie, it's *fine*," I said.   "Please, you promised."

"If you want another partner -"

"I don't." I made myself look at him. "But if you do, I'll understand why."

"I don't," Matt said. "You're one of my best friends, Mia, and I don't want to be in this ambulance with anyone but you."

"Then we're good," I said. "I'll be right back."

I grabbed the trash, opened the door and hopped out of the ambulance. I took my time walking to the trash can, even though technically our lunch had ended five minutes ago. I needed the extra few minutes though. My shame was a living, pulsing thing inside of me and for about the hundredth time in the last month, I wished I could go back and change what I had done.

I couldn't though. I didn't have a time machine that could whisk me back a month and tell my past self to absolutely, under no circumstances, go to Matt's house wearing nothing under my coat but pasties, a barely-there thong, and a smile.

I tossed our lunch trash into the can and took another deep breath. It was what it was. I had taken a chance on love and got shot down. It happened, right? The ironic thing was – Mattie felt way worse than I did. I hated myself for doing that to him, but I also couldn't bring myself to have a conversation with him about it. It just brought back the deep humiliation from that night.

"Mia?" Matt's voice called out. "We got a

call."

Thankful for the distraction, I turned and jogged back to the ambulance.

❧ ❧

"You want Ranch dressing or Thousand Island?" Isabelle asked.

"Either is fine. Where's Knox tonight?"

Isabelle pulled the chicken out of the oven, lifted it out of the roasting pan, and set it on the cutting board. "He and my brother are doing some kind of guys night. Which means they're probably eating cheezies, drinking beer, and playing video games. Poor Luna. I invited her to come over here and hang out with us, but she has a bit of a cold and didn't want to pass it on."

As Isabelle grabbed the knife to carve up the chicken, I heard my cell phone buzz. I pulled it from my purse and said, "I'm happy for you, Isabelle."

She smiled at me over her shoulder. "I'm happy for me too. I know it's only been a couple of months since Knox and I got together, but man, I'm just happy. You know? And he is too... I can see it in him."

"The entire town can see it," I said with a grin. "You two are adorable together." I checked my message and quickly sent off a return message.

"Who ya textin' with?" Isabelle plopped down next to me and handed me the platter of chicken. "Help yourself. Max...no. Back to the living room, big guy."

The big mastiff cross who had suddenly shown up in the kitchen, snorted loudly before staring

4

longingly at the pile of chicken sitting on the table. He was big enough to just help himself, but instead he heaved a loud sigh before ambling back out of the kitchen.

"Thanks, Isabelle. This looks really good." I added some chicken to my plate and then poured a bit of dressing on my salad. "I was texting with Elijah."

Isabelle paused with a forkful of chicken. "You guys are friends now, huh?"

I shrugged. "Well, we always knew each other. You can't work as an EMT without getting to know the firefighters, you know? But the gym I joined is the same gym he goes to, so I see him there. He helped me out with the machines when I first started and gave me some tips on lifting with free weights. We usually act as spotters for each other if we're there at the same time."

My best friend was giving me a weird look and I said, "What? Why are you looking at me like that?"

"You sure that Elijah only wants to be friends with you?" She asked.

I nodded. "Yep, no doubt about it."

"Why do you say that?"

I laughed and waved my fork at her. "Girl, have you seen Elijah?"

"Of course I have."

"Well then, you know why. The man has the body of an ancient God. Do you know I once saw him bench press three hundred and seventy-five pounds? It was incredible, Isabelle. That guy is like, Superman strong. His muscles have muscles."

"I know what he looks like, Mia, but what does

5

that have to do with anything?" Isabelle asked.

"Uh, a guy like him would never go for a girl who looks like me," I said.

"Stop it. You look fantastic," Isabelle replied.

"I've been going to the gym for nearly two months and I've only lost ten pounds," I said. "Ten freaking pounds."

"One, you looked amazing before you started going to the gym, and two, it isn't always about weight loss. Weren't you just telling me the other day that your clothes fit better, you're stronger, and," Isabelle gave me a smug look, "you have more stamina than you did before. Right?"

"Yeah, I do. Still," I stared down at my muffin top and the way my thick thighs touched, "I'd be happier if I lost another twenty pounds or so."

"You don't have to lose twenty pounds to get Elijah Thomson."

I swallowed my bite of salad. "Why are you so insistent that I should be trying to get Elijah Thomson?"

Isabelle stabbed another piece of chicken with her fork. "I think he has a secret crush on you."

My mouth dropped open, and I stared at Isabelle before bursting into laughter. "No, no he doesn't."

"I don't know." Isabelle ate her piece of chicken. "Remember that night I got super drunk at Ren's Bar, before Knox and I started officially dating?"

"I remember," I said.

"I danced with Elijah that night, and he was checking you out the whole time we were on the dance floor. He was jealous that you were dancing with Matt."

I ate some more salad. "Nope, you're wrong."

Isabelle gave me an indignant look. "I'm not."

"You are. Isabelle, I love you, but you were completely hammered that night. You saw what you wanted to see. Trust me, Elijah isn't into me. We're just friends, nothing more."

"I think he -"

"We're just friends," I said firmly. "Believe me on this."

Isabelle rolled her eyes. "Maybe you only think that because you were wrong about Matt. Just because Matt only wants to be friends, doesn't mean that every guy in your life does."

"Oh God," I groaned, "why does this keep coming up today? First Matt and now you. Can we please not talk about the most humiliating moment of my life?"

"You and Matt talked about it today?" Isabelle dropped her fork, her enthusiasm for her chicken buried under her enthusiasm to hear all the dirty details. "Why the hell didn't you say something when you first got here?"

"Because we didn't talk about it," I said. "Matt *tried* to talk about it, and I shut him down. He promised me that night that we would never talk about it again, remember?"

"I still can't believe you went to his house wearing nothing but a thong."

"There were also pasties," I protested. "Besides, you told me to make a move, Isabelle!"

"Yeah, but I was picturing something a little less big," Isabelle said solemnly.

7

"Now you tell me."

"Well, if Matt didn't take one look at your mostly naked, smoking hot body and want to bang you right then and there, then he's obviously not the one for you. Your tits are a man's wet dream. Hell, even I fantasize about them sometimes," Isabelle said.

I laughed and rolled my eyes. "Thanks, I think? It's been so long since I've had sex that if you weren't with Knox, I might try and convince you that we should give it a go."

"Vibrator just ain't doin' it for you, huh?" Isabelle replied.

"Nope. But it's all I've got. That reminds me – do you have a couple of D batteries I can steal? Charlie's magic vibrations aren't so magical anymore."

"Oh God, now you've named your vibrator? We definitely need to get you laid, girl."

"Tell me about it."

Isabelle reached out and took my hand, squeezing it gently before letting go. "Seriously, though, honey. Do you think maybe you only see what you want to see when it comes to other guys because of what happened with Matt? I know what it's like to be secretly in love with someone, you know that I do, but -"

"I'm not in love with Matt anymore," I said.

Isabelle gave me a cautious look. "Do you really believe that, or are you just saying what you think I want to hear so I'll shut up?"

I gave her a faint smile. "I'm telling you the truth, and you know what? It makes me feel even worse."

"What do you mean?" Isabelle asked.

I sighed and set my fork down before taking a sip of wine. "I've spent the last two years in love with Matt. I finally work up the courage to tell him how I feel, he rejects me, and a month later, I'm not in love anymore."

"Well, that's a good thing, isn't it?" Isabelle said slowly. "It's torture to be in love with someone who doesn't love you back."

"Yeah, I know," I replied. "But what does it say about me that I can just fall in and out of love so quickly?"

"Well, you've always been very practical and level-headed." Isabelle picked up her fork again. "Maybe, it's just your survival mode kicking in. Your brain is telling your heart to knock it off, so you aren't miserable for the rest of your life. You know?"

"Maybe," I replied.

"Are you telling me though, that if Matt suddenly changed his mind, if he realized that he was in love with you, that you wouldn't go out with him?" Isabelle said.

I thought about it for a few minutes before shaking my head. "No, I wouldn't. The look on his face that night, Isabelle. It wasn't – it wasn't disgust, thank God, but...the dismay on his face and in his eyes..."

Another wave of humiliation rolled through me at the memory. "I'll never get that image out of my head. It was like I had hurt him – hurt our *friendship* – so badly." I gave Isabelle an earnest look. "Honestly, at this point, I'm just glad that we still have a friendship. I came stupidly close to ruining it. I think, I *hope,* that the reason I could stop loving him so quickly is not because I'm shallow and awful, but because deep down I know how important my friendship with Matt is. After you, he's my best friend. And I think, maybe, that being with Matt in a sexual way would end our friendship."

I sat back in my chair, staring at my half-eaten salad and chicken. After a few moments, Isabelle added more wine to our glasses before lifting hers up. "A toast to Mia. For being a damn fucking adult and knowing exactly who she is."

I smiled a little and clinked my glass against hers before taking a sip. "Not sure if that's completely true, but I'll take it."

"I think you might be wrong about Elijah though," Isabelle said.

"One more word about Elijah having a crush on me and I'll stab you in the thigh with my fork. I swear to God, Izzy."

Her nose wrinkled. "You know I hate being called Izzy."

"Yeah, well, stop trying to make Melijah a thing."

Isabelle laughed so hard that Max wandered back into the kitchen to stare at her. "Melijah?"

I grinned at her. "What? All the cool kids mash their names together."

"You would make a fun couple." Isabelle tossed Max a piece of chicken and he caught it with a quick snap of his jaws that belied his age.

"Just friends," I said. "Elijah could have any woman he wanted in this town. He's not gonna choose me."

"Could he, though?" Isabelle said. "I'm not trying to be mean, but Elijah isn't the best-looking dude in the town."

I frowned at her. "There's nothing wrong with the way Elijah looks."

"I'm not saying there is," Isabelle replied. "He's not the *Hunchback of Notre Dame* or anything, but if you look at him objectively, he might have an incredible body, but his face…"

"What about his face?" I said.

"If he were a woman, he'd be what guys call Butterface," Isabelle said bluntly. "You know, because the body is incredible, but her face…"

"I get it," I said irritably. "God, people are horrible. What exactly are they saying about Elijah?"

"I have no idea if anyone says anything. If they're smart, they won't," Isabelle replied. "He could crush them with one fist. You know, my brother might be bigger, but I think overall Elijah is stronger than Ash."

"He is," I said. "Elijah is, like, ridiculously strong. He spends so much time at the gym – it's insane."

"Explains the body, then," Isabelle said. "Again, he's not ugly, but he isn't handsome either so your belief that he could have any woman in town isn't exactly accurate. Plus, he's just as friggin quiet as Ash, so it's not like he's out there charmin' the ladies. Right?"

I shrugged. "He is pretty quiet. Anyway, it doesn't matter. Elijah is just like all the other guys in my life – only interested in friendship."

"Phillip wasn't like that," Isabelle said.

Now my appetite really did disappear, and I pushed my plate away before draining most of my wine in one big gulp. "Don't remind me."

"I'm sorry," Isabelle said.

"It's fine," I sighed. "I'm learning to accept that men either plant me firmly in the friend zone, or they put me on a damn pedestal and then dump me when I fail to live up to their expectations."

"Phillip's been your only serious steady boyfriend," Isabelle said gently. "Just because he did that doesn't mean that every guy will."

"Maybe," I said.

"What Phillip did wasn't fair, Mia," Isabelle said. "The friggin' Pope couldn't have lived up to his expectations."

"Maybe," I repeated. "Anyway, I don't want to talk about this anymore. Let's finish eating and then go for a walk before it gets too cold."

Chapter Two

Elijah

I ducked my head under the hot spray of water and let it beat down on my neck. Showering before going to the gym was stupid, but it hadn't stopped me from doing it. Not when I knew I was going to see her there. I couldn't do much about the way I looked, but I'd be damned if I showed up smelling like a rank gorilla.

I closed my eyes, knowing it was dangerous to picture her beautiful face and her gorgeous curvy body, but I couldn't help it. As steam filled my small bathroom, I thought about Mia's mouth, that full bottom lip and the way she ran her tongue over it when she was really concentrating.

My dick was hardening, and I groaned and tried to think of something other than the way Mia's ass looked when she was doing her squats. Fuck, the flex of her thighs and ass was mesmerizing. When we were at the gym, I couldn't even glance her way when she was doing them. Mia and everyone else in the gym seeing my shorts tenting would be the humiliation to end all humiliations.

Just watching her at the gym was becoming a turn on. In the last two weeks, she'd started jogging on the treadmill, and the way her tits bounced was gonna fucking kill me. Could a man die from blue balls? From a build-up of too much cum? If I didn't stop going to the gym when Mia was there, I was gonna find out.

I couldn't stop though. The last two months had been some of the happiest of my life. I was friends with Mia. Friends with the woman I'd been in love with for over a year. I'd never even thought she'd talk to me, let alone be my friend.

I thought about her laugh, about the low sexy sound of her voice, and my dick throbbed anew. Without thinking, I reached down and gripped my cock, stroking it roughly as I braced one forearm against the slick tile.

I pictured Mia's mouth again, pictured kissing it, imagined Mia kissing down my chest and stomach, her low laugh as she kissed each hip bone, teasing me, making me beg for her mouth.

I rubbed harder and faster. My balls were tightening, and I was so close. Maybe Mia would blow me in the shower, or maybe she'd let me fuck her in the shower, let me shove my aching dick into her tight pussy until that maddening need for her was finally eased.

I rubbed my thumb over the tip of my cock, gasping Mia's name as my hips pumped back and forth. Maybe she'd let me fuck her on her hands and knees, let me cup those amazing tits of hers as I fucked her until she was begging me for release. Until she came all over my cock, screaming my name.

I arched my back, my hand tightening around the base of my cock. One more stroke was all I needed to –

Dirty boy! Sinner! Fornicator!

My hand clamped around my dick hard enough to hurt, and I released it with a hoarse shout of pain, my urge to cum disappearing immediately.

On your knees, dirty boy! You will pray for your sins to be forgiven. Pray to be relieved of the burden of your filthy, dirty mind! Pray for forgiveness for your lustful, wicked thoughts! Dirty boy! Vile boy! Sick boy!

My gorge rose, and I could barely contain my urge to vomit as shame and – I hated to admit it – fear flooded through me. I ripped open the shower curtain, not caring that water sprayed onto the bathroom floor, and stared at the small room.

My heart was thumping along like an out of control bass, and adrenaline kept my dick ramrod stiff. Trying to cover it with one hand, I listened intently for any small sound, but the whoosh of blood in my ears and the sound of the shower made it difficult to hear anything.

I was just about to get out of the shower when common sense roared back in. I sagged back against the wet wall, my stiff muscles and dick both wilting.

"They're not here. They're not here and they'll never find you again," I said in a low voice.

My pulse still thudding, I stared at my limp dick

and tried not to feel disgust and shame about what I was doing. It was natural. It was normal. I wasn't a damn freak.

I repeated it to myself, but even just the thought of continuing made me sick to my stomach. I pulled the shower curtain back in place and reached for the soap. I had to stop doing this. I had to stop thinking about Mia as anything other than a friend.

Mia was beautiful and perfect, and a woman like her would never want a man who looked like me.

∾ ᰛ

"Elijah, I don't mind. I swear." Mia, her face flushed from her workout, wiped the hand towel across her forehead before draping it over her arm. "I'll just pick you up at the station tomorrow before work and drop you off. Did you take your car to Jack Williams' shop?"

I nodded and ignored my urge to check out her tits in her tight tank top. "Yeah. But I can ask one of the other guys at the station to -"

"I don't mind," she said again. "It's on my way to work anyway. But I usually stop for coffee for Matt and me, you okay with that?"

I nodded, trying not to let her see the way my jealousy reared its ugly head at just the mention of the guy she was in love with. "Yeah, that's fine."

"Okay, good. You're done at seven?"

I nodded again, and she smiled at me before dabbing at the sweat on her upper chest.

Do not get an erection. Do not get an erection.

"Perfect. I'll be there by seven-thirty at the latest."

"Thanks, Mia. I appreciate it."

"Anytime," she said. "Hey, would you mind spotting me? I want to try and -"

"Elijah? Dude! I didn't know you went to this gym!"

I gave the man who'd joined us a cursory grunt. "Yeah."

"Cool, cool." He looked Mia up and down, and I was one hundred percent not okay with the way his gaze lingered on her crotch and then her tits. "Hey, how are ya?"

"Good," Mia said.

There was a moment of silence and both of them looked at me expectantly. I wanted to pick up Mia and carry her away. Instead, I said, "Mia this is Buck. He's new at the station. Buck, this is Mia. She's an EMT."

"Nice to meet ya, Mia," Buck gave her *that* grin. The grin that said - yeah, I'm a fucking stud, and you and I both know it.

"You as well," Mia said politely.

"You need some help with lifting?" Buck said.

He ignored my furious glare and gave Mia an idiotic wink. "I couldn't help but overhear you."

Mia shook her head. "I'm good. Elijah will help me. Right?"

I nodded, feeling my own smug sense of satisfaction even though Mia didn't belong to me and never would. "Yeah."

"Hey, that's cool. That's cool." Buck gave me another shit-eating grin, this one more along the lines of – I'll stop hitting on your woman now.

Mia wasn't mine, but I nodded to Buck like she

was, before turning to Mia. "Ready?"

"I am. Nice to meet you, Buck," Mia said.

"You too, Mia. See you at the station, Elijah," Buck said.

"See you." Keeping my gaze on the back of Mia's head and not on her amazing ass, I followed her toward the weights.

જ્જ જ્જ

"Mia, are you sure it's okay?" I repeated.

"I'm positive. Nana loves it when I bring my friends over," Mia said with a grin. "Says it reminds her of when I was a teenager."

I shifted in the seat, pulling at the seatbelt. Mia's car was on the smaller side and even though I was slouched down, the top of my head still brushed the ceiling of the car.

Mia gave me an apologetic look. "Sorry about it being so cramped."

"It's fine. Listen, maybe you should just drop me off and -"

"Don't be silly. Nana is a fantastic cook, and I know you're hungry. I heard your stomach growling at the gym. We'll have a bite to eat and a quick visit and then I'll drive you to the station for your shift. Okay?"

"Okay," I said. "Your nana raised you, is that right?"

"Yep. Me and my cousin Wyatt." Mia turned left and gave me a quick smile. "You remembered."

I remembered every single thing she said to me, but admitting it made me sound like a crazed stalker.

"Do you ever talk to your mom or dad?" I asked.

"Mom calls about once every year or so. It's always awkward. I mean, what do you say to the woman who abandoned you when you were two years old, you know?" Mia said. "My dad – I don't even know where he is and neither does Nana. I've asked Mom a few times, but she refuses to tell me anything about him."

She turned left again and slowed her speed a bit. "It used to bug me, but now…" she shrugged, "I'm kind of over it. In fact, I think I'm luckier than most. So many parents screw their kids up, but Nana was an awesome parent. Neither my mom nor dad would have done as good of a job as Nana did in raising me. What about your parents? You never really mention them. Are you close?"

Sweat immediately broke out on my back. "No," I said and then quickly changed the subject. "Why did your nana raise your cousin as well?"

"Wyatt's parents died in a car accident when he was four," Mia replied. "Drunk driver. I think it's partially why he decided to become a cop. Speaking of Wyatt…looks like he's gonna be eating with us."

She parked in the driveway behind the police cruiser and shut the car off. I unfolded my large body out of the front seat and cracked my neck as I waited for Mia to join me on the sidewalk.

"You look nervous," she said.

"I'm not."

She put her hand on my upper arm and squeezed it in a friendly way, but all of my nerve endings jolted to life like she'd grabbed my dick. Her hand was so soft. How would it feel on my dick? Would she know exactly the right way to touch me?

Buddy, you don't even know the right way to touch yourself. Why the fuck would she? Besides, she's not into you and even if she was, you wouldn't have a fucking clue what to do. Remember? You really wanna embarrass yourself like that in front of Mia?

The stiffy I was starting to sport just from Mia's innocent touch, vanished like a rabbit in a magician's hat.

"Elijah?" Mia was giving me a concerned look. "If you really don't want to have dinner with us, you don't have to. I'll take you to the station right now."

"No, I do," I said.

She stared at me doubtfully and I forced myself to smile at her. "Really, I want to have dinner with you and your family. Thank you for inviting me."

"Okay," she said.

I followed her up the sidewalk, trying desperately not to stare at her ass, to the small pale blue bungalow. Decorative shrubs were planted along the front of the house and there was a small wooden plaque on the front door engraved with the words 'Nana's Place' on it.

"Wyatt made that for Nana when he was fifteen," Mia said as she opened the door and stepped inside. I followed her in, and we removed our jackets before Mia hitched her thumb over her shoulder. "Kitchen's this way."

We followed the mouthwatering scent of beef

stew down the narrow hallway to the first door on the left. Feeling a little self-conscious, I stood in the doorway as Mia walked into the kitchen.

"Hey, Nana."

"Hi, sweetheart."

Mia's nana was standing at the counter with her back to us. She was short, plump and had long silver hair that hung to her waist. It was braided with a bright pink ribbon weaved throughout the braid. Mia tugged gently on the braid. "I like your hair today, Nana."

"Thanks, honey. Chelsea next door did it. She's such a sweet child. Only twelve years old and already knows what she wants to do. She's going to be a hair stylist to the stars, she says, and you know what? I believe her." Mia's grandmother turned and smiled at her. "The girl's got – oh, hi there."

I stepped into the kitchen, holding my hand out as Mia's grandmother looked me up and down.

"Nana, this is my friend, Elijah. He works -"

"At the fire station," Nana said. She shook my hand, her grip was dry and strong. "I've seen you around town. You're kind of hard to miss – just like that Stokes fellow. Oh, what's his first name again?"

"Asher," a voice said behind us.

I turned and nodded to Mia's cousin and sheriff's deputy, Wyatt Reynolds. "Hey, Wyatt."

"Hello, Elijah."

"You two know each other?" Mia's grandmother asked.

"In passing," Wyatt said. "We see each other at

work sometimes."

"I suppose you do," Nana said. "Is that how you and Mia met?"

"Yes, ma'am," I said.

"Oh please," Nana waved her hand in front of her face. "You may call me Nana or Martha, all right? I assume you're joining us for dinner?"

I glanced at Mia who grinned at me and said, "He is, Nana."

"If you have enough food," I said.

Nana laughed. "There's always enough food."

"I'm just going to use the bathroom quick," Mia said. "Elijah, have a seat."

I sat down as Mia left the kitchen. Wyatt sat next to me. He was wearing his uniform and he ran a hand through his dark hair as Nana placed a glass of lemonade in front of him.

"Elijah, what would you like to drink?"

"Water, please, ma'am. I mean, Martha."

"Such a polite young man," she said as she handed me a bottle of water. "I like you. How long have you and Mia been dating?"

My face went an embarrassing shade of red and I twisted the cap off the water bottle so hard that the cap cracked. "We're not dating. We're just, uh, friends. I gave her some tips about lifting and then we, uh, became friends."

Martha gave me a puzzled look and Wyatt said, "He means lifting weights, Nana."

"Oh." Nana glanced at Wyatt before smiling at me. "Well, isn't that nice."

I drank a few swallows of water, as Wyatt said, "I'll have the last of the renovations done on the guest house by the weekend."

"Oh, that's brilliant," Nana said happily. "You did the renovations so quickly, my sweet boy." She smiled at me. "I have a small guest house in the back that I've decided to rent out. If you know of anyone in town who's looking for a one bedroom, one bath, darling little cottage type place, send them my way."

"Um, okay," I said.

Mia returned and slid into the seat next to mine. "What did I miss?"

"We're just discussing the guest house, dear heart," Nana said. "It's almost ready to rent out, thanks to Wyatt's hard work."

"Nice work, Wyatt." Mia held her fist out and Wyatt bumped it before grabbing a bun from the basket on the table.

"Do you need help, Nana?" Mia asked.

"Maybe I'll get you to bring the pot to the table," Nana replied. "It's heavy and my arthritis is acting up this week."

"Sure." Mia bounced to her feet and I gave her jean-clad ass a quick glance before looking away.

Wyatt was giving me an inscrutable look, and my fucking face turned crimson again. I stared at the empty bowl in front of me, Wyatt's gaze boring into the top of my skull. I was stupidly grateful when Mia set the pot on the table and Martha patted Wyatt's shoulder. "Help yourself, sweet boy."

As Wyatt ladled some stew into his bowl, Mia leaned close and said in a low voice. "You okay?"

"Fine," I said as Mia's scent washed over me. Fuck, she always smelled so good. "The stew smells delicious."

Mia smiled at me and handed me a warm roll. "My nana's the best cook in town."

∂~ ∞

"Thank you again for inviting me to dinner," I said as Mia pulled into the station.

"You're welcome," she replied. "Thanks for coming."

Like a thirteen-year-old boy, my mind immediately went to sex. What would it be like to cum inside of Mia? I'd cut off my right hand to find out. I gave Mia a strained smile. "I had fun."

She studied me for a moment. "I'm really glad we're friends, Elijah."

My stomach twisted but I widened my smile. "I am too."

"Okay, well have a good shift. I'll see you tomorrow morning around seven-thirty, okay?"

"Sounds good. Bye, Mia."

"Bye, Elijah."

I waited until she drove away before walking into the station. Buck was washing down the truck while Peter, the oldest of our crew, was watching.

"You missed a spot on the bumper." Peter picked at his teeth as I joined him.

"Yeah, yeah," Buck said with a good-natured roll of his eyes. "I see it, old man."

"Kids these days," Peter said. "No fucking respect."

"Hey, my dad says the same shit," Buck said. His grin widened when Peter flipped him the bird.

"See what I mean?" Peter said to me.

I didn't reply. I was only a few years older than

Buck and when I first started at the station, Peter had said and did the exact same things to me that he was doing to Buck. It was a time-honored ritual at the station to rag on the new guy.

"Hey, Peter? Did you talk to your wife about switching shifts?" Charlie joined us and barely gave me a passing glance.

I resisted the urge to punch his face. Up until six months ago, Charlie hadn't been just a coworker. He'd been my best friend. I knew most people in town considered Matt to be my best friend, but while we were close, it was Charlie who I'd spent most of my time with.

"Yeah, I can switch." Peter found something interesting between his teeth, examined it briefly on the tip of his finger and then wiped his fingers on his pants.

"Thanks, man," Charlie said.

"Yeah, don't mention it."

Charlie left, and Peter gave me a scrutinizing look. "The fucking tension between you two is a real drag, you know that?"

"Yeah, well maybe he shouldn't have been such an asshole, then," I snapped.

"Hey," Peter gave me a commiserating look, "I'm not saying him spilling your condition to the whole crew wasn't a shit move, but -"

"It's not a condition," I snapped again.

Peter waved his hand at me, "Okay, okay, don't get snippy with me. Listen, if you want some help with your problem, the missus knows a few single ladies at work. She sure as hell would love to set you up with one of them. She says she's real sweet and won't care that you haven't -"

"You told Barb?" I glared at Peter. "Thanks a lot."

Peter just shrugged. "I tell her everything. Besides, she thought it was kind of sweet that a man your age hasn't -"

"I gotta go." I walked away before Peter could finish his sentence, my shame and anger buzzing in my gut like an enraged swarm of bees.

Chapter Three

Mia

I checked the entire bay area of the fire station before climbing the steps leading upstairs to the living quarters. I glanced at my watch. It was twenty to eight, and I was a little surprised that Elijah wasn't waiting for me outside of the station for his ride to the repair shop.

As I crested the stairs, I could hear the loud voices of the other firefighters and smell the tantalizing scent of cooking bacon. I scanned the dining area of the living quarters. There were four men sitting at the table, but no Elijah. They didn't notice me and were digging into the food in front of them as they talked.

I froze on the top step, my hand gripping the rail, when one of them said. "Hey, how long has Elijah been dating that Mia chick?"

I couldn't see his face, but I recognized the voice. He was the guy from the gym yesterday, Chuck or Buck or something like that.

The three other men fell dead silent, and Chuck/Buck said, "What?"

"Mia the paramedic?" One of the men said.

"I dunno. She's curvy, got dark hair and great tits," Chuck/Buck said. "She was at the gym with Elijah yesterday. Are they serious?"

Another man burst into laughter before nudging the man sitting beside him. "You think Elijah finally got laid?"

"Shit, no. Not by her, anyway. She's too fucking hot for his ugly mug."

My skin prickled, and I could feel anger seeping into me on Elijah's behalf. My hand clenched down on the railing when Chuck/Buck said, "Wait, so they're not dating?"

"No, Buck." The man dipped his toast into the pool of egg yolk on his plate. "They're not dating. They're just friends, work out at the gym together."

"You sure?" Buck asked. "He was giving me the eye like she belonged to him."

"Trust me," the man said, "they're not."

"Hey, we need to confirm that, Rudy," the other man said. "I had last month in the pool. Elijah and Mia have been hanging out for like a month now, and if Elijah's been laid, then I want to collect the fucking prize money.

"Enough, Frank." The third man, who'd been silent the entire time, finally looked up from his plate. "It ain't no one's business."

"Oh, c'mon, Peter. Everyone else knows, thanks to Charlie. Why shouldn't Buck know?"

"Know what?" Buck stopped eating and gave the guy named Frank a curious look.

"Elijah's a virgin," Frank said with a certain amount of glee.

My mouth dropped open and if I hadn't still been clinging to the handrail, I would have fallen down the damn stairs. Elijah was a…virgin?

"You're fucking kidding me," Buck said. He stared at each man before shaking his head. "No, you're pulling my fucking leg."

"We aren't," Frank said. "Elijah's never been laid. Never had his dick in a pussy."

"Frank, knock it off," Peter growled.

"What? It's true. Unless he's been playing hide the bishop with that Mia chick. In which case, I want my goddamn prize money."

"There's no way he's a virgin. He's gotta be what? Twenty-five?" Buck said.

"At least. I think he's actually closer to thirty," Rudy replied. "But he's a virgin."

"How do you know?" Buck asked. "Sure as shit, he isn't telling everyone."

"He and Charlie used to be best friends. Until Charlie got drunk at the summer barbeque and told all of us about Elijah being a virgin. I guess Elijah told him a few months before that. See," Rudy leaned forward and snagged the ketchup bottle off the table, "Elijah ain't the best-looking guy, right? I mean, he's jacked as shit now and could probably fucking lift a car if he had to, but apparently, he used to be a fat kid. So, he was fat *and* ugly. Plus, his parents were these ultra-strict religious freaks, and he went to an all-boys school when he was a teenager."

"Holy shit," Buck said. "It's the perfect non-fucking storm."

Both Rudy and Frank roared laughter, but nausea was swirling and dipping in my belly. Elijah and I hadn't been friends very long, but I'd noticed how close-mouthed he was about his childhood and his parents.

Frank nudged Rudy's arm. "You think Mia's giving Elijah a ride to pound-town every night? Because I could seriously use that prize money."

"What prize money?" Buck asked.

"Some of us," Frank glanced at Peter who had pushed his plate away and was giving all of them a disgusted look, "have a bet on when Elijah's cherry finally gets popped. I picked a date last month and if Mia has popped his cherry, then I fucking win."

"She hasn't," Rudy said. "Elijah would be a lot happier if he was getting pussy on the regular."

"He does seem pretty intense," Buck said.

"Wouldn't you be if you never had sex?" Rudy said. "Especially if he's hanging out with Mia and not fucking her. I was thinking about asking her out myself, just for a chance to titty-fuck her. You've seen her tits, right? If Elijah's hanging out with her and not banging her, then that guy's balls must be bluer than a fucking Smurf."

"Enough," Peter said. "Don't talk about the ladies that way, ya little punk. It's no goddamn wonder you're fucking single. Hell, I'm surprised you're not a damn virgin just like Elijah is."

I backed down a step. My face was hot, and my heart was racing like I'd just ran a marathon. I shouldn't have been listening to them talk about stuff that wasn't any of my business. I swung around, ready to bolt back down to the bay area. My breath wheezed out of me in a low groan when I saw Elijah standing on the steps below me.

From the look on his face, and the way his big hands were squeezing the handrails, he had heard everything. We stared silently at each other for a moment, before I whispered, "Elijah, I didn't -"

He turned and walked down the stairs without saying a word. Feeling sick to my stomach, I hurried after him, catching up to him just as he was walking out of the station.

"Elijah, wait!" I placed my hand on his arm, wincing when he tore his arm free. "Please, I'm sorry. Please, just wait, would you?"

He paused on the sidewalk, staring grimly at his feet.

"I didn't mean to eavesdrop. I was just looking for you and…"

I had no fucking idea what to say. Despite my shame at eavesdropping, I was intensely curious to know if what they had said was true. But asking Elijah if he actually was a virgin was a terrible idea.

"Elijah, please say something," I said.

"I gotta go get my car."

He started off down the sidewalk again and I scrambled after him. "My car's back there."

"I'll walk."

"What? No, you can't. Jack's repair shop is on the other side of town."

"It's fine."

"Elijah, please." I hesitated before resting my hand on his forearm. "Let me give you a ride."

His face went even redder and mine turned an

unholy shade of tomato as well. "I mean, let me drive you to the repair shop. Please."

He sighed and, without looking at me, said, "Yeah, fine."

I dropped my hand from his arm, inwardly sighing with relief when he trudged after me to my car. We climbed into the car and I drove away from the station. After only a few seconds of silence, I said, "I'm very sorry."

"You don't have to apologize." He refused to look at me.

"I do. I didn't mean to eavesdrop, but I thought you would be upstairs and I -"

"I was at my locker," he said.

"Oh." I stopped at a red light. The tension was thick, and I could almost feel the shame coming off of Elijah in slow waves. The light turned green and I stepped on the gas. We drove silently, me giving Elijah small glances every few minutes, Elijah staring studiously out the passenger window.

I wanted to say something, *needed* to say something, and my curiosity was almost overwhelming. As we turned onto the street leading to the repair shop, I said, "It doesn't matter, you know."

When he didn't reply, I hurried on, "It's kind of, uh, cool that you're still a virgin. Really. Lots of women would think it's sweet."

His face turned even redder and his hands clenched into fists as he shook his head.

Shit. Had the others been lying to Buck? It made sense. Men were always doing stupid hazing shit. Jesus, why had I even for a second believed them?

"They were lying," I said. "God, what dicks." I laughed nervously as I pulled into the repair shop. "Sorry for believing them. I should have known they -"

"It's not a lie," Elijah suddenly blurted.

I put the car into park and cleared my throat. "Oh. Well, that's cool."

He suddenly swung his head toward me, and I was nearly scorched by the blazing fury in his gaze. "That's cool? You think it's cool that I was so fat and ugly as a teenager that no girl would look twice at me? That my parents were religious nutjobs who taught me that sex is wrong and a sin? That I'm nothing more than a lonely freak who can't find a girl? That sounds cool to you, Mia?"

"No," I whispered.

He glared at me before yanking open the door handle. "Thanks for the ride to the shop."

He climbed out of the car and slammed the door so hard, my car rocked a little. I watched him walk stiff-legged and with his back ramrod straight, into the repair shop before rubbing at my forehead.

Well, fuck. I'd just ruined my friendship with Elijah.

ॐ ॐ

"Nope, I don't believe it." Isabelle paced back and forth in my small living room later that night. I had called her for an emergency best friend's meeting as soon as I was finished my work shift. Like a true friend, she had dropped everything and joined me at my apartment. "It's not possible in this day and age for a man his age to be a virgin. I

33

don't care how unattractive he is."

I glared at her from my spot on the couch. "Elijah is not unattractive! Besides, he told me himself that it was true, Isabelle. Elijah's a virgin."

Isabelle dropped into the armchair and took a sip of her wine. "That's messed up."

"Why?" I said. "Who cares if he's had sex or not? It doesn't change who he is."

"I know," Isabelle said. "I'm just really…surprised, you know? Also, I feel bad for the dude."

I sighed and took my own sip of wine. "I feel bad for him too. Not because he's a virgin, but because he obviously had a fucked-up childhood and it's really affected him."

"Well, you know what you have to do, right?" Isabelle said.

I gave her a blank look and she wiggled her eyebrows at me. "You gotta pop Elijah's cherry."

"Are you crazy? Did you not hear the part where I said I ruined my friendship with Elijah? The guy will never speak to me again."

"He will," Isabelle said. "Especially if you volunteer to participate in sexy times with him."

"We're *friends*, Isabelle. Or were," I said morosely.

"It's called friends with benefits, Mia," Isabelle said.

"I can't – I mean… that isn't something I do."

"Why not?" Isabelle asked. "Weren't you just telling me that you missed sex? Here's your chance to get some *and* help a friend out. He said he was lonely. He obviously wants a girlfriend, but he doesn't have a clue what to do in the bedroom department which, at his age, makes him look weird and awkward as shit. If you teach him about sex, it'll help him find a girlfriend. Right? You want to be a good friend to him, what better way than helping him get laid and find a girl?"

"Elijah doesn't want my help with sex or finding a girlfriend," I said.

"Oh, please. He's a virgin, and what guy wouldn't want no-strings-attached sex? Jesus, Mia, stop being so naïve."

I scowled at my best friend. "A guy has to be attracted to a woman to have sex with her."

"Elijah is attracted to you," Isabelle said. "That night at the bar -"

"You were drunk, Isabelle."

"I know what I saw," Isabelle replied stubbornly. "Listen, what do you have to lose by offering to help Elijah out with his problem?"

"His friendship?"

"You said you've already lost that," Isabelle pointed out.

"Fuck," I muttered.

Isabelle leaned forward. "Look, you obviously don't have to do it if you don't want to, but isn't there some small part of you that wants to show Elijah how fantastic sex can be? I mean, if I wasn't ridiculously in love with Knox, I would totally volunteer to teach Elijah how to sex."

"Isabelle!"

"What? I'm just being honest. It's a win-win situation, Mia. Elijah loses his v-card, and you get a huge ego boost when he worships you like the sex goddess you are."

I shook my head. "You're nuts. Besides, maybe the whole traumatic childhood isn't the only reason Elijah is still a virgin. Maybe he just wants to wait until he's married."

"Only one way to find out." Isabelle took another gulp of wine. "Like I said, there's no harm in asking."

I stared into my wine glass. I hated to admit it, but there was a part of me that thought Isabelle's suggestion made perfect sense. Elijah was my friend and if being a virgin wasn't a choice, I would be helping him out, right?

Not to mention getting your own itch scratched.

Yeah, there was that. I'd be lying if I tried to tell myself that every single thought about Elijah had been strictly PG. In fact, in the last couple of weeks, it had become increasingly more difficult to concentrate on lifting when I was at the gym with him. Watching him work out had started making me feel things that definitely weren't based in friendship. Elijah wasn't interested in me as more than a friend – if he was, wouldn't he have asked me out or made a move by now? – but I'd seen him checking out my tits occasionally.

Despite my protests to Isabelle, I know that he was at least somewhat attracted to me. And if he wasn't and rejected my suggestion of friends with benefits? Well, it wouldn't be the first time a guy turned me down, right? If I could survive Matt's rejection, I could survive Elijah's.

"Mia? What are you thinking over there?"

I sighed and lifted my head to stare at Isabelle.

"That I'm gonna volunteer to pop Elijah's cherry and help him find a girlfriend."

Isabelle let out a screech of excitement and raised her wine glass in salute. "That's my girl."

Chapter Four

Elijah

I knew it was Mia knocking on my door. From my living room window, I'd seen her car pull up on the street, watched her walk down the sidewalk to the front door. But like a little kid not allowed to open the door to strangers, I stood in the hallway, my heart beating too fast and my face burning hot as she knocked repeatedly.

What was she doing here? It had been three days since she'd discovered my biggest secret and after how I'd reacted, after what I'd said to her, I knew she would never speak to me again. She hadn't texted or called me once and I couldn't bring myself to text her, not even to apologize. What was the point? I believed Mia wanted nothing to do with me anymore and I couldn't blame her for it. I was an asshole, plain and simple.

Except, here she was, knocking on my door.

"Elijah?" Her low voice drifted through the closed door. "I know you're home. Please let me in. I want to apologize in person."

Apologize? What did she have to apologize for?

"Please," she said again and this time I could hear the break in her voice. She sounded near tears and my immediate horror at upsetting her, had me hauling ass down the hallway and yanking open the door.

She blinked at me. "Um, hi."

"Hey."

"Can I come in?"

I hesitated, and she gave me a pleading look, her dark brown eyes shiny with unshed tears. "Please, Elijah?"

I stepped back, and she walked through the door. We'd been friends long enough that Mia had been to my place before – although I'd never been to hers – and she took off her jacket and hung it in the closet before giving me a nervous look and walking toward the kitchen.

I trailed after her, my face still hot and my stomach as jumpy as a frog on meth. When we were in the kitchen, she gave me another nervous smile. "I'm sorry about Tuesday morning. I shouldn't have -"

"You don't have to say sorry," I said. "I'm the one who needs to apologize. I shouldn't have yelled or said what I did."

"You didn't yell," she replied.

"I did," I said.

She just shook her head and gave me a small smile. "Can we both just agree that we handled the situation badly and leave it at that?"

"Sure." My relief that Mia still wanted to be my friend was stupidly high. High enough to ignore the fact that she knew just how pathetic I was now. I tried to ignore the shame twining its way through my body. I couldn't do anything about the fact that she knew, and my shame wasn't enough to make me stop being friends with her. I loved her too much.

She was still giving me a weirdly nervous look and I said, "What's wrong?"

"Nothing," she said quickly. She crossed her arms over her torso, and I kept my gaze firmly on her face. I didn't need to look to know that her t-shirt was snug across those amazing tits. Didn't need to look to know that her jeans were tight, that her milky skin looked as soft and touchable as ever.

My cock was already starting to harden, and I immediately sat down at the table to hide my stiffy. Fuck, my control around her was getting worse and worse.

Yeah, well maybe if you fucking masturbated occasionally, it wouldn't be so difficult to keep your dick under control.

My face flushed hot again and I must have looked sick to my stomach because Mia sat down next to me and touched my forearm. "Elijah? Are you all right? You look like you're going to vomit."

"I'm fine," I muttered. "Just...I'm fine."

"Okay." She gave me a doubtful look before clearing her throat. "There was something else I wanted to talk to you about."

"What's that?" I asked, thankful for the

distraction.

She took a deep breath, another flicker of nervousness crossing her face, "I want to help you find a girlfriend."

My jaw dropped, and I stared silently at her as she chewed on her bottom lip before saying, "You're lonely, you said, right? Well, I can help you find someone."

Some of my shock was wearing off, and disappointment and anger were starting to sink in. Mia, the woman I was in love with, wanted to help me find a girlfriend. She didn't want to *be* my girlfriend, of course she fucking didn't, but she was willing to help the poor lonely virgin find a woman to bang.

"No," I said.

"Don't say no right away," she replied. "Just think about it and -"

"I said no, Mia," I snapped.

She scowled at me. "Don't be angry with me. I want to help you."

"I don't need your help," I said.

"You haven't had a girlfriend since you moved here. I can find you a nice girl, someone who doesn't care that…"

My face went bright red. "Doesn't care about what? That I'm a virgin? Yeah, because there's so many to choose from."

"My nana's church has a lot of nice women who -"

Fear skittered down my spine at just the mention of church. "No! I'm not interested in a woman who goes to church."

"Okay," she said. "Well, there are plenty of -"

"Are you insane?" I said. "Is that it, Mia?"

"Of course not," she said.

"You must be. It's the only explanation."

Her scowl got deeper. "Don't be a dick, Elijah. I'm not insane. I want to help my friend find a girlfriend. What's wrong with that?"

"What's wrong with that? You know I can't have a girlfriend, Mia!"

"Why not?"

"Look at me! I'm almost thirty years old and a virgin. I'm ugly, and I barely even know how to talk to women. Even if I could convince a woman to sleep with me, I wouldn't know what the hell to do with her! I've never even fucking kissed a woman in my entire goddamn life!"

I stopped, my breath roaring in and out of my lungs and my pulse thudding heavily. I waited dully for Mia to just get up and leave. It was the second time I'd lost my temper around her in less than a week. Instead of leaving, she reached out and squeezed my forearm.

"You're not ugly. Don't ever say that to me again or I'll punch you right in the dick," she said.

I gaped at her and she shrugged. "I'll do it, I swear. Do you want to test me on that?"

"No," I said.

"Wise idea." She squeezed my forearm again. "I'm going to ask you a question and I want you to answer me honestly, okay?"

I nodded, and she said, "Are you a virgin because you're waiting until you're married?"

"No," I said shortly.

"Okay. Do you know what a friends with benefits relationship is, Elijah?"

"Yeah." I had no idea where she was going with this.

"Well," she hesitated and took a deep breath, "we could have a friends with benefits relationship."

This time my mouth dropped open so far that I was certain you could drive a fucking train into it. She sat patiently as I processed her statement. After what felt like an eternity, I croaked, "What?"

"Your concerns about your lack of experience at your age are valid," she said. "I want to help you find a woman and it'll go much smoother and easier if you're not a virgin. We'll have sex, I'll teach you some stuff about pleasing a woman, and then we'll find you a girlfriend. What do you think?"

"I...what?"

She smiled at me and patted my arm. "I know it's a lot to think about and I'll give you some time to consider it. I know I don't have the perfect body or a super model face, but I know what I'm doing in the bedroom. I can help you get comfortable with sex, I promise. But if you're not interested, that's perfectly fine. I won't be insulted or get upset. Don't feel any pressure to say yes. You're my friend and I want to help you, but I definitely don't want you doing something you're not comfortable with. All right?"

I nodded dumbly, and she squeezed my arm for a third time before standing. "Okay, good. I'll, um, leave now and give you some time. Take as much time as you need. Just text me when you've made your decision."

She hesitated and then leaned down and pressed a light kiss against my cheek. "Bye, Elijah."

She started toward the doorway and I swallowed hard, the dry click in my throat sounding excruciatingly loud in my head. "Yes."

She turned to stare at me. "Yes?"

I nodded, my head screaming at me and my dick already rising with excitement. What the fuck was I doing?

We're getting laid, my inner voice crowed. *Finally!*

"You sure?" Mia asked.

I nodded again, not trusting myself to speak. My dick was a throbbing bar of steel, and I was extremely thankful the table hid my lap. I was going to sleep with Mia. I was going to be in Mia's pussy. There was an almost painful cramp of pleasure in my belly and for one heart stopping moment, I thought I'd cum right there at the kitchen table.

After a moment, I realized my dick was still steel-hard and while I probably had a fucking wet spot on my jeans from the precum streaming out of it, I hadn't actually cum.

I waited for Mia to ask me if I was sure again, but instead she smiled and said. "Good. Come over to my place tonight for dinner around six."

"Okay." My voice didn't sound anything close to normal. "Should I, uh, buy some condoms?"

My face went a fiery shade of red and I wanted to punch myself in the face for sounding so pathetic and eager. Of course I needed to buy condoms.

Why would I even ask that? Mia wouldn't let me fuck her bareback.

Mia shook her head. "I have some. But I'm on the pill and I can show you my medical records, so we can have sex without condoms if you want. Totally up to you."

"Without," I said.

She grinned a little. "Shocker. Okay, I'm gonna go. I'll see you at six, all right? Park in the visitor parking."

"All right."

I should have walked her to the door, but I couldn't. Not just because I was afraid I had a wet spot on my crotch, but because even sitting, my legs felt dismayingly weak and trembly.

"Bye, Elijah."

"Bye, Mia."

She walked out of the kitchen and I continued to stare blankly at the table after I heard the front door close. I was going to have sex with Mia. After tonight I would finally know what it was like to fuck a woman.

Sinner! Fornicator! Sex before marriage is a sin. You'll burn in hell, Elijah.

Their voices crowded into my head, making me feel guilty and sick at the same time. I shook my head and tried to shut them down before they became overwhelming. There was nothing wrong with having sex with the woman I loved. I wouldn't let them ruin this for me. They'd ruined almost everything, I wouldn't let them destroy my chance to have one perfect night with the perfect woman.

Perfect night? Dude, you'll be lucky if you don't embarrass yourself by cumming the second she touches you.

I winced, but my inner voice had a point. Maybe jacking off a couple of times before I went over there would be a good idea.

Dirty boy! Sinner!

Hating the power they still had over me, but not able to break it, I slumped in my chair and kept my hands away from my dick. I couldn't masturbate, not today. The occasional time I gave in to the temptation to touch myself, I spent days afterward feeling sick to my stomach and guilty as hell. If I masturbated now, it would ruin my night with Mia. I would just have to hope she understood when I came like a fucking firehose the minute she touched me.

Chapter Five

Elijah

I'd barely knocked on Mia's apartment door when she opened it and smiled at me. "Hi, Elijah. Come in."

I lurched forward, my throat already dry and my stomach in knots. Mia was wearing a green dress that hugged her tits and stopped about mid-thigh. I stared at her pale smooth legs, pictured them wrapped around my hips and lost the little ability I had left to think rationally.

My urge to just pick her up and carry her to her bedroom was so intense, I had to shove my hands into the pockets of my jeans to stop from doing it. God, I wanted her so bad. I had no idea how I'd even be able to eat dinner. All I could think about, the only thing I could think about since the moment Mia left my house earlier today, was fucking her.

"Come into the kitchen, okay?" Mia took my jacket and hung it on the coat rack. I took off my boots and followed her into the kitchen. It smelled good, but I barely noticed the delicious scent of food. I couldn't stop staring at the curve of Mia's neck and the smooth skin of her upper chest. Soon, I would be touching her skin. Touching her and kissing her and –

You don't know how to kiss, remember?

My inner voice had been going back and forth between elation and terror all goddamn day. One minute it was over the moon about having sex and the next it was listing all the ways I was gonna fuck it up. It was enough to drive a man crazy.

"Elijah?"

"Sorry, what?" I rasped.

"I asked if you got my email with my medical records?"

"Yeah. Yeah, I did."

"Okay. Good. Do you want something to drink?"

I shook my head. Even the thought of drinking made my stomach churn. Shit, I'd never get through dinner. I couldn't eat a fucking thing. How could I eat when I was this close to having exactly what I'd been dreaming of for the last two years?

Not exactly what you wanted, my inner voice was quick to remind me. *Mia isn't in love with you. Don't go thinking she is.*

"I know you're in love with Matt. Why are you doing this?" I suddenly blurted. I wanted to kick myself in the nuts, but I needed to know.

Mia gave me a startled look. "I'm not in love with Matt. Who said I was?"

"People talk," I said.

She sighed and shook her head. "Stupid small

48

town. I used to be in love with Matt, now I'm not."

"That isn't how love works," I said.

"I guess it does with me," she replied.

"I don't believe that."

She sighed again and my curiosity about the embarrassment on her face was answered when she said, "I told Matt how I felt, and he didn't feel the same way. That was over a month ago and I've moved on."

I didn't quite believe her, but I didn't push her on it. Maybe sleeping with me was her way of making Matt jealous. I should have hated myself for being so willing to sleep with a woman who was most likely in love with another man, but apparently my pride had taken a backseat to my lust. "So, why are you doing this?" I asked again.

"Well, you're my friend and I want to help you find someone and be happy. That's my main reason. But I'm not going to lie and say that's the only reason," Mia said.

My heart was pounding so loudly, I could barely hear Mia's soft voice. "What do you mean?"

"It's been a while since I've had sex and I miss it," she said.

I hated that my laugh was bitter. "Seriously? If you're looking for good sex, you're barking up the wrong tree, Mia. I don't know what I'm doing, remember?"

"I remember," she said. "But you're a smart guy and I'm a good teacher. You'll learn quickly."

"What if I don't?" I said. "I don't even know how to kiss for Christ sake. I kissed a girl once when I was in seventh grade."

"Wait, you said earlier that you'd never kissed a girl." Mia gave me a teasing grin. "Next you'll be confessing that you've done some heavy petting. Are you sure you're even a virgin, Mr. Thomson?"

"I'm sure," I muttered.

The smile fell from her face. "I'm sorry, Elijah. I was only teasing but I shouldn't have -"

"It's fine. I'm just...this feels weird."

"If you've changed your mind, you can tell me," Mia said earnestly. "You know that, right? In fact, if you change your mind at any point while we're in bed together, just say something and I'll stop right away."

"Jesus, it feels like I'm in an after-school special," I said.

She burst into laughter, and my anxiety eased enough for me to take my first deep breath since Mia had offered to teach me how to fuck.

"It kind of does." She giggled. "I'd suggest you give me a safe word, but with how tense you are, I'm afraid even thinking you need a safe word might make you run."

I gave her a half-smile before my gaze dropped to her tits again. Soon, I'd see what they looked like. She'd let me touch them and -

"Elijah?"

I looked up to see Mia smiling knowingly at me. I blushed immediately. "I'm sorry."

"Don't be sorry. I don't mind." She smiled again before pointing to one of the kitchen chairs. "Have a seat, okay?"

"Yeah, okay." I dropped into the chair, surreptitiously smelling my pits when Mia turned away to the oven. I had showered right before I came over, but I was so fucking nervous, I was getting sweaty as hell.

Mia opened the oven and brought out a roasting pan. She set it on the stove and lifted off the lid. The smell of roast beef intensified, but despite not eating at all today, I didn't feel a lick of hunger. How could I when I was about to be inside Mia? When I was about to see her pussy, feel her soft skin against mine?

"Okay, well the roast is done and so are the potatoes. I just need to make the gravy and steam the vegetables and we can eat. Sound good?"

"Yeah," I said, even though I knew I wouldn't be able to eat a thing.

Mia studied me for a moment before shutting off the oven and putting the lid back on the roasting pan. She moved the pot of potatoes to the back burner and stuck the vegetables back in the fridge before moving toward me. She held out her hand. "C'mon, Elijah."

"What – where are we going?"

"To my bedroom."

I peeled my tongue off the roof of my mouth and gave her a look ripe with panic. "Uh, what?"

She gave me a sweet smile. "At this moment, you want sex more than food. Don't you?"

"I, um…"

"Be honest, Elijah."

"Yes," I said. "I want sex more."

"Then let's go have sex. We can eat dinner after we're done."

"Are you sure? I don't mind waiting."

She arched her eyebrow at me. "I'm fairly confident that's a big fat lie. Come on, big guy."

She took my hand and tugged on it. Feeling numb and disconnected from my body, I followed her down the hallway to her bedroom. It was on the smaller side, but I barely noticed. I couldn't stop staring at her bed. Soon, I'd be on that bed with Mia.

"You okay?" She asked.

"Yeah."

"It's okay to be nervous. You know that, right?"

I nodded, and she squeezed my hand. "Still want to do this?"

"Yes." Even I could hear the excitement in my voice.

Mia smiled, a brief look of relief flickering across her face. "Good. Me too."

"Should I, uh, get undressed?" I asked.

"How about we start with teaching you to kiss?" Mia said.

I blushed furiously at my eagerness and nodded. "Right, yeah, okay. Sorry."

"Again, you don't have to be sorry. But," she gave me another sweet smile, "we have all night so don't worry about rushing anything."

I wanted to take my time, especially since I was pretty sure Mia wasn't interested in more than one night of teaching me how to fuck, so making the experience last as long as possible was my goddamn goal. Only, my throbbing cock had other plans and I was still one hundred percent certain I would go off like a bottle rocket, the second I was inside of

Mia's pussy.

"Come sit on the bed," Mia said.

I froze and stared wide-eyed at the bed as Mia made an encouraging sound and tugged on my hand. "C'mon, Elijah."

I followed her to the bed and sat down next to her when Mia patted the mattress. She moved closer, until her thigh was pressing against mine and her shoulder was touching my arm. My cock hardened but if she noticed the bulge in my jeans, she didn't say anything.

"So, the key to good kissing is starting off slow," she said. 'You don't want to be shoving your tongue into the woman's mouth immediately. Make sense?"

"Yes," I said.

"Good."

I jerked all over when her soft hand slid around my neck and she tugged lightly. "Time for your first lesson, Elijah."

I bent my head until my mouth was just above Mia's. When she pressed her mouth against mine, I made a low groan.

"Remember, soft and slow," she said as she pressed feather-light kisses against my mouth. "You try."

I kissed her gently, brushing my mouth across hers a few times before pulling back a little.

"Okay?" I said.

Her eyelids fluttered open and she smiled at me. "Perfect."

I dipped my head and kissed her again, twitching when her lips parted, and the tip of her tongue brushed across my mouth.

"Open your mouth," she breathed.

I parted my lips, groaning again when she sucked on my bottom lip. When her tongue slipped into my mouth, I leaned into her, I couldn't help it. She grabbed my arm and slid it around her waist. I held her tightly as she explored my mouth with her soft tongue.

She pulled back and gave my lower lip a light nip. "Your turn."

We kissed again and when I licked her bottom lip, she parted her mouth. My entire body on fire with need, I slid my tongue into her mouth. She let me taste and explore for a few seconds before she sucked on my tongue.

Our kissing turned hot and heavy, our tongues sliding in and out of each other's mouths as we both tasted and teased. Holy shit, I had no idea kissing could be like this. Had no concept of just how amazing it was to kiss the woman you loved.

My hips arched, and I made a loud moan of pleasure before pulling away. I was already short of breath and I studied Mia's swollen mouth as she rubbed the back of my neck with her soft hand.

"You okay?" She asked.

"Yeah, I – that was good."

"It was," she said. "You're a natural at kissing."

"Thank you."

She laughed and tugged on my hair. "You're welcome."

Before I could reply, she was nuzzling my neck and at the feel of her soft tongue licking my neck, I almost came in my goddamn pants again. My cock was a fucking rock against the stiff material of my jeans. When Mia ran her hand over my chest, I knew without a doubt that I wouldn't make it to the fucking.

Embarrassed beyond belief, I pulled away from her touch and gripped my knees with both hands.

"Elijah? What's wrong?" She asked before leaning against me. Her left breast pushed against my arm, and I groaned before trying to ease away. "Are we moving too fast?"

I shook my head and made myself say it. "No, but I don't think I'm gonna last. I'm sorry."

Thank fucking Christ, I didn't have to explain myself, nor did Mia even seem all that put out. Instead, she said, "That's all right. Why don't we make you cum right now and get it over with?"

I gave her a wry look and she blushed. "Oh God, that didn't come out right at all. What I meant is that − I feel like a good deal of your anxiety is stemming from your worry that you're gonna...you know... before we even have sex. Am I right?"

"Maybe," I said.

"Well then, let's make you cum right now. It'll take some of the pressure off you. In more ways than one." She grinned, and I had a moment to appreciate just how sweet she was being to me before she placed her hand on my thigh and I lost any and all ability to think properly.

"Fuck," I said as my pelvis jerked.

"Does that mean you like the idea?" She said.

"It's a really great idea," I said fervently.

She smiled again and leaned back. "Awesome. Undo your jeans."

My hands shaking, I unbuttoned and unzipped my jeans. My dick strained at the cotton material of my briefs and I was a little embarrassed at the prominent wet spot on the front of them.

"Pull them down." Now Mia's voice was a little shaky and it weirdly helped ease some of my embarrassment.

I shoved my jeans and briefs down my legs until they were below my knees. I meant to kick them off, to reach down and remove my socks, but the look on Mia's face made me still. "Mia? What's wrong?"

"Nothing's wrong." She was staring at my cock and more precum spilled out when she licked her lips. "You, um, you have a really nice dick."

"Oh, uh, thanks."

She was still staring at it and I was starting to feel a little weird. I'd never really given any thought to whether my dick looked normal or not, but now I was starting to second guess myself. Maybe there was something wrong with it.

"Mia? Please tell me what's wrong."

"I swear there isn't anything wrong," she said. She raised her gaze to mine and I was a bit puzzled by the apprehension in her gaze. "You're, just, uh, really big."

"Am I?"

She nodded. "Porn star big, buddy."

"I'm sorry?" It felt like a weird thing to say sorry for, but the look on Mia's face made me feel like I should be apologizing.

She smiled at me. "Oh, honey. *Never* apologize for the size of your dick."

The weird moment passed as quickly as it appeared when she gave me another smile and said, "You're just bigger than my previous lovers and I was having a teensy bit of anxiety about taking you, but it'll be fine. We'll just need to go slow, okay?"

"Okay."

"Good." She leaned close again and wrapped her hand around the back of my neck once more. "Kiss me again."

I kissed her, sliding my tongue into her mouth when she parted her lips. She was making soft little moans and sighs that a man could quickly become addicted to. I nibbled on her bottom lip and tentatively slid my arm around her waist again. I wanted to touch her tits, but I wasn't sure if that was being too bold or – oh holy fucking hell...

I tore my mouth from Mia's and sucked in a gasping gulp of oxygen. Mia had wrapped her long fingers around my dick, and I made another loud groan of pleasure, my hips jerking compulsively when she stroked me firmly.

"Mia, oh fuck, Mia!" My voice was a hoarse shout as she stroked me again.

Her other hand cupped the back of my skull and with surprising strength, she tugged my head down until our mouths met. She thrust her tongue into my mouth, muffling the sounds of my cries as she stroked my dick.

The feel of her soft hand, the way she rubbed me up and down without any tentativeness or hesitation made me delirious with pleasure. I cried out into her mouth again, my hips rocking back and forth like a piston as she stroked me harder and faster. When her thumb rubbed across the wide head, my orgasm rolled over me like a tsunami wave. Pleasure skated up and down my spine as cum shot out of my dick. I shuddered and moaned as she continued to pump me until every last bit of cum was wrung out of me.

She pulled her mouth away and watched my face intently as I fell back on the bed and moaned her name. She released my dick and rested her hand on my thigh, rubbing gently as I twitched and moaned and tried to breathe through the orgasm induced heart attack I was currently experiencing.

After a few minutes, I cracked open one eye and stared at Mia. She smiled at me. "Hi there."

"Hey," I rasped.

"You okay?"

"Fucking awesome."

She giggled and squeezed my leg. "Good, I'm glad."

I glanced down at myself, fresh embarrassment spilling through me at the amount of cum that was splattered across my thighs and lower abdomen. I pulled my shirt off but before I could use it to wipe myself clean, Mia plucked it from my hand and dropped it on the floor.

"Stay there, I'll get a towel."

She left the room and returned with a towel in her hand. I was still feeling embarrassed, but Mia wiped my legs and abdomen clean without any visible signs of disgust. When she gently wiped my cock with the towel, I inhaled sharply, and she gave me a little smile when my dick visibly hardened.

"Getting hard again already? Oh, honey, this is

gonna be so much fun…"

Chapter Six

Mia

Okay, so Isabelle was right. Teaching Elijah how to have sex made me feel like a damn sex goddess. From the moment he'd stepped into my apartment, the hunger and need in his gaze was more than apparent.

For a few seconds, I'd wondered if maybe Isabelle wasn't also right about his crush on me, until reality came crashing in. I'd offered to bang a guy who was nearly thirty and had never had sex, of course he was gonna look at me like I'd given him the key to the kingdom of heaven.

Still, I'd never felt more attractive or sexy than at this moment. Elijah's need for me was a drug I could quickly become addicted to.

Keep it together, Mia. You're doing this to help him find a woman, remember? Nothing more.

My inner voice was right, and I definitely needed to remember why exactly I was doing this. Elijah wanted me, but he wasn't in love with me or anything. And I could sugar coat this as much as I wanted, but there was a big part of me that offered to help solely because I wanted to get laid too.

Speaking of big...

I tossed the towel that I'd been using to clean Elijah's cock, to the floor and then tugged his jeans and briefs off his legs. I tossed them on the floor, then yanked off his socks and dropped them.

"Thank you," he said.

I smiled a little. God, he was so cute and polite. And now that I'd seen him naked... holy shit. I knew his body was incredible but seeing him naked brought on a whole new appreciation for how much he worked out.

I was certain that Elijah had no idea just how fantastic his body was and how many women at the gym probably drooled over him daily. He didn't seem to have an ounce of fat anywhere on his body, and one could almost believe that he'd been carved from stone rather than born like a mere mortal.

His entire body was made of granite-hard muscle and warm skin, and I was itching to lick that truly impressive v-line. Giving Elijah a blow job was high on my list of things to do to him, but I had a feeling the only thing he was really thinking about was sex. Once I'd deflowered him, then I could blow his mind with, well... a blow job.

But first, I wanted my own release. Kissing Elijah was a surprising turn on – I wasn't lying when I told him he was a natural at it – and the way he'd picked up so quickly on it was also a bit of a surprise. My concern that teaching such a big, strong man to be gentle was, so far anyway, a non-issue. Now, just thinking about Elijah kissing my breasts, sucking on my nipples, and his big hands touching my pussy made me soaking wet.

I turned around and smiled at him over my shoulder. "Can you unzip me?"

His cock – his gloriously large and amazingly thick cock – twitched again. He was already sporting a semi and another trickle of smugness went through me. He sat up on the bed and with a visible tremor in his hands, pulled down the zipper of my dress.

As I slid my dress down and let it pool on the floor, my usual trepidation about a man seeing me in my underwear reared its ugly head. I took a deep breath, straightened my shoulders, and spun around. I might have a round stomach and my thighs might touch, but I was still beautiful. I was still…

The thought died in my head as I studied Elijah's face. The look of pure delight and wonder on his face made me feel sexy and powerful. I was wearing a matching set of black bra and panties, and my own lust kicked up a notch when Elijah stared hungrily at my tits.

He was still sitting on the side of the bed and I stepped between his legs. He was so tall that even with him sitting and me standing, he was eye-level with my mouth. Not that he was looking at my mouth. He couldn't tear his gaze away from my chest, and my feelings of sexiness and power increased.

I reached behind and unclasped my bra, smiling teasingly at him. "I'll let you practice how to undo a bra later, all right?"

He nodded, his gaze still planted firmly on my chest. It was a little adorable the way he lost the ability to speak when seeing me half-naked.

My usual shyness had completely disappeared, and I let my bra slip off with a wiggle and dip of my shoulders. I dropped it on the floor with my dress and watched the muscle in Elijah's temple tick, tick, tick.

He was breathing rapidly and when I glanced down, his cock was fully hard again. Good lord, did I love me a man with a quick recovery time.

His hands were clenched into fists on his knees. Smiling a little, I said, "You can touch them, Elijah."

He didn't move. I wasn't sure if he was frozen to the spot with lust or fear, so I reached down and wrapped my hands around his fists. "Give me your hands, honey."

He uncurled his hands and I guided them to my breasts. He cupped them gently and reverently and while I appreciated his gentleness, he was acting like I was made of fragile glass. I put one finger under his chin and tipped his head up until he was staring at me. His dark blue eyes were stormy with lust and desire, and another muscle in his jaw had joined its brethren in ticking.

"I won't break, Elijah. Touch me."

His shy smile sent a weird trickle of tenderness through me. I studied his face for a moment, taking in the broad nose, heavy brow, and wide cheekbones. Maybe Isabelle was right, maybe Elijah wasn't the best-looking guy in town, but if she could see him now, she'd realize that he was far from unattractive.

"I don't want to hurt you," he said.

"You won't. Trust me." I rubbed his forearms and gave him an encouraging look. "If you do something I don't like, I'll tell you. Okay?"

"Yeah, okay."

His gaze dropped back to my breasts and when he gently squeezed them and then ran his thumbs over my nipples, I made an encouraging moan. He circled my nipples again, groaning under his breath when they hardened. When he tentatively plucked at my right nipple with his thumb and forefinger, I inhaled sharply, my back arching as pleasure arrowed from my breast straight to my pussy.

He gave me a worried look and I shook my head. "I liked it. Do it again."

He lightly pinched both my nipples at the same time. I moaned happily before sliding my hands into his hair and tugging his head toward my breasts. His warm breath washed over my nipples and when he kissed my right nipple and then my left, I made another encouraging moan.

He pressed a kiss between my breasts, both hands squeezing and kneading them lightly, before he kissed across my left breast to my nipple. When his hot mouth closed around the tip and sucked lightly, I cried out with pleasure. I squeezed his skull and arched my back, encouraging him to suck harder.

"Oh God," I moaned, "good, that's good, honey. Just like that."

He grinned up at me, the shyness replaced by an almost boyish confidence. He played and toyed with my tits, alternating between using his fingers and his mouth to tease and torment.

"Fuck, you're a really fast learner," I groaned.

"I like pleasing you," he said.

I smiled down at him as he kissed between my breasts again. His sweetness and his tenderness were a welcome change from my previous lovers. Whether it was just his personality or the fact that he'd never been with a woman, his vulnerability was achingly appealing to me.

His big hands were rubbing the front of my thighs as he kissed my breasts. I already knew he'd be too shy to touch my pussy without prompting, so I pushed lightly on his shoulders and stepped back. It was time to teach Elijah how to make me cum.

"Lie back on the bed, Elijah."

He did what I asked, lying on the right side of the bed. His cock was still rock hard and when I curled my fingers into the waistband of my panties, a look of almost painful need crossed his face. His hand went to the base of his dick and squeezed. He stroked himself twice before suddenly snatching his hand away, the lust on his face replaced with guilt.

It struck me as a little strange, but I chalked it up to general nervousness. I smiled at him. "Go ahead and touch yourself. I don't mind."

He shook his head, red infusing his cheeks as more guilt flooded his face. I ignored the way my weirdness meter was rising and slowly slid my panties down my thighs. I stepped out of them and watched the emotions cross Elijah's face as he stared at my pussy. Lust was prominent but, weirdly, there was still guilt as well.

Suddenly worried that I was pushing him to do something he didn't really want to do, I said, "We can stop, if you want, Elijah."

His gaze whipped up to mine and he immediately shook his head. "Christ, no. Please."

Relief replaced my doubt and I climbed onto the bed and laid on my back next to Elijah. He immediately turned on his side and cupped my breast, giving me a quick look. I tugged his head down to mine and we kissed again. God, I was rapidly growing addicted to Elijah's kisses.

After a few minutes, Elijah pulled back and studied my mouth. "I want you so much, Mia."

"I want you too," I said. His hand was still cupping my breast, his thumb rubbing back and forth over my aching nipple. I took his hand and grinned at him. "Time to teach you how to make me cum. You good with that?"

"Yes," he said. "Hell, yes."

I giggled and parted my legs before guiding his hand between them. He cupped my pussy gently, staring into my face as I said, "Just like kissing, the key is to start off soft and slow. Okay?"

"Okay."

"Good." I gave him a saucy smile before tucking my hands under my head. "Touch me, handsome."

"I'm not sure, I mean…"

"It's all good. Let's get you familiar with a pussy first, and then I'll show you what I like best. Okay?"

A grin crossed his face and I said, "What?"

"After school special again," he said.

I laughed and cupped his face, pressing a kiss against his mouth. "Should I be threatening you with a pop quiz after the lesson?"

He laughed, and the sound brought a twinge of pleasure to my belly. I kissed his mouth again. "Touch me, Elijah."

I gave him an encouraging look as he gently rubbed my wet pussy lips with the tips of his fingers. I found his look of studious concentration truly charming. When his finger slipped between my lips and rubbed across my clit, pleasure flickered through my veins. I arched, grabbing his forearm and moaning softly when he rubbed it again.

He stopped, giving me an uncertain look, and I shook my head. "Nope, don't stop. That feels really good."

I clung to his arm, my pelvis beginning to rise and fall as he rubbed small circles over and around my clit. He was touching me gently, maybe a little too gently, but there was something to be said about a man with a soft touch. I squirmed a little on the bed, letting my thighs fall open when he slid his fingers down my slit to my entrance. He pushed one thick finger into me, and our loud groans intermingled.

"Oh," I moaned when he slid his finger in and out with slow strokes.

"You're so wet, so tight," he whispered.

I smiled at him, "You make me wet, honey. Touch my clit again."

He moved to my clit obediently and rubbed it. I placed my fingers over his and rubbed in small, fast circles. "Like this."

He let me take control, watching my face as I rubbed his fingers against my clit. "The closer I get, the harder I like to be touched," I said. It was becoming increasingly difficult to concentrate on teaching him. "You can also tug or lightly pinch my clit to – OH! Oh shit, yes."

He had given my clit a light tug and I moaned loudly. "Good, honey. So good."

I rubbed his fingers against me again. It had been so long since I'd had a man touch me and Elijah's hard body pressed against mine, the feel of his rough fingers against my clit, had me ready to explode.

"Harder," I moaned. I clutched the bedsheets with one hand, my pelvis pumping rapidly against Elijah's hand. When he dipped his head and sucked on my nipple, the hot wet pressure of his mouth and tongue tipped me over into my climax. I cried out, my back arching and my body stiffening as the pleasure washed over me. Panting, I collapsed against the bed, holding his hand still when he tried to touch my clit again.

"No," I panted. "Too sensitive."

He nuzzled my neck. "I'm sorry."

"All good," I panted again. "God, really good…"

"You sure?"

I nodded, my chest rising and falling as my body made little tremors. "Nice work."

He smiled a little. "I think it was more you than me."

I shook my head. "You definitely made it

better. Next time you can try on your own, yeah?"

"I'd like that." He bent and pressed a kiss against my breast. "You're beautiful when you cum, Mia."

"Thank you." I rubbed his big forearm. His cock was pressing against my thigh, hard and hot and leaking precum. "Are you ready?"

He nodded eagerly. "Yes. Are you – are you sure about this?"

"No doubt at all," I said before spreading my legs wide. "Time to get rid of that pesky v-card, big guy."

Chapter Seven

Elijah

As long as I lived, I would never see anything more beautiful than the way Mia looked when she was cumming. Her soft sounds, the way her perfect, curvy body moved on the bed, and the flush in her cheeks as she came were like a drug. I wanted to make her cum over and over again.

"C'mon, honey," Mia urged.

I liked it a little too much when she called me 'honey'. I knew it didn't mean anything, but it certainly helped my fantasy that what was happening between us was based on love. I groaned inwardly. Fuck, I was an idiot. I was finally about to get laid and what was I doing? Thinking about love. Not only was that a stupid idea, but it was dangerous too. Mia might be the perfect woman for me, but there were very specific reasons she was doing this and none of them involved her falling for me.

Why would she? She was beautiful and funny

and smart, and I was all sorts of fucked up. Every time I thought I was starting to be okay, starting to be *normal*, memories of my past brought me crashing back to reality. I would never be normal.

"Elijah?" Mia was leaning over me now. "What's wrong?"

"Nothing," I said.

"Are you sure?" She said. "We can take a break, or we can stop if you're not -"

"I don't want to stop," I said hoarsely. I might have had a sudden moment of feeling sorry for myself, but it hadn't affected my dick. It was still hard as a rock and my balls were heavy and aching. I needed to be inside of Mia. Needed to finally know what it was like.

"If you're sure," she said hesitantly.

"Positive."

"All right." She relaxed on her back again and stroked my hip. "I'm assuming you want to be on top for your first time?"

I nodded. Missionary position was probably considered boring as hell but when you'd never had sex before, the idea of being on top of a woman, of having her legs spread wide around your hips as you fucked her, was intoxicating. I had one chance at sex with Mia and I wanted her under me for it. "If you're okay with that?"

"Totally," she said with a small grin. "I know some people find missionary boring, but secretly, I love it."

Her grin widened. "Climb on, cowboy. Let's get this party started."

Feeling a little awkward and uncoordinated, I

kneeled between her open legs.

"Elijah?" Mia's voice had turned serious. "I'm about to ask you to do something that's going to be really difficult. I need you to try and go slow at first, okay?"

I nodded before leaning over her and propping myself up on my hands. The head of my dick brushed against her wet pussy and I hissed out a breath. She cupped my face and stroked my cheekbone with her thumb before staring directly at me.

"I'm sorry, I know how difficult this will be for you, but I really do need you to be slow when you enter me. You're," she paused, "really big and if you aren't careful, you'll hurt me. Okay?"

I knew she was worried, I could see it in her face and hear it in her voice, and my chest tightened. I didn't doubt that it was going to be difficult, hell, I already wanted to just push in to the hilt inside her pussy, but I would never hurt my Mia. Just the thought of hurting her made me sick to my stomach.

"I won't hurt you, Mia." My voice was hoarse but steady. "I promise I will never hurt you."

She studied me, a small line appearing between her eyebrows as she absorbed what I said. She brushed her fingers across my mouth before lifting her head and pressing a kiss against my lips. "Thank you."

I smiled at her and carefully pressed my cock against her wet warmth. Fuck, did it feel good. I rubbed back and forth, the head of my cock sliding up and down her slit, but I couldn't seem to find her tight entrance. I was starting to feel self-conscious and sweat was sliding down my back. I wasn't sure if I should keep trying the way I was, or reach down and... oh, holy hell.

Mia had reached between us and I groaned out loud when her soft hand gripped my dick.

"Steady," she whispered before guiding me forward. The head of my dick pressed against her wet hole, then slipped inside, and I moaned with need.

"Slow, honey," she said.

"Slow," I gritted out. Ignoring every part of me that was screaming to shove my dick deep inside of her, I kept my thrusts short and light. With every stroke, I went a little deeper. I clenched my jaw, the vein in my temple pulsing heavily as I slowly – agonizingly slow – slid deeper into Mia.

Mia wrapped her hands around my arms, squeezing tightly as I stared down at her.

"Good, honey," she praised. "Your cock feels so good, so thick and hard."

I moaned again and stopped, trying not to blow my load right then and there.

"You okay?" Mia asked.

"Baseball," I groaned. "Thinkin' about baseball."

She laughed, and her pussy squeezed around me. I groaned again, making an involuntary thrust. She gasped, and I froze. "I'm sorry."

"No, it's... oh fuck, it's good. Keep going."

I continued my slow slide and retreat until I was completely sheathed. I stayed still, my eyes squeezed shut and my heart thumping in my chest.

Mia's pussy was incredible. Smooth and wet and warm and fucking amazing.

I wanted to stay in her forever, but I also wanted – *needed* – to move.

"Mia," I groaned. "Please."

She lifted her head again and kissed my chest. "I'm good, honey. Fuck me."

With a low moan, I thrust in and out. I tried to go slow, I wanted to go slow, but after only a few strokes, I was moving hard and fast. The sensation of being in Mia, the feel of her tight, smooth pussy gripping my aching cock, made me lose control.

I thrust wildly, my breath coming in harsh pants and the blood roaring in my ears. I stared at Mia's tits. They bounced with every thrust and it further weakened my control.

Mia's hands slid around me and rested on the scarred landscape that was my lower back. I could see the confusion cross her face, but I couldn't worry about her reaction, not when I was so close.

"Mia, oh God, Mia," I groaned again. My balls were tightening, and the base of my spine was tingling, and I couldn't last a second longer. I made one final hard thrust, my back arching and a low howl of pleasure spilling from my mouth as my climax fucking exploded over me. I thrust and thrust again as Mia's pussy squeezed around me, milking my cock of cum.

I shook and cried out again before collapsing on top of Mia. She made a low grunt and patted my back. "Honey, too heavy."

I heaved myself to my knees again, slipping my dick out of her amazing pussy, and fell on my side next to her. She turned to face me and rubbed my chest. She didn't speak, just watched my face as I came down from the high of my orgasm.

When my pulse was almost back to normal and my breathing not quite so labored, she smiled and kissed my chest. "You okay?"

"Oh my God," I said. "That was... I mean, that was amazing."

"I'm glad you liked it," she said.

"Liked it? Liked it doesn't quite describe how I felt about it."

She laughed and kissed my chest again. "You came really hard, huh?"

I nodded and then suddenly gave her a worried look. "Did I hurt you? Shit, was I too rough or -"

"No," she said.

"Are you sure?" I searched her face. "I didn't go slow and I -"

"You went slow at the beginning, that's all I needed," she said. "I promise you didn't hurt me. It was good."

"Did you cum?" I was a little embarrassed that I had no idea if Mia had even climaxed or not.

"No, but I didn't expect to," she said. "It's why I had you make me cum before we had sex."

"I'm sorry."

"Stop apologizing," she said. "Honestly, I was super surprised by how much control you had and how long you lasted once we started having sex. Good job, Elijah."

I grinned at her and she laughed. "Oh God, I'm sure there's nothing sexier than a woman giving a man a performance review after sex, but seriously...

you did so well."

Without thinking, I pulled her into my arms. I wanted that connection with her again, wanted to feel close to her even though I knew this meant nothing to her. She didn't seem put out by it. She rested her cheek against my chest and traced circles on my abdomen with her fingertips.

"Your heart is still beating a mile a minute," she said.

"Best work out of my life," I said.

She giggled, and I stroked her long dark hair before saying, "Thank you, Mia."

"You're welcome."

We laid quietly together for almost ten minutes. My body had never been so relaxed before and I was almost asleep when Mia sat up and peered over my body.

"Oh my God," she whispered.

I gave her a sleepy look of confusion. "What's wrong?"

"Your back," she said. "Elijah, are those scars?"

I tensed, my sleepiness gone immediately. "Yeah," I grunted.

"How did you get them?" Her fingers were tracing the scars and I rolled onto my back and stared up at the ceiling.

"Elijah?" She touched my chest. "How did you get them?"

"I've had them since I was a teenager," I said.

Dirty boy! Fornicator!

I winced inwardly at their voices, immediately feeling small and worthless and ashamed.

"A teenager?" I could hear the horror in her voice.

Fuck, why did I think she wouldn't notice the scarring? I'd been so anxious to be with her, that I'd talked myself into believing that I could keep Mia from seeing them.

"How?" She said.

I didn't answer, and she patted my chest. "Elijah, how did you get the scars?"

"It was an accident," I lied.

"An accident," she repeated.

"Yeah."

"Like a car accident?"

"Not exactly."

She frowned at me. "What type of accident?"

"I don't want to talk about it."

She paused and then rubbed my chest. "Where were your parents? How could they let you be hurt so badly, or -"

At the mention of my parents, I sat up in bed and pushed away from her. "I said I don't want to talk about it. Jesus, Mia, mind your own business."

I regretted my harsh tone the second the words came out. The soft look in Mia's eyes disappeared and she folded her arms across her breasts. "You're right. I apologize. It's none of my business and I shouldn't have pushed."

Her gaze drifted to my back and I couldn't take it. If I stayed here any longer, I'd tell her exactly what happened and then she'd know what a freak I was. I climbed out of her bed and grabbed my clothes, yanking them on as Mia watched silently.

"It's late, I should go." I walked toward the

door, pausing when Mia called my name.

"You don't have to -"

I shook my head. "It's late. Thanks for the lesson. Good-bye, Mia."

Chapter Eight

Mia

"So, he said the scars were from an accident?" Isabelle sipped at her glass of wine.

I nodded and poured myself another half glass. "Yeah. But they didn't look like they were from an accident."

"What do you mean?"

"They looked like... well, like scars a person would get from being hit with a belt or something." I gave Isabelle a sick look.

She'd paused with her wine glass at her mouth. "Seriously?"

"Yeah."

"Do you think his parents did it?"

"I do. We've only been friends for a couple of months but anytime I bring up his parents, he changes the subject. The most he's ever said about their relationship is that they aren't close."

"Makes sense they wouldn't be close if the assholes beat him as a kid."

"Right?" I sighed and took a sip of wine. "I feel so awful, Isabelle. The whole night was going great and then I fucked up by pushing him to tell me something that was none of my business."

"You've been a little close-mouthed about how the sex went," Isabelle pointed out. "Did you guys even…"

"We did," I said. "It was good. I mean, it was fast, but I expected that. What I didn't expect was how gentle and…almost tender, he would be. I mean, he's such a big guy, you know?"

Isabelle nodded before giving me a cheeky grin. "Was he big…everywhere?"

I gave her a disapproving look. "Isabelle, you know I don't share details like that. Not even with my best…"

Both of us dissolved into giggles before I nodded. "God, yes. Biggest dick I've ever seen, Isabelle. Swear to God."

Isabelle held up her wine glass and I clinked mine against it. "Good for you, Mia."

My good mood deflated. "Not really. I totally screwed up. I'll never get to see that gloriously large cock again."

"I don't know, once a guy has had a taste of pussy, it doesn't take much for him to want more," Isabelle said.

"Yeah, but he'll find it with someone else."

"Well," Isabelle gave me a delicate look, "wasn't that the plan all along anyway? You were going to take his v-card, so he could find a woman."

"Yes, it was the plan – *is* the plan – but I just…" I sighed and shook my head. "I don't know. I had plans to give him a blow job, teach him how to fuck in a few different positions, that sort of thing. I'm really disappointed that it'll be some other woman teaching him those things now."

"Why?" Isabelle asked bluntly.

"Well, because he's my friend and I -"

"I smell such bullshit," Isabelle sang out. "Never bullshit a bullshitter, Mia. You know better than that."

"Fine," I glowered at her. "I wanted to teach him those things because being with him was fun and surprisingly sexy and... I felt like a goddess when I was in bed with him."

"And he has a really big dick," Isabelle said.

"And he has a really big dick," I echoed

I drank some more wine before studying Isabelle. "You know what the worse part is? I've ruined my friendship with him. It's been four days and I haven't heard a single word from him."

"He's probably working," Isabelle said.

"He is. I saw him at the scene of a car accident yesterday."

"You didn't talk?"

"No, I was working and so was he. Plus, Matt was with me and there were other firefighters around. It wasn't exactly the time to try and apologize again, you know?"

"Have you texted him?"

"After he left, I tried calling him. When he didn't answer, I sent a text saying I was sorry again," I said. "He read it but didn't reply."

"Oh."

"Yeah." I stared morosely at my wine glass. "I

feel awful, Isabelle. And now I have two days off and all I'm going to do is sit around moping and feeling sorry for myself, and wishing I'd just kept my damn mouth shut about -"

My door buzzed, and Isabelle said, "Are you expecting someone?"

"No." I walked into the hallway and pushed the button. "Hello?"

"Hey, Mia. It's Elijah."

My eyes widened, and I hesitated before pushing the button again. "Hi. Um, c'mon up."

I buzzed the lobby door open before returning to the kitchen. "It's Elijah."

"Really?" Isabelle said. "That's great! Okay, I'm gonna get out of here."

"You don't have to leave," I said. "He probably just…"

Isabelle was already putting on her jacket. "Text me tomorrow and let me know how it goes."

I walked her to the door, and she gave me a quick peck on the cheek. "Good luck, Mia."

She opened the door, smiling at Elijah who was just about to knock. "Hey, Elijah."

"Hi, Isabelle. I'm sorry, I can come back. I didn't mean to -"

"Nope, it's all good. I was just leaving. Bye!"

She left, and Elijah stood awkwardly in the hallway for a minute before I gave him a tentative smile. "Come in."

"Thanks." He took his boots off and followed me into the kitchen.

"Do you want some wine?"

He shook his head, his big body looking tense

and uncomfortable. Before he could say anything, I said, "Elijah, I'm really very sorry. I shouldn't have pried into your personal business."

"I'm sorry," he said. "I was being a sensitive jackass and it was a real dick move to ignore you for the last four days."

"That's okay," I said. "I'm just glad we're still friends."

He didn't reply, and I cursed inwardly. "I mean, are we still friends?"

"Yeah, of course."

I wanted to ask him if he meant that, but I also didn't want to look pathetically eager. Instead, I said, "So, uh, what are you up to tonight?"

He shrugged. "Not much. Just finished my shift. I'm off for a couple of days."

"Me too," I said. "Do you wanna watch a movie with me tonight?"

He hesitated, and my heart sunk.

"Sure," he finally said.

"You don't have to," I said. "You don't have to do anything you don't want to."

"No, I want to watch a movie with you." His gaze landed on my tits and then bounced away. "A movie would be nice."

His body was still tense but when he took another quick glance at my chest, I realized how stupid I was. Elijah had come here not just to apologize but because he wanted more sex. Weirdly, instead of being offended, I was excited and more than a little turned on. He still wanted me. He could have gone out to find another woman, but he'd come to me.

He was too shy to come right out and ask for more lessons and although I'd always been on the shy and timid side myself, something about Elijah made me want to be bold. Or... maybe I just really wanted another taste of his giant dick.

I took a deep breath and moved across the kitchen to stand in front of him. His hard and deliciously muscular body was trembling minutely, and another wave of lust washed over me. His obvious need for me only made my need for him stronger and sweeter.

"Elijah?"

"Yeah?" He lifted his gaze to mine and I gave him a slow and seductive smile. His nostrils flared, and the muscle in his jaw started ticking when I put my arms around him and pressed my body against his.

"We could watch a movie, or we could go to my bedroom and have another...lesson."

Surprise flickered across his face. "You want to give me another lesson?"

"Yes. If that's what you want." I pressed my pelvis against that growing bulge in his jeans, knowing damn well that was what he wanted.

"I – I thought it was just one lesson," he said.

"Did you?" I tilted my head at him. "How strange. There's still so much I can teach you. If you're interested?"

"I don't want you doing something you're not really into," he said.

I shook my head. "Believe me, I'm into it. We have a choice to make. We can find a movie and watch it while we make small talk and pretend that you're not checking out my tits and I'm not checking out your dick. Or, we can spend the next two days in my bed fucking each other repeatedly.

"Fucking," he said immediately.

"Excellent choice." I took his hand and led him out of the kitchen. When we got to the bedroom, I tugged Elijah's shirt over his head and gave his naked chest an appreciative look. "You have an incredible body."

"Thank you." He leaned down to kiss me, and I pressed myself against his warm, hard body as we kissed with growing urgency. When he slid his tongue into my mouth, I sucked hard on it and his pelvis bucked against mine, almost knocking me over.

I giggled as he grabbed my hips to steady me. "Have you missed me?"

"Yes," he said. "So much, Mia."

I blinked up at him, the affection in his voice taking me off-guard. He was giving me a weirdly tender look that sent shivers of awareness up my spine. Had any man ever looked at me like that before? I didn't think so.

Before I could think too much about what it meant, Elijah was pulling my shirt over my head. He stared hungrily at my breasts before leaning down and pressing a kiss against my collarbone. His big, warm hands slid up my back to my bra and I grinned at him. "Time to learn how to undo a -"

My bra loosened, and I gave Elijah a surprised look. "That was pretty good. Do you practice at home on some weird and totally creepy mannequin?"

He laughed and shook his head. "Just really nimble fingers."

"Well," I shimmied out of my bra and let it fall to the floor before reaching for the button on his jeans, "let's see what else those nimble fingers can do. Shall we?"

I unbuttoned his jeans. His hands were already cupping my breasts and those nimble fingers were teasing my nipples into hard buds. I shoved his pants and underwear down his legs. He stepped out of them and I giggled and tugged his hands away. "Socks off, buddy."

He yanked his socks off before reaching out and cupping my hips. He pulled me up against him and we kissed again. His chest had a light layer of dark hair, and I stood on my tiptoes and rubbed my sensitive nipples against the rough hair, moaning into his mouth.

"You're so gorgeous, Mia," he whispered.

"You are too," I said. "Help me take my pants off."

He immediately yanked my yoga pants down, dragging my panties with them. He inhaled sharply at the sight of my pussy as I kicked my pants and underwear off. I stood naked in front of him, glorying in the look of utter enthrallment on his face as he stared at me.

"Do you want to touch my pussy, honey?"

"Fuck, yes," he said.

My soft giggle died out when he pulled me up against him with one arm around my waist. His free hand was already reaching between my legs, and when he cupped my pussy and rubbed his rough fingers against my clit, I grabbed onto his shoulders and arched my back.

His head dropped down and he kissed my neck before licking his way to my earlobe. He sucked on my lobe, his hot breath sending shivers down my spine as his fingers rubbed small circles over my clit. Already, there was a noticeable difference in how he touched me. His earlier tentativeness was gone, and I shivered again when he slid one finger deep inside of me and made a low growl.

"I love how wet you are, baby."

I spread my legs, giving him a wordless look of need as he angled his hand so his thumb could brush against my clit while he finger fucked me. God, he was learning so damn fast. I rocked back and forth against his hand, surprising both myself and him when my climax washed over me.

My legs trembling violently, I leaned against him, trusting him to hold me up as I rocked harder against his hand. The pleasure flooded through my entire body, making my nipples rock hard and my pussy quiver around his finger.

"Feel good, baby?" His voice was a low rasp in my ear.

"Yes," I muttered. "Shit, that was unexpected."

He smiled at me as I stared up at him. "I've never cum that fast before."

"Glad I could be here to see it."

He gently slid his finger out of my pussy, and I kissed his broad chest. "Lie on your back on the bed."

He did what I asked, and I quickly straddled him, smiling down at him when he gave me an eager look of desire. "I was thinking I'd be on top this time. What do you think?"

"I think that's a great idea." His hands cupped my tits and I arched into his touch, giving him a slow smile.

"Ready, handsome?"

"So ready. You're all I've thought about for the last four days, Mia. Your beautiful smile and perfect body."

I ignored the tingle of unease that went down my spine at his words and braced my hands on his chest before lifting myself up a little. "Put your dick in me, Elijah. Right now."

He reached down and after a moment of fumbling, guided his dick into my pussy. He automatically cupped my hips, helping me as I slowly sunk down over his dick. Like before, his thickness stretched my inner walls to the limit, and I took a deep breath, trying to adjust to his width as I sheathed him entirely.

"Okay?" He asked.

I nodded, a little breathless already. "Yeah. You're just so fucking thick. It feels really good though."

I stayed still, studying his face as his big hands slipped around me to cup my ass. He kneaded it gently, and even though I could see the need on his face, he didn't move.

"You know," I said, "for someone who's having sex for only the second time, you have a lot of self-control."

"I want to please you," he gritted out. "I want you to cum this time when we're...oh Jesus, Mia!"

I had made a slow thrust on his cock and I grinned at the look on his face. "I'm more than up to the idea of cumming on your cock, big guy."

"Fuck," he muttered. "Maybe you should stop talking like that."

I laughed and leaned over him, letting my tits brush against his chest. "You don't like the dirty talk? Or you don't like the idea of my pussy cumming on your dick?"

He made two uncontrollable thrusts, his hands digging into my ass. "Mia! Are you trying to kill me?"

"Of course not." I traced my fingers over the hard line of his jaw before leaning back a little and pinching his flat nipple. "A little teasing never killed anyone."

"Mia," he moaned. One hand left my ass to cup the back of my skull when I sucked on his flat nipple. "Oh fuck, Mia. Please."

I straightened and braced my hands on his chest. "Do you want me to fuck you now, Elijah?"

"Yes." He was already making small thrusts against me and I moved up and down, matching his rhythm.

His cock felt so good. I shifted my hips a little, switching up the angle, and moaned happily when the new position brought new pleasure.

"Oh God," I muttered. "That's the spot."

We moved faster, my desire to tempt and tease gone under my overwhelming need to cum. I moved harder and faster, our harsh breathing the only sound in the room as Elijah met each of my strokes. He gripped my hip with one strong hand, the other one reaching up to tease my tits.

"Fuck, yes. Just like that," I moaned. My orgasm was fast approaching and as I teetered on the precipice of my climax, I reached down and rubbed furiously at my clit.

"Fuck!" I screamed as my back arched and I came hard on Elijah's cock. He echoed my cry, his big body arching up as his fingers dug into my hips with brutal intensity. Fresh new wetness flooded my pussy and I ground myself against his cock, my nails scratching across his chest as the pleasure went on and on.

He was gasping and moaning my name and when I collapsed on his broad chest, he lifted one shaking hand and cupped my skull, holding me against him.

"Oh my God," he whispered. "That was even better than the first time."

I made a tired little giggle and nuzzled his chest. "Glad you liked it."

"It was incredible. The way your pussy squeezed when you were cumming. Holy shit…" He sounded completely awestruck and I lifted my head to grin at him.

"You're welcome."

He laughed as I let my head clunk back down to his chest. "I want you to cum on my dick every time we fuck. All right?"

"Sure," I said before yawning. "S'no problem."

He kissed the top of my head. "Should I go?"

I slid off of him, my bones like jelly, and curled up on my side. "Spoon me, please."

He did what I asked, pulling the covers up over

us and pressing his warm body along my spine and ass. He cupped my breast before moving his hand down to my hip.

I moved it back to my breast, squeezing his hand lightly. "If you leave, how will we fuck again after we nap?"

He kissed the back of my shoulder. "I guess I'd better stay then."

"Guess so," I said.

Chapter Nine

Elijah

"Hey, Mia?"

"Hmm?" She lifted the spoon to her lips and tasted the chicken soup before adding a bit more seasoning.

"I don't have to stay the entire two days if you have other things to do. You can just call me when you're ready to have sex and I'll come over."

She turned and frowned at me. "Don't be silly. I'm having a good time, aren't you?"

"The best time," I said, "but I don't want to intrude on your personal space."

"You're not." She stirred the soup again. "Besides, with you here, it gives me the excuse to cook. I love cooking but when it's just me, it feels like a bit of a waste."

"The soup smells delicious." I stared at her ass as she bent and checked the biscuits in the oven.

"Thanks. It's actually Nana's recipe, but I did add a few changes to make it my own." She turned and caught me staring at her ass.

I blushed, but she just grinned and wiggled her ass at me. "Like what you see, big guy?"

"Very much. Can I help you with lunch?"

"Nope. Sit right there and relax," she said. "I know some people like help, but I prefer to be the only cook in the kitchen."

I leaned back in the kitchen chair and...well...ogled Mia shamelessly as she set the table and checked the biscuits again. Last night was amazing. After our nap, we'd had sex again. Mia was more than willing to let me be on top again and having her cum on my dick was just as incredible the second time.

She'd made a quick supper for us and we'd watched TV for a little while before she invited me to spend the night. I could tell she was tired, but she'd insisted we have sex again. I should have said no, but resisting Mia was impossible. I thought after having sex a few times, my obsession with it would ease, but it had only increased.

Still... I watched as Mia sat down across from me and winced. Guilt flooded through me. She was sore and that was my fault. I'd been too rough with her. She was up and showered and downstairs before I'd even woken up this morning, and I wondered if it was a self-preservation thing for her. Get out of bed before the stupidly horny guy started groping her again.

"Mia?"

"Yeah?" She smiled at me.

"Am I being too rough?"

"No, why?" She replied.

"You're in pain," I said.

"I'm not."

I gave her my own scowl and she sighed. "Fine, I'm a little sore but it has nothing to do with how rough you are. You're not rough, Elijah. It's just been a while for me, and we've had sex three times in the last twenty-four hours, and you have a big dick. I've got some muscle ache, that's all."

"I could run you a bath after lunch," I said.

She grinned at me. "That's very sweet of you, but I'll be fine."

"Maybe we should give it a couple of days before we have sex again," I said.

Are you crazy? Shut up! We just started having sex and now you want to cut us off?

"No," she said. "Absolutely not. I promised to teach you sex stuff and I'm gonna. I mean, maybe we won't be banging after lunch or anything, but there are other things I can show you."

Was it wrong that I immediately hoped she meant letting me eat her pussy? I'd been dreaming for a year about tasting Mia, about hearing her soft cries as I tongued her wet clit, and to think that it might actually come true, made me feel a little crazy with need.

She stood and shut off the burner. She brought over the pot of soup, set it on the hot pads in the middle of the table and carefully ladled soup into both our bowls. As she took out the biscuits from the oven and set them in a basket next to the soup, I tried to concentrate on how good lunch looked and smelled, rather than how I might be fulfilling a year-long fantasy this afternoon.

"You okay?" She sat next to me and gave me a curious look.

"Yes, why?"

"You have a weird look on your face."

"I'm fine," I repeated.

She crinkled her nose at me – shit, she was so fucking adorable – and said, "You don't have to hide things from me, Elijah. We're friends and friends share stuff. Right?"

"I want to eat you out," I blurted. "Shit. I mean...that was rude."

She was giggling like crazy and some of my embarrassment eased when she said, "I want that too. But how about you taste my soup first and then you can taste my pussy. Deal?"

"Deal," I said.

ॐ ॐ

"You're so beautiful, Mia." I cupped her breast and pressed a kiss against her collarbone.

She smiled and stroked my hair. "Man, you're good for my ego."

"I mean it," I said earnestly. "You're beautiful and perfect and I can't get enough of you." I frowned at the look that crossed her face. "What's wrong?"

"Nothing," she said. "But I'm not perfect. No one is."

I just shrugged before dipping my head and tracing along her collarbone with my tongue. I didn't care what she said, Mia was perfect and being in her bed was something I would never grow tired of.

Yeah, well, it's not gonna last, so don't get used

to it.

I ignored the stray thought and concentrated on Mia. I sucked on her nipple, tracing it with my tongue as my hand gently kneaded her other breast. When she was making the soft noises and moans that never failed to make me horny as hell, I raised my head and smiled at her. "I love your breasts."

She laughed and gently poked me on the top of my head. "I'm glad. Now, wander on down the bed and discover how much you love my pussy, would you?"

I tried to hide my excitement as I kissed my way down Mia's body, over the gentle curve of her belly and across her smooth thighs. I deliberately avoided the dark curls at the top of her mound before sliding down the bed. Mia spread her legs apart and I moved my body between them. My wide shoulders nudged at her thighs and she smiled softly before letting her legs drop open farther.

"You are seriously the biggest man, ever."

"I like to stay in shape." I kissed the inside of one creamy thigh, and she made a sharp inhale.

"Mmm... you definitely have an incredible body."

I kissed her other creamy thigh before giving it a soft nip. She jerked and made another soft and sexy giggle that stiffened my cock until it was aching.

"Hey, get to the good stuff." She bonked my butt with the heel of her foot.

I took a deep breath. Fuck, would there ever be a moment where I wasn't so goddamn nervous about touching Mia?

"Elijah?"

I lifted my head. She was giving me her sweet smile and my anxiety disappeared. "As long as you don't bite me like you're a vampire, whatever you do will feel good so don't be nervous. Start off -"

"Soft and slow," I finished.

She laughed. "Exactly. Now get to the pussy eating, big guy."

"Yes, Mia." I bent my head and inhaled again. Fuck, her pussy smelled so goddamn good. We'd only been making out for about ten minutes, but already her pussy was glistening wet and I could see her soft, pink clit peeking out from between her pussy lips.

I kissed her inner thigh again before licking her wet lips with the tip of my tongue. She moaned, her pelvis already arching a little and I licked her again before tentatively licking her clit.

I groaned when her hand immediately dropped on my head and she practically pushed me face-first into her hot pussy. Her reaction made precum spurt from my cock, and I ignored my urge to fist my cock as I pressed a kiss against the soft curls at the top of her pussy before licking her lips again. I avoided her clit, just tasting and kissing and making light nips across her pussy. If these two days were all I had with Mia, I wanted to make the most of them, which meant taking my time eating her sweet pussy.

Mia had other plans though. She fisted her hand in my hair and yanked my mouth toward her clit. "Elijah, please."

Her voice had a breathless need to it that I'd

never heard before. It made me ache to give her exactly what she wanted so I tossed my plan to go slow and attacked her clit with soft wide licks of my tongue.

"Oh fuck!" She rocked her pussy against my face, both hands holding my head steady now as I licked her repeatedly. "Good, so good, honey. Just like that… keep licking. Fuck…oh fuck, that's so good."

I was drowning in the sweet scent and taste of her pussy. My cock was hard and pulsing, and I was helpless to stop from rubbing it against the mattress as I buried my face in Mia's pussy and licked like a fucking mad man.

"Suck my clit, honey," Mia gasped. "Suck it, right now."

I parted her pussy lips with my thumbs and exposed her entire swollen clit. I licked it once and then sucked it into my mouth, applying gentle pressure. Mia's reaction was explosive. Her thighs clamped around my head, her fingers dug into my skull, and her lower body lifted until I was completely surrounded by her wet, damp heat.

She made a low scream of pleasure and wetness flooded my lips and tongue. I sucked on her clit as she came, and she cried out, her body trying hard to toss me to the floor as she bucked her pelvis against my face.

I licked her clit a final time and pushed her thighs apart so I could lift my head and suck in a breath of oxygen. Mia was moaning and shuddering, and I rubbed her thigh lightly as she collapsed against the bed.

I crawled out from between her thighs and stretched out on my side next to her. I wanted to fuck her so bad, but she was sore and just the thought of hurting her was enough to make my cock wilt a little.

I rested my hand on the curve of her belly and pressed a kiss against one diamond-hard nipple as she took in breath after ragged breath. After a few minutes, she cracked open one eye and smiled at me. "Sorry."

"For what?" I asked.

"I didn't last very long, and I got demanding at the end there."

"I didn't mind," I said.

"Well, it wasn't exactly helpful for you to learn how to eat a woman out," she said. "But, hell, it's been a long time since I've had a tongue in my pussy, and you did a great fucking job for your first time."

"Flattering but most likely inaccurate," I said.

She shook her head. "Nope. You did really well for your first time. You did better than my last boyfriend and he'd been having sex since he was fifteen."

I had no sense that she was trying to flatter me, and so I gave her a pleased look. "Thanks. I appreciate the feedback."

She laughed. "Oh God, we're such... nerds, maybe? I don't even know the word to describe it."

I pressed a kiss against her shoulder. "Thank you for letting me do that, Mia."

"Trust me, honey, it's me who needs to thank you. It was great, and I promise the next time you eat me out, I'll try and let you go slower and do your own thing."

A stupid grin crossed my face. Just knowing that Mia wanted more made me happy.

"Now, since you've taken care of my need so sweetly, I think it's time I helped you out. What do you say?"

I thought about Mia's soft hand, the way it felt when she gripped my cock, and nodded eagerly. "Yes, I'd like that."

"Lie on your back, honey."

I flipped to my back, smiling at Mia when she hovered over me and kissed my mouth. "Are you ready?"

I nodded, giving her a puzzled look when she said, "Don't worry if you cum quickly, okay? It's to be expected."

She kissed my chest and then my stomach as I tried to figure out what the hell she meant. Was I still cumming too quickly for her? I thought over the last twenty-four hours that I'd been getting better at controlling my urge to cum when she touched or fucked me, but maybe it wasn't good enough. Maybe she wasn't –

Her warm breath washed over my pubic hair and all rational thought fled. Holy fucking shit. Mia was going to blow me. Mia was going to suck my cock. My pelvis rose a little and I groaned loudly when she kissed my pubes and her soft hand stroked my inner thigh.

"Mia," I whispered.

She raised her head, her long hair tickling my thighs as she smiled at me. "Yeah?"

"Please," I moaned. "Oh please."

"Have you thought about me sucking your cock, Elijah?" She asked. The tips of her fingers traced my balls before running up and down my aching shaft.

"Yes," I groaned.

"Before we started having sex?" Her thumb rubbed across the head and I nearly fucking lost it when she sucked my precum off of her thumb.

"Oh fuck. Oh, Mia, please."

"Answer the question, Elijah." She bent her head and my heart thudded in my ears as I waited for her soft mouth to slide over my cock. Instead, she licked a slow path down my v-line as her hand curled around the base of my dick. "Answer me, please."

"Yes. God, yes."

"Really?" She gave me a smug little grin that only made me hotter for her. "Tell me one of your fantasies."

"Mia, later, for the love of Christ," I groaned.

"No, now," she replied.

I fucking loved and hated her at the moment.

"In the shower," I moaned. "I would fantasize about you giving me a blow job in the shower."

"Hmm, that does sound like fun," she said. "We'll definitely make that fantasy come true for you later. All right?"

I nodded, unable to form words as her breath washed over my aching, throbbing dick.

"But for now, let's stay right here and," she licked away the precum that had beaded up on the tip of my cock again and I gasped, "you can give me a nice long taste of your delicious cum. What do you think?"

"Please," I begged incoherently. "Please."

"Such a sweet, polite boy," she said with a cheeky smile.

I was getting ready to beg again – I didn't fucking care how pathetic it made me look – when Mia's hot mouth slid over the head of my cock. She sucked lightly, and I made a hoarse shout, my hands clawing into the sheets as I stared at the ceiling. I couldn't look at her, couldn't watch her lips stretch around my cock or I'd cum for fucking sure.

"So yummy," Mia whispered. She sucked again on the head before sliding more of her mouth down over my cock. She bobbed her head up and down my cock as she sucked firmly. Her hand stroked and teased the base of my shaft as she sucked, and I couldn't stop my pelvis from rising with every long pull of her mouth.

I was moaning her name repeatedly as she sucked and licked and stroked. My balls were tightening, and I tried desperately to stop myself from cumming. When Mia lifted her head and said my name, I continued to stare grimly at the ceiling.

She gave my dick a hard squeeze that sent lightning bolts of pleasure down my legs. "Mia, please!" I gasped.

"Look at me, honey," she said.

"No, no I can't."

"Yes, you can," she said. "I want you to watch as I suck you off, Elijah."

I tore my gaze from the ceiling and stared at her. She was lying across my thighs, her dark hair tucked behind her ears and her full mouth red and swollen from sucking on my cock. Without breaking eye contact, she leaned down and took my dick into her mouth. As I watched her lips stretch around my width, I cried out and dug my hands into the sheets again.

I couldn't look away. Couldn't stop watching as Mia sucked on my throbbing cock. Her mouth slid up and down, and the combination of the way she looked with her mouth stuffed full of my cock and the gentle scrape of her teeth against my flesh sent me over the edge.

I arched, my low howl of ecstasy echoing through the room as I came hard into Mia's mouth. She sucked me dry, her smooth throat swallowing repeatedly as she worked to take every bit of my cum. I watched through half-lidded eyes as the pleasure washed over me in slow waves of pure bliss. When she licked my cock clean and then licked away the cum on her lower lip, more cum spurted out of my dick.

She grinned and bent her head, licking the cum away as I moaned and shivered and rocked back and forth on the bed. She sat up and gave me another smug grin before pulling the covers up over both of us and lying on her side. I immediately turned to face her, my big body still shaking, and she wrapped her arms around me and kissed my chest.

I wanted – needed – to be close to her and she seemed to understand. She didn't protest when I plastered my entire body against hers, my cock pressed against her stomach and my chest smashed against her breasts.

She kissed my chest again and stroked my upper back as I labored to catch my breath. "Oh my God, Mia, that was…"

She smiled up at me. "I'm glad you enjoyed your first blow job."

"It was fucking perfect," I said, "just like you are."

A small line appeared between her eyebrows for a few seconds before she smoothed it away. "Next time, we'll do it in the shower and fulfill that fantasy of yours. Okay?"

"Jesus, you're the best," I said weakly.

She grinned and rested her head against my shoulder. I lazily stroked her hip and thigh as my body slowly recovered from the orgasm. Nearly fifteen minutes later, I was nearly asleep when Mia touched the scars on my lower back.

I wanted to tense, but my body was so goddamn relaxed, that I couldn't muster up the energy. Besides, the way Mia stroked them, the way she seemed to memorize the pattern and shape of the raised skin with the pads of her fingers, was weirdly soothing. She hadn't touched or brought up the scars once since our first night together and I still felt guilty for making her feel bad about asking questions.

Maybe it was the lingering guilt, or maybe it was just how damn relaxed I was, but I didn't pull away when Mia kissed my chest and said, "Elijah, you don't have to tell me why you got the scars but will you tell me if it was your parents who did this to you?"

"Yes. My father, but my mother wanted him to do it."

"Oh, honey," she said softly. "Did he – did he use a belt?"

I nodded, keeping my eyes closed. "Yeah. My parents are very religious and strict. I'd done something they considered sinful and that's how they punished me."

"How old were you?" She asked.

"Fourteen."

Her hand tightened for a moment on my scars. "That's child abuse, Elijah."

I shrugged, and she sighed before saying, "Do you have any siblings?"

"No. It was just me."

"No one saw what they did to you? You didn't have a teacher you could go to or -"

"I went to an all-boys school that was just as strict with religion as my parents were. They still used the strap for punishment at the school."

"Holy shit, how is that even possible?" She whispered.

"They were shut down a few years ago," I said.

"Thank God," she replied. "How often did your father beat you?"

"Whenever I did something he or my mother didn't approve of or thought was sinful. They were difficult to…please, so I was punished a lot. He only really did real damage that one time though."

She was quiet, and I knew she was about to ask me what I had done, even though she'd promised not to. I didn't blame her, but I couldn't – wouldn't – talk about it with her. My body had stiffened, and

I waited for her to ask the question that would drive me from her bed again.

"I'm so sorry, honey."

I jerked in surprise and stared down at Mia. She was giving me a soft look of compassion, and every muscle in my body tensed again before relaxing.

"What your parents did you to you was terrible and abusive and I'm sorry you had to go through that alone. I'm sorry they hurt you the way they did."

She pressed a kiss against my mouth, and I rested my forehead against hers, breathing in her soft scent. "It wasn't that bad."

"Wasn't it?" She said.

"I… it was awful."

She wrapped her arms around me and held me tight. "I'm sorry, Elijah."

I buried my face in her neck and breathed deep before muttering, "I ran away when I was seventeen and I haven't talked to them since. They're still alive and my father is still a pastor, but that's about all I know. I don't want to have anything to do with them."

"Of course you don't," she said.

"I'm a bad son."

"No, you're not." She cupped my face and stared at me intently. "They were bad parents, Elijah. They're to blame, not you. Short of murdering a human or an animal – nothing you could have done was bad enough to warrant that type of abuse. Do you hear me?"

"I didn't murder anyone," I said.

She smiled a little and kissed my mouth. "I

know.   You don't have a bad bone in your body, Elijah Thomson.   You're the sweetest, gentlest man I know, and I adore you.   You know that, don't you?"

I nodded, and she kissed my mouth again before resting her head on my chest.

It wasn't love she was offering, but it was enough.   When she was done with me, when she wanted to go back to being just friends, the memory of this moment would be enough.

It had to be enough.

Chapter Ten

Mia

"Wait, so you're telling me you're still giving Elijah sex lessons?" Isabelle stared at me over her cup of coffee.

"Keep your voice down," I scolded before glancing around Mugs Coffee Shop.

"It's been two weeks," Isabelle said. "You said before that he was a fast learner. Were you lying? How bad is the dude in bed?"

"He's not bad," I said defensively. "In fact, he's really good and he is a fast learner."

"Then why are you still giving him lessons?" Isabelle asked.

"Because I…"

I didn't know what to say. I should never have told Isabelle that I was still banging Elijah, but she had outright asked me, and I couldn't lie to my best friend.

"Are you falling for Elijah?" Isabelle asked.

"What? No, of course not," I said.

"Why not? Obviously, you two are compatible in bed, and you're really great friends. Why shouldn't you just start dating? And don't give me that bullshit about Elijah not liking you that way. He does, Mia."

I sighed and picked at the sleeve on my coffee cup. "Okay, fine, maybe he does like me, but he's bordering on being a Phillip."

"No way. Phillip was a dickwad. I know I don't know Elijah very well, but you can tell he isn't a dickwad."

"He isn't," I said. "But he keeps making these little comments about how perfect I am, and -"

"That doesn't mean he's a Phillip," Isabelle said. "Look, I get why you're paranoid, Phillip did a real number on your head, but you can't just hide away from love."

"I'm not. I just – I need more time to get over the mindfuck games that Phillip played with me. Okay?"

"So, what? You're gonna date a few assholes first? Guys who don't tell you that you're awesome? Is that how you're gonna get over him?" Isabelle scowled at me.

"No, but dating someone who occasionally reminds me of Phillip, is definitely not the way to go."

"Fair enough," Isabelle said. "But, if you're not interested in dating Elijah, then you need to stop leading him on and find him a woman like you told him you would."

I winced. Isabelle was always blunt and honest, and I loved her for it, but, man, did it hurt to hear the truth. I didn't want to lead Elijah on, hated the idea that I was, but Isabelle was one hundred percent correct.

Just because I loved how damn amazing Elijah was turning out to be in bed, was no excuse for what I was doing.

It's not just the sex, Mia. You like him. He's sweet and smart and funny. You know you like him. Give him a chance. Please?

I sipped my coffee. Was there a big part of me that wanted to ask Elijah if he'd like to date? Hell, yes. But the thought that he might even be a little like Phillip, and that he'd place me on this pedestal that I had no right to be on, was devastating. Losing Phillip had hurt, but losing Elijah? I couldn't even fathom it. If I couldn't have him in my bed forever, I could at least have him as a friend.

"You're right," I said. "I'm going to find him a girlfriend."

"Find who a girlfriend?"

I glanced up and smiled at the handsome dark-haired man who had stopped at our table. "Hey, Knox."

"Hey, Mia." He bent and kissed my cheek before grinning at Isabelle and giving her a slow kiss on the mouth. "Hey, sexy."

"Hey, yourself. You on a break from work?"

Knox nodded. "It's my last job of the season, but I probably should have put it off until spring. It's starting to be a little too cold. If it freezes overnight, I'm hooped."

Isabelle gave him a sympathetic look. "Sorry,

babe. I'll keep my fingers crossed that it's -"

She was interrupted by the small redhead who was falling face-first into our table. Before she could smash her face into the hard surface, Knox's arm shot out and hooked around her waist. She stopped inches from our table and hot coffees, her face as red as her hair.

Knox hauled her back into a standing position and grinned at her. "Hey, Luna."

"Oh my God, I'm so sorry," Luna said. "I tripped over," she glanced behind her at the smooth floor, "something."

"It's fine," Knox said.

"Thank you so much, Knox," Luna said. "You're as fast as Ash when it comes to saving me from faceplants."

Knox laughed and wiggled his eyebrows at her. "I've got lightning quick reflexes."

"You okay, Luna?" Isabelle asked. "Did you hurt yourself?"

"Nope, I'm good. Thanks to your man." Luna grinned at her. "Are you and Knox coming to Ren's tonight?"

"We are," Isabelle said. "I won't be singing, but I'm looking forward to hearing you sing. Oh, and Mia and Elijah will be there too."

"We will?" I said.

Isabelle nodded. "Yes. Operation 'find Elijah a girlfriend' starts tonight."

"Elijah Thomson?" Knox said. "The giant, sullen firefighter?"

"He's not sullen." I gave Knox an indignant look. "He's a sweetheart."

"Sure, he is," Knox said.

"Okay, well, I gotta get back to work. We'll see all of you tonight!" Luna waved at us and returned to the counter.

"Am I the only one who holds my breath whenever that chick walks?" Knox asked.

Isabelle laughed. "Nope." She turned toward me. "Don't tell Luna this, but Ash totally Luna-proofed his place for her. He made me come over and walk through the house, pointing out any sharp objects or things Luna could impale herself on that he might have missed."

"That's adorable," I said.

"Are you seriously trying to find Elijah a girlfriend?" Knox asked.

"Yes. He's my friend and I told him I'd help him find someone," I said. "Why?"

Knox just shrugged. "He just seemed like the loner type to me. I better go too. I need a coffee and I want to get back to work before it just gets colder. See you at home, Isabelle."

"Bye, honey." Isabelle patted him on the ass as he walked away before smiling at me. "So, we'll see you and Elijah at karaoke around eight tonight. All right?"

"I'll double check with Elijah, but yeah, sure, it should be fine."

"Perfect." Isabelle said before passing her phone to me. "Now, take a look at this dress I found online and tell me if you think it's a yay or a nay for me."

❧ ❧

"You want to go to karaoke at Ren's Bar

tonight?" Elijah gave me a confused look as he loaded the dishwasher.

I finished wiping down the counters and hung the dishcloth over the tap. "Yes."

"I don't sing." There was a note of alarm in Elijah's voice.

"I don't either," I said.

"Then why are we going?" Elijah's thick arms slid around my waist and he pressed a kiss against my neck. Like always, my pussy began to throb the moment he touched me. "We should just stay home, and I'll eat your pussy and then you can ride my dick."

I shivered with pleasure when his big hand cupped my breast and he toyed with my nipple through my shirt and bra. He gave me another persuasive kiss on the neck. "We only have a limited time before I'm back to work, and then I'll have to go three days without being inside your sweet pussy. Don't make me waste a single minute on karaoke."

I was tempted to give in. Tempted to take Elijah to my bed and keep him there for the next forty-eight hours, just like I'd been doing with every single free moment we both had in the last two weeks. What was the harm of spending a few more days with him before I found him a girlfriend? No harm, really.

Plenty of harm. Stop doing this Mia. If you're not going to date this perfectly sweet and amazing man, then stop leading him on. You're being a total selfish bitch.

I winced inwardly but my inner voice was right.

I couldn't keep doing this to Elijah.

I took a deep breath and put my hand on top of Elijah's when he started to slip it into my pants. "Actually, the reason we're going out is not the karaoke."

"Then what is it?" Elijah nipped my neck.

"I think it's time I did what I said I would and help you find a girlfriend."

I could feel his body stiffen behind me, and dismay and regret flooded through me when he stepped away immediately. Feeling like I was making a giant mistake, I turned around and did my best to smile at him. "What do you think?"

"I," Elijah paused, "I'm not sure I'm good enough in bed yet."

"You are," I said. "Elijah, you're fantastic in bed. I mean that. You're the best lover I've ever had."

He didn't reply and I cleared my throat. "I just – I mean, I promised you I'd find you a girlfriend and I'm going to keep that promise."

"Right." He folded his arms across his chest and stared at the ground. "Okay, fine."

"Are you sure?" I wanted to touch him but restrained myself. He looked stiff and upset, and I'd been friends with him long enough to know that he needed physical space when he was upset. Probably because his asshole parents beat the shit out of him as a kid.

My anger over what his parents did to him was rearing its head, but now wasn't the time. If Elijah no longer wanted my help to find a girlfriend, I wasn't going to force him to accept it.

"If you don't want my help, that's okay. I get it and I -"

"No," he said. "No, that was that the deal, right? You teach me how to fuck and then find me a girlfriend. So, let's find me a girlfriend."

"Elijah, *are* you okay?" I swallowed hard when he lifted his head and glared at me.

"Perfectly fine. I should go home and have a quick shower."

"You can shower here," I said.

He shook his head. "No. I need to change my clothes anyway." He glanced at his track pants and t-shirt before heading for the front door of my apartment.

"I told Isabelle we'd be there around eight. I'll pick you up at quarter to eight, okay?" I followed him to the door.

He grabbed his jacket and yanked open the door. "I'll meet you there."

"I don't mind driving you."

Without looking at me, he said, "If I meet someone, I'll need my car."

"You don't have to, like, sleep with them tonight, Elijah. I just meant that we should get you out there and meet some ladies. The odds of you finding someone tonight -"

"I'll see you at Ren's at eight." He walked out of my apartment and slammed the door shut.

๛ ๛

I was waiting outside for Elijah when he pulled into the parking lot of Ren's bar. My nerves jagged and my body shivering with cold, I gave him a nervous smile when he joined me. "Hi there."

"What are you doing outside?" He said gruffly. "It's freezing out."

"I wanted to double check that you actually wanted to do this, and also to, um, apologize for earlier. I said or did something that upset you and I feel awful about it."

"You didn't," he said with a deep sigh. "I'm the one who should be apologizing to you. I was being an asshole, but it had nothing to do with you."

"Are you sure?" I searched his face. "I hate upsetting you, Elijah."

"You didn't," he repeated. He gave me a smile that almost looked normal. "C'mon, let's go in there and find my ugly mug a girlfriend."

"You're not ugly," I said sharply, but he had already turned away to open the door.

He held the door open for me and then followed me toward the table that Isabelle and Knox, and Ash and Luna were sitting at. Karaoke hadn't quite started yet, but the place was already packed with people. We'd find Elijah a nice girl for sure.

Jealousy rippled in my stomach and I swallowed it down as we joined the others. "Elijah, this is Isabelle and Knox, and Asher and Luna."

"Nice to meet you." Elijah shook Knox's hand and then Asher's before pulling an empty chair out for me.

"Thanks," I said and sat down. Elijah sat next to me and there was a moment of awkward silence.

"So," Luna said brightly, "you're a firefighter. That's a super dangerous job. What made you decide to become one?"

"I like helping people," Elijah said.

"That's really sweet." Luna smiled at him and I could see Elijah blushing lightly.

Ash glanced first at Luna and then at Elijah, a frown marring his heavy brow. "How long have you and Mia been dating?"

"We're not," I said quickly. "In fact, Elijah is looking to meet someone tonight."

"Luna's with me." Asher placed a proprietary hand on Luna's slender thigh.

"He knows that, ya big lug," Isabelle said with a roll of her eyes. "Everyone in town knows you and Luna are dating."

Luna squeezed Ash's hand before smiling at Elijah. "Okay, so what type of woman are you interested in?"

"Oh, uh," Elijah's face was growing redder by the second, "I don't really know."

"He's looking for someone sweet and funny," I said. "Someone who appreciates how amazing he is."

"Seems like half the goddamn town is here tonight." Knox took a long pull of beer. "You're bound to find someone to hook up with."

"Knox!" Isabelle frowned at him. "He's not looking for just a hook up." She hesitated. "I mean, it's fine if that's what you're looking for, but is it, Elijah?"

"Uh, no, not really."

"We'll find someone," Luna said confidently.

"What about Sonja? She's single." Knox pointed to the pretty brunette who was sitting with a group of other women about four tables away from us.

"No," I snapped. "Absolutely not."

"Why not?" Knox said.

"Because she's not right for him," I replied. "She's a jerk."

Knox glanced at Isabelle who nodded. "She kind of is. She's been awful to Lily Carson ever since Lily had that run of bad luck."

"Lily was awful to her in high school," Knox said.

"People change," I replied before Isabelle could. "Besides, it's not just that. She's always been kind of awful, trust me."

I pulled self-consciously at my shirt. Even with the weight I'd lost, my shirt still clung to my muffin-top. I tried not to notice the way every other woman in the room seemed thinner and prettier than me. Elijah was attracted to me and he found me sexy, that was obvious.

So, what? Who cares if he finds you sexy? You're here to find him a woman, remember?

Yeah, I remembered. Still, the last two weeks with Elijah had made me feel confident and sexy and wanted. It was a real blow to go back to my usual self-consciousness and doubt about the way I looked. I hated that I needed a guy's interest in me to make me feel good about myself. It was why I'd stayed so long with Phillip, even when it started to become obvious that I would never live up to his expectations.

Elijah was staring at me and I forced myself to smile at him. "Don't worry, Elijah. We'll find you the perfect woman, I promise."

Chapter Eleven

Elijah

I nodded my thanks to the bartender, Ren, and picked up the two beers before turning around. The little redhead, Luna, was standing behind me with a slender blonde woman who looked as nervous as I suddenly felt.

"Hey, Elijah," Luna said.

"Hi, Luna," I paused for a second, "Uh, you're doing a great job with the karaoke singing."

"Oh, thanks!" Luna smiled at me before turning to the woman standing next to her. "This is my friend Natalia. Natalia works as a server at the Farmhouse Diner. She comes into the coffee shop all the time. She loves coffee. Right, Natalia?"

"Yes." Natalia gave me another clearly nervous smile.

"This is Elijah. He's a firefighter," Luna said.

"It's nice to meet you, Elijah," Natalia said.

"Uh, nice to meet you as well." My hands were gripping the bottles so tightly I was about one squeeze away from shattering them.

"Anyway, I ran into Natalia here at the bar tonight, and I thought I should introduce the two of you. Natalia was just saying the other day in the coffee shop that she wanted to do some weight training and since you're, like, the strongest guy I know, I figured you could give her some tips. Maybe even show her some stuff at the gym sometime. What do you think?" Luna asked.

"Oh, uh, sure, yeah, maybe," I said.

"Great!" Luna smiled happily at the both of us before prying the beers from my hand. "Here, I'll take these to Mia and Isabelle. Why don't you stay and chat with Natalia for a bit?"

She took off like a shot, weaving her way through the crowd of people. I glanced over at our table. Mia was staring anxiously at me, but she gave me the thumbs up, her mouth curving up in the approximation of a smile.

I hated this. I wanted to go to Mia, throw her over my shoulder and carry her out of this place. I wanted to take her back to my house, back to my bed where I could bury myself in her warm, wet pussy and fuck her senseless while her cries for more echoed through the room.

She doesn't want that. What the two of you had is over now.

"So, this is totally awful and awkward, isn't it?"

I dragged my gaze away from Mia and studied the small blonde standing in front of me. She was pretty with light blue eyes and pale skin and a tight, athletic body.

She didn't do a thing for me.

I preferred Mia's soft curves, Mia's dark eyes filled with need as she begged me to fuck her harder and faster.

"Um, would you prefer if I just go?" Natalia gave me an uncomfortable smile.

I needed to forget about Mia and concentrate on finding someone who would actually love me back. The least I could do was have a conversation with Natalia. Maybe I'd start to feel a flicker of lust for her once I got to know her a little better.

I shook my head no and said, "I'm sorry. I'm being rude. Um, can I buy you a drink?"

"No, thank you. I've already had my one drink for the night."

"Oh, okay," I said.

"I have to pick up my daughter at the babysitter's later," Natalia said.

"Right. How, uh, how old is your daughter?"

"She's three. I don't usually go out on a Wednesday night, but Mel – I work with her at the diner – wanted to go out tonight." She glanced behind her at the small dance floor. A few people were dancing to the music that was blaring from the karaoke machine. "She met some guy about half an hour ago and ditched me."

"Oh, uh, that's too bad."

She just shrugged. "Eh, good for her, right? Anyway, I'd decided it was time to call it a night when I ran into Luna. She insisted that you and I should meet. So, here I am."

"Well, it's, um, nice to meet you."

"You too." She glanced at my body before smiling up at me. "So, you're a firefighter, huh?"

"Yeah. Are you actually interested in learning about weight lifting or…?"

"Or was that just Luna's incredibly awkward way of introducing us?" Natalia laughed.

Her laughter was genuine and infectious, and I grinned at her. "Yeah."

"I am actually interested in learning more about weight training. But I figured I'd watch a few YouTube videos or -"

"No, you shouldn't do that," I said. "Videos can't really show you proper lifting techniques. It's always best to have a qualified trainer show you how to lift."

"Makes sense. Unfortunately, I'm on a budget. Shockingly, working as a waitress at a diner does not pay nearly as much as you would think it does."

"I am shocked," I said.

She laughed. "Right? So, since I'm just a poor, broke waitress, I'm going to take advantage of you and get some free advice on weight lifting." She eyed my body again. "Assuming you didn't get all of those amazing muscles from your heroic job of protecting and saving the people of our good town?"

I blushed, and Natalia's smile widened. "Are you blushing? That's kind of adorable."

I ignored her comment, not quite sure what to do with it… women didn't find me attractive. "I do lift, yeah. I could get you a free guest pass at my gym for a week, if you're interested? I could show you some lifting techniques during that week."

"Really? That would be amazing, Elijah. Thank you. I'll definitely take you up on that,"

Natalia said.

"Sure, it's no problem." My throat was suddenly dry, and I swallowed hard. "So, uh, have you lived here your entire life?"

"Yep. How about you?"

"No, I moved here for the job."

Natalia glanced around the crowded bar. "It's funny how in such a small town, there can still be people you've never met. You know? I don't think I've ever seen you in the diner."

"I don't eat out much, I, um, watch what I eat a lot. I used to be fat and ate pretty unhealthy stuff."

Smooth, idiot. Real smooth.

Natalia eyed my body again. "Well, good for you for eating healthy now. It looks really good on you."

She gave me a slow smile of appreciation, and I stared blankly at her. Was she actually flirting with me? The thought that she might be, made me feel uneasy and anxious. I glanced again at Mia.

She was staring at us and her face was pale, and that familiar anxiety line was between her eyebrows. Isabelle tugged on her arm, and she turned away reluctantly. She shook her head, a brief look of anger crossing her face when Isabelle spoke into her ear.

"So, what do you like to do for fun, Elijah?" Natalia asked.

Before I could answer, Luna's name was called by the guy running the karaoke machine. A loud cheer broke out among the crowd, along with some whistling and catcalling. Luna, her face red, made her way up to the karaoke machine and took the microphone.

A slow song started up and as Luna's clear alto voice washed over the crowd, Natalia smiled up at me before glancing at the dance floor. "Would you like to dance, Elijah?"

"Oh, um…"

I'd only danced with one woman before – Isabelle. I'd chosen her because I knew she had zero interest in me which kept my anxiety about dancing to a minimum. I'd spent the entire dance watching Mia dance with Matt and trying not to burst into flames of jealousy.

"That's okay, we don't have to. I didn't… I mean, I wasn't…"

Now Natalia looked completely embarrassed and guilt surged through me.

"I'd like to dance," I said abruptly. "But, uh, I'm not very good at it."

"Luckily for you," Natalia held out her hand, "you happen to be talking to the grade eight square dance champion. I've got moves, my friend."

I laughed and took her hand. "In that case, I'll let you lead."

We walked to the dance floor, and I put my arm around her waist and held her other hand in a loose grasp as she reached to place her other hand on my shoulder. She was too short, and she settled for resting it on my chest. "Good God, you are one tall guy."

"Sorry," I said.

"Why? I'm not gonna apologize for being the height of a leprechaun. You don't need to say sorry for being the height of a giant."

I laughed again. "You're not leprechaun height."

"You're just saying that to be nice."

"I'm not. I'd say you're at least a few inches taller than the average leprechaun."

"Such a charmer," Natalia said with a laugh. "What woman doesn't want to be told she's slightly taller than the average -"

"Can I cut in?"

We stopped and stared in silent surprise at Mia who'd appeared beside us. She gave Natalia a stiff smile. "Do you mind if I cut in?"

The look on Mia's face was a mixture of jealousy, proprietorship, and anger. Weirdly, it sent a surge of lust through me. I stared hungrily at her as she folded her arms across her chest and gave Natalia a pointed look.

Mia was jealous. She was jealous that I was dancing with Natalia.

"Elijah?"

It took me a few seconds to drag my gaze from Mia. Fuck, I wanted her so bad. Her jealousy was like some weird sort of aphrodisiac.

"Yeah?" I glanced briefly at Natalia before my gaze was drawn back to Mia's face. Christ, she was gorgeous when she was pissed off.

Natalia dropped my hand and stepped away from me. I turned back to her, "Natalia, I'm, uh…"

She shook her head and gave me a soft smile. "Nope, no need to explain. I'm not blind. Enjoy your dance. I should go pick up my kid anyway. It was nice to meet you, Elijah."

"You too, Natalia."

Natalia left the dance floor and Mia gave me an angry look as she pressed her soft body against mine and grabbed my hand. I put my arm around her waist and rested my hand in the curve of her lower back, pulling her into me even tighter as she stared at me.

"You seem to be having fun," she said.

"Natalia is nice," I replied. "I'm going to teach her some weight lifting stuff."

Her body stiffened and I rubbed her lower back soothingly, as another look of jealousy flashed across her face. "You're going to see her again?"

"At the gym."

"That's a weird place to have a date," Mia snapped.

Was it wrong that I was enjoying her jealousy? Probably. But I'd never had a woman be jealous over me before and I couldn't resist teasing her a little.

"She seemed excited about it."

"What does she need to lift weights for?" Mia said. "She's already perfect. With her perfect blonde hair and her slender perfect body."

"She wants to do some strength-training," I said.

"Oh."

We were silent for a few moments before Mia said. "She's not right for you."

"Is that why you interrupted our dance?"

She blushed furiously but gave me a defiant look. "I'm your friend and I know what's best for you. Natalia isn't the right woman."

"Why do you say that?"

"Because she's..." Mia's tongue lashed across

her lower lip and Christ was it distracting. "Because she just isn't. Listen, I'm the one supposed to be finding you a woman, remember? Not Luna."

I shrugged. "Luna seems to think we'll get along well."

"Well, she's wrong," Mia said. "That Natalia chick is too small for you. You'd have to be careful not to crush her tiny, perfect body."

I bent my mouth to her ear, hesitated briefly and then sucked on her lobe for a few seconds before murmuring, "You taught me to be gentle."

Her back had arched a little and I could feel her hand tightening in mine. "I – you need someone different."

"Hmm," I licked her lobe and then nipped it, "you sound jealous."

"I'm not," she said. "I'm just looking out for you."

"Is that right?" I reached down and cupped her ass, giving it a hard squeeze. I had no idea why, but Mia's jealousy had set off some kind of weird sexual confidence in me.

She moaned softly. "Yes, I'm... I'm being a good friend."

"Is that what this is about?" I said. "You being a good friend?"

"She's too little for you." Mia stared up at me. "She probably couldn't even take all of your cock. Is that what you want?"

I bit back my grin and instead solemnly shook my head before pressing my mouth against her ear again. "No, Mia. In fact, one of my favourite things about you is how well your tight pussy takes all of my dick."

"Elijah," she moaned.

"You like that too, don't you? You like being stuffed full of my cock. Don't you, Mia?"

"Yes," she said in a low voice. Her cheeks were red, her eyes were bright with excitement, and she had never looked more beautiful to me.

"You want my dick right now, don't you?"

"Yes," she said. "I do, Elijah."

"I know. C'mon."

I stepped back and when I started off the dance floor, she resisted a bit. "Where are we going?"

I pulled her close again so the people around us wouldn't hear me. "Back to my place. You're gonna get on your hands and knees, spread those soft thighs of yours and I'm gonna fuck you until you can't think straight. Do you have a problem with that?"

Christ, I could almost smell her lust.

"No, Elijah," she whispered.

"Good. Let's go."

࿊ ࿊

I was undressing the minute I ushered Mia into my bedroom. I stripped off all my clothes in record time before raising my eyebrow at the still fully-clothed Mia. "Take off your clothes, Mia."

She stared wide-eyed at me. She'd said nothing the entire ride to my place, but the way she kept squirming in her seat as I rubbed my hand up and down her thigh, made me confident she was soaking wet already.

Normally, I'd undress her, but this time I

reclined on the bed and stared at her. "Undress."

She reached for the hem of her shirt and I said, "Slow."

She blushed but slowly pulled her shirt over her head before dropping it on the floor. Her dark hair was down, and I studied the way it gleamed in the light as she reached to unclasp her bra. She held it against her tits for a moment before letting it slide down her arms, revealing those beautiful pale globes slowly.

"Touch them," I demanded. My voice was hoarse, and I watched eagerly as Mia cupped her tits and rubbed her nipples with her thumbs. "Does that feel good, baby?"

"Yes," she moaned. She squeezed them harder and I groaned when she unbuttoned her jeans and eased them down her legs. She kicked them off and gracefully removed her socks before standing in front of me. Only a scrap of silk separated my hungry gaze from her pussy.

"Are you wet, Mia?"

"Yes." She spread her legs just a little, and it was my turn to moan when I saw the growing wet spot on her silk panties. Her hands were cupping and kneading her tits again and I watched, my excitement growing, as she tugged and pinched her nipples until they were hard and swollen.

I glanced up at her face and then followed her gaze to my crotch. Shame flooded through me and I snatched my hand away from my dick. I'd been rubbing and squeezing my cock without even realizing it.

"Don't stop," Mia said. "I want to watch."

"No," I said. "Get on the bed, Mia."

She shook her head and gave me a sexy, stubborn look. "No, I want to watch you touch yourself, Elijah."

Dirty boy! Sinner!

More shame filled me, and my dick shriveled. "I said no."

"Why not?"

"Drop it, Mia," I said.

She shook her head and embarrassed and angry, I turned on my side and stared at the wall. "You know what? I'm tired. Let's do this another night."

"Oh, no fucking way," Mia said.

I tensed when Mia climbed into the bed behind me and pressed her warm tits against my back. Despite my shame and bad memories, my cock immediately hardened again.

"Why do you look like you're gonna barf whenever you start touching yourself?" Mia said.

"I don't want to talk about it," I replied.

Her soft hands traced the scars on my back. "Did your parents teach you that masturbating was wrong?"

Jesus, she was too perceptive for her own good. I kept my mouth shut as she pressed a soft kiss against my back, her fingers still tracing the ridges of healed flesh on my lower back.

"Tell me why you have these scars, Elijah." Her voice was loving but firm.

My stomach churning, my dick back to being completely out of the game, I said, "I knew it was wrong. I'd been told repeatedly that touching yourself was a sin, but I was fourteen and I couldn't help it. I didn't want to sin, but I just... I couldn't help it."

God, I sounded pathetic, but Mia made a soothing sound and pressed herself even closer against me.

"My mother came into my room. She was supposed to knock first, that was the rule, but she-she didn't follow the rule. When she saw what I was doing, she freaked out. I begged her not to tell my father, but she dragged me downstairs and made me confess to him."

I tried to drag in a breath, old shame and guilt making the air turn to soup around me. "My father made me get on my knees and then he-he took off his belt and hit me with it until I passed out."

"Oh, Elijah." Mia sounded close to tears.

When I woke up, I was still lying on the floor and there was blood everywhere. My parents were praying and calling me dirty and a sinner and a fornicator. They made me get on my knees again and pray for God's forgiveness while my mother wailed and screamed about how I was going to hell, and my father threatened to beat me again if I didn't pray hard enough. After that night, I didn't touch myself again until I was in my early twenties. And even then, I felt dirty and guilty and awful for days after. I've mostly gotten over the idea that sex is a sin, but masturbating... it-it's more difficult to let go of my guilt."

I fell silent, my body stiff and my stomach feeling like an entire football team was stampeding through it. I waited dully for Mia to get up and leave. Now that she knew how truly fucked up I was, she'd be gone. I wouldn't blame her either.

"Elijah, turn over."

I didn't want to, but I couldn't deny her. I rolled over, staring at her perfect tits, until she cupped my face and made me look at her.

"Your parents are monsters," she said softly. "They took what is natural and normal and turned it into a perversion. They made you believe it was sick."

She squeezed my face and gave me a grave look. "It isn't. There is nothing wrong with touching yourself, Elijah. Nothing. Sex isn't a sin, and masturbating isn't a sin. What they did to you was abuse and they're the ones going to hell. Not you. You are a good, sweet, kind man. You're not dirty or sick or a sinner. Do you hear me?"

I didn't reply and she gave my face a little shake. "Do you hear me?"

"Yes, Mia," I whispered.

She stroked my face and pressed a soft kiss against my mouth. "I'm so sorry your parents did this to you, Elijah. You didn't deserve it."

I studied her face as she stroked my chest with soft, light touches. "I'm not going to ask you to touch yourself tonight, but will you do something for me?"

"What?" I rasped.

"Watch me touch myself. Watch how good I can make myself feel and try to see that it isn't bad or wrong. Everyone touches themselves, Elijah. It's normal and appropriate and a good thing. Will you watch me?"

"Yes," I said. "I – I want to watch you, Mia."

"Good."

She relaxed on her back and pushed her panties down her legs and off of her feet. I reached to cup her breast and she gave me a cute little wink before pushing my hand away. "Nope. Not this time, mister. This is a solo mission."

I smiled a little and she stroked my face tenderly. "Watch, honey."

Her soft hands cupped her breasts again and she tugged on her nipples, toying with them lightly as I watched. My cock was starting to stiffen and when she slid her hand down over her stomach and touched the soft dark curls at the apex of her thighs, I made a low groan.

She spread her legs wide until I could see the glistening wetness of her pussy lips and clit. Her fingers brushed against her clit and she moaned, her back arching a little as her other hand cupped one breast.

I watched in fascination, my heart beating humming-bird fast, and my cock rapidly stiffening, as Mia stroked her clit in tiny circles. Her low moans were growing louder and when she gave her clit a soft tug she gasped and her hips rose up off the bed.

I glanced at her face. Her eyes were closed, her cheeks were rosy, and she was biting compulsively at her bottom lip as she pleasured herself. A small tiny voice deep inside my head was trying to tell me it was wrong, that what Mia was doing was a sin and dirty, but I found it remarkably easy to ignore. Mia touching herself was one of the most beautiful things I'd ever seen.

It couldn't be wrong or bad. Not when it was my Mia.

Mia's sharp gasp made me drag my gaze back to her pussy. She'd slid two fingers deep into her pussy and was slowly finger-fucking herself. I clenched my hands into fists. I wanted to touch her so bad. Instead, I said, "Does that feel good, baby?"

Her eyes popped open and she gave me a lazy smile of pure need. "Yeah. Not as good as your dick though."

I smiled at her. "I can't wait to be inside your tight pussy, baby."

"Not too much longer now," she panted. "Will you fuck me on my hands and knees like you promised?"

"Yes," I said. "As soon as you cum, I'll fuck you."

"Oh God," she moaned. Her fingers left her sweet, tight hole and rubbed furiously at her clit. Her hips rose and fell with her strokes and she squeezed and kneaded her tits as her groans grew louder. "Oh fuck, oh, I'm so close, I'm so…"

Her voice trailed off into a long, drawn-out moan and her curvy body stiffened and then shook wildly. Her fingers rubbed for a few more seconds at her clit before she pulled them away and collapsed against the bed. "Fuck, that felt good."

I picked up her hand and she moaned again when I sucked both her fingers into my mouth and licked them clean.

"Oh my God, Elijah…"

"Your pussy tastes sweet, baby. Get on your hands and knees."

"I just need a couple of minutes to catch my breath and -"

"No, baby. Do what I tell you." My shame and guilt had disappeared, and I wanted Mia with a deep seated need that was almost painful.

Mia studied me for a moment before smiling slowly. "Yes, Elijah."

She rolled to her hands and knees. A wave of overwhelming lust washed over me when she spread her legs wide and I saw the wet, slick lips of her pussy and her tight hole waiting to be filled with my dick.

She stared at me over her shoulder, giving me another slow and lazy smile. "Are we fucking or not?"

I growled at her and gave her a light slap to the ass as I knelt between her legs. She squealed and giggled before wiggling her butt at me. "Am I gonna need a safe word or – ohhhh. Oh fuck!"

I had lined my dick up to her pussy and pushed in to the hilt with one hard thrust. Her back arched, her head fell back, and her hands dug into the sheets as she tried to adjust to my size. I reached over her and gathered her hair into one fist. I tugged hard, making her gasp, as I gripped her hip with my other hand.

I didn't move and she made a whining noise. "Elijah, please."

"Tell me what you want."

"I want you to fuck me."

I grinned and tightened my grip on her hair before thrusting steadily in and out of her soaking wet pussy. She cried out and when she tried to wiggle forward, I clamped my other hand down on her shoulder. "No, take my cock, Mia. All of it."

"Oh my God!" Her pussy tightened around me, and I groaned before making two hard pumps into her.

My need for her was out of control, and I held tight to her hair and her shoulder as I fucked her with hard and rough strokes. She widened her thighs and moaned loudly, her hips meeting each of my thrusts with unrestrained enthusiasm. The only sound in the room was our harsh breathing, the wet sucking sounds of her pussy as it took my invading cock over and over, and the slap of my pelvis against her perfect ass, as we fucked hard and fast.

I drove harder and deeper, my hand still wrapped in Mia's dark hair. I tugged her head even farther back until she was staring straight up at the ceiling, her cries and gasps of pleasure growing increasingly louder.

"Cum for me, Mia," I growled. "Cum for me right now."

She made a loud wail of pleasure and came hard. I drove deep a final time as her pussy squeezed exquisitely tight around me. I roared her name and let my own climax roll over me, my hand squeezing her shoulder hard, keeping her in place as I pumped her tiny pussy full of my cum.

When my body had finally stopped shaking, I released Mia's hair and shoulder. She collapsed face-first on the bed, her body heaving for air as I eased out of her. I laid on my side next to her and rubbed her back.

"Oh my God." Her voice was muffled by the

pillows. "That was – that was the best sex of my life."

I grinned and pulled the covers over both of us before turning her on her side and spooning her.

"I hope you're okay with me staying the night," she said. "My body is like a damn noodle right now. Pretty sure I won't be able to walk on these spaghetti legs for at least a few hours."

"You're not going anywhere. Go to sleep, baby." I kissed the back of her shoulder and snuggled in closer, my hand cupping her breast and our legs entwined.

Chapter Twelve

Mia

I studied Elijah's sleeping body before sitting on the side of the bed. I'd woken up almost an hour ago and had a quick shower and dressed before returning to Elijah's bed. Last night was amazing and incredible, and I'd loved every moment of it.

This morning though... I felt terrible for what I'd done. I needed to apologize to Elijah, but I was dreading it. I'd been so horribly selfish all goddamn night and I hated what I'd done to him.

Yeah, well, you were awful and it's time to stop dragging your damn heels and do the right thing, Mia. You distracted him with sex last night, but as soon as he wakes up, he's gonna be pissed about what you did. You need to apologize.

I wanted to strip off my clothes and crawl back into bed with Elijah. Instead, I squared my shoulders and rubbed the wide expanse of his back. He made a cute little snore before stretching and then rolling onto his back.

He gave me a sleepy smile and I held up the mug of coffee. "Morning, Elijah."

"Hey." He sat up, tucking the pillow behind his back and taking the coffee when I handed it to him. "Thank you. What did I do to deserve coffee in bed?"

"I need to apologize for last night," I said.

He opened his mouth and I shook my head. "No, can you… I mean, I just need to get this out, okay? Then you can yell at me."

"Why would I yell at you?"

I took a deep breath and blew it out. "I'm sorry for my behaviour last night, Elijah. I acted like a horrible, jealous bitch and I'm ashamed about that. You were making a connection with Natalia and I ruined it."

"Mia -"

"It's not just that," I said. "I used sex as a weapon to-to get you to go home with me. Then I pushed you to talk about something that you didn't want to talk about. I forced you to tell me a secret that you weren't ready to share, and I am truly sorry. I should never have pried into your personal life the way I did, and I hope you can forgive me. I know you're angry with me and I -"

"I'm not angry with you," Elijah said. "Mia, I'm not."

I gave him a blank look of shock. "What? You are. Of course, you are. I was awful last night. I was an awful person, Elijah."

He laughed and took a sip of his coffee. "No, you weren't. You're fucking perfect, Mia." He gave me a tender look that hinged on worship and every nerve in my body pinged in alarm.

He reached out and squeezed my thigh. "Everything you do is amazing and perfect, and last night was -"

"I'm not perfect." I could hear the anxiety in my voice tinged with the slightest bit of anger.

Elijah shrugged. "You are to me. You're beautiful and perfect, and you don't need to apologize. I'm not angry."

"You should be angry," I said slowly. "Elijah, what I did wasn't fair to you. I promised to help you find a girlfriend and instead I – I sabotaged it."

He shrugged again. "I wasn't attracted to Natalia. Don't worry about it."

"That's not the point."

He gave me a cheeky grin. "Then what is the point? That you find me so hot, you can't resist me? Mia, I don't want another woman. You're the perfect woman and -"

"Stop it!" My voice was loud and this time the anger was evident. "Stop saying that!"

"Stop saying what?" Elijah blinked at me.

"Stop saying I'm perfect! What's wrong with you? You need to be angry, you need to be upset with me."

"Well, I'm not," he said.

I threw my hands up in the air. "Elijah, I am not perfect, and you need to stop saying that I am. You need to stop *believing* that I am."

He gave me a stubborn look. "What is going on? Since when is it a bad thing to give a woman a compliment?"

"Being told you're perfect is not a compliment,"

I snapped.

His big hand tightened around his coffee mug and a flicker of anger crossed his face. He set the mug down on the nightstand with a harsh thud, coffee sloshing over the edge. "I don't know what you want from me, Mia."

"I want you to stop thinking I'm perfect!" I was almost yelling now, and I tried to take a deep breath and just chill the fuck out a little. It didn't work. Elijah being like Phillip was more than I could stand. Not when I was falling in lo-

Nope! Nope, don't you say it, girl.

"Seriously? You want me to stop complimenting you? Jesus..." Elijah ran a hand through his thick hair. "I can't do a thing right, can I, Mia? It doesn't matter what I do or what I say, it's always wrong. Why did you even agree to sleep with me?"

"Because I..."

I pressed my lips together, feeling sick to my stomach when Elijah made a bitter laugh. "Right. Because you had an itch that needed scratching. That's all it is, right? I'm good enough to fuck, but not good enough to date."

"No! That isn't it at all! Elijah, I just – I don't want you thinking I'm perfect. Okay? I need you to -"

"Fine," he said. "I don't think you're perfect. Does that make you happy?"

"I'm sorry," I said.

"Don't," he said. "I don't want or need your pity. Thank you for teaching me how to fuck, but I think I'm good now."

I glared at him. "Listen, I'm asking for something simple. Realize that I'm not as perfect as you think I am. I'm not saying I want to stop what's happening between us, and in fact, I was thinking maybe we could try dat -"

"I want to stop," Elijah said.

I swallowed hard. "W-what?"

"I want to stop," he repeated. "I don't need any more lessons and I can find a girlfriend on my own. Someone who wants me for more than itch scratching"

I blinked back the tears and cleared my throat. "Elijah, I -"

"Can you go, Mia? I'm tired and there's nothing left to say. I'll see you around." He stared at a spot over my shoulder, his face closed off and withdrawn.

Tears starting to drip down my face, I turned and practically sprinted for the door.

❧ ❧

I stood in Nana's driveway, staring at my hands. In the three days since my fight with Elijah, I hadn't left my house once. I had to work tomorrow, and I was already dreading it. If there was an accident and I saw Elijah at the scene, I didn't know what I would do. Burst into tears would be my first guess.

I sighed and trudged toward the front door. I hadn't wanted to leave the house today either, but Nana had called and insisted I come over this afternoon. Unable to think of a reason why I couldn't, I'd dragged my sorry ass into the shower, threw my hair up into a bun, put on my least stained yoga pants and t-shirt, and drove over here.

I walked up the front steps and rapped on the door before walking inside. Nana's house smelled exactly like it always did, warm cinnamon and crisp apples, but even the familiar smell couldn't lift my depression.

"Nana?" I hung my jacket in the closet and removed my boots. "I'm here. Why did you ask me to park down the street? I thought the driveway wasn't being repaved until next week."

"I'm in the kitchen, sweetheart."

I walked down the hallway to the kitchen. "What is it that you needed? I can't stay very long. I'm sorry, but I…. Isabelle? Wyatt? What are you doing here?"

I stared in confusion at my best friend and my cousin who were sitting at the table with Nana. A plate of cookies was in front of them, and Wyatt grabbed a cookie and ate it as I continued to stare at them.

"Sit down, Mia," Isabelle said.

"What's going on?" I gave Isabelle a suspicious look. Although I hadn't said a word to Nana about what happened, I'd already cried on Isabelle's shoulder twice since the fight.

Isabelle glanced at Nana. "This is an intervention."

"What? What do you mean an intervention?"

"Just sit down, Mia. Please."

I began to back out of the kitchen. "Nope, no way. I don't know what's happening here, but I -"

"Mia Margaret Martin," Nana said. "Sit your cute butt in that chair immediately."

Sulking, I walked into the kitchen and parked

my butt in the chair, folding my arms across my chest.

"Your middle name is Margaret?" Isabelle said.

"Cork it, Izzy."

She grinned at me and folded her hands together on top of the table. "This is a love intervention, Mia."

"Whoa, a what now?" Wyatt paused with a second cookie at his mouth.

Isabelle ignored him. "Mia, you love Elijah and Elijah loves you. It's more than apparent. You need to talk to him and work this shit out."

"Wait… Elijah? Elijah Thomson? You're in love with that jacked firefighter?" Wyatt said.

"No!" I snapped.

"Yes, she is," Isabelle said. "Wyatt, I told you we were doing an intervention on Mia."

"I didn't know it was a," Wyatt made a face, "love intervention."

"What kind of intervention did you think it was gonna be?" Isabelle gave him an exasperated look.

"I dunno… a cheese intervention, maybe."

"A cheese intervention?" I sputtered.

"You have an addiction to cheese," Wyatt said solemnly.

"I do not!" I turned to Isabelle who shrugged.

"He's right. You do have an addiction to cheese."

"I don't!" I said indignantly. "Just because I love cheese doesn't mean -"

"You have a drawer in your fridge dedicated to just cheese," Wyatt said. "You need help, Mia."

"Wyatt, sweetie, perhaps we can talk to Mia

about her cheese addiction at another intervention," Nana said gently. "Right now, this intervention is about her love for that sweet boy Elijah."

Wyatt rolled his eyes and took a bite of cookie. "Worst. Intervention. Ever."

"I don't need a love intervention," I said. "I'm perfectly fine."

Nana leaned forward and took one of my hands in hers. "Oh, dear heart, you're not fine. You're heartbroken."

She gave me a look of compassion and love, and the tears immediately started to spill down my cheeks. "I-I-I'm fine."

Isabelle handed me a tissue. "You're not, honey. And it's okay that you're not. But we want to help you get better. The only way to do that is by forcing you to see that you need Elijah in your life. You are miserable without him."

"He thinks I'm perfect," I whispered.

"Obviously, he doesn't know you well enough yet," Wyatt said.

"Wyatt!" Isabelle glared at him.

"What? She's not perfect. She has weird looking feet, she's addicted to cheese, she can't ride a bike, and," Wyatt gave me a smug look, "she cheats at Scrabble."

I wanted to flip him the bird, but with Nana in the room, I settled for giving him a dirty look. "Just because I beat you every time at Scrabble, doesn't mean I'm cheating."

Wyatt mumbled something under his breath before stretching his long legs out under the table and nudging my calf with his foot. "Izzy's right,

Mia. You look miserable."

"Don't call me Izzy," Isabelle said automatically. "Mia, Elijah is not like Phillip, okay? You panicked and you made a wrong decision when you and Elijah had your fight, and that's understandable, considering what you went through. Phillip was a total dickhe – jerk – sorry, Nana."

Isabelle gave Nana an apologetic look and Nana made a 'go on' motion with her hand.

"Phillip was a jerk and like I told you before, no one could have lived up to his expectations. Okay? Maybe Elijah thinks you're perfect right now and maybe eventually he'll start to see your flaws, but regardless, he's not Phillip. He adores you, Mia. The way he looked at you that night at the bar… he is in love with you. He will still be in love with you even when he recognizes your flaws," Isabelle said. "Don't throw that away, honey."

I swiped at the tears with the tissue. "It's too late. I wrecked everything by acting like an idiot. He said we were done, remember? He's probably already friggin' moved on by now."

"Doubtful," Wyatt said. "I saw him last night at an accident and -"

"Accident?" I froze in my chair and gave Wyatt a look of terror. "Is he okay? Is he hurt? What happened? How did he -"

"Mia, relax," Wyatt said. "He wasn't in the accident, he was at the scene of the accident. It's his job, remember? Shit, you do have it bad for this guy." He shook his head. "Anyway, he was there, and he looked like shit. I mean, he looked worse than the guy who actually *was* in the accident. It's obvious that he's just as miserable as you are."

"See?" Isabelle said. "You need to talk to him."

"I don't know," I said. "What if he -"

The doorbell rang and Nana popped out of her seat like a jackrabbit. "Who could that be?" She gave me a guilty look before hurrying out of the kitchen. "I'll just go check."

"Why does Nana look guilty?" I asked Wyatt.

Wyatt shrugged. "How should I know? I'm just here for the cookies."

Isabelle squeezed my hand. "Don't be angry, honey. Okay? Remember that we did this because we love you."

"Isabelle?" I gave her a warning look. "What have you done? Please tell me that you -"

"Thank you so much for coming by, sweet boy," Nana's voice drifted down the hall. "I've asked Wyatt a couple of times to look at the sink, but he's just so darn busy lately. Mia said you were pretty handy so I figured I'd see if you could help."

"Isabelle," I said in a fierce whisper. "Please tell me you didn't -"

"Oh, Mia, dear heart, look who's here."

I swiveled in my chair, my heart thumping in my chest and my face bright red. Elijah stared back at me before beginning to back out of the kitchen. "Uh, I should go. I can come back -"

"Don't be silly." Nana took his arm and tugged him forward. "Stay and have a cookie, Elijah. They're freshly baked."

"Um…"

She smiled up at him. "You're not going to break an old woman's heart by refusing to try one of her freshly-baked cookies, are you, sweetheart?"

Helpless against the relentless force that was my grandmother, Elijah shook his head. "No, ma'am."

"Good, good. Remember, I told you to call me Nana or Martha. Have a seat. Would you like a glass of milk with your cookies?"

Elijah dropped into the chair next to me. "Um, sure, that would be nice."

"Good." As Nana grabbed two glasses from the cupboard and the milk from the fridge, Isabelle stood up and stared pointedly at Wyatt.

"Hey, Wyatt? Can you come help me with that *thing* now?"

Wyatt grinned at her. "I already helped you with that *thing*, Izzy. I think I'll stay in the kitchen and have some more milk and cookies."

He flinched when Nana gave him a hard poke between the shoulder blades. "Go and help Isabelle with the thing. Right now, young man."

"Yes, Nana." Wyatt made a face at me and I stuck my tongue out at him as he stood and grabbed another cookie. "Good seeing you again, Elijah."

"You too, Wyatt," Elijah replied.

Isabelle and Wyatt left the kitchen and Nana sat the glasses of milk in front of us before clearing her throat. There was a moment of awkward silence and then Nana said, "I should go help the kids with their...thing. You two stay here."

She hurried out of the kitchen and I stared at the glass of milk in front of me. Without speaking, Elijah held the plate of cookies out to me and I took one with a small nod of thanks. He took one as well and we each ate a cookie. I was so nervous and sick to my stomach, that I could only eat half of mine before I set it down.

"So, uh, I guess there's nothing wrong with your Nana's sink, huh?" Elijah finally said.

"Nope."

"Why are Isabelle and your cousin here?" He asked.

"They're having an intervention for me," I said.

"For your cheese addiction?"

I glanced up at him. "Why does everyone think I have a cheese addiction?"

"You have an entire drawer in your fridge for cheese, Mia."

I stared at him, and when his lips curled up in a smile, I leaned over and rested my head on his thick arm.

"I'm so sorry, Elijah. So damn sorry."

"I am too," he said. "I shouldn't have gotten angry with you. It was stupid."

"No, I was being stupid." I sighed and lifted my head before taking his hand.

He squeezed it gently and, staring at the kitchen table, I said, "I used to date this guy named Phillip. Met him at the bar one night. He wasn't from here, had just moved to town like two months before that. He was a chef over at Josie's Bar and Grill."

I poked at the half-eaten cookie in front of me. "We got along really well, and we started dating. He-he was always talking about how I was the perfect woman and how everything I did was amazing and wonderful. After a few months, we moved in together."

I fell silent and Elijah squeezed my hand again. "It's okay, Mia. You don't have to tell me."

"I want to tell you," I said. "After we moved in together, it – it wasn't that Phillip changed exactly. He just, well, I guess he just had a side to him that I hadn't noticed or didn't want to notice. He'd put me up on this pedestal of perfection and when I couldn't keep up his standard of perfection, it was almost…crushing to him, you know? Like I fell off that pedestal and I fell hard, and that was it. Then I couldn't do anything right."

My stomach churned but I forced myself to go on. "He constantly criticized me about everything. Before, he used to love my body, told me I was sexy and beautiful, but it switched to I was too fat and I needed to lose weight. If I had a bad day at work, I couldn't tell him about it because he would twist it around on me, make it sound like it was bad because I wasn't working hard enough to be good at my job."

"You're good at your job," Elijah said.

"Yeah, I am," I replied. I smiled up at him. "I know that I am, but at the time… I let him say those horrible things to me because I was lonely. Even worse, I let him put me on that damn pedestal of perfection, even knowing that I wouldn't be able to stay there. It just, it made me feel good, you know?"

Elijah pressed a kiss against my forehead. "Sounds like he had unreasonable expectations, Mia."

"Yeah, that's what Isabelle and Nana said, and I

know they're right. I do. But then every time you said I was perfect, it freaked me out because I was already falling in love with you and thinking that you might be like Phillip really scared me. Even though, deep down I knew you weren't like him, Elijah. I *knew* it. But it's like a damn trigger for me or something."

I sighed and rubbed at my forehead. "I probably need some serious therapy."

Elijah didn't say anything, and I glanced up at him, expecting to see pity and disgust on his face. Instead, there was a look of shock and - my pulse zinged, zagged, zigged - was that happiness?

"Elijah? You okay?"

"You love me?" He whispered.

Shit. I hadn't meant to say that out loud, but it was too late to take it back. I nodded. "Yeah, I do. I know it's quick and weird, and I swear I'm not trying to really freak you out, but I'm like a hundred percent positive that I love you, Elijah. But you don't have to – oh my God!"

Elijah, the muscles in his arms bulging, had turned and scooped me up out of the chair with ease. He sat me in his lap, cupped my face and kissed me hard on the mouth. I made another muffled sound of shock before sinking into him and returning his kiss eagerly.

I wasn't exactly sure what was happening, but God had I missed his kisses. I pressed myself up against him, sweeping my tongue across his lips. When he parted them, I practically shoved my tongue into his mouth, tasting him with greedy desire.

He pulled back after a few moments and studied my swollen mouth before smiling at me. "I love you, Mia."

"You love me," I said.

He nodded. "You can't be all that surprised."

"I am," I said. "I mean, I knew you liked me and that you wanted to maybe date, but I -"

"I've had a crush on you for over a year," he said. "When you offered to teach me how to have sex, I couldn't believe it. It was like every one of my fantasies had come true."

"Over a year?" I whispered. "Why didn't you say something before."

"Because you were in love with Matt, and because I was a virgin and embarrassed," he said.

"I don't love Matt now," I said quickly. "I swear, Elijah. Honestly, what I thought was love was more a combination of loneliness and convincing myself he was the one for me because he knew me so well and knew I was far from perfect. But I don't love him as anything more than a friend. I love you and only you."

"I believe you," he said. "I'm sorry again for what I said."

"No," I said. "You don't have to apologize."

He kissed my mouth, pulling away before I could deepen it. "I know you have flaws and make mistakes just like everyone else, but, Mia, I will not stop telling you that you're the perfect woman. Because you're the perfect woman for me and I love you."

He wiped away the tear that was sliding down my cheek and I gave him a soft smile. "Elijah

Thomson, you just might be the perfect man."

The Cop
(Book Eight)

Ramona Gray

Chapter One

Maggie

"Shit." I looked in the rearview mirror as the flashing lights lit up the growing gloom and the siren broke the silence.

I glanced at my speed before slowing down, pulling over to the side of the road and stopping. I put the car in park and rubbed at my temples. I wasn't speeding and I had zero idea why the cop was pulling me over.

I was about five miles from some small town I'd never heard of, a blip on the map, just another place to get through on my way to…. well, I had no idea where, but what I did know was that the last thing I needed was a damn ticket.

"All right, Maggie. You know what you need to do," I said to my reflection in the rearview mirror.

I cringed but unbuttoned the first couple of buttons on my shirt, giving my small breasts a quick adjustment. I didn't have much in the chest department, but maybe the cop was into chicks with tiny tits. I took a deep breath and blew it out.

"You can do this, Maggie. Flirt your way out of this ticket, girl. Flirt *hard*. You can't afford a ticket, so smile pretty, let him have a look at your cleavage, and -"

The sharp rap on my window made me startle and I jerked, my seat belt cutting into my chest. I rolled the window down, the flirtatious smile dying before it really started as I stared at the magnificent god standing next to my car.

Holy shit, Mags, if this is how they grow 'em in small towns, maybe you should reconsider your idea to find a big city.

The cop stared silently at me as my gaze roamed his face. Tanned skin, sharp cheekbones, a narrow nose and... oh God, total cliché – but piercing, and I mean, piercing, blue eyes that were staring straight into my damn soul. I wanted desperately to take a look at the tall, lean body attached to the most beautiful face in the universe, but I couldn't seem to look away from his gaze.

Snap out of it, Mags. Start flirting, for God's sake.

Right. Flirting. No problem.

"Good evening, Officer." I pasted that flirtatious smile on my face and thrust my chest out. Shit, I should have undone my seat belt first.

The cop's gaze never wavered from my face. "Ma'am. License and registration, please."

Holy hell... what a voice. My pussy actually quivered in response to the deep, gravel-filled rasp.

"Of course." My smile widened, and I unclicked my seat belt before leaning over and digging the registration out of the glovebox, then snagged my license from my wallet.

I cocked my head and bit my bottom lip, arching my back and working my tiny tits with everything I had as I handed over my information.

C'mon, tiny tits, don't fail me now.

The cop took my license and registration, his gaze still firmly on my face.

Houston, we have a problem. It's a tiny tits failure. We're asking for permission to abort.

Abort? Not with my limited funds, dammit. I let my fingers trace the soft skin of my upper chest as I bit my bottom lip again. "What seems to be the problem... Officer?"

For the size of my body, I had a weirdly deep voice, but I had been pitching it higher, making it breathy and squeaky. It didn't have the desired effect on the cop, but I kept trying. "I wasn't speeding."

He studied my license before lifting those stormy ocean eyes back to my face. "Ma'am, are you aware that it's a crime to provide false ID to a police officer?"

I sighed, admitted failure, and aborted the mission. "It's not a false ID, Officer."

If he was surprised by the sound of my normal speaking voice, it didn't show on his face. "Is that right?"

"Yes," I said.

"Your name is," his gaze dipped to my license again, "Magnolia Blossom?"

I rattled off my regular spiel whenever someone discovered my full name. "Yes. First name

Magnolia. Last name Blossom. Like the flower. My parents were hippies."

He didn't reply, and I made a show of checking my watch before giving him a clearly irritated smile. "Can you tell me why I've been stopped, Officer? The speed limit is fifty and I was doing fifty."

"Your tail light is out."

"Oh. Okay, well, I'll get that fixed. Thanks for letting me know." I held my hand out for my license and registration.

"Where are you headed, Ms. Blossom?"

After a week on the road, rapidly dwindling funds, and no solid idea of where I was going or what I was doing, my already-frayed nerves took another hit. I was suddenly and irrationally angry at the stupidly handsome cop.

Or, maybe I was just pissed that my flirting hadn't worked one single bit.

"How is that any of your business, Officer..." I squinted at his nametag in the rapidly growing dark, "Reynolds?"

Annoyance flickered across his face and he stepped back. "Wait here, please, Ms. Blossom."

"Oh, for heaven's sake," I muttered as he took my license and registration back to his car.

My temper steadily rose as I waited nearly five minutes for Officer "How Could Such a Beautiful Man be Such a Dickhead" to return.

The cold air drifting through the open window was making me shiver, and I cranked the heat in my car and rolled up my window. I rubbed at my temples. It was getting late and dark, and snow was starting to fall. My plan to drive through the one-horse town I was on the outskirts of and hit the bigger town after it was rapidly changing. I hated driving to begin with, and driving in an unfamiliar area after dark and during a snowstorm? No, thank you. I'd just have to hope the rinky-dink town had at least one motel.

Officer Muscles rapped on my window again and I rolled it down. Snowflakes were starting to cling to his dark hair, and he was wearing just a t-shirt under his vest, but the cold and the weather didn't seem to affect him at all. I looked away from the hard line of his biceps as he held my paperwork out.

Yeah, because he's already stone-cold, Mags. He might be handsome, but his arrogance is a total turn-off.

Right, a total turn-off.... no lingering attraction here at all.

"What's this?" I stared blankly at the piece of paper he handed to me with my license and registration.

"It's a ticket for your broken tail light."

My jaw dropped and I stared at him. "You're kidding me."

"I am not, Ms. Blossom. A broken tail light is a fineable offense."

I stared at the amount of the ticket, my stomach churning. "Isn't this a bit excessive? It's a broken tail light. I'll get it fixed."

"When you do, bring the receipt to your court date, and the judge will dismiss the fine," he said.

"The court date is a month from now. I'm just

passing through." I hitched my thumb at my backseat that was covered with three suitcases.

"Then I guess you'll need to pay the fine."

My temper flared and I glared at Officer Hot and Arrogant. "Look, can't you just give me a warning and let me go? I promise I'll fix the tail light first thing in the morning."

"Rules are rules, Ms. Blossom. You can pay the fine or, in a month, you can bring your receipt to the court and have the fine dismissed."

"I – *seriously*? It is a broken tail light." I spoke slowly, as if that might knock some sense into him.

"I am aware." He gave me a steely stare. "Drive safe, Ms. Blossom."

He turned to walk away, and I muttered "arrogant asshole", under my breath as I tossed the ticket and my license and registration onto my passenger seat.

Apparently, Officer Bulging Biceps also had the hearing of a hawk, because he immediately turned back. "What was that, Ms. Blossom?"

Jesus, why did his low voice saying my name make my nipples go hard?

It's not his voice, it's the cold air, idiot.

Right. The cold air.

"Nothing," I said.

He studied me, those blue eyes making my insides feel weirdly hot. I had a sudden desire to confess my insult to him. What the hell was wrong with me?

I straightened my back and gave him my best ice-cold court stare. "Thank you, Officer Reynolds. It's been a pleasure."

His nostrils flared just the tiniest bit and the exasperation on his face was fleeting, but a wave of perverse pleasure washed over me. I had gotten under his skin, just a little. He turned to leave, and weird disappointment washed over me.

I had no idea what my odd compulsion to interact with him just a little longer was about, and it was more than a little alarming. Still, it didn't stop me from saying, "Officer Reynolds?"

"Yes?"

"Uh," I searched desperately for something to say. "Does your tiny little town even have a motel?"

"We have two. One is," he paused, "a Best Western, and the other is a smaller locally-owned motel."

"What's the name of the motel?" I asked.

"Park Motel. It's over on Park Street. You'll want to stay at the Best Western," he said. "It's more expensive but cleaner and safer for a woman traveling on her own."

"Thank you." I gave him a frosty smile and he nodded before walking back to his car.

I stared at – goddammit, the most amazing ass I'd ever seen in a pair of jeans – in the side mirror before he climbed into his SUV and shut the door.

I googled the Park Motel and put the address into my GPS. The Best Western might have been safer, but with my limited cash, I needed the cheapest option. The questionable Park Motel it was.

I put the car into drive and with another quick glance at the cop car behind me, pulled back onto the road. He stayed where he was on the side of the road, and I blew my breath out again as I drove around a curve in the road and Officer Fine Ass disappeared from my rearview mirror.

ॐ ॐ

"Ugh. Officer Hot Pants was right." I stared in disgust at the motel room before closing the door behind me and dropping the key card on the desk. I studied the covers on the bed then gingerly pulled them back.

"Oh lord, oh god, no thank you... nope, not crawling in there." I whipped the covers back over the bed and headed into the bathroom. It was... almost clean, and the stack of towels on the shelf below the sink were at least cleaner than the bedding.

I laid the towels across the bed and laid another one across the pillow before propping it up against the headboard. I grabbed the bottle of water and bag of chips I'd bought from the vending machine near the lobby, then sat down on the bed. I rearranged the pillow between my back and the headboard and leaned back. My stomach growled and I drank some water.

I probably should have stopped at that diner I passed on the way to the motel and had a proper meal, but I wasn't sure I had enough money for gas. Buying an entire meal was a luxury I couldn't afford.

I crammed some chips into my mouth, crunching them down and taking another drink of water. I cringed when the shouting started in the room next to mine. Shit. My plan to get a good night's sleep was already shot, the walls were paper thin. Not surprising, considering how little I paid for the room, but still…

The two men's voices grew louder, and I listened in on their argument without a lick of shame. If a person didn't want someone eavesdropping, they should speak at normal decibels, right?

"God, Jerry," I murmured as I snagged my phone from my purse, "just let him hold the remote. Then maybe we can all get some sleep tonight."

The man named Jerry must have heard me because the shouting ended abruptly, and their TV blared as the volume was turned to maximum. I ignored it and tried to automatically open my Facebook app on my phone before reality set in. Right. I had turned my Facebook profile to inactive. Not that I thought she could track me through it if I didn't post anything, but I wasn't taking any chances.

Besides, it's not like anyone would miss me on Facebook. I had less than fifty friends and most of them were from an online book club I belonged to. I'd always had trouble making friends, thanks to my parents' gypsy like tendencies. Moving every six months to a year made it difficult, if not downright impossible to make friends. Even after I moved out and lived in university housing, I still didn't make friends easily. The combination of my lack of social skills and the insanity of trying to earn my law degree didn't leave much time or energy for friend making.

I dropped the empty chip bag on the nightstand

and ignored my still-growling stomach. I rested my head on the wall behind me and closed my eyes. I didn't want to think about my past, but it kept creeping in, refusing to let me go.

Images flickered through my head – walking across the stage to accept my degree, identifying my parents' bodies at the morgue, sitting for the Bar exam, those first two insane years of being a lawyer. I had almost quit. The insane work hours, that feeling of being thrown in to the deep end without a life jacket was almost too much. But my parents would have been disappointed – they'd been so proud when I told them I was going to be a lawyer – and disappointing them, even if they were dead, wasn't an option.

I'd stuck it out and in my third year started working for a small firm that specialized in family law. I'd finally felt like I belonged. Helping a woman divorce her abusive husband, getting child support from deadbeat dads – it was my calling and I was damn good at it.

Until I met her.

I crossed my arms over my torso and shook my head. "No. Don't think about her, it'll only upset you."

That was true. But it was kind of hard not to think about her when she was the reason that I had to leave a job I loved and a city I thought of as home, and run away in the night like a coward.

You're not a coward, Mags. She's insane and dangerous. You did all the right things – you got a restraining order, you changed the locks and installed security cameras. And she still nearly killed you. Disappearing was your only choice.

Yeah, maybe. But thanks to student loans, a car payment and living expenses, I didn't have a lot of cash on hand. Which meant I needed to find a new job and fast. I couldn't work in a law firm again. They'd plaster my face on their website, announce my employment with them and if Ruby was watching for me, if she was trying to find me, I'd be an easy target to find.

My stomach churned and I wiped away the tears that were starting to leak down my face. All of that time, and effort, and money to become a lawyer and now I couldn't even do it anymore.

I didn't want to cry but it was growing more difficult to hold back the tears. My life may not have been perfect, I may have worked too much, and, okay, maybe I'd been really lonely, but it had been *my* life, and to lose it all through no fault of my own was horrible.

I should have been in my small but cozy apartment watching bad reality television and waiting for my microwave frozen dinner to heat up. Instead, I was in some disgusting motel in the middle of nowhere, starving and alone, and listening to two men fight over a stupid TV remote. The loss of what I'd used to have washed over me in a tidal wave of regret and sorrow. I buried my face in the crook of my arm and wept bitterly.

Chapter Two

Wyatt

"You working tonight, Wyatt?"

I took the bag from Sally and the receipt for the gas. "Just finished."

The older woman leaned against the counter and stared out the window at the falling snow. "Looks like we're gonna get one hell of a snowstorm."

"That's what they're saying," I replied. I started toward the door, turning when Sally called my name again.

"You sure you don't want to buy a lottery ticket? Fifty million this week."

I shook my head. "No thanks. I have better ways to waste my money."

She grinned at me, revealing the chiclet size gap between her front teeth. "You're not much for taking chances are you, Wyatt? Never have been."

"Good night, Sally."

"Night, Wyatt."

I stepped outside and walked toward my SUV

parked beside one of the two gas pumps. The air was freezing, and the large snowflakes were wet and dense, but I didn't bother to grab my jacket before I pumped the gas. The weather might have been cold, but I was burning up inside. Had been, ever since I'd pulled over Magnolia Blossom for a burned-out tail light.

Just thinking about her made my cock stiffen and, after a quick glance at the store to make sure Sally wasn't still staring outside, I reached down and adjusted myself through my jeans. My breath hissed out between my teeth at just my own touch and I muttered an expletive.

What was wrong with me? The woman I pulled over tonight had me turned inside out. I'd wanted her from the moment she'd rolled down her window and stared up at me with those big blue eyes of hers. Her dark hair and pale skin, those pouty lips…fuck, what I wouldn't do to see them wrapped around my dick.

Her clumsy attempts at flirting had even been sort of cute, but when she'd dropped the act? Fucking hell, my need for her had almost become unbearable. She'd lost the annoying breathy little girl voice and her real voice… low and smoky sounding with a rasp to it that made my balls heavy with cum just hearing it. It was surprisingly deep for a woman her size and just thinking about how she'd sound saying my name when she was cumming made my cock swell and ache.

I adjusted myself again, my breath steaming out in front of me as I tried not to think about Ms. Magnolia Blossom. I failed miserably. I couldn't get her out of my damn head which was beyond stupid. I'd never see her again, and fantasizing about handcuffing her to my bed, spreading her soft thighs and burying my tongue deep inside her wet pussy was ridiculous.

Of course, it wouldn't stop me from jacking off to that very fantasy later tonight. It had been over a year since I'd been laid, and I wasn't going to deny myself a fun little fantasy that involved the possible woman of my dreams.

Maybe I should stop in at Ren's Bar and see if I could find someone who was interested in nothing more than a night of fun. It wasn't my usual thing, but I wasn't feeling like my own hand would be enough. Not tonight.

No. If I can't have Magnolia, I don't want anyone.

I froze, my hand clenching around the cold gas pump. Where the hell did that come from?

I hung up the pump, put the gas lid on and climbed into the vehicle. Judy, our dispatcher, was talking over the radio and I listened for a few minutes before joining in.

"Judy, did I hear right? There's been shots fired at Park Motel?"

Judy's voice, crackling with static, came back. "Yeah. Jerry and Roger are fighting again."

I groaned. Jerry and Roger had been together for thirty some years and while I had no doubt they genuinely loved each other, they also had a tendency to fight like cats and dogs.

"Why are they at the hotel and when the hell did they get a gun?" I asked.

"No idea about the gun," Judy replied. "But they've been staying at the motel for over a month now, ever since they got kicked out of their apartment building on a noise complaint."

"Christ," I said. "Tell me Roger didn't shoot Jerry."

"Nah, they're both fine, but they're in a heap of trouble. Roger shot through the wall of their room and almost killed some woman in the room next to them. An out-of-towner."

My blood turned to ice. It couldn't be her. If she even stayed the night in our little town, I told her to go to the Best Western. "What's her name?"

"Um, not sure." The indifference in Judy's voice made me want to reach through the radio and throttle her.

"Check for me, please." I tried to keep the sudden panic I was feeling out of my voice.

"Hold on."

I waited an eternity for Judy to come back over the radio.

"Oh, for Pete's sake, this can't be right," Judy grumbled. "I can't believe Alex has been a cop for two years and still can't figure out when someone gives him a false name."

My entire body froze. "The name, Judy. What is it?"

"Magnolia Blossom." Judy made a harrumph noise that was distinct even over the crackling of the radio. "Ridiculous."

The edge of panic turned bright, bold, brash.

My heart beating so fast it threatened to trample out of my chest like a herd of rhinos, I flicked on the lights and the siren and tore out of the gas station.

❦

"Wyatt?" Alex gave me a startled look. "What are you doing here? I thought you were done your shift."

I studied the parking lot of the Park Motel. Three police vehicles plus mine were parked in the half-full lot, and I could see Jenny and Mark, two of our other deputies, talking to Jerry and Roger.

"Where is she?" I asked.

"Who?" Alex said.

"Jesus Christ, Alex," my usual patience was wearing thin, "the woman. Magnolia."

"Oh. She's still in her room. She was sitting up in bed and the bullet, like, grazed right by her head and lodged in the far wall." Alex held his thumb and pointer finger up until they were only inches apart. "If she'd been sitting even an inch to the right, she'd have a bullet in her head, and we'd be cleaning up a real fucking mess. I tried to take her statement, but she's super freaked out, so I decided to give her a couple of minutes."

"You left her alone?" I snarled.

Alex gave me another confused look. "Do you know this woman, Wyatt?"

"What room?" I said.

"Right there." Alex pointed to the door just behind us and I pushed past him without another word and practically ran toward the door.

I knocked lightly before opening it and stepping inside. The room was freezing cold and I hurried over to where Magnolia was sitting at the small desk. She had her arms wrapped around her slender body and she was shaking so hard, I could hear the loose rail on the chair rattling.

She was staring at the dirty carpet, her sneaker-clad feet tapping back and forth with nervous energy. I crouched in front of her and said, "Magnolia?"

She continued to stare at the carpet and I briefly touched her knee. "Magnolia, look at me."

She lifted her head and I quelled my immediate urge to pull her into my arms when I saw her face. Gone was the cheeky attitude from earlier. In its place was a terrified vulnerability that made me want to drop to my knees and promise her she would never be this afraid and alone again. That I would always keep her safe and never let her go.

"Officer Hottie?" she whispered. She paused, her mouth trembling. "I mean, Reynolds?"

"Magnolia, are you all right?" It was a stupid question, she obviously wasn't, but my terror that she almost died was a living, breathing thing inside of me and I was having trouble thinking straight.

"I – Maggie," she said.

"What?"

"I go by Maggie."

"Okay. Maggie, is there someone I can call for you? A," I swallowed hard, "boyfriend or husband?"

She shook her head and the relief that poured through me made me a right bastard. "No, I - there's no one. My parents are dead, and I was an only child."

"What about a friend?"

She stared blankly at me. "No."

My hand inched out on its own and tucked a lock of her dark hair behind her ear. "All right. Everything's going to be okay."

She blinked, her pupils so large that only a thin ring of blue could be seen around them. "I almost died."

I winced. "I know."

"I almost died," she repeated. She pointed to the bed and I stared at the hole that pierced the faded wallpaper above the headboard. "A bullet came through the wall right there. I was sitting right there, and a-a bullet came through the wall."

Her face had turned the colour of the snow falling outside and even her pink lips had paled. "The men were arguing over a TV remote. I almost died because of a TV remote."

"You're safe now," I said.

She surprised me when she staggered to her feet. I straightened as, rocking lightly back and forth, she said, "I felt the bullet brush by my face, Officer Reynolds. I – I felt the wind of it and I... just an inch to the right and it would be in my head. My-my brains would be splattered all over the wall."

Her face crumpled and when she started to cry, I couldn't help myself. I pulled her into my arms and pressed her head to my vest, kissing the top of her head and rubbing her back. "Shh, baby. Shh, it's okay. You're safe now. I won't let anyone hurt or scare you ever again, baby. I promise."

She put her slender arms around my waist and clung to me, crying brokenly into my vest. I held her tight and rocked her back and forth, rubbing her back and trying to warm her with my body heat as she cried.

To my surprise, she didn't cry very long. After only a couple of minutes, she pulled a tissue from her pocket and wiped her face before blowing her nose. She was still shaking wildly, but when she glanced up at me, the blank look of shock had disappeared.

"I'm sorry," she whispered.

With far more intimacy than I should have been comfortable with, I cupped her face and ran my thumb over her damp cheekbone. "It's okay. Do you feel a little better?"

She nodded. "Surprisingly, yes. I mean, no, but yes. If that makes sense? God, I'm being an idiot."

"You're not," I said.

"Wyatt?"

I immediately stepped away from Maggie, dropping my arms and ignoring my sense of loss. "Yeah?"

"Um," Alex was giving me a look that suggested he'd thought I'd gone crazy, "I need to get Ms. Blossom's statement."

I nodded and turned back to Maggie. "You need to tell Officer Peterson what happened for a formal statement. Are you okay to do that, or do you need more time?"

"No, I can do it right now," she said. "But," she gave me another aching look of vulnerability, "will you stay with me while I do it?"

"Yes," I said. "I'll stay."

❧ ❦

"Maybe I should drive you to the Best Western." I watched the way Maggie's hands shook as she tried to unlock the door of her car.

I took the keys from her and unlocked the door before opening it and placing her suitcase in the backseat with the others.

"Uh, no, I'm fine. I'll drive myself to the hotel."

Her eyes cut away from mine and even though I knew nothing about her, I was certain she was lying about going to the hotel. I studied her car and then the clothes she was wearing. Neither screamed money, but she also didn't look like she was under the poverty line either. Still, the only possible reason she could have chosen the Park Motel was because of money.

"Maggie, look at me," I said.

"I really should get going before the snowstorm gets worse." She stared fixedly at the ground at her feet.

"Maggie," I said again.

She sighed and looked up at me. "What?"

"Why don't you want to stay at the Best Western?"

She scratched her throat and tapped her fingers against the car door. "Uh, I'm going to stay there."

I didn't reply and as the silence drew out, she said, "I'm not going to fold and tell you the truth just because you stay quiet, Officer Reynolds. Give me my keys back, please."

I held onto her keys, staring silently at her, and she rubbed at her temples. "You're not going to give me my keys, are you?"

"Tell me the truth and I will," I said.

She stared up at me. She was average height for a woman, but I was almost 6'3" and standing close enough to her that she had to crane her neck to look me in the eye. "How do you know I'm lying?"

"Tell me, Maggie." I made my voice low and coaxing.

"Fine," she said. "I don't have the money for the Best Western, okay? It's why I stayed at this stupid murder motel in the first place."

My lips twitched. The fact that she could almost joke about what had happened not three hours earlier, showed me just how resilient she really was.

"So, you're going to stay here at the motel?" I said.

She shuddered all over, her hands coming up to cup her elbows. "God, no. I'm sleeping in my car tonight and in the morning, I'm getting the hell out of this godforsaken town." She glanced at me. "No offense."

"You can't sleep in your car," I said. "It's supposed to dip below zero tonight."

She shrugged. "I'll survive, I've got a blanket in the trunk."

"No," I said.

She glared at me. "Yes."

"No."

"Oh my God, are you always this-this infuriating? I almost died tonight, remember? Cut me some slack and just let me sleep in my stupid car. Hell, if you wanna give me a ticket for car sleeping, give me one. I'll add it to your earlier ticket."

Her low voice was rising and had an almost hysterical tone to it. She gave me a wild look of anger and confusion. I had a feeling that Maggie rarely felt this unbalanced and overwhelmed, and I had the immediate urge to soothe and comfort her again.

When fresh tears ran down her face, I pulled her into my arms again. I suddenly didn't give a rat's ass that the rest of my coworkers were still milling around the parking lot.

"It's all right, baby," I said. "But you can't sleep in your car."

"I have no place else to go." Her breath hitched. "Please, just let me sleep in my car."

"I can't, Maggie. You'll freeze to death. You're already half-frozen now." I rubbed her back through her jacket. "I have a place that you can stay for free."

"I- I can't stay with you," she mumbled into my chest. "I don't even know you."

"It's not with me," I said. "It's with my grandmother."

She lifted her head and stared at me, the snowflakes catching on her long lashes. "Your grandmother?"

I nodded. "Yeah. She's got a small guesthouse behind her house. You can stay there tonight, okay?"

"I – are you sure? It's late and she doesn't know me. What if she doesn't want a stranger staying there?"

I smiled and brushed back a lock of hair that

was blowing against her mouth. "Nana won't mind. I promise."

Chapter Three

Maggie

"This is nice." I studied my surroundings as Officer Reynolds shut the door and set my suitcase down.

"It's small, but it works well for one person. Here, I'll take your coat."

I handed him my coat and he hung it on the hook. I took off my sneakers and he removed his boots before walking to the kitchen. The guesthouse was an open floor concept with the small kitchen opening into the even smaller living room. Two doors were on the far end of the living room. One was open and I could see part of the vanity and the toilet.

"It's really nice. Officer Reynolds?"

He paused with his hand on the fridge door. "You can call me Wyatt."

"Wyatt," I said. I ignored how weirdly intimate it felt to call him Wyatt. "Are you sure that your grandmother is okay with a stranger staying in her guest house for the night?"

"Yes. I texted her and told her you'd be staying here," he said.

"You did? When?" I asked.

"When you were getting your money back from the motel manager."

"Thanks for that, by the way," I said. "It was really nice of you to, um, get the guy to refund my money."

He just nodded and opened the fridge. "So, there isn't any food in here but there is some leftover juice and bottled water from when I was doing repairs. I could go and get you something or -"

"I'm not hungry," I said.

He gave me a stubborn look. "You need to eat."

"Trust me, if I try and eat anything right now, it's just gonna come right back up."

Nice, Maggie. Why don't you talk some more to the sexiest cop in the universe about how you're gonna throw up? It'll definitely turn him on.

"So, um, you did renovations on this place?"

He shut the fridge door. "Yeah. The plumbing needed replacing, and the bathroom needed an upgrade."

"Wow. A man who can do household repairs... your wife or girlfriend must be happy."

Smooth, Maggie. So smooth.

"No wife or girlfriend." He glanced at his watch. He was clearly ready to leave, and I couldn't blame him. I wasn't exactly an expert at flirting with men and it was getting late.

Why exactly are you trying to flirt with him,

Mags?

I didn't have an answer for my inner voice. Or, maybe I did, and I didn't want to think too hard about it.

You almost died, sweetheart. You almost died and there's so much you haven't done or experienced. You would have died a virgin at twenty-eight and that's just about the saddest thing I've ever heard.

I winced inwardly. I could almost hear the *Price is Right* loser horn blaring in my head.

Life is short, Mags. Stop waiting for Mr. Right and go for Officer Right There.

"Maggie?"

Wyatt had moved until he was standing right in front of me and I tried to smile at him. "Sorry, just, uh, up in my head for a minute there."

He studied me, God I wish I could convince myself there was a little bit of lust in his gaze, but there was nothing, nada, zilch.

Flirt harder!

I tried to block out inner Maggie. I'd just been through a traumatic experience... of course, I was going to have weird and wild thoughts about my life. Maybe even a few regrets about what I had and hadn't done, but tonight wasn't the night to start rectifying it.

Sure it is! You've got a cop standing in front of you who looks like he could be an extra in the Magic Mike movies. Now is the goddamn perfect time to give up your virginity.

I cleared my throat and smiled at Wyatt. "So, um, what do you have planned for this evening?"

Do you hear that sound, Mags?   That's the sound of your flirting attempt sinking faster than the Titanic.

Wyatt picked up my suitcase. "Here, I'll show you the bedroom."

Fuck me! It worked!

I followed Wyatt to the bedroom, trying vainly to ignore my inner voice.   My emotions and thoughts were all over the goddamn place and I didn't know what the hell to do. I'd almost died tonight, was it really the time to be admiring Wyatt's ass as he walked in front of me?

"Again," Wyatt pushed open the bedroom door and stood back so I could walk in first, "it's small but…"

"It's perfect." I ran my hand across the quilt on the bed. "This is beautiful."

"My grandmother made it," Wyatt said.

"Wow. She's very talented."

"She is." He set my suitcase down as I gave him a nervous smile.

For the first time since I met him, he looked a little flustered and uncertain. There was a moment of awkward silence and then he was brushing past me and moving to the window. He checked the lock before turning back to me. His gaze flickered down my body and then back up to my face. "So, uh, I should go."

Panic and lust and loneliness washed over me, and I grabbed his arm when he walked by me. "Wyatt, wait."

"What's wrong?" He stared at a spot over my head.

I could feel his arm thrumming lightly under my hand and when I stepped closer, he made a sharp inhale.

Holy shit… did he want me?

Only one way to find out, Mags.

"I don't want to be alone," I whispered.

He swallowed hard. "Understandable. You've had a traumatic experience. I can, uh, see if my grandmother is awake. She's a night owl and she -"

"Wyatt?" I said. "Please look at me."

His gaze flickered to mine and a low throb immediately began in my pussy. The look on his face – I might have been a virgin, but I knew lust when I saw it.

"Maggie, I should go," he rasped.

"No," I said. "I don't want you to leave."

"This isn't a good idea," he said when I stepped closer and draped my arms around his broad shoulders. "You've had a terrible night and you're not thinking straight and -"

I stood on my tiptoes and pressed my mouth against his. His big hands clamped around my waist and I moaned when his tongue immediately invaded my mouth. He pulled me even closer, nipping and licking at my mouth with a need that matched my own.

I was overwhelmed by the sensation, by the way he just took control without any hesitation, but there was a part of me – a big part – that was totally digging it. There was no tentativeness in his kiss, no sweet coaxing. He was all hard demand and need and a take no prisoners attitude when it came to kissing and holy God… it made me hot.

His big hand cupped the back of my head, threaded through my hair and pulled. The sharp bite of pain made me gasp, but if he felt bad about it, there was no indication. Not that I needed an apology. His rough handling was weirdly... enjoyable?

Ooh, we're kinky!

My inner voice was delighted by this revelation. Me? I was too busy getting all turned on by the feel of his hard dick pressing into my hip. Officer Hot Pants wanted me as much as I wanted him.

As if he heard my inner thoughts, Wyatt kissed his way to my ear. I cried out when he bit it and he gave my lobe a quick soothing suck before saying, "We shouldn't be doing this."

"Yes, we should," I moaned. "This is exactly what I need."

When he didn't reply, I rubbed against that hardness pressing into my hip. "And from the feel of it, you need it too."

He took a step back, his big hand still threaded through my hair and holding me tight. He licked those beautiful, firm lips and said, "That's my gun."

I blinked at him. "It's your gun digging into my hip?"

He nodded, and I blushed to the goddamn roots of my hair. *Of course,* I was rubbing myself like a horndog against his gun. I was punching way above my weight with Officer He Bites and I Kinda Like It, and there was no way I would make him that hard that quickly. Hell, I was lucky he even seemed to enjoy kissing me.

"Near death experience and the most

humiliating moment of my life both in one night. Super," I said.

Wyatt frowned, his hand tightening in my hair when I tried to move away from him.

I stared at his broad chest, my shame growing. What kind of idiot mistook a gun for a dick? I might have been a virgin, but I wasn't a complete novice about penises. I had touched them before and -

One. You touched one in your first year of university and it ended badly. Remember?

How could I forget? I hadn't been expecting Reggie's penis to just gush semen like a geyser the minute I touched it. Two seconds after seeing and touching my first penis, I'd taken a cum shot to the face that would have made a porn star proud.

My respect for porn stars had skyrocketed in that moment. The burning sensation in my eyes, the wretched taste in my mouth… ugh. I had managed not to actually barf all over Reggie's rapidly deflating dick, but my retching and the way my eyes had gushed tears had sent Reggie, a relative novice when it came to sex himself, fleeing in horror.

And so ended my one and only introduction to the penis.

"I'm sorry," I said as Wyatt took my hand with his free one. "I thought you wanted me like I wanted you and now I'm really embarrassed and… holy crap."

Wyatt had pressed my hand against his dick, and it didn't seem possible, but his dick was even harder than his gun.

"I do want you, Maggie. Very much." His

voice was a low rasp that sent literal shivers down my spine.

"I want you too," I whispered.

I was, in fact, almost desperate to have sex with him. I kept my hand perfectly still against him, even though I really wanted to curl my fingers around that almost alarmingly thick steel pole he seemed to be hiding in his underwear. But I was worried I'd turn his penis into a cum spouting fountain and be denied my chance at sex.

"Are you sure?" He searched my face.

I nodded. "Positive. Please, Wyatt, I need this."

He searched my face a few seconds longer before releasing my hair and stepping away. My immediate disappointment disappeared when he said, "Take off your clothes."

My hands shaking, I pulled my shirt over my head and dropped it on the floor before unbuttoning my jeans and pushing them down my legs. I peeled off my socks and then hesitated. I'd been completely naked in front of Reggie – I'd been planning on losing my virginity to him and being naked had seemed necessary to the procedure – but I was suddenly self-conscious.

I had an okay body, if you looked past the tiny tits, and I tried to eat well and exercise despite my busy work schedule, but still... Reggie had been thin and a bit spindly and Wyatt was... well...

I believe the term you used earlier was magnificent god.

Right.

Currently, the magnificent god was standing

over near the chair tucked into the corner of the small bedroom. He'd removed his belt – good gravy, cops carried a lot of shit on one belt - and placed it on the chair before laying his vest on top of it. He took a condom from his wallet then stripped off his t-shirt. I stared in awe at his flexing back muscles as he shucked his jeans and underwear and socks in two graceful movements.

I stared at the most perfect naked ass I'd ever seen in my life, swallowing hard when he turned around and the naked ass became the largest and thickest dick I'd ever seen. Hmm, maybe it wasn't the best idea to have a giant dick be my first.

Oh my God, you are not bailing out now, girl. I want that massive dick and you're gonna give it to me.

I honestly had no idea if that was my inner voice or my crotch talking.

"What's wrong?" Wyatt was standing in front of me now and I dragged my gaze from his magnificent dick back up to his face.

"Uh, nothing," I said. "Nothing's wrong."

"Are you sure? You're still dressed." He placed the condom on the small nightstand next to the bed.

I plucked nervously at my bra strap. "Wearing a bra and underwear isn't really *dressed*."

He grinned at me – oh dear lord, the man had a *dimple* – and some of my nervousness just floated away. Damn, he was hot when he smiled full on like that.

"You're overdressed for what I'm about to do to you," he said with another grin.

I squeaked nervously when he pulled me into his arms. His dick brushed against my flat stomach and he made a low moan that made my pussy gush wetness. He flicked open my bra and pulled it off to land on the floor somewhere behind him.

He eyed my tits and before I could give him a self-conscious apology for how small they were, his big hands were cupping them, and he was pinching and pulling on my nipples.

"Holy God," I moaned as my back arched.

"So beautiful and perfect," he murmured before bending his head.

I had a moment to realize what he was about to do before his mouth closed over one nipple and he sucked hard. My back arched again, my hands clutching at his short, dark hair as he licked around my nipple before sucking on it again. His hand continued to pinch and pull my other nipple and what kind of freak was I that the pain only made the pleasure sweeter?

Before I could dwell too much on my newly discovered freakiness, he was sucking on my other nipple, soothing it with soft licks that made my toes curl. He kissed between my breasts before pressing hot, open mouthed kisses across my chest and up my neck.

"I want you so much, baby," he breathed into my ear.

I rubbed my fingers across his biceps, kneading and squeezing the hard muscles. "I want you too."

"Good." His fingers curled into the waistband of my panties and he pushed them down my legs. I stepped out of them but automatically covered my crotch with both hands.

He cocked his head at me. "Are you playing shy?"

"Um, maybe a little," I said.

"No need to be. Show me your pussy, baby."

I continued to hold my hands in front of my crotch. It wasn't that I no longer wanted to bang Wyatt, but I had pictured it as more of a 'we both get under the covers and just do it' scenario. This standing here completely naked with the light on was a little too much for me.

I turned around and quickly pulled back the covers on the bed. "Why don't we just get into bed and -"

Wyatt's thick arm curled around my waist and pulled me back against his hard chest. I slammed my hands over my crotch again as Wyatt nipped the base of my neck hard enough to leave a mark.

"Show me your pussy." His voice was firm and demanding.

I ignored my immediate and weird urge to obey him and said, "It's just a pussy, same as every other one you've seen. You don't need, like, an up close and personal look at it."

He laughed and I squeezed my thighs together, a little worried that the fresh wetness in my pussy would drip to the floor.

"Baby, I intend to have a very up close and personal look at your sweet pussy."

"Wh-what do you mean?" I craned my neck to stare up at him.

His grin turned predatory and I made an unladylike squeal when he lifted me and tossed me onto my back on the bed. He pushed open my flailing legs and stretched out on his stomach between them. His big hands closed around my wrists and held them tight against my outer thighs.

"Wyatt!" I tried to wiggle free, but it wasn't possible. He was too strong, and I was trapped.

"Hold still, Maggie, or I'll give you a spanking."

My entire body stilled, and I stared down at him. He stared calmly back at me and I forgot about the fact that my crotch was directly in his face and said, "You'd spank me?"

"Yes."

"Like an honest to god, over the knee spanking?" I said.

"Yes," he repeated.

A deep and unexpected spasm of pleasure went through my lower body and my pelvis twitched upward. It was only a little, but a look of satisfaction crossed Wyatt's face.

Oh, girl. We are sooo kinky!

"I don't want a spanking," I said quickly. I couldn't be positive if I was talking to my inner voice or to Wyatt.

"Then be a good girl and you won't get one." His gaze dropped to my pussy and I squirmed with embarrassment when he inhaled.

"Wyatt, please, this is…"

My voice stopped dead in my throat, the air rushed out of my lungs in a long drawn out 'unggh' sound, and my entire body stiffened, my hands clenching into tight fists.

I had a tongue in my pussy.

I had Wyatt's tongue in my pussy, and it was... holy smacking snappers it was incredible.

"Wyatt!" I cried, my pelvis bucking upward as he licked my slit from my hole to the top of my clit. "Oh my God, Wyatt!"

"Does my girl like that?" He lifted his head and gave me a lazy grin.

"Yes! Yes, your girl likes that very much. Do it again, oh my God, do that again," I babbled as I thrust my crotch at him like an out-of-control marionette.

He laughed. "Spread your legs wide, baby."

I let my legs drop open, no longer even remotely embarrassed about my pussy being directly in Wyatt's face. Not when he had a hot and wet tongue that was rapidly becoming my new addiction.

He was still holding my wrists and when he bent his head and licked my pussy repeatedly, I squealed happily and strained against his tight grip. I wanted to grab his head, wanted to guide that soft tongue back to my clit.

"Wyatt, let me go!" I moaned.

"No," he said.

"Oh fuck!" Just that one word, that oh-so-calm and decisive 'no' that fell from his perfect lips was almost enough to make me cum.

Or maybe it was the tongue currently buried in my aching hole. I rocked my pussy against his face as he tongued my hole before nibbling on my wet pussy lips. I tried desperately to free myself from his hard grip, my lust ratcheting up to a whole new level when he gave my inner thigh a hard nip as punishment.

"Oh, oh, oh god," I chanted, my head whipping back and forth mindlessly as Wyatt worked me over with his lips and tongue. He slicked it over my clit, and I shrieked happily, my fingers digging into my own thighs.

He kissed my inner thigh and I moaned in disappointment. "No, Wyatt!"

"Do you want more clit licking?" He asked.

"Yes!" I glared at him and he laughed before kissing my thigh again.

"Ask me nicely."

I kicked him in the thigh with my foot, cursing under my breath when it hurt. "Dammit, Wyatt! Do it!"

"That's not asking nicely, baby."

I squirmed against the bed. "Oh god. Okay, please do that again."

"Be specific, Magnolia. Tell me exactly what you're asking for."

My scowl deepened but he just stared patiently at me.

"Please, Wyatt, lick my pussy."

"Not bad, but you need to be more specific and maybe just a," he grinned at me, "touch more respectful."

"Wyatt," I moaned, "please." My clit was aching and throbbing and I was on the edge of going completely insane.

He bent his head and gave my clit a brief gentle brush with the tip of his tongue that only made me ache more.

"Wyatt!"

"Repeat after me, sweet Magnolia," he said. "Will you please lick my clit, sir?"

"Will you please lick my clit, sir?" I repeated immediately. "Please, sir?"

"Yes, baby, I will." He bent his head and proceeded to do exactly what he promised. His tongue licked across my clit with wide, soft strokes and I was brought to the edge of my climax instantly.

When he sucked on my clit, I lost total control. My hips bucked up, my legs locked around his head, and I was engulfed by the hardest most intense orgasm of my entire life. His hands released my wrists, and I grabbed onto his head, grinding my pussy against his face as I rode out the rest of my orgasm.

His hard hands pried my thighs apart and I collapsed against the bed, moaning and shuddering, my pussy quivering wildly with the aftershocks of my orgasm. I was barely aware of Wyatt getting off the bed and the sound of the condom being opened.

When he knelt between my open legs and propped himself up on his hands above me, I smiled weakly at him. "Oh my God, Wyatt, that was... I mean..."

He grinned at me. "You came fast. Has it been a while since you had your pussy eaten out?"

"Hmm," I said. I'd never actually had a tongue in my pussy before, but now that I had, I planned on it being a much more frequent occurrence.

I relaxed beneath him, my muscles like jelly. Had I ever cum that hard before? I thought I was an expert at masturbation, at giving myself the best damn orgasms a girl could have, but I'd never been more wrong in my life.

I gave him another soft smile when he bent his head and pressed a kiss against my rock-hard nipple. The head of his cock probed at my opening and before my climax-rattled brain could even begin to send a warning signal to my pussy, he had thrust into me to the hilt.

The pain was immediate and intense. I cried out, my thighs clamping around his hips and my hands slapping up against his chest. I dug my nails into his hard chest, barely feeling the rough hair beneath my palms as the pain radiated across my lower body.

I sucked in a breath, trying to breathe through the pain as Wyatt gave me a look of complete horror.

"Oh, baby," he groaned, "no."

I couldn't stop my ridiculous urge to apologize. "I'm sorry."

He shook his head. "No, I'm sorry. I'm so sorry."

He started to ease out of me, and I hooked my legs around his hips, holding him as tight as I could. "No, don't do that."

"Baby, I can't…we shouldn't…"

"Yes," I insisted. "We can. It doesn't hurt anymore. I don't want you to stop."

I wasn't lying to him. The pain had already faded, although I suspected that tomorrow I'd be sore as hell, and I had the weirdest feeling of fullness.

It might have felt strange to have my pussy

completely filled with Wyatt's cock, but oddly, it felt good too. Like, my pussy was meant to have Wyatt's dick in it.

Girl, you're trippin' balls over there.

"Magnolia," Wyatt said. "I don't think – oh fuck, baby, don't do that."

I had rocked my pelvis against him experimentally, and the look of pure pleasure that crossed his face sent an answering bolt through my own belly. I was pretty sure I wouldn't be able to cum again, but I suddenly and desperately wanted to see him cum.

"It doesn't hurt anymore," I repeated. "Please, Wyatt. I want you to cum."

"Fuck," he muttered, but he made a slow, soft thrust. "Does that hurt?"

"No."

He stared down at me and I cupped his face and pressed a kiss against his mouth. "It didn't. Keep going."

"Christ," he moaned as he moved with long, slow strokes that rocked us gently on the bed, "you're so goddamn tight."

"Does it feel good?" I asked shyly.

"Yeah, so good," he groaned.

I rubbed the ball of my thumb over his flat nipple and he jerked and moaned before increasing the pace of his thrusts. I tried to meet his rhythm, but I felt awkward and uncoordinated so gave up. Instead, I held on to his hips and watched his face as he fucked me.

I blinked in surprise when he shifted a little and reached between us with one hand. "Wyatt, what are you – oh!"

His rough fingers were rubbing against my sensitive clit, and I squirmed beneath him. "Oh, don't – don't do that."

"Does it hurt?"

"No, I just… I don't think I can have another… oh God!"

"You can have another orgasm for me," he said.

"No, I can't, I … oh, right there." I wrapped one hand around his wrist, the other clutching at his broad shoulder as he slid in and out of me and rubbed my clit.

"Right here?" He whispered as he rubbed my clit with hard firm circles.

"Yes!" To my surprise, I was already climbing toward a second orgasm. As the pleasure grew in my belly, I bucked my hips against his, meeting each of his thrusts with an erratic rhythm.

He was groaning softly under his breath, his face a mixture of pleasure and concentration and as much as I wanted to watch him cum, I was suddenly too wrapped up in my own reach for pleasure.

I moaned his name again and he rubbed harder before whispering, "Cum for me, Magnolia. Right now, baby."

His low command sent pleasure skyrocketing through me and I arched with a broken cry, cumming again with less intensity than the first one, but no less pleasure.

He groaned again and propped himself back up on both hands, his hips thrusting back and forth as he buried his cock in my body repeatedly. I quivered beneath him, the pleasure spreading throughout my entire body, and barely even noticed when he said my name like a prayer and his big body stiffened against mine.

I kept my eyes closed, listening to his harsh breathing and holding his shuddering body tightly. He kissed my shoulder and eased out of me before leaving the bed. I curled into a ball on my side, reaching out blindly for a pillow and tucking it under my head.

I was mentally exhausted and physically completely sated. I grunted in annoyance when Wyatt returned and placed a hand on my hip. "Magnolia, we need to talk."

"No," I said. "Tired. Talk tomorrow, kay?"

He slipped into the bed behind me and I sighed happily when he tucked his big body against mine and put his arm around my waist. "Yes, but we're talking in the morning."

"Yeah, okay," I muttered before burrowing deeper under the covers. "Talk in the morning."

Chapter Four

Maggie

"Hi there, you must be Magnolia."

I groaned inwardly, but turned around, smiling at the older woman with the waist length silver hair. "Hi, uh, it's Maggie."

"Hi, Maggie. I'm Martha."

I shifted my suitcase to my other hand, my breath steaming out like smoke in front of me as I glanced down the empty street. My plan to sneak out of the guesthouse while Wyatt slept, had fallen flat on its face the minute I walked past the main house.

Man, why hadn't I thought to check the porch for Wyatt's grandmother before sneaking out?

Because it's six in the morning and Wyatt said she was a night owl?

"Wyatt said you were a night owl," I blurted and then wanted to kick myself in the butt. "Sorry, that's rude."

Martha laughed before slipping into a pair of rubber boots and tramping down the steps of the porch to join me in the driveway. "Usually I am."

She was wearing a long nightgown, covered by a flannel robe, despite how cold it was, and she gave me a cheery grin before glancing at Wyatt's police vehicle in the driveway. "I didn't realize Wyatt was spending the night as well."

I turned bright red and Martha gave me an apologetic look. "Oh, dear, I'm sorry. I've embarrassed you."

"No, uh, you didn't. But I should, I should get going."

"Why don't you come in and have a cup of coffee and some breakfast first?" Martha said.

"Oh, no, I couldn't. I'm not hungry and -" my stomach growled loudly, and Martha gave me a delighted smile.

"Come, dear heart, you're not going to turn down a lonely old woman's invitation to join her for breakfast, are you?"

I glanced at the guest house again, biting my lip with indecision. I really was starving, apparently sex with a total stranger burned a lot of calories, and it would be one less meal I'd have to buy. Of course, if I didn't make a decision about where I was going and find a damn job soon, I'd be completely out of money and then I really would starve.

Still… it didn't exactly seem smart to have breakfast with your one-night stand's grandmother the morning after.

"Come, dear heart," Martha coaxed, "Wyatt

isn't a morning person and won't be up for a while. Which means you'll need to wait for him to drive you, right? You really can't walk in this snow with that suitcase."

I had no intention of ever seeing Wyatt again – oh my God, what had I been thinking when I just gave up my v-card to him last night? The look on his face... nope, no way. I was not thinking about that. What was done was done. Maybe I had some regrets about what I had done, but there was nothing I could do other than get my ass out of this town and forget all about Officer Big Dick.

Do you regret the sex or regret that you're leaving without saying goodbye to Wyatt? Or maybe just that you're leaving in general and you'll never see him again?

The smart thing to do would be to politely but firmly turn down Martha's invitation and call a damn Uber. Of course, history had proven that I wasn't always smart.

I smiled at Martha and said, "Breakfast sounds really nice. Thank you, ma'am."

"Oh, please, call me Martha or Nana," she said before putting her arm around my shoulders and guiding me toward the main house. "Now, we'll have a bite to eat and a hot cup of coffee and you can tell me a little bit about Ms. Magnolia Blossom."

❧ ❦

Wyatt

"What's going on with you today?" Elijah set down the weights he was holding in both hands and gave me a curious look.

"Nothing." I grunted my way through two more sets before setting the weights next to Elijah's.

"Something's wrong," he said.

I sighed and wiped the sweat from my forehead. The massive firefighter looked rough and tough, but in the six months that he'd been dating my cousin Mia, I'd seen the real side of him. He was thoughtful and maybe a little sensitive, and it hadn't taken more than a couple of family dinners at Nana's house for us to become friends.

Now, we worked out together, had coffee once a week and did guys' night every couple of weeks. And, both Elijah and his EMT friend, Matt, joined me and the other cops for our monthly poker night.

"I fucked up last night," I said.

"How?" Elijah asked.

I glanced around to make sure none of the other gym rats were close enough to overhear before telling Elijah what happened with Maggie last night. I left out the virginity thing. It didn't feel right to share something so personal about Maggie with him.

When I was finished, Elijah wiped down the weights he'd been holding before giving me a thoughtful look. "So, are you upset because you had a one-night stand, or upset because she left before you woke up?"

"I'm not sure."

It wasn't a total lie. I was pissed that she'd snuck out this morning and that I hadn't woken up when she left, but what was upsetting me the most was hurting her last night. I couldn't stop remembering the way I'd entered her so roughly. Her cry of pain, the way her tiny body had tensed around me… I scrubbed a hand across my jaw.

"Well," Elijah said, "you're a cop and you know her name. Can't you look up her information in some database or something?"

"That's an abuse of power," I said.

Elijah gave me a sympathetic look. "Then I guess you'll never see her again."

"Yeah." I didn't want to admit this to Elijah, but I'd driven over to the Park Motel this morning. Maggie's car was gone and although I wasn't surprised, I was disappointed.

≈ ≈

I slid into a booth at the Farmhouse Diner, nodding my thanks to the hostess when she handed me a menu. I studied it unseeingly, my thoughts still wrapped up in the intoxicating and gone forever Magnolia Blossom. Why the fuck hadn't I woken up when she left? I slept light, always had, so how'd she manage to sneak out without me knowing?

"Hey, Deputy Reynolds. How's it going today?"

"Good, Natalia." I looked up from the menu. "How are…"

My voice died and I stared dumbly at the woman standing next to Natalia. She was wearing the same salmon-coloured polyester uniform that Natalia wore, and she gave me a look that was half dismay and half panic.

"This is Maggie," Natalia said. "She started this morning and is training with me. Maggie, this is

Deputy Reynolds. He's a regular."

"Nice to meet you," Maggie said in that weirdly low voice of hers.

The crotch of my jeans was immediately too tight, and I shifted in my seat before nodding. "You as well."

Natalia stared at me and then at Maggie, her forehead creasing a little. "Do you want a coffee, Deputy?"

"Uh, yeah. Yes, please," I said.

I was still staring at Maggie and her cheeks were going a light shade of pink that matched her lips perfectly. Natalia's frown deepened before she said, "Coming right up."

Maggie turned and followed Natalia back to the counter. I sank back against my seat, my heart pounding and sweat forming at my temples. Maggie was still here. If she'd gotten a job at the diner, it meant she was staying in town. Which meant I had a chance to fix my fuck-up.

☙ ❧

I parked in Nana's driveway next to my cousin Mia's car. I stared blankly at Nana's house before climbing out of the vehicle and slamming the door shut. I trudged up the driveway, the snow crunching under my boots. My urge to duck into the guest house and stare at the bed where I'd been with Maggie was almost too much to ignore. I would have to go in there eventually, not just because Nana had reminded me last week that the pantry door was stuck shut, but because I needed to wash the sheets before Nana discovered the evidence of Maggie's virginity.

I paused at the bottom of the stairs, my hand clutching the cold wooden banister. Yesterday at the diner, there'd been no opportunity to talk with Maggie – not with Natalia there – and today when I'd dropped in to the diner, neither Natalia nor Maggie were working.

I climbed the stairs of the porch. I just needed to be patient. This was a small town and there was no way Maggie could avoid me forever. Once she was done shadowing Natalia and was alone, I'd simply ask her to have coffee with me so I could apologize for what happened.

Apologize or beg her for the chance to fuck her again?

I yanked open the front door a little harder than necessary and stepped into the warm hallway. The idea of sleeping with Maggie again was becoming an obsession. I had masturbated twice last night to the thought of her and then again, this morning in the shower.

Becoming an obsession?   More like, is an obsession.

I removed my boots and hung my coat in the closet. "Nana, it's Wyatt. Where are…"

I stared at the tiny blonde girl standing in the hallway and staring solemnly at me. She was holding a doll in one arm and she had large blue eyes and a smatter of freckles across her nose. She couldn't have been more than two or three, and we stared silently at each other for almost thirty seconds.

"I'm in the kitchen, Wyatt," Nana's voice called out.

"I'm in da kitchen, Wha-at," the little girl mimicked. She turned and skipped down the hallway before turning into the kitchen.

Feeling a little like I'd stepped into the Twilight Zone, I followed her to the kitchen. "Nana, who is…"

I stared in surprise at the women gathered around Nana's table. Brightly coloured yarn littered the scarred wooden table and the kitchen smelled like coffee and freshly baked cookies. The little girl climbed into Nana's lap and leaned against her. Nana kissed the top of her head before smiling at me. "Hi, sweet boy."

"Hi, sweet boy," the little girl repeated.

"Uh, what's going on?" I said.

"Didn't I tell you I started a knitting class?" Nana asked. "It must have slipped my mind."

"Oh my God, Nana, I dropped a stitch *again*." My cousin Mia's voice was full of exasperation.

"At least it was only one. I think I've lost at least five." The brunette sitting next to her gave me a cheerful grin. "Hey, Wyatt."

"Hey, Isabelle."

"Do you know Lily Carson?" Isabelle hitched her thumb at the woman sitting on the other side of her. "Lily, this is Mia's cousin, Deputy Wyatt Reynolds."

"Nice to meet you," I said. I knew Lily, everyone knew the story of the former rich girl's family and their fall from grace, but I'd never formally met her.

"Nice to meet you too, Deputy Reynolds."

"Call me Wyatt," I replied.

"Wha-at," the little girl said before sliding off of Nana's lap. Natalia from the diner was sitting to Nana's left and the little girl leaned against her legs before smiling up at her. "Cookie, Mama."

"You've had two, sweetpea. No more cookies."

The little girl crinkled her nose before pointing at the cup on the table. "Milk?"

"What do you say?" Natalia replied.

"Milk, please."

Natalia handed her the cup and the little girl took a swig of milk. "Hi, Wyatt."

"Hi, Natalia. How are you?"

"Good, thanks."

"Hi, Wha-at."

Natalia smiled a little and held her knitting in one hand before stroking the little girl's hair. "Phoebe, his name is Deputy Reynolds."

I grinned a little at the thought of Phoebe trying to say Deputy Reynolds. "She can call me Wyatt."

"Wha-at," Phoebe said.

"Wy-att," Natalia said slowly and clearly. "Wy. Att."

Phoebe cocked her head. "Wy-hat."

"Almost," Natalia said with a grin.

There was movement behind me, and I turned, my jaw dropping when I saw Maggie standing behind me.

"Maggie? What are you doing here?"

"Uh, hello again, Deputy Reynolds." Maggie brushed by me, her scent immediately driving me to distraction, and sat down between Nana and Mia. She picked up her knitting and stared studiously at it.

"You know Maggie?" Mia asked.

I wasn't sure what to say, but Nana smiled at Mia. "Didn't I tell you? Wyatt was the one who introduced me to Maggie. She's such a lovely girl, I'm so glad he did." She squeezed Maggie's hand who blushed but smiled at Nana.

"How do you know Maggie?" Mia asked.

"Uh…"

"I was staying at the Park Motel," Maggie said, "and there was an incident and -"

"Oh my God," Isabelle said. "You're the woman who almost died when that idiot Roger shot through the wall."

Maggie winced, and Mia elbowed Isabelle in the side. "Izzy, c'mon."

"Sorry, Maggie," Isabelle said. "I shouldn't have said it like that."

"How did you, uh, even know?" Maggie asked.

Lily gave her a small smile. "Small town, Maggie. Everyone knows everyone's business."

"Oh," Maggie said.

"You're from a bigger city, right?" Mia said.

Maggie nodded and Mia grinned at her. "You'll get used to small town gossip." She glanced at me. "So, I'm still not sure how you met Nana?"

"Oh, you can imagine that sweet Maggie didn't want to exactly stay in another motel room after that dreadful incident, so Wyatt brought her to the guesthouse. Wasn't that nice of him?" Nana said.

"Very nice." Mia gave me a way too perceptive look. The two of us had been raised together by Nana after my parents died in a car accident and Mia's mother abandoned her, and we were as close as siblings.

A hand tugged on my jeans and I looked down to see Phoebe standing next to me. She held her arms out. "Up, Wy-hat."

"Phoebe, honey, don't bother Wyatt," Natalia said.

"Uh, it's fine." I bent and picked up Phoebe a bit gingerly before settling her in the crook of my arm.

She studied my face before turning to her mother and smiling. "I'm up, Mama."

"I see that," Natalia said. She gave me an apologetic look when Phoebe rubbed her small hand across the scruff on my jaw. "Sorry, she's not usually this friendly with men."

"It's fine," I repeated.

"Anyway," Nana said. "I invited Maggie to have breakfast with me in the morning and we got along like a house on fire, didn't we, dear heart?"

"We did," Maggie said.

"Maggie mentioned she was looking for a job and I had just found out the day before that Rhonda over the diner was looking for someone after Mel up and quit on her."

"She met a guy at the bar six months ago and moved to Europe with him last week," Natalia said.

"So, I texted Rhonda and told her I was bringing Maggie over for an interview. Rhonda loved her and Maggie got the job on the spot. She started that very morning." Nana smiled with satisfaction.

"Cool." Mia handed her knitting to Nana. "It's hopeless, Nana. If you couldn't teach me to knit as a kid, it's not gonna work now."

"Oh hush, sweetheart, you can do it." Nana took her knitting and examined it. "You just need to keep practicing."

"Did you find a place to stay, Maggie?" Lily asked.

"Actually," Maggie gave me a quick look, "I'm renting Martha's guest house."

My arm tightened around Phoebe and the little girl made a squeal of protest. "Too tight, Wy-hat."

"Sorry, Phoebe." I relaxed my grip and she studied me for a second before patting my face.

"That's otay. Down, please."

I set her down and she patted my cheek again before skipping over to Natalia. "Go home, Mama?"

Natalia nodded. "Yes, sweetpea. We should get going. Thank you, Martha, for the lesson."

"You're so welcome, honey. Does next Saturday work for everyone?" Nana asked.

"I'm working," Mia said.

"Me too," Isabelle replied.

Natalia helped Phoebe into her coat. "I'll be working which means Maggie will be too. We get rotating weekends off at the diner."

"All right, perhaps a weekday evening then," Nana said. "Lily, don't forget to text me your email address so I can add you to the group emails."

"I will. Thank you, Martha."

"You're welcome, dearest." Nana fixed her gaze on me. "Wyatt, could you please walk Maggie back to the guesthouse and fix the pantry door while you're at it? Your tools are still on the back porch."

"Yes, Nana," I said. Holy hell, I had never

loved my grandmother more than in this moment.

"Oh, um, he doesn't have to fix it today," Maggie said.

"I don't mind," I said quickly.

"He does," Nana said. "You were just saying this morning that the door won't open at all. It won't take him long to fix it. Isn't that right, Wyatt?"

"Yes, ma'am," I replied.

"Good. Go on then."

Maggie started gathering up her knitting as Lily, Isabelle and Mia walked by me. Mia tapped me on the hip and muttered, "Wipe the drool off your face, horndog."

I poked her in the butt, and she grinned at me before following Isabelle down the hallway.

"Bye, Wy-hat," Phoebe said as she and Natalia walked past.

"Bye, Phoebe," I replied. "Ready, Maggie?"

"Yes." She followed me to the front door, slipping her feet into her boots.

"Where's your jacket?"

"I left it at the guest house," she said. "It's not a long walk – oh, um, thank you."

I had draped my jacket around her shoulders, and she smiled nervously as I opened the front door. "After you."

I followed her to the guest house. "Where's your car?"

"I parked it down the street." Maggie unlocked the front door and stepped inside, holding the door for me.

She hung my jacket on the hook and gave me

another nervous look. "You really don't -"

"Excuse me." I pushed past her and walked to the kitchen before she had the chance to kick me out. I studied the pantry door as Maggie joined me in the kitchen.

"Wyatt, maybe you should -"

"Why did you sneak out yesterday morning?" I turned to face her.

She stared at the floor. "I don't – I mean, I was kind of embarrassed. Sleeping with someone I don't know isn't my…usual thing."

"Yeah, that was kind of obvious," I said.

Her face turned bright red and she hugged herself, her hands cupping her elbows.

"Why didn't you tell me you were a virgin?"

"Because it wasn't any of your business."

"None of my business? Magnolia, you gave your virginity to me. Don't you think I deserved to know beforehand?"

She scowled at me. "Don't make it into a thing, Wyatt. Okay? It's not a gift or something stupid like that. It's just a thin little piece of flesh. It means nothing."

"You don't believe that."

"You don't know that," she said.

I just stared at her and she sighed before squeezing her elbows. "Can we not talk about this?"

"Why did you give it to me?" I said. "Just tell me that."

"Because I almost *died*," she said angrily. "I almost died and I – I'm impulsive and don't always think before I act and-and this is who I am. I do stupid things and don't always make the most rational decisions."

My blood ran cold and I couldn't stop from moving forward and cupping her arms. "Do you regret what happened between us?"

She stared at the floor and dismay shot through me like a bullet. The idea that she regretted what happened between us made me feel sick to my stomach. I cupped her face and gently made her look at me. "Do you?"

"No," she said. "I don't regret what happened between us."

"I'm sorry that I hurt you," I said. "I swear, if I had known -"

"If you had known, you wouldn't have had sex with me," she said.

I hesitated and she sighed. "Which is why I didn't tell you. I needed it that night, Wyatt. I needed to feel wanted and connected to someone and you were in the right place at the right time. But I'm sorry that I used you that way. It was a really shitty thing for me to do."

"So, you only slept with me because I was convenient?" Christ, I sounded like a whiney ass baby, but I was stupidly hurt by what she'd said.

"Yes…no, I don't know…" She gave me a look of confusion. "I don't know anything anymore, okay? My life is so…it's upside down and crazy, and I almost died two days ago."

She looked close to tears and I immediately pulled her into my arms. "I'm sorry, baby. Don't cry."

She buried her face in my chest and I kissed the

top of her head. "I feel terrible about hurting you."

She raised her head. "Don't. It wasn't that painful and -"

I squeezed her waist. "Don't lie to me, Magnolia."

A cheeky sort of defiance crossed her face. "Why? Will you spank me if I do?"

Her voice had gone even lower and I knew the aching need in it wasn't my imagination. My nostrils flared and lust immediately flooded through me. I wanted to rub my hardening dick against her. My own voice low, I said, "Does my girl want a spanking?"

She stared up at me, her eyes wide and her mouth trembling lightly. "I think, maybe, um…"

I leaned down and placed my mouth against her ear. "Lying *will* get you a spanking, Magnolia."

"Yes," she said breathlessly. "Yes, I want a spanking."

"Then come with me." I took her hand and started toward the bedroom.

Before we even left the kitchen, she pulled her hand from mine and gave me a horrified look. "Oh my God, what -what am I doing?"

"It's all right, baby," I said. "We'll start off slow and you'll have a safe word."

Her face went red. "No, I mean, I can't – I can't do this with you."

"Why not?" I asked. "Give me the chance to make up for hurting you the last time."

She licked her lips. "Uh, pretty sure that a spanking is gonna hurt."

"You're right, but it'll be a sweet pain, I

promise. And the sex will definitely not hurt. Let me show you."

I reached for her hand again and she tucked both hands behind her back. "I can't, Wyatt. I'm sorry, I shouldn't have – I mean, I don't know what came over me just now, but I can't sleep with you again."

I swallowed down my disappointment. "Is it because I hurt you? Because I swear that -"

"It isn't that," she said.

"Then why -"

"I'm not staying," she blurted out.

"What do you mean?"

"I'm just working long enough to get some money saved up and then I'm moving on," Maggie said. "So, sleeping with you, being with you – isn't a good idea."

"To where?" I asked.

"What do you mean?"

"You said you'd be moving on... to where?"

"I don't know yet. What does it matter?"

I'd been a cop long enough to recognize when someone was in trouble. "What or who are you running from, Maggie?"

All of the colour drained from her face and she gave me such a look of sheer terror that I wanted to pull her back into my arms. But when I reached for her, she staggered away, wetting her lips nervously.

"Baby, it's okay. Tell me who you're running from. Maybe I can help," I said.

"I'm not running from anyone," she said. "Can you please go, Wyatt? I'm tired and have a bit of a headache. I'd like to lie down."

I didn't want to leave her. The realization that I

never wanted to leave her didn't even freak me out that much. Although it probably fucking should have. But I couldn't work up the energy to let it freak me out. I had no idea what it was about Magnolia Blossom, but from the minute I'd seen her, I'd known deep down that she was mine and I was hers.

Now, I just had to convince her. But today wasn't the day. She needed some space.

"I'll go," I said. "But if you need anything at all, I want you to call me or text me." I grabbed a pen from the magnetic cup on the fridge and pulled off a piece of paper from the pad sitting on the counter. I wrote my cell number on the paper and set it on the table. "This is my cell number. Put it in your phone. All right, baby?"

She nodded and I smiled at her. "I'll come back another time to fix the pantry door."

"Okay," she whispered. "Thank you."

"Bye, Maggie."

"Bye, Wyatt."

Chapter Five

Maggie

"What's up with you and Wyatt?"

I froze with my sandwich halfway to my mouth. "Nothing. What do you mean? Nothing's up with us. Why? Did he say there was something up with us?"

Stuff that sandwich into your mouth before you make things worse.

I took a giant bite of my sandwich, giving Natalia what I hoped was a casual look as my cheeks bulged with bread.

"Oh, now I know there's definitely something up with the two of you."

"Thev's noffing mup mith fuss."

Natalia laughed. "Good God, you're like Phoebe with a mouthful of food. Try that again."

I chewed, swallowed, and repeated. "There's nothing up with us."

Natalia bit into her pear. "Oh yeah? So, he just comes into the diner every day and sits in your section because he likes the food here?"

"The food is good here," I said.

"Yeah, but a guy who looks like Wyatt, doesn't eat the food in this diner every day. Not with his body. I know it's hard to tell when he's wearing that thick police vest, but I'm pretty sure he's got a smoking hot body."

"He has a six pack," I said and then froze again. "Shit."

"A-ha! I knew it!"

"A-ha?" I said. "What are you – a cartoon villain?"

We were sitting in the quietest spot in the diner, a booth close to the kitchen that Rhonda kept reserved for staff when they were on their break. Natalia leaned over the table and stole a cracker from the container in front of me. "Don't deflect. I know you and Wyatt had sex. Admit it."

"Fine, yes we had sex."

Natalia's mouth dropped open. "Holy shit. You did?"

"What? You knew we did, you just said so," I said.

"I was lying," Natalia said.

"Nat!" I threw another cracker at her and it was my turn for jaw dropping when Natalia caught it neatly in her mouth. "Holy shit. How did you do that?"

"I'm really good at using my mouth," Natalia said and then laughed when I blushed. "So, give me all the details. He seems totally tough and kind of rough. Is he the exact opposite and all sweet tenderness in bed, or is he rough? Does he act like a cop when he's banging? Ooh - did he handcuff you to the headboard?"

I dropped my sandwich to the table in front of me and wiped the crumbs from the hideous salmon-coloured uniform. "God, these uniforms are ugly."

"Tell me about it," Nat said. "Now, stop stalling."

I had only known Nat for a week now, but already I loved her. She was funny and kind, and I'd been to her small apartment twice for dinner and to hang out with her and Phoebe. It was nice having a girlfriend again. Ruby had systematically cut me off from the few friends I had, doing it so slowly and insidiously that I hadn't even realized until it was too late.

She'd insisted that she was the only one who understood me, the only one I needed in my life and, still grieving the death of my parents and drowning in work, I'd believed her.

"Maggie?" Natalia touched my hand. "You don't have to tell me anything. I'm sorry, I'm being nosey and -"

"He is sort of rough in bed and I-I liked it. A lot. He doesn't act like a cop, but he wants to be in charge. He didn't handcuff me to the bed, but he did say he would spank me if I wasn't a good girl. Which made me super turned on, and it's super weird that I'm a grown-ass woman who wants to be spanked. Oh God, I said too much. Oh, and he also is really good at using his mouth, and I was a virgin and I had no idea that a man could do those types of things with his tongue, and now I think I might be addicted to oral sex with Officer Six Pack... and why am I still talking? Oh God, please make me stop talking."

I stared wildly at Nat, a cracker in one hand and my embarrassment in the other.

"Okay," Nat said slowly. "That's... a lot to digest."

"I'm sorry," I said.

"Don't be," Nat replied. "I asked."

I took a deep breath as Natalia said, "We've got another half hour left on our lunch break. Do you want to tell me the whole story from the beginning or should I change the subject?"

I took another deep breath. "It all started the night I almost died."

ॐ ॐ

I parked my car next to Martha's in the driveway and rubbed at the delicate skin under my eyes before grabbing my purse and opening the door. My feet hurt and my back ached and while I was extremely grateful to be working, the fact that I was working in a damn diner instead of as a lawyer, stung like a bitch.

It's only temporary, Mags. Don't worry about it. Just make some money, smile your stupid face off to get those tips, and then you can move on.

Right, move on. That's what I needed to concentrate on. Not a certain dynamite hot police officer who sat in my section every day, looking and smelling delicious.

Girl, that ship has sailed. He doesn't even flirt with you. He's lost interest and it's all your fault.

I ducked my head against the cold wind and hurried toward the guest house. I felt sick to my stomach and I wanted to pretend that inner Maggie didn't know what the hell she was talking about, but I couldn't. Wyatt *was* over me. If I wasn't sure before, I was positive after the text that Martha sent me this afternoon.

Wyatt knew I was working today, he'd been in this morning for coffee and a stack of pancakes, but Martha's text said he would be at the guest house fixing the pantry door this afternoon. If he wanted me, wouldn't he have fixed the door when he knew I was at home? It was the perfect excuse to be around me.

He tried. You kicked him out, remember?

I winced and moved a little faster, trying not to slip in the snow. I'd actually felt a little better after spilling my guts to Nat during our lunch break, but the text from Martha had made me feel blue and disappointed. Which was stupid, because I had specifically told Nat it was for the best that I didn't see him anymore.

I opened the door and slipped inside, hanging my jacket on the hook before dropping my purse and kicking off my shoes. I stood on one foot like a stork and rubbed the other, groaning loudly at the shooting pain up through my arches. God, I had to get better shoes. My feet were –

"Maggie?"

I screamed and jerked back, my heart fluttering like a panicked bird trapped in a room. I tripped over my boots and went sprawling, the skirt of my ugly uniform hiking up to nearly my crotch. I banged my head against the hardwood floors and groaned loudly, rubbing the back of my head as

Wyatt's face appeared in front of me.

"Shit. Are you okay?"

His big hands cupped my waist and he helped me to my feet, steadying me as I shoved my uniform down and stared up at him.

"What are you doing here?" I asked.

"Didn't Nana text you? I'm fixing the pantry door."

"She did, but I, uh, thought you'd be finished by now."

He grimaced. "The door was a piece of crap. A big chunk of it cracked off when I tried to fix it. I had to buy a new door and now I'm just about to hang it."

"Oh," I said. "But, uh, your car isn't here."

"Nana borrowed mine to run a few errands. It's better in the ice and snow than hers."

"Right," I said.

He hesitated. "I meant to be finished before you were done work. I can come back tomorrow."

"No, that's okay. I don't mind."

"All right." He was still holding me around the waist, and I was way too aware of the way his shirt clung to his broad shoulders. God, I wanted to kiss him. I wanted him to kiss me. I wanted him to strip me naked and bury his face in my pussy and then fuck me and maybe finally give me that spanking that I couldn't stop thinking about.

Hey, Maggie? That's real sweet, but you remember that you're wearing a truly revolting uniform that makes you look like you have a uni-tit, you have a stain on the front from that milkshake that kid dumped on you, and you smell like a grease bucket. Right?

Dammit!

I pulled away from him and folded my arms across my chest to hide both my uni-tit and the milkshake stain. "Um, I was just going to go have a shower so, uh…"

"Sure, of course. I'll try and finish this up quickly."

"No, that's fine. Take your time." I fled down the hallway, wondering if Wyatt was looking at my ass. I stopped at the bedroom door, checking quickly behind me. Disappointment flooded through me. Not only was Wyatt not checking out my ass, but he'd already gone back into the kitchen.

I sighed and ducked into the room, unzipping my uniform and tossing it into the hamper. I had to get over this unhealthy obsession with Officer I Want his Tongue Down my Throat. He was over me and - I glanced ruefully at my chest - my tiny tits.

I took a quick shower, scrubbing the old milkshake and grease smell away, before slipping into a t-shirt and yoga pants. No bra, but it wasn't like I needed one anyway, right? Besides, Wyatt had already seen my boobs and he was over them.

And you're going without panties because…?

Resolutely ignoring my inner voice and pasting a smile on my face, I stepped into the kitchen. Wyatt was just packing up his tools, the new door already hung and looking perfect. A wave of disappointment washed over me. He'd leave now and I'd be alone.

And horny. Don't forget the horny part.

I grimaced inwardly. How could I forget the horny part? It was like a damn part of me now. It didn't help that I saw Wyatt every day at the diner, that I couldn't stop thinking about how talented he was with that damn tongue of his.

I stared at his ass in those tight jeans, watched the flex of his back muscles as he carefully piled the tools into his totally manly toolbox. Lord, the guy had a great ass. Very…

Biteable?

I swallowed hard as my cheeks flushed and lust rocketed through me. Just thinking about Wyatt and his biteable, yummy butt, made my nipples hard and my pussy wet and, oh boy, going without panties was a very, very bad idea.

It couldn't be normal for a vagina to get this wet just looking at a man, could it? I mean, obviously there was something wrong with my hoochie that required immediate tongue attention.

Medical. I mean it requires *medical* attention.

"What requires medical attention?"

Sweet mother of mercy… did I just say that out loud? I lifted my gaze from Wyatt's ass to his face. "Um, sorry, what?"

"What needs medical attention?" Wyatt's face was a mixture of confusion and concern.

"Oh, uh…"

Don't say vagina. Don't say vagina. Don't say…

"Vagina!" I blurted.

Goddammit!

His gaze dropped to my crotch. "Your vagina requires medical attention?"

"It's wet," I whispered. "I mean...it's aching."

He moved closer and when his gaze dropped to my tits, I followed it. My nipples were rock hard and poking against my shirt. I watched the muscle in Wyatt's jaw tick as he stared at them. He inched even closer, until I could feel the heat of his body, see the small spot of stubble on his jaw that he'd missed with the razor. I wanted to touch that spot, wanted to lick it with my tongue until he moaned.

"Is your pussy wet or is it aching?" He asked.

I stared mutely at him and he gave me a stern look that sent a new wave of liquid to my pussy. "Answer me, Magnolia."

"Um...it's not, I mean, it's kind of achy?" I said like an idiot.

"Maybe I should take a look at it," he replied.

"You're not a doctor."

Before he could answer, I said, "But you play one on TV, am I right?"

I giggled, the nerves clearly audible in it, and raised my hand for a high five.

He folded his arms across his chest, and I stared at the light dusting of dark hair across his forearms, and the sinewy muscle just below the skin before slowly lowering my hand. "Sorry."

"As an officer of the law, I have some medical training," he said.

"Right," I said. "Well, if you don't mind, maybe you could take a quick look at it. For, uh, medical purposes, not, um, licking purposes."

Oh.My.God.

His lips twitched and that muscle in his jaw ticked faster before he said. "I don't mind at all."

He walked to the sink and washed his hands before returning to me. I was still standing next to the table, my heart beating too fast and the heat in my cheeks matching the heat in my possibly broken vagina.

I squeaked when in three swift moves, he yanked my yoga pants to my ankles, picked me up, and plopped me down on the table. I sat there in surprise, my bare ass smushed against the cold wood, as Wyatt pulled my yoga pants completely free and dropped them on the floor.

"No panties, Ms. Blossom?"

"I, um, I didn't... shouldn't we go to the bedroom for this?"

"What for?" He asked with a hint of amusement. "The kitchen has better lighting and I'm doing this for medical purposes not... licking purposes. Remember?"

My blush was moving down my face and into my chest but there wasn't a single part of me that wanted to stop.

"Lie back."

I hesitated, and Wyatt placed a warm hand right between my tiny tits and pushed gently. "Lie back, please."

Feeling silly and embarrassed and wickedly horny, I collapsed on my back, staring at the ceiling as Wyatt lifted my legs until my feet were resting on the table. My knees were locked together, and I jerked when Wyatt rested his big warm hands on them.

"Open, Magnolia."

I peered at him over my raised legs. "Wyatt,

maybe…"

"Open for me. Now."

I opened my legs. How could I not when his deep voice demanded it?

Wyatt's hands slid down my inner thighs, leaving a searing path of heat wherever he touched. He pressed until my legs were spread as wide as they could go and my pussy was fully bared to him. He stared silently at it before lifting his gaze to me.

I moaned at the hunger on his face and his hands tightened against my inner thighs. "Your pussy is very wet, Magnolia."

"I -I know," I said.

One finger traced across my wet lips and I moaned, my hips rising compulsively. "Oh, please."

"Where does it ache?" He asked. "Here?" The tip of his finger probed between my pussy lips, and I made a strangled cry of need when it brushed against my swollen clit.

"Yes! Please, Wyatt."

He ignored my whimper of need and slid his finger back down my slit to my aching hole. He pushed his thick finger deep inside of me, a low groan escaping his throat when I clenched around him.

"Is it aching here, baby?"

"Yes!" I nodded frantically, my hands reaching down to clutch at his forearm. "Yes, it aches, Wyatt."

"Hmm. Does this help?" He added another finger and slowly moved them in and out.

"Oh God, yes. A little… kind of. Please!" I

said.

He smiled before tugging on the hem of my shirt with his free hand. "Take this off. I think my girl needs to be completely naked for me. Don't you?"

"Sure, yeah, okay," I said and yanked off my shirt.

"Good." He was studying my breasts but for once I wasn't thinking about how tiny they were. I was too distracted by the pressure of Wyatt's thumb as he rested it against my throbbing clit.

"Wyatt, rub," I whined.

He shook his head. I immediately wiggled my hips, rubbing my pussy against his hand. Oh God, it felt so good. The pressure, the roughness of –

"Ow! Oh…"

The stinging slap to my inner thigh made me squeal in surprise. He gave me another stern look. "Stay still, baby."

"That hurt!" I pouted.

He rubbed the pink mark on my thigh. "I'm sure it did. Stop moving, Magnolia."

I desperately wanted to rub against his thumb again, but it really had hurt when he slapped my thigh. I made myself stay still as he stared at my breasts again.

"Pull on your nipples," he said. "Make them hard for me."

I cupped my breasts, weirdly not self-conscious at all, and pulled and tugged on my nipples until they were swollen and diamond hard.

"Such pretty tits," Wyatt crooned. "I can't wait to suck on your nipples again, baby."

I cried out with pleasure when he rubbed my clit with his thumb.

"Does that help with the ache?"

I rubbed and kneaded my breasts, my hips rocking against Wyatt's hand. "Yeah," I gasped out. "A little."

He stopped rubbing. "Only a little?"

"Oh, please," I begged. "Fuck, Wyatt, please. I want more."

He just stared at me and I was pretty sure he saw the lightbulb go off over my head only a few seconds later.

"Please lick my clit, sir," I moaned.

He immediately bent his head, his fingers still firmly wedged in my pussy, and licked my swollen clit.

I wound my hands in his thick hair and held tightly as he licked my clit repeatedly. I ground my pussy against his face, crying out when he nipped my wet lips before sucking on my clit.

He lifted his head, his beautiful, talented mouth soaking wet. "Don't cum, Magnolia."

"What?" I glared at him. "No, I have to."

"No," he said. "Not yet."

"Yes."

"No." He punctuated the no with a long, wet lick of my clit that brought me to the very edge of my orgasm.

"Yes!" I shrieked. "Wyatt, yes!"

"No." He was as relentless as the tide. "Do not cum, Magnolia." Another wet lick that brought a strangled cry from my lips.

"If you cum, I'll spank you," he said.

With a loud shriek, I came all over his face, my hips pumping like a piston, my hands holding his face tight against my pussy. He growled, the sound vibrating against my pussy and sending another shockwave of pleasure through me. He gave my clit one final slow slide of his tongue that made me moan with delight before pulling my hands free of his hair and straightening.

He was giving me a look of disapproval, but I didn't care. The orgasm had been worth every bit of his disapproval. I gave him a languid smile. "Sorry about that."

"No, you're not," he replied.

"I am. But really, it's your fault," I said with a soft and sated giggle. "You and your magic tongue."

I lolled on the table, naked as a jaybird and not caring at all, my eyes half closed as my pussy throbbed pleasantly with the last of my orgasm. I could hear Wyatt rustling around the kitchen, and I smiled. Maybe he was making me something to eat. It was dinner time and I was kind of hungry now that my little lust problem was taken care of.

"Stand up, Magnolia."

I forced myself into a sitting position, the soft smile on my lips dying when I saw Wyatt. He was naked and sitting on a kitchen chair, the condom already on his perfect erect cock. He patted his lap. "Come here, please."

I swallowed heavily, my gaze trained on that sexy and large – very large – dick of his. Just the tiniest bit of lust was flickering back to life in my belly. I licked my lips. "Wh-what are you planning on doing to me?"

"You know what I'm going to do to you," he said. "You disobeyed me. What happens when you disobey me?"

"I get a stern talking to and another orgasm?" I said.

His perfect lips twitched again, but his gaze was solemn when he said, "Come here, Magnolia. I won't ask again."

I hopped off the table and stood next to him. He patted his lap again. "Over my lap, please."

"Wyatt, this is kind of ridiculous. I mean, a spanking is one thing, but does it have to be over your -"

"The more you argue, the more spanks you'll get," he said.

"You're kidding!"

"Do I look like I'm kidding?"

I folded my arms across my chest and studied him for a minute before shrugging. "Okay, fine."

Feeling a little awkward, I leaned over his lap, squeaking when his heavy hand pressed on my lower back and I fell into his lap. His erection pressed against my stomach, and I stared at the floor as he rubbed my lower back.

I was head down and ass up and while it felt weird and a little humiliating, that flicker of lust in my belly was becoming a tiny flame.

"I need a safe word, Magnolia." His warm hand rubbed over my bare bottom and I shivered against his thighs.

"Do I really need one?" I craned my neck to stare at him. "I mean, this is like a sexy spanking, not a real spanking, right? I don't need a safe word."

He smiled at me and squeezed my right ass cheek. "Baby, with this type of play, I always require a safe word."

"But if it's just for fun, then…"

"Those are the rules," he said. "Without a safe word, this doesn't happen."

"Fine," I huffed. I glanced around the kitchen for inspiration. "Uh, spatula. Spatula is my safe word."

I expected him to roll his eyes or tell me to pick another, but he just nodded and stroked my ass again. "All right. If you want me to stop, you say spatula. Understood?"

"Yeah, sure."

"Magnolia," his tone was firm, but his touch was gentle, "this is very important. I won't stop for anything but your safe word. Do you understand?"

I stared into his stormy ocean eyes, my throat suddenly dry, and that flame of lust burning a little brighter. "Yes, Wyatt. I understand."

"Good. Relax, please."

"It's kind of hard to relax when you're naked and draped over a man's lap for a spanking," I said.

He grinned at me and any trepidation I might have been feeling disappeared the moment I saw that damn dimple. "Fair enough."

He rubbed my ass again. "I love your ass, baby. I can't wait to spank it."

"Then what are you waiting for?" I said cheekily. "I haven't got all – shit! Ow, ow, ow!"

Wyatt had slapped my right ass cheek and it was

not the sexy little love slap I was expecting. Nope, this was a full-on spank and when his hand came down on my left cheek, I was no less prepared for the harsh sting of pain it sent through my lower body.

I immediately flailed around on his lap like a wounded bird, trying to slide off his lap to the floor. His hand pressed down on my lower back, pinning me in place, and he spanked me again.

I squealed in outrage and tried to protect my already painful butt with my hands.

"Wyatt, no!" I shouted when he grabbed my wrists and pinned them behind my back. I stared at the floor, my poor defenseless ass already on fire as Wyatt spanked me again.

"Goddammit!" I shouted. "That hurts. You son of a bitch!"

He spanked me again and I wiggled wildly on his lap. I don't know how he did it, but my thrashing legs were suddenly pinned under one of his legs and I was completely trapped. I arched my back when he rubbed my burning ass.

"Wyatt, it hurts!"

"I know," he said. "Only ten more, baby."

"Ten!" I turned my head to give him a look of outrage. "Ten? No, no way. I am not... oh fuck!"

He spanked me twice more, each one sending a line of fire across my ass.

"This is not sexy!" I moaned. "This isn't sexy or fun or... oh, oh, oh my God!"

His horrible, terrible, wonderful hand had slipped between my legs and when he rubbed my clit, I made a screeching inarticulate sound of pleasure. My ass was burning, but the sensation had paled with the sudden realization that the flame of lust burning in my belly had become an out-of-control wildfire.

"Look, baby."

I shook my head, staring grimly at the floor as Wyatt moved his hand away from my pussy.

"Magnolia, look."

I lifted my head and studied his fingers, staring at the way they dripped with liquid.

"Your sweet pussy is soaking wet, isn't it?" Wyatt said.

I pressed my lips together, a little ashamed at myself and my reaction to the not-at-all sexy, but somehow unfucking-believably sexy, spanking.

"Answer me," Wyatt said.

"Yes." I glared at him. "Yes, it's wet."

He smiled at me. "Soaking wet."

I could feel that shame growing, but underneath it was the almost desperate need for him to finish the spanking so that he would fuck me.

"Wyatt," I moaned.

"Yes, Magnolia?"

"Please."

"Please what, baby?"

"Just finish it already," I snapped.

He laughed and gave me a spank that brought a plea for mercy flying from my mouth.

"Ask me nicely," he said.

"I won't!" I glared at him again. "You can't make me – oh, oh, yes, right there."

His hand had dipped between my legs again and he was rubbing firm circles against my clit. I rocked against him, gasping and moaning, my head down and my hair hanging in my face as my orgasm grew closer and closer.

"Oh, oh, yes, oh, honey, that's so good, that's so... no! Goddammit, no!!"

Wyatt's hand was back resting on my ass. He gave me a sweet smile and if my hands had been free, I would have done my best to punch that sweet smile right off of his face.

"Don't stop!" I begged.

"You know what I want from you, Magnolia."

I gritted my teeth, my pussy dripping and aching with the need to cum, as my inner self warred between asking for my ass to be spanked or giving up on the idea of finding relief for my aching pussy. When Wyatt's fingers traced my pussy lips, my need to cum won the war raging inside of me.

"Please finish spanking me, sir," I said.

"That's my girl." Wyatt smoothed his hand over my burning ass. "If you're very good and hold still for the rest of your spanking, I'll give you an orgasm before I fuck you. Would you like that, baby?"

"Yes, sir," I moaned.

His hand came down on my ass with a loud crack, the burning pain making me squeeze my ass cheeks together and drum my feet against the floor. I dropped my head, trying to breathe through the pain of the next seven slaps. He was mercifully quick, no hesitating or making me wonder when the next spank would be.

When he finished, the silence in the kitchen was broken only by my labored breathing.

"You did so well, baby," he said. "Time for your reward."

His hand slipped between my legs again and I cried out with pleasure when he rubbed my clit. He circled it and when he gave it a quick, hard pinch, I screamed, and my orgasm burst over me in a glorious wave of indescribable pleasure.

I'd never cum so hard in my entire life. My body shook wildly, lights exploding behind my tightly-closed eyelids as my orgasm went on and on and on. I was only vaguely aware of Wyatt releasing my hands, of his warm hands holding me against his legs as I moaned and shook and twitched on his lap.

"Oh my God," I whispered. "Oh my God."

"Stand up, baby." He helped me into a standing position, my knees buckled, and he quickly pulled me into his lap until I was straddling him. My legs hung over his, my toes just brushing the floor. I let my head fall to his chest with a clunk, feeling a little lightheaded and weak.

"All right?" His big warm hands rubbed my back, brushed my hair out of my face, massaged the back of my neck.

"That was amazing," I whispered.

"Good," he said.

He reached between us, one arm wrapping around my waist to lift me a little. I felt the head of his cock probe against my pussy and then it was sliding into me, hard and thick and perfect.

"Oh," I moaned, pressing my face into his chest. "Oh, that's nice."

He gathered my hair into a low ponytail and

tugged lightly until I lifted my head.

"Sit up, baby."

I struggled to straighten, I was still weak and a bit twitchy, and I stared at him as he put his arm around my waist.

"Okay?" He asked.

"Yes, it doesn't hurt at all."

"Good."

He didn't move, and I braced my hands on his shoulders and made a tiny experimental bounce. He moaned loudly, that mask of control slipping from his face, and I realized for the first time just how turned on he was as well.

"Baby," he whispered, "just give me a minute, okay? You're tight and wet and I just need a minute to -"

"No," I said. "I want you to fuck me, Wyatt." I bounced on his cock again, giving him a delighted look when he shuddered and his arm tightened around my waist. "You want to fuck me, so do it."

"Christ," he muttered before his hips started pumping and his cock was sliding in and out of me in a delicious rhythm that tore another crow of delight from my throat.

He fucked me hard and steady, his hips thrusting up and down, the chair creaking underneath us as I held onto his broad shoulders and let him take what he wanted.

"Kiss me," he rasped.

I kissed him hard, angling my mouth over his and opening for his tongue. I could taste myself on him, and I moaned happily, licking and sucking at his tongue as he moved faster beneath me.

He pulled his mouth from mine and I gasped in a lungful of oxygen as he threw his arm around my waist. He made a low roar of pleasure and thrust so hard, I would have been thrown from his lap if he hadn't held me so tight.

His body shook, the veins in his neck standing out as he made another low groan and two more hard, choppy thrusts before collapsing on the chair. I rested my head on his chest, listening to the rapid beat of his heart as he slowly rubbed my back.

His cock was softening inside of me, but he made no attempt to move as he came down from the high of his orgasm. I rubbed my hand across his ribs before kissing his chest.

"Hey, Wyatt?"

"Yeah, baby?"

"My ass is killing me."

He laughed, the sound rumbling out of his chest and warming me to my toes. He kissed my forehead and squeezed the back of my neck. "C'mon. Let's get an icepack for your sore ass."

Chapter Six

Wyatt

"This is really good. Thank you." I stuffed the last of my omelet into my mouth as Maggie grinned.

"It's only an omelet, not beef wellington, Wyatt."

I laughed and finished off my water. "Yeah, but it's the best damn omelet I've ever eaten."

"I doubt that." Maggie loaded the dishwasher and I studied her ass. The yoga pants hid how red her delightful ass cheeks were, but both me and my dick remembered what they looked like.

I adjusted the front of my jeans as Maggie put the pan in the sink to soak before returning to the table. She sat down and winced before reaching under her and rubbing at her ass. "I think I need another ice pack."

I smiled and she crinkled her nose at me. "You're enjoying my pain, aren't you?"

"No, but I do enjoy that your ass is covered in

my handprints."

I thought that would get me a laugh, but instead she said, "I'm sorry."

"For what?"

"I said we couldn't do this anymore and then I basically begged you to eat my pussy."

"I didn't mind."

"I'm giving you mixed messages and that's a dick thing to do."

"Look, there's an attraction between us – one that's hard to ignore. I get it, I promise you."

"So," she glanced at the clock on the wall, "now what?"

I leaned forward and took her hand. "Now, we go to your bedroom and I give you another orgasm"

Her cheeks flushed and she bit at her bottom lip. "I'm leaving. Remember?"

My guts clenched and I wanted to tell her that she wasn't. That she was mine now and there was no way in hell I was ever letting her go. Instead, I forced a smile and said, "I remember. But that doesn't mean we can't have some fun while you're here. Right?"

"I guess not," she said slowly.

Now my stomach was churning, and I released her hand. "If you're not into that, then obviously I'm not going to pressure you -"

"No! No, I'm into it. I just – I want to make sure we're both clear on what this is."

"We are," I said. "You're leaving as soon as you've made an undisclosed sum of money. But until you do leave, we can enjoy each other's company and I can make amends for hurting you that first night."

She rolled her eyes. "Seriously, Wyatt? You've got to get over that. Half an hour ago, you spanked me so hard, your handprints are probably permanently etched into my ass cheeks. But you feel bad about a little hymen tearing?"

I couldn't help but laugh. "You asked for the spanking, you didn't ask for the abrupt hymen tearing."

"I didn't ask for the spanking!" She gave me a look of outrage.

"Oh, please, sir. Please finish my spanking, sir." I pitched my voice into a falsetto and her outrage deepened.

"I do not sound like that, Wyatt Reynolds! Besides, what else was I supposed to do or say? I was on the verge of the best orgasm of my life."

"You're welcome." I gave her a smug little grin.

"Your arrogance is not the least bit attractive," she said.

"Lying will get you a spanking, Magnolia." I deliberately deepened my voice and gave her the look that I knew would make her squirm.

It didn't fail me. She cleared her throat and shifted on her chair before saying, "Do you spank every woman you sleep with?"

"No, not every woman. Some of them aren't into it."

"Are you – have you always been like this in bed?"

"Yes. I've always liked control, in and out of bed, and spanking a woman is just one way of maintaining that control, I suppose."

She gave me a shy look that I found utterly intoxicating. "I–I liked the spanking a lot."

"I know."

"Arrogant jerk," she muttered under her breath.

I laughed. "No, just honest." I stood and walked over to the counter, wiping the spots clean that Maggie had missed when she was tidying, before scrubbing the pot and putting it in its spot in the cupboard. I opened the dishwasher and rearranged the dishes. When I was finished, I turned to see Maggie grinning at me.

"What?"

"You know we are exact opposites, right?"

"Are we?"

"Um, yeah. I have poor impulse control and I don't always think before I act. I was literally raised by hippies."

"So?" I said.

She cocked her head at me. "Have you ever done anything illegal?"

"No. But that doesn't mean we're completely different."

"You like order and control. You admitted that yourself. I mean, you just rearranged the dishes in the dishwasher, for God's sake. You've lived your entire life in this town, haven't you?"

I sat down beside her. "Yes. Why?"

She smiled a bit wistfully. "The longest I've ever lived in one place was four years, and that's because I was doing my bachelor's degree and had to stay."

"You have your bachelor's degree?"

An 'I've said too much' look crossed her face. "Uh, yeah. Anyway, my point is, even if I wasn't leaving, we'd never last."

"You can't possibly know that."

"I do," she said with a heavy sigh.

That sigh made me wonder if there was a part of her that wanted more with me, and I had to stop from giving myself a fist bump of victory. Maybe I could convince Maggie to stick around a little longer.

"You don't," I said. "Opposites attract, remember?"

"So, what, you're gonna go around behind me straightening up and rearranging the dishes in the dishwasher for the rest of our lives?"

I shrugged and gave her a small grin. "I did it for the entire time I lived with Mia at Nana's."

She giggled. "Man, if my parents could see me dating a cop, they'd never believe it." Her eyes widened as she realized what she said. "Not that we're dating. Because obviously we're not... I mean, I don't think we're dating or anything or... oh shit, Maggie, stop talking."

I laughed and said, "Relax, Maggie. I knew what you meant. But, hey, if I ever do happen to meet your parents, I promise to try and be more hippie-like, so they're not completely freaked out."

The look of sadness on her face made me curse under my breath. I knew that look, had seen it staring back at me in the mirror too many mornings to count. I took her hand and kissed the knuckles before giving her a gentle look. "When did they die?"

She pressed her lips together and studied the table. "My first year of university. Car accident. They were coming to visit me for the weekend." Her voice turned dull. "We were supposed to go for dinner that night. Instead, I went to the morgue and identified their bodies."

"Oh, baby. I'm so sorry." I moved my chair closer and pulled her from her chair and into my lap. She winced a little but settled on my thighs, her lower lip trembling.

"Thanks," she whispered before resting her head on my shoulder. "I know it isn't my fault, but there's a part of me that won't shut up about how they'd still be alive if I hadn't been such a baby and asked them to come see. I just – I really missed them, you know? I wanted to see them, but if I had been stronger, they wouldn't have -"

"No." I kissed the top of her forehead and gave her a gentle shake. "No, that isn't true. Your guilt and your grief are lying to you, baby. Their car accident was no more your fault than my parents' car accident was mine."

She sat up, her soft hand cupping my face. "Oh my God. Your parents died in a car accident too? That's why you were raised by your nana?"

I nodded and sorrow crossed her face. "I'm so sorry, Wyatt. How old were you?"

"I was four."

"Oh my God. I'm very sorry. Here I am complaining about my parents and you didn't, I mean, you never really had the chance to…"

She rested her forehead against mine. "I'm sorry for your loss, honey."

"Me too," I said. "I have a few memories of them, they're more like hazy dreams than memories, but Nana made sure to tell me lots of stories about them when I was growing up, and she has pictures of Mom and Dad all over the house."

"That's good," she said. "I really like your nana."

"Everyone does," I said. "She's wonderful."

"She really is," Maggie said. She raised her head and studied my face before stroking her fingers along my jawline. "She raised an amazing guy."

I cupped the back of her head, her delicate skull resting in my palm, and pressed a kiss against her mouth. She moaned, her lips parting and her soft tongue touching mine when I slipped it into her mouth.

I cupped one breast in my hand, teasing her nipple as I deepened the kiss. She moved closer, her tiny hands running across my shoulders and down my bare chest. When her fingers grazed one flat nipple, I groaned and broke the kiss.

"Bedroom, now," I said hoarsely.

"Yes, sir," she replied.

Shit. Magnolia Blossom was going to be the death of me.

☙ ❧

"Baby," I moaned, "touch my dick. Please."

We were in Maggie's small bed, both of us naked, the room lit by the small lamp on the nightstand. It had started to snow again while we were eating our omelets, and the only sounds in the room were Maggie's soft moans and the hard pellets of snow hitting the window with a regular and rhythmic tap-tap-tap.

We'd been making out for almost ten minutes. Although Maggie's soft hands had roamed across my body while I'd teased and tormented her sweet tits until her nipples were rock-hard and a delightful shade of dark pink, she hadn't gone near my cock.

"I would, but I really want to have sex." Her voice was breathless in my ear.

I gave her swollen clit a soft pinch. "So do I. But I also want your hands and your mouth on my dick. We can do both."

She sat up and gave me a weirdly suspicious look. "Are you sure?"

"Yes," I said.

She stared at my dick, her hand resting on my lower abdomen. Christ, her hand was so damn close, and I could almost see how it would look with her fingers wrapped around my shaft.

She took a deep breath and slowly slid her fingers around my width. My cock twitched and she jerked her hand away like she'd been burned. "Shit!"

"What's wrong?" I said.

"Nothing." She gave me a giant-sized false smile. "Okay, here we go!"

I groaned when she put her tiny hand around me and made a few rapid jacking off motions. I was so hot for her that it was almost sexy, despite the way she rubbed my dick like it was a poisonous snake that was going to bite her.

I glanced at her face. She was leaning back, her head half-turned away and her eyes squinted almost closed as she watched her hand move up and down my dick. The look on her face would have made me laugh if I wasn't so worried that she was suddenly afraid of my dick.

I reached down and put my hand over hers, peeling it off my cock and then linking our fingers together. "Magnolia, what's wrong?"

"Nothing," she said.

Her face was still all squinched up and I said, "Then why do you look like you ate something rotten?"

She bit her lip. 'Oh my God, I am totally ruining the moment, aren't I?"

"Just tell me what's wrong, baby."

She hugged her knees to her chest with one arm and gave me an embarrassed look. "I've only touched one penis before yours."

"All right," I said. "No big deal."

She rested her chin on her knees. "His name was Reggie. I met him in university, and I was going to have sex with him."

Jealousy niggled in my stomach over a man that she'd obviously never had sex with. Yeah, I was a total fool for her.

"We made out for a while and I – he wasn't very experienced either. You know? Like, when he touched my, um, clit, he was way too tentative, and it didn't really do anything for me. Anyway, I decided that I'd touch him for a while."

She gripped her knees a little tighter. "Only, I gave his dick a couple of, um, strokes, and the damn thing just... like, it just exploded – I mean, it was a cum fountain, Wyatt. It was everywhere and I had made the mistake of leaning over him, so it went in my face and in my mouth and, oh my God, it tasted so bad."

The story was fucking hilarious, but I fought against my urge to laugh as Maggie said, "I didn't throw up, but I couldn't stop retching and I was, like, half-blind because it got in my eyes. Reggie's dick had basically deflated after he came, and all I kept thinking was – well, that's not gonna work now and what the hell did he eat to make his cum taste that bad?"

Her mouth went down in a moue of disgust at the memory. "I couldn't stop gagging and my eyes were watering so bad it looked like I was crying. Reggie was mortified. He jumped out of the bed, got dressed, and then spent the next three years avoiding me on campus."

She sighed deeply. "After that, I decided it was best to focus on my studies rather than losing my virginity. Which is why I was a twenty-eight-year-old virgin."

I reached down and stroked her smooth shin. "That sounds like a really traumatic experience."

She stared at me before rolling her eyes. "I know you're trying not to laugh, Wyatt."

The grin spread across my face despite how hard I was trying to keep it contained. "I'm sorry, but it's a pretty funny story."

She poked me in the thigh. "It wasn't funny at the time."

I squeezed her calf. "If I promise that I won't 'explode' all over you, will you let me teach you how to give me a hand job and a blow job?"

She nodded. "Yeah, I want to learn, but – and don't take this the wrong way – what if you taste bad and I start gagging again?"

I wanted to laugh but she was giving me an adorably earnest look. I gave her calf another reassuring squeeze. "I haven't had any complaints about my taste before, but if I taste bad to you, you have my permission to gag. I won't be offended."

"But you will leave," she said with a sigh.

"I won't. I promise."

"Really?" She eyed me carefully.

"Really, really."

"All right," she said. "I'll give it a shot."

"That's my girl," I said with a grin. "Watch what I do, okay?"

"Okay," she said.

I sat up and stuffed a pillow behind my back before leaning against the headboard. I reached down and gripped my cock and stroked from root to tip. I did it a few times, my cock hardening under both my hand and Maggie's watchful gaze. I stroked lightly and then firmly before rubbing my thumb over the head.

I groaned, and Maggie licked her lips before whispering, "Can I try?"

"Yeah, baby," I said. "I want you to touch me."

She scooted closer and wrapped her soft little hand around the base of my dick. My cock twitched but this time she didn't flinch. Instead, mimicking the movements I had made, she stroked my cock with a surprisingly firm grip.

I moaned, my hips rising up and down. I was weirdly proud when she leaned a little closer and studied my dick. I loved that she trusted me enough to no longer worry I would 'explode' in her face.

"Is this right?" She asked.

I nodded. "It's so good. You're a natural."

She gave me a pleased look and continued to rub my cock. Precum was beading out of the tip and she gave it a look of both fascination and trepidation. When her little tongue wetted her bottom lip, I made a harsh groan.

"Baby, are you ready to try with your mouth?"

She paused in her stroking, her hand halfway down my cock, as she gave me a look of apprehension. "Um, yeah, I think so. You're not, um, close…are you?"

I shook my head. "No, baby. I promise I won't cum in your mouth."

"Okay." She got up on her knees and leaned over me. The look on her face one of 'let's get this over with', she bent her head and tentatively licked up a bit of the precum.

Fuck me! It was all I could do not to grasp her head and push her mouth down over my dick. I clenched my hands into fists and kept my body still as she licked her lips. She raised her gaze to mine, the surprise evident in her eyes.

"You – you taste good." Her voice was full of soft wonderment. "Really good."

I gritted my teeth when she bent her head and licked the rest of the precum away.

"Oh, this is much better," she muttered to herself before sliding her hot wet mouth over the head of my dick.

I cried out, my hips rising up off the bed and she

immediately released me, giving me a nervous look. "Was that wrong?"

"Fuck, no. Maggie," I groaned, "put your mouth back on my dick right now." I cupped the back of her neck, unable to stop myself from pushing her head back toward my cock. I didn't want to overwhelm her, but fuck, I was only human.

To my relief, she slid her mouth back down over my cock and sucked enthusiastically. She tongued the shaft, bobbing her head a bit awkwardly up and down.

"Good, baby," I moaned. "That's good." I took her hand and wrapped it around the base. "Stroke while you suck."

She rubbed the base up and down, her mouth meeting her fist with every downward stroke. I groaned and gathered her hair into one fist, watching her lips widen and stretch around me. "Good, baby. Take more with your mouth." I tugged on her hair to guide her down.

She made a muffled sound of protest, her free hand digging into my thigh. I shook my head, holding her head still when she tried to move back. "No, you're doing well. Take a breath through your nose."

She paused and took several breaths through her nose, her beautiful lips still wrapped around my cock the way they were meant to be.

"That's my girl," I said. "Suck harder."

She sucked hard, staring up at me with her big blue eyes. I could see lust swirling in their depths, and it made me pump my hips a little harder into her mouth. She continued to suck, gasping around my thickness when I reached under her and gave her nipple a pinch.

"Is my girl getting horny again?" I asked.

She nodded and I smiled at her before running my hand down her satin-smooth back. "Do you want to be fucked?"

Her reply was muffled by my cock and I tugged on her hair, lifting her mouth from my cock with a wet pop.

"Yes," she panted. Her mouth was swollen and red and I'd never seen anything more beautiful in my goddamn life.

"Ask me nicely, Magnolia."

"Please fuck me, sir," she said immediately.

My dick leaked more precum and my plan to teach her how to put a condom on me went out the fucking window. If I didn't get my dick inside of her in the next few minutes, I'd lose my fucking mind.

"Hands and knees," I said.

My voice was harsher than I meant, but she didn't hesitate. She swung around and bent over, bracing her hands on the mattress as I grabbed the condom I'd already placed on the nightstand. I ripped it open and rolled it down my dick as I stared at Maggie's ass. It was still red from my spanking earlier, and fresh lust rolled over me.

"Spread your legs, baby. Show me your pussy."

She spread her legs wide and I made a hoarse sound of approval as I got on my knees behind her. "Your little pussy is so wet, isn't it?"

"Yes," she said. "Yes, it's wet for you, sir."

Fuck! I smoothed my hand over her ass,

making a soothing sound when she tensed. "Don't worry, baby, you're not getting a spanking. My girl's been so good, and good girls get a fucking, not a spanking."

"Please," she moaned.

I grinned and lined my dick up at her wet hole. Reminding myself to go slow, I pushed into her, watching and stifling my groan of pleasure as her little pussy took every inch of my cock. "Good, baby. So good," I breathed.

I went deep, deeper than I'd gone before and I wasn't surprised when she made a moan of protest and tried to wiggle forward. I gripped her hips tight, ignoring my urge to give her upturned ass a spank, and said, "No, Magnolia. Hold still for your fucking."

"It's too much," she moaned. "Please, Wyatt."

"It isn't," I said. "My girl needs to take all of my cock."

"I'm trying," she grumbled, and I grinned before slapping the back of one creamy thigh.

"Hey!" She jerked wildly and I groaned when her pussy tightened around my cock. "You said you wouldn't spank me."

"Then be a good girl and hold still," I said.

I pushed on her upper back, forcing her chest and head to the bed. Her upturned ass and her soaking wet pussy stuffed full of my cock was a beautiful sight and I took a moment to admire it.

"Wyatt," she whined. "Please. I need you to fuck me."

"I know," I said. I reached between her legs and rubbed her clit, groaning again when she cried out and her pussy clamped like a vice on my dick. "Oh fuck, you're so tight."

She was straining against my grip, trying to rock her hips back and forth, and I lifted my hand from her back and gave her full control. She immediately lifted up and braced her hands on the bed again, practically ramming her pussy back and forth over my dick.

I held her hips loosely, watching her pussy lips stretch around my dick as she fucked me with an out-of-control need that was quickly bringing me to the edge as well.

"Oh," she moaned, "oh, I think I-I might cum like this. It feels so good, sir!"

Her low voice calling me 'sir', ruined my own control and I dug my hands into her hips, holding her tight before pounding into her. She cried out, tossing her head from side to side as I fucked her.

It only took a few minutes for her to cum hard on my dick. As her pussy squeezed and released me, I gasped her name and thrust wildly. She cried out again, her whole body shaking on the bed as I drove into her for a final time and came. Pleasure rolled over me, making my body shake and my lungs gasp for air. Her pussy tightened again, and I squeezed my eyes shut, shouting her name this time as another lightning bolt of pleasure ran down my legs.

I wanted to collapse on top of her, but I forced myself to pull out of her still quivering pussy and collapse on my back instead. She moaned and crawled to me, lying down next to me and resting her head on my chest. I stroked her back as we both shook lightly, our legs twitching with the aftershocks of our orgasms.

"Holy God," she moaned. "That was…"

"Incredible," I gasped. "Fucking incredible."

Chapter Seven

Maggie

"My feet are killing me. This was the longest shift ever." Natalia slid into the booth across from me and slumped against the seat. Her normally cheerful face was strained and pinched looking and I gave her a worried look. I'd never seen her look down before and even though I knew it was hard for her being a single mom, she'd never once complained.

Hoping to cheer her up, I said, "The hot guy sitting with Elijah at table seven during the lunch rush was totally into you."

Natalia rolled her eyes. "That hot guy is Matt Andrews and he's a total dog. He hits on anything in a skirt. Even," she glanced down at her uniform, "when it highlights your muffin top and washes out your skin tone."

"You haven't got a muffin top," I said. "Is Matt the EMT who works with Mia?"

She shrugged. "Thanks to the magical sucking-in power of Spanx. Trust me, after having Phoebe, my flat stomach is a thing of the past. And yes, Matt is the EMT who works with Mia."

"Hey, is everything all right?" I asked.

"So, you and Officer Reynolds officially dating yet, or what?" She replied.

I shook my head. "No, of course not. You know it's just a casual thing."

"Is it?" she asked. "Because it's been three weeks now and everyone in town is talking about how much time our handsome deputy is spending with the out-of-towner."

"God, the gossip in this town is insane," I said.

"It's not exactly gossip if it's true," she replied.

"It's casual," I insisted.

"He dropped you off at work this morning and is picking you up tonight, isn't he?"

"My car's getting an oil change," I said.

"Fine," she said. "But tell me again how casual it is even though you and Wyatt, and Mia and Elijah had a double date last weekend."

I wanted to scowl at her, but we had sort of gone on a double date. Mia had asked and I couldn't think of a way to say no. It felt weird telling her that I was only banging her cousin for the orgasms, not his company.

That's not true though, is it, Mags? If you only wanted Wyatt for the orgasms, would you spend every free moment you have with him? If you're only in it for the sex, why did he spend the night last night and you didn't actually have sex?

He was really tired, I argued inwardly. *He'd had a long day at work, and he had a headache and*

I could see how tired he was. I wasn't gonna force him to have sex with me.

No, but you certainly seemed to enjoy the cuddling you did all night instead.

"Hey, you still with me?" Natalia tapped on the table.

"Yes, sorry. Just thinking."

"About Wyatt and the fact that you're in love with him?"

"I'm not," I snapped. "God, Nat, give it a rest, would you?"

Her face fell and I was submerged in guilt when a tear slipped down her cheek. I reached across and grabbed her hand. "Nat, I'm sorry. I shouldn't have snapped."

She shook her head as more tears dripped down her face. "No, it's my fault. I was being way too pushy and -"

"You weren't," I said. 'But will you please tell me what's wrong? You've been upset all day, I know you have."

She sighed and dug a tissue out of the pocket of her apron before wiping her face. "It's not that big of a deal."

"Tell me, honey," I said.

"Money is a little short right now and I'm having a hard time covering expenses. I've already got poor Phoebe in a second-rate daycare – which I feel terrible about – but I can't afford the better one. My heat got cut off last night."

She dabbed at her eyes again. "I bundled Phoebe up and put her into bed with me and we have a small space heater, but it's only going to get colder. I'll have the money to pay the bill and have it turned back on by Friday, but if it happens again and it's the middle of goddamn winter…"

She sighed and gave me a despondent look. "I'm failing Phoebe so badly, Maggie."

"Honey, no, you're not." I squeezed her hand. "You're an amazing mom."

"Some weeks I can barely afford to feed her," Nat said. "I take as many extra shifts at the diner as I can get. I grit my teeth and smile and pretend to be flattered when someone like that douchebag Matt hits on me, just so he'll give me a bigger tip, and we're still barely scraping by."

"I'm sorry," I said. "I can loan you some cash if –"

"No," she said. "Absolutely not. You need your money and besides," she squeezed my hand when I tried to protest, "I'd never be able to pay you back anyway."

We sat in silence for a few minutes. Our shifts were over and I knew Wyatt was probably waiting for me in the parking lot, but Natalia wasn't making any move to leave, and she looked so sad and lonely, there was no way in hell I was leaving her.

"Honey, what about Phoebe's dad? If you're going through a rough patch financially, you can ask for increased child support."

Nat's laugh was only a little bitter. "He doesn't pay any child support anymore."

"What?" I leaned forward. "Why not?"

"Because he moved out of state when Phoebe was about a year and a half and stopped sending payments. It's almost impossible to contact him.

When I do, he says he'll send me a cheque and then he changes his cell number, it takes me another six months to track him down and we just have the exact same conversation."

"He is legally obligated to pay child support," I said. "You can have a portion of his pay cheque garnished to pay it."

"Really? Boris didn't tell me that," Nat said.

"Who's Boris?" I asked.

"Boris Galthwaite. He's the only lawyer in town. About four months ago, I scraped up some cash and made an appointment. When he found out that Evan had moved out of state, he told me that trying to get child support was a losing battle and to just cut my losses. Basically, I paid him a hundred and twenty-five bucks to tell me I was on my own."

"What?" I gave her a look of outrage. "What kind of fucking lawyer is this guy? He's full of shit, Nat."

"I – he seemed to know what he was talking about," she said. "He's like eighty years old and has been a lawyer forever."

"He's full of shit," I repeated. "What a stupid, lazy motherfu – look, it doesn't matter that Evan is out of state. He is still required to pay child support. There's something called the Uniform Interstate Family Support Act. It sets a national standard for each state to follow in enforcing child support orders. Basically, you just need to take your order of child support from here and register it with the courts of the state that the father resides in. Once that's registered, if that dickhead Evan still doesn't pay, then we can enforce the child support order by garnishing his wages, revoking his driver's license, or seizing any property he owns. You told me he was an accountant, right?"

Natalia nodded, and I gave her a smug grin. "I could get his professional license suspended if he doesn't pay the child support."

Nat stared at me. "How do you know all of this?"

Shit.

"Oh, uh… I watch a lot of *Law and Order* reruns," I said feebly. "It's amazing how much you pick up from that show."

"Right," Natalia said. I knew she was about to grill me for the truth and I made a show of glancing at my watch. She checked hers as well and immediately slid out of the booth. "Shit, I gotta go. I'll be late to pick up Phoebe if I don't move my ass."

"See you tomorrow," I called as I climbed out of the booth and grabbed my purse and my jacket that were lying on the seat. I turned and ran into a solid wall of Wyatt.

His big hands cupped my hips and, despite the prying eyes of the customers in the diner, I gave him a delighted smile. "Hey, you."

"Hey, yourself."

"I'm sorry to keep you waiting. I was talking to Natalia."

"I heard," he said.

A thread of unease went down my spine. "You were eavesdropping?"

"I didn't mean to," he said as he guided me toward the door.

We stepped outside into the cold air and hurried toward the SUV. I climbed into the passenger side and Wyatt slid in behind the wheel. He turned it on and clicked the heat to high.

"It's rude to listen in on other people's conversations," I said.

"It is," he agreed. "It wasn't my intention though. I came inside to find you and when I realized you were still talking to Natalia, sat down in the booth behind yours and decided to let you finish your conversation."

"Oh, well, I'm sure Natalia doesn't want anyone knowing her business, so keep it to yourself, please."

He backed out of the parking spot and pulled out onto the street. "You know I'm not a gossip, Maggie."

"I know, I was…"

What I was, was panicking that he'd overheard my conversation. I'd messed up by giving Natalia all of that advice, but I was also still bristling with indignance over what that so-called lawyer, Boris, had said to her.

"So, Maggie…"

Shit.

Double shit.

He was gonna ask me about how I knew the legal stuff he'd overheard, and I needed a better excuse than *Law and Order* reruns.

"What do you think about going out for dinner tonight?"

"I'm sorry?" I gave him a blank look.

"Dinner. Baker's Steakhouse. You and me. A

bottle of wine. Two very large and medium rare steaks."

I grinned at him. "Make mine medium well, and you've got yourself a dinner date."

"Good." He reached across and I took his hand, squeezing it lightly. "I picked up your car from Jack's shop and took it back to your place."

"What? You did? That's so nice."

"I'm a nice guy," he said with a grin that made his dimple deepen.

"Most of the time," I said. "My ass didn't think so the other night."

He laughed and rested his big hand on my leg, his fingers stroking my inner thigh. "You know the rules, Magnolia. No cumming until I say you can cum."

"You were sucking on my clit like it was a damn lifesaver," I protested. "No woman could have stopped from cumming."

"You just need to learn better control." He gave my leg a little squeeze. "Besides, didn't you say that having my dick shoved up that pretty little pussy while you were being spanked, made it less painful?"

My pussy was already starting to get wet and I was certain he could see the way my body was quivering in my seat. Two nights ago, after I'd disobeyed him by cumming, Wyatt had put me on my hands and knees and put his hard and deliciously thick cock deep inside my pussy before starting the spanking. He'd alternated between fucking me and spanking me, until my resulting orgasm was so strong, it'd almost blown the top of my head off.

"Answer me, Magnolia," he said.

"Yes, it made it less painful," I said. "Other than the damage I did to my vocal chords."

He laughed again. "You were rather loud when you came all over my cock. I'm surprised my grandmother didn't come running out to the guesthouse to find out what was wrong."

"Oh God," I said as a blush covered my cheeks. "Don't even joke about that. I would be mortified."

"You and me both," he said with a cute little grin. "So, maybe you should try and scream just a little softer when you cum. What do you say, Ms. Blossom?"

"Maybe you shouldn't make me cum so hard, Officer Reynolds," I said.

He pulled into the parking lot of Baker's Steakhouse and parked before grinning at me. "Baby, I can't help it if I'm a god in bed."

I burst into giggles and gave his hand a light slap. "Again, your arrogance is not the least bit charming."

"We both know that's not true. C'mon, hot stuff. I'm gonna buy my girl a steak dinner and then take her home and fuck her."

"Sure, but are you buying me a steak as well, or do I just have to watch you and *your girl* eat?"

I expected him to threaten me with a spanking for my cheekiness and was surprised when he leaned over and cupped the back of my neck. He pulled me forward and kissed me hard on the mouth, his tongue dipping between my lips.

When he pulled back, I was breathless and more

than a little turned on. He studied me, his eyes turned a dark blue by lust and another emotion I couldn't identify.

"You're my girl, Magnolia Blossom," he said in a low voice. "All mine. Do you understand?"

I wet my lips before taking a shaky breath. "Wyatt, I -"

"My girl," he said. "Say it."

"Your girl," I whispered.

The dimple appeared and he kissed me lightly before releasing me and opening his door. "Good. Let's eat."

৵ ৎ

"How's your steak?" Wyatt asked.

"So good," I replied. "But I'll never be able to eat all of it. It's ginormous."

He just grinned at me and ate another bite of his. "This is my favourite spot to eat in town."

"It's really good," I said. "Thanks for bringing me here."

"You're welcome."

"So, how was work today? Are you glad to be back on the day shift?" I asked.

"Yes, and no," he said. "More shit goes down at night, obviously, but the day shift can drag on. I had a domestic disturbance call today that was a pain in the ass."

"Oh yeah?"

He nodded. "Yeah. They've been fighting for the last three years. It never gets physical or anything, but they scream at each other until the neighbours get sick of it and call us. We get called out there at least once a week. He keeps cheating on her and she wants to kick him out, but she's afraid he'll get half the house."

I ate a bite of salad. "Are they married or common-law?"

"Common-law, but for over ten years."

"Do they jointly own the house?"

"I'm not sure," he said. "I think she owns it, but I'm not positive."

"Well, if they own it jointly, then the likelihood of him getting half of it, is pretty strong. The court will basically treat it like they're married, it doesn't matter what his behaviour is or if she paid more into the mortgage, that sort of thing. However, if she owns it herself, then she's entitled to receive her own property without sharing its value. Basically, he gets nothing. So, if she owns the house, tell her to dump his cheating ass and give him the boot."

I took a sip of wine. "But if he owns the house, the same rules apply. So, make sure you mention that to her the next time you're there. God, it's so frustrating how many women don't know their rights when it comes to stuff like this."

"Maybe you should open up your own law firm here in town and then you could tell them."

I smiled. "Owning my own law firm is my ultimate goal, but I probably need a bit more experience before... oh, shit. You son of a bitch."

Wyatt gave me a pleasant grin before popping another bite of steak into his mouth.

"You did that on purpose," I said.

"Not entirely," he replied. "The story was true, and I will happily pass on the information to her the next time I'm called out there."

"So, is it too late to convince you I watch a lot of *Law and Order* reruns, or should I give it a go?"

"You're hilarious." He took a drink of beer. "So, why exactly is a lawyer working as a waitress in some diner with mediocre food and questionable food safety practices?"

"Hey!" I gave him an indignant look. "The food is really good at the diner, and I'll have you know Cook Stanley washes his hands almost seventy-five percent of the time after using the washroom."

"Oh God," Wyatt made a face, "I'm never eating there again."

I laughed. "You've been eating there since you were a kid, Wyatt. I'm pretty sure your immune system has built up a defense against Stanley's germs."

"So, you're doing a wonderful job at trying to change the subject, but I repeat – why is a lawyer working at a diner?"

I shrugged. "It's not like this place is teeming with job offers for lawyers."

"True. Where did you work before?"

"Uh, just a small firm in the city. You won't have heard of it. I specialized in family law, helping single mothers get child support, that sort of thing."

"You enjoy it, obviously."

"I do," I said.

"So, why did you leave?"

"Boy, this steak is just way too much to eat." I pushed away my plate and glanced around the restaurant for the server. "I'm going to get the rest packed up."

"Magnolia."

"Are you done? Should I get a take-out container for you?" I refused to look at Wyatt.

"Magnolia, look at me, please."

I gave him an irritable look. "What?"

"Who are you running from, baby?"

"Oh my God, I'm not running from anyone. I just – I needed a new start, so I left. Okay? Can we just leave it at that?"

"Why are you afraid to tell me?"

"I'm not afraid," I said. "There's nothing to tell, Wyatt. I needed a fresh start, so that's what I'm trying to do."

"By working as a waitress at a diner?"

"This is just to make enough money so I can move on. Remember?"

Hurt flashed briefly across his face. "I remember."

I was instantly feeling guilty and sick to my stomach. Fuck. Why the hell did I let myself get so attached to the man across from me?

Attached? That's a real funny way to say love, Mags.

I took a deep breath, pushing that thought out of my mind like it was a hissing, spitting snake. I couldn't love Wyatt. I couldn't. Because if I did love him, then leaving this town wasn't an option, and I couldn't stay. What if Ruby found me here?

My brain knew it was a real stretch to think her obsession would continue once I was gone, but… what if it had? What if she found me and she realized I was in love with Wyatt? She was certifiably insane and I had the restraining order to prove it.

She wanted me all to herself and if she thought that I cared for Wyatt, if she thought that he was more important to me than she ever would be...

Mags, you're overreacting. Yes, she's crazy. Yes, she's dangerous. But she won't find you. How could she? This isn't some movie where the bad guy has tons of resources to find the good guy. She's gone from your life forever. You love Wyatt, you should be with him.

My inner voice made some good points, so why couldn't I believe it? Why was there this niggling, jiggling, squiggling little part of me that knew Ruby would find me?

"Maggie? You okay, baby?" Wyatt was giving me a look of concern and the part of me that was attached – attached, definitely not love – almost melted. God, I was being a real bitch to him, and he was still being sweet.

"I'm sorry," I said. "I don't mean to be so awful to you and I apologize. But there isn't anything wrong and I'm not – I'm not running. It's been a long day and I'm tired. Can we drop it?"

"Sure," he said. "Any decisions on when you'll be leaving our small town?"

I winced and studied my half-eaten steak. "No, not yet. But if you don't want to, um, continue this, I totally get it and -"

"I want to continue." He reached across the table and grabbed my hand. "I'm sorry, Maggie. Now I'm being a dick."

"You're not," I said. "Can we go home now?"

"Yes," he said, "we can go home."

࿔ ࿔

"Wyatt, please." My voice was soft and hoarse from all the moaning and begging I'd been doing.

He lifted his head from my breast and gave me a teasing smile. "Soon, baby."

"No, now. I need you." I pushed on his broad shoulders as he dipped his head back to my breast and licked a slow circle around my swollen and pleasantly throbbing nipple.

"Oh God," I muttered, "I'm gonna go crazy, honey."

He laughed before kissing the tip of my nipple. "I doubt that, but since you've been such a good girl tonight, I'll give you what you want."

"Can I be on top?" I asked when he leaned back.

"Yes." He rolled to his back and when he grabbed the condom from the nightstand, I plucked it out of his hands.

"Let me, sir," I said with a little giggle.

He grinned and tucked his hands behind his back, watching as I carefully rolled it down over his dick. "I'm getting really good at this."

He didn't reply, but I was too busy straddling him and carefully sliding his dick deep into my pussy to notice. As his now familiar width stretched my inner walls, I made a happy little coo and glanced up at him.

"Wyatt?" I froze on top of his hard body. "What's wrong?"

"Nothing."

He was still rock-hard inside of me, but his face

was closed off and withdrawn. I leaned over and stroked his chest. "Something's wrong, please tell me."

He looked away, his hands still tucked under his head. "I don't like the thought of you putting a condom on some other guy's dick."

My entire insides actually rolled with nausea at the thought. Without thinking, I said, "I'm not gonna sleep with another guy, Wyatt."

He made a low snort of anger. "That's bullshit and we both know it."

"It isn't," I insisted. "I won't sleep with anyone but you." I cupped his face and made him look at me. I stroked his jawline with my thumb and whispered. "I'm your girl."

His face deepened into the grin that I'd grown to love, and he said, "You're my girl."

His warm hands cupped my hips and I moaned happily when he made two slow pumps into me. I braced my hands on his chest and rode him with slow and gentle movements, watching his face as we brought each other closer to the edge.

"Wyatt," I moaned when he wouldn't let me move faster. "Please."

"Nice and slow, baby," he whispered.

I moaned again and dug my nails into his chest, each slide of this thick cock sending little quivers of pleasure through my body. I loved it when Wyatt fucked me hard and rough, but this tender, slow slide and retreat was incredible.

He reached up and cupped the back of my skull, smiling sweetly at me as our bodies worked together to bring us both pleasure. "That's right, baby, just like that," he panted. "So good."

"Mmm," I agreed. I arched my back, meeting each of his thrusts with the same slow and deliberate pace. "I want to cum, honey. I'm so close."

He reached between us and the moment his rough fingers brushed against my clit, my orgasm washed over me. It was sweet and intense and perfect. I shuddered wildly, my pussy clamping around his dick, my head dropping back as I rode out my orgasm. Beneath me, Wyatt was arching, his fingers digging into my ass as he gave in to his own need to climax.

I collapsed against him, pressing light kisses against his chest as he stroked my hair and our frantic heartbeats slowly returned to normal. I stayed where I was as he softened inside of me, enjoying the feel of his hard warmth below me.

"Maggie?"

"Hmm?" I replied.

"Does this mean you're staying?" His delightful and perfect hands rubbed my back in long, soothing strokes.

I raised my head and gave him a sleepy, sated smile. "I'm staying."

ॐ ॐ

"Breakfast was delicious. Thank you." Wyatt bent down and kissed me. He tasted like bacon and coffee and I grinned at him.

"You're welcome. Have a good day, honey."

He laughed and gave me a light slap to the butt. "You too. Do you need me to pick up anything from the store on my way home tonight?"

"Actually, if you can pick up some mushrooms and a bag of salad, that would be super helpful."

"Will do." He kissed me again and shrugged into his vest. "See you tonight, baby."

"Bye." I watched his amazing ass walk out of the kitchen before leaning against the counter and sipping at my coffee.

I was happy. Blissfully happy. Sure, there was still a small part of me worried about Ruby, but I had to put that out of my head. Even if she was looking for me, she wouldn't find me. How could she?

Deciding to stay here, deciding to stay with Wyatt, was the right decision. I loved him and, even though he hadn't said he loved me, I knew he did. It was quick, I hadn't even known him a month yet, but my parents fell in love after two days and were married in two months. Sometimes love happened fast.

From the moment the words "I'm staying" came out of my mouth, I'd been... at peace, I guess you could say. My worries and fears were still there, I suppose, but they were muted by the realization that I had a man I loved and a place that was starting to feel like home.

Hell, I was even considering the idea of starting my own law firm. I might have been young, but I would do a hell of a better job than that lazy ass Boris Galthwaite.

"Shit!" I glanced at the clock on the microwave. I'd been standing here like a love-struck fool for almost five minutes and if I didn't get my ass moving, I'd be late for work. I dumped the rest of my coffee down the sink.

The doorbell rang and I headed toward the front door. A smile spreading across my lips, I opened the door and said, "Hey, handsome, did you forget…"

"Hello, Maggie. Have you missed me?"

I stared wide-eyed at the woman standing in my doorway. The gun pointed at me made fear claw and tear its way into my chest.

"Ruby," I whispered, "Ruby, how did you find me?"

"Did you really think I wouldn't, Maggie?" She said as a tender smile crossed her face.

I couldn't stop staring at her. She'd cut and dyed her hair into the same style and shade as mine, and her formerly brown eyes were covered with blue contacts.

My gaze flickered to the cluster of three freckles that dotted her left temple, the exact shape and size of the freckles that were on mine. Her right hand still holding the gun, she used her left hand to touch the freckles. "Do you like? I had them tattooed on. A bit painful, but worth it."

"Ruby, what are you -"

"No." She shook her head. "It's time for you to listen, Maggie. Invite me in."

Chapter Eight

Wyatt

I stepped into the diner, the smile on my face fading when I didn't see Maggie. It was almost eleven and although I was taking an early lunch, it was too early for her to be on her lunch break. Natalia was walking by, her arms loaded down with a tray of dirty dishes, and she gave me a distracted smile.

"Hey, Wyatt."

"Hi, Natalia. Do you know where Maggie is?"

She stopped and my pulse turned into a heavy drumbeat when she said, "She called in sick this morning."

"She called in sick," I repeated.

"Yes. Is something wrong?" Natalia gave me a worried look.

I made myself smile at her. "No, everything's fine. Thanks, Natalia."

"Sure." Her face still worried, she walked away.

I turned around and headed out the door and straight for my vehicle. Dismay and a surprising amount of panic were swirling in my guts.

"Just cool it," I muttered to myself as I climbed behind the wheel. "She didn't leave. She just said last night that she was staying. She didn't leave you."

I wanted to believe that was true, but... she'd been saying for weeks that she wasn't staying, and her sudden change of heart last night was a bit of a surprise. I'd been so insanely happy that she wasn't leaving me that I hadn't even thought to ask why she'd changed her mind.

It's because you want to believe she loves you. Admit it.

I pulled out of the parking lot of the diner and headed toward Nana's house. All right, maybe that's what I was hoping, but, hell, you couldn't blame me. I was stupidly, ridiculously, head over heels for Magnolia Blossom and the thought of her not in my life made me feel sick.

If she's gone, you can just track her down and make her come back.

Jesus, my inner self had gone full-on stalker.

If she was gone, maybe I would use my connections as a cop to find her, but I would be respectful and understanding and just talk to her about coming back to me. I wouldn't demand that she return, wouldn't demand that she love me like I loved her. I would be...

You'd be a stalker, but a totally considerate stalker.

Panic still an unwelcome guest in my belly, I

stepped on the gas. I didn't want to believe that Maggie had left me, but she had seemed perfectly healthy when I left this morning. And if she had gotten sick after I left, why didn't she text me and tell me?

As if my very thoughts had summoned her, my cell phone rang. I hit the speaker button, trying to keep the panic from my voice. "Maggie? Hi, where are you?"

There was silence and I was just about to say her name again when she said, "Hi, Wyatt. I'm, uh, I'm at home."

"Are you sick? I stopped in at the diner and Natalia said you called in sick."

"Yeah, I'm not feeling great."

I frowned. Maggie sounded off, but she didn't sound sick. She sounded scared.

Before I could say anything, Maggie said, "I hate to ask, but do you, uh, do you think you could pick me up some, um, Advil and drop it off. I have a terrible headache and I'm all out."

"Yes," I said. "I'm on my way."

"Okay, thanks." Weirdly, there was dismay and guilt in her voice.

She hung up before I could reply. I drove down the slick roads, tapping my fingers on the steering wheel. What the fuck was going on? Maggie could have easily texted Nana and asked her to bring over some Advil.

She's running from someone, Wyatt.

I took a deep breath and turned down Nana's street. Maggie denied it repeatedly, but I hadn't been able to shake the idea that she was on the run.

If she was on the run and they'd found her…

Fear spiked through me. I parked in Nana's driveway and climbed out of my vehicle. Nana glanced out the big bay window of her living room and waved at me. I waved back and headed toward the guest house. I knocked and then opened the door, stepping inside and listening carefully.

"Maggie, I'm here."

There was silence and then Maggie's voice, small and undeniably afraid, drifted to me. "In the bedroom."

Alarm bells went off inside my head. Without even thinking about it, I pulled my gun from my holster and walked quietly past the kitchen and living room. A chair was missing from the kitchen and while nothing else looked out of place, my spine was tingling, and my nerves were pinging.

Something was terribly wrong. I'd been a cop long enough to trust my instincts.

I paused at the closed door and keeping my gun raised, turned the handle and lightly pushed the door open without entering. I could see the empty bed but nothing else, and I stepped into the room.

"Maggie, are you -"

All of the breath got sucked out of my lungs as I stared at the gun held to the head of the woman I loved.

"I'm sorry, Wyatt," Maggie whispered. She was sitting on the kitchen chair a few feet back from the bed, rope and duct tape wrapped around her slender body to bind her to it. "I'm so sorry. I didn't want to call you, but she threatened to kill Nana if I didn't, and -"

"Hush, Maggie." The woman holding the gun said. "It's time for you to listen, remember?"

"What the fuck?" I said. The woman could almost have been Maggie's twin. Her hair was cut and styled the same, she had blue eyes like Maggie's, her makeup was identical right down to the shade of lipstick on her mouth, and she even had the same cluster of freckles on her left temple.

Even weirder - she was wearing Maggie's uniform from the diner.

The woman frowned at me. "Such foul language, Wyatt."

"Who the fuck are you?" I had my gun pointed at her and she made a little tsking noise.

"Be careful, Wyatt. You're not the only one with a gun, remember?" She pressed the barrel of the gun against Maggie's temple.

Maggie moaned quietly, and I immediately lowered my weapon and raised one hand. "Okay. It's fine. No need to do anything rash. Let's talk. You know me, but I don't know you. What's your name?"

She smiled at me before standing behind Maggie and gently stroking her hair. "My name is Ruby, and Maggie is mine. She's mine, Wyatt. You can't have her."

"He doesn't want me," Maggie said quickly. "I keep telling you, Ruby, he doesn't mean anything to me. All right? He was just a fling, that's all. Just let him go, and you and I will leave together. We'll go wherever you want."

Ruby sighed. "I know you, sweetie. I know everything about you." She leaned down and pressed a gentle kiss against Maggie's cheek. "I know your every thought, Maggie. You can't hide from me."

"So, you're in love with her," I said. "I understand, but -"

"In love with her?" Ruby gave me a look of impatience. "It's not – God, men are so stupid." She kissed Maggie's cheek again. "Why you would ever want him over me… why you would even be attracted to men, is beyond me. They're idiots, Maggie. All of them."

She straightened and gave me a look of disdain. "It isn't just about love, Wyatt. It's about knowing what she wants and needs and being the person to give it to her. I am exactly who Maggie needs. I know everything about her. I love her, but I also… am her. Do you understand?"

Cold fear ran down my spine. The woman was batshit insane.

"No, help me to understand, Ruby," I said. I needed to keep her talking, needed to figure out how the fuck I was going to save the woman I loved.

"Oh, for heaven's sake," she said irritably. "Why do you even love him, Maggie?"

"I don't," Maggie said. "I keep telling you that I don't."

"Lies!" Ruby suddenly screamed. She slapped Maggie hard across the head with her free hand. "Stop your fucking goddamn lying, Maggie! You know how I hate it when you lie to me!"

"It's okay," I said. "Calm down, Ruby."

"Don't tell me to calm down," she snarled.

"Don't ever tell me to do anything, Officer Wyatt."

I made a small sound of acquiesce and she stared sullenly at me for a moment. "I asked Maggie to be with me, did she tell you that? I even got her drunk one night and tried to show her how much better sex would be with me than with a man. But she refused. She just kept saying, 'No, Ruby. I'm not into you that way. We're just friends, Ruby. I'm straight, Ruby.'" Her upper lip curled up and she scowled at me. "I know you fucked her. Did you like it? She was a virgin, right? She never came right out and told me she was, but I knew she was. I liked that about her. Liked that she'd never been fouled by the touch of a man."

She stroked Maggie's hair again. "Although, that's changed now, isn't it? She's no longer pure, but that's okay. I still love her. I still want to be her - I mean - be with her. She made a mistake and when the people you love make mistakes, you forgive them. Isn't that right?"

"Yes," I said. "How did you and Maggie meet?"

"Oh, it's the most wonderful meet-cute story." Ruby's eyes glowed with happiness. "We met at the library. We literally ran into each other at the corner of biographies and true crime. Maggie's arms were loaded down with books and they all went flying and they made the loudest noise when they landed. Everyone in the library was staring at us. I looked at her and she looked at me and we both got the giggles. Do you remember, Maggie?"

"Yes," Maggie said.

"It was the best day of my life. I knew that

Maggie was meant for me. Has that ever happened to you, Wyatt? Have you ever just met someone and knew they were destined to be your soul mate?"

"Yes." I stared at Maggie and Ruby made an angry sound of disapproval.

"No. Not Maggie. She's my soul mate. Not yours."

"She left you," I said.

Ruby's face drew down in a scowl. "That was a mistake. She was – was confused, that's all. But now that we're together again, she understands that she needs me. Isn't that right, Maggie?"

"That's right," Maggie said. "So, why don't you untie me, and I'll grab my things and we'll leave. We'll get out of this stupid town and we won't look back, Ruby. Just you and me. Together forever."

"Mmm, I don't think I'm quite ready to trust you yet, sweetie. You did after all, put a restraining order against me." Ruby giggled and gave me a I-did-a-bad-thing look. "I guess I'm kind of breaking the law, huh, Officer Wyatt?"

"How did you find her?" I inched a little closer and Ruby shook her head before running the barrel of the gun through Maggie's hair.

"No, no. Don't do that, Wyatt."

I backed up a step. "Tell me how you found her."

"Oh, you'll love this. So, I have a friend. His name is Frank. I fuck him from time to time, but not because I enjoy it or want it. Oh God, he has the smallest dick, I swear. But the benefits of fucking small-dick Frank, is that when I need something computer related, he's my guy."

She gave me a thoughtful look. "I suppose he's what the movies would refer to as a hacker. He lives in the basement of his mom's house – Lord, he is just the biggest cliché, isn't he?" She laughed before continuing, "Anyway, he lives in the basement of his mom's house and spends most of his time watching porn and using his computer to find out all sorts of information he really shouldn't know."

She leaned down, keeping her gaze on my face, and kissed the top of Maggie's head. "Maggie was pretty clever though. Do you know she hasn't used her credit card or her debit card once since she ran away like a coward? Not once, Wyatt. I was so worried about her. Where was she sleeping? Was she eating enough? How was she getting money? For a while I even worried that she was," she lowered her voice, "prostituting herself like a dirty little whore. I told Frank to keep looking though, because I knew sooner or later, she'd fuck up. She couldn't help it."

She kissed Maggie's head again. "And she did fuck up. By getting herself a ticket for a burned-out tail light in some backwater, pissant little town. Frank came across the ticket and I figured it might be worth it just to take a drive out to your little town. You never know, right? And wouldn't you know it… my very first day, I decided to stop in at the Farmhouse Diner for a bite to eat and who does my spying eye see through the window? Sweet Maggie."

She smiled happily. "I've been here for a week,

being a sly little mouse, just staying out of the way and never poking my nose out too much. I've been watching you come and go from this awful little," she gave the bedroom a look of disdain, "house for days now, Wyatt. Just between you and me – you're not a very good cop. You didn't even notice me."

She studied me carefully, a sly grin crossing her face. "Ah, Officer Wyatt, you look so upset. Are you just realizing that you're the reason I found my Maggie again?"

"Maggie, baby, I'm sorry," I said. "I'm so sorry."

"It's okay," she whispered. "It isn't your fault."

"It kind of is," Ruby said cheerfully. "Now, I think I've done enough of the proper movie villain thing and spilled all the details of my nefarious plans. Don't you, Wyatt? I mean, I've given you plenty of time to come up with a plan to stop me and you've got nothing. Isn't that right?"

"Let's just leave, Ruby," Maggie said again. "Please. I swear to you that Wyatt means nothing to me. You don't have to hurt him, okay?"

"Oh, sweetie," Ruby said gently, "I'm not going to hurt Wyatt. I am going to kill him though."

"No!" Maggie cried. She rocked against the ropes and the duct tape, trying desperately to free herself. "Ruby, no! Please! I am begging you, let's just leave. Okay?"

"For someone who says she doesn't love him, you're awfully concerned about good ole' Wyatt." Ruby grinned.

"Because I'm a decent human being who

doesn't want to see someone die. Jesus Christ, Ruby," Maggie shouted, "for the last time, he means nothing to me, and I mean nothing to him. Let's just leave!"

"Calm down, sweetheart," Ruby said. "No one likes a hysterical woman. The thing is, you can tell me all you want that you don't love him, but you've forgotten how well I know you." She gave Maggie a tender look. "You can't hide anything from me, sweetie. You love him and he loves you. It's written all over his face."

She glanced up at me. "Isn't that right?"

"Yes," I said. "I love her."

"Wyatt, no," Maggie moaned.

"It's all right," Ruby said. "I already knew, Maggie. I already knew."

She kissed Maggie's head again. "Time to say goodbye to him."

"No," Maggie said, her voice on the edge of hysteria. "No, Ruby, please don't."

"Shh," Ruby said. "It's what's best for you."

"NO!" Maggie screamed. "Ruby, goddammit, no!"

Ruby flinched and plugged one ear. "Jesus, Maggie, that's kind of shrill. Tell you what, I love you so I'm gonna be sweet and let you give Officer Wyatt over there one last kiss goodbye. Okay?"

"Please, Ruby." Maggie was crying now, and Ruby lovingly wiped away the tears on her face.

"Shh, sweetie, don't cry. Say goodbye to him and make it a good kiss. It's the last one he'll ever get."

Ruby straightened and pointed the gun at me.

"Toss your gun to the middle of the bed, please, Wyatt."

I hesitated and she gave me a weary look. "Either you toss your gun to the bed and I let you say goodbye to Maggie, or you die right now. Your choice."

I tossed my gun to the middle of the bed, watching as Ruby backed away until she was in the furthest corner of the room. She kept the gun pointed at Maggie as she said, "Now you head on over to that far corner, just behind Maggie, please."

I did what she asked. The distance between us was too much for me to even try and tackle the gun away from her. I passed by Maggie, she was still weeping softly, and stood in the corner as Ruby moved to my spot in front of the doorway.

"There," she said. "Aren't I clever, Wyatt? I've watched a lot of movies and I know better than to let you get anywhere close to me. That's how we lose guns." She laughed in delight before making a 'go on' motion with the gun. "Go ahead and give Maggie a kiss goodbye."

I crossed to Maggie and crouched next to her chair. She gave me a stark look of despair. "I'm so sorry, Wyatt. I'm so sorry. I never meant for this to happen."

"I know, baby. Shh, it's okay. Everything is going to be okay."

"It isn't," she whispered. "I can't – I can't live without you."

"You won't be," I said. "I'm not dead yet."

She studied me, her eyes glistening with tears. Her voice so soft and quiet I could barely hear her, she said, "I love you, Wyatt."

"I know, baby." I cupped her face. "I love you."

I kissed her, tasting cold fear and salty tears on her mouth. My heart was a jittering, out-of-control beat in my chest and sweat was sliding down my back. I pulled back and made myself smile at Maggie again. "I love you, baby. Don't ever forget that."

I stood, and Maggie made a loud sobbing cry that tore my heart wide open.

"Please, Ruby," she sobbed, "please don't kill him. I'll do whatever you ask, just let him live. Please."

"I can't do that, Maggie," Ruby said as she raised her gun and pointed it at me.

My gaze skittered to the bed, wondering if could dive forward and get my gun before she shot me dead.

"Sorry about this, Wyatt," Ruby said with a small smile. "It really isn't anything personal, in fact, I -"

There was a hollow thudding noise. I watched in disbelief as Ruby's eyes rolled up in her head and chocolate chip cookies flew past her face. She crumpled to the ground, falling flat on her face, the gun falling from her hand to land on the floor with a heavy clunk.

I stared in quiet disbelief at my grandmother standing in front of us. She held a heavy ceramic plate in one hand, and I watched as a cookie, clinging tenuously to the smooth surface, slowly slid down the plate and landed on Ruby's back.

"Nana?" I said.

She gave me a shaky smile before holding out the plate in her hand. "I didn't even break the plate." She glanced at Ruby's prone body. "Oh dear, do you think I killed her? I hope not. I'm too pretty for prison."

ॐ ॐ

"Sheriff Roberts, are you sure I can't interest you in some cookies to take home?" Nana held out the Tupperware container and gave my boss a sweet smile.

"Well, maybe just this once." Grant took the cookies from her. "Thanks, Martha."

"You're so welcome." She waved across the street at the group of neighbours who had gathered and were unabashedly gawking at the four police vehicles parked in and around Nana's driveway.

"Hi, Helen!" Nana shouted.

As Alex pulled out of the driveway, I stared at the back door. Thanks to the tinted windows, I couldn't see Ruby sitting there, her hands handcuffed behind her back and one hell of a goose egg on the back of her head, but I could picture her face. It'd probably be a long time before I stopped seeing her face.

"You okay, Wyatt?" Grant asked.

"Yeah," I said. "I'll come back to the station and write -"

"Nah," Grant shook his head, "it can wait until tomorrow. Take the rest of the day off."

"You sure?"

"Yep. I'll see you tomorrow."

"Okay, thanks."

The sheriff and the rest of my coworkers left, leaving just me and Nana standing in the driveway. The neighbours drifted away one by one, and Nana smiled at me. "You should go to her, honey."

"Nana, are you sure you're all right?"

"I'm fine. Why would you ask that?"

"Um, because you knocked a woman out cold with a plate of cookies? A woman who was about to shoot your grandson."

"Pshh," she said with a wave of her hand, "that was nothing. You forget I coached high school basketball for years. If I can handle a bunch of hormone-filled teenage girls, I can handle a crazy stalker with a gun."

My laugh was shaky. "Yeah."

She stepped close and took my shoulders in her hands, peering up at me. "Are you okay, dear heart?"

"I think so. Just really glad that you decided to stop by with a plate of cookies."

She smiled. "Me too. You know, your grandpa always said that my cookies were deadly, but he really had no idea, did he?"

"No, I guess not."

She studied me closely before putting her arms around me and hugging me hard. I returned her hug. "I love you, Nana. Thank you."

"I love you too, sweet boy. So much. Now, go to Maggie. I know she's upset, and she needs you. The both of you can come by the house tomorrow night for dinner. All right?"

"All right." I kissed her cheek and she gave me another hard squeeze before patting my face.

"Go on now."

She headed toward the house and I walked to the guest house. I let myself in, taking off my boots and hanging my jacket on the hooks. The kitchen chair had been returned and I frowned at the mess of rope and duct tape that was piled on the table. I would take it out back to the firepit and burn it, I decided. But first...

"Maggie? Baby, where are you?"

"I'm in the bedroom." Her voice was muffled and distant, despite the door being open.

I walked into the room. "Baby, are you – what are you doing?"

She came out of the closet, her arms stuffed full of clothes. She tossed them haphazardly into the open suitcase and slammed the lid shut, zipping it closed. "I'm packing my stuff."

"Why?" I said.

She gave me a look like she thought I might have been the one cracked over the head with a plate of my grandmother's cookies. "I'm not leaving my stuff here."

"It's fine if you don't want to stay in the guesthouse, baby, I get it. But you don't need to pack everything up tonight. Just bring a few days' worth of clothes to my place and we can come back later and pack up everything else."

She paused in the doorway of her closet, more clothes tangled up in her arms. "Your place? I'm – I'm not going to your place, Wyatt."

"Where are you going then?"

"I don't know." She threw another load of clothes in the second suitcase. "I'll figure it out later."

"Magnolia, stop." I walked toward her and pulled her into my arms. "Why are you leaving?"

"Why am I leaving?" Her face was a mask of disbelief. "I almost got you killed, Wyatt. You almost died and your nana almost died, and it was all my fault."

"Technically," I said with a small grin, "it was my fault for giving you that ticket."

"This isn't funny," she said. "Ruby almost killed you, would have killed you, if…"

Her face contorted and I pressed her head against my chest, rocking her back and forth a little. "Shh, baby. It's okay."

She sobbed hard for a few minutes before wiping her face and lifting her head to stare at me. "Why don't you hate me?"

"Magnolia, I love you."

More tears ran down her face and I kissed them away. "It's not your fault, baby."

"It is," she said. "It is my fault."

"It isn't." I gave her a firm little shake. "You are not responsible for Ruby being batshit crazy. Do you hear me? You did all the right things – you cut off contact, you got a restraining order, and, when she still went after you, you -"

"I ran away," she said dully. "I ran like a coward and -"

"You ended up exactly where you were supposed to be. In my arms," I said. "I love you and I know you love me too."

"I do," she said. "I love you so much."

"Then, that's all that matters," I said.

"Is it?" There was a note of hope in her voice.

"Yes," I replied. "You're my girl, Magnolia Blossom, and I'm never letting you go."

She gave me a soft smile. "I'm your girl."

ॐ ॐ

The Paramedic
(Book Nine)

Ramona Gray

Chapter One

Matt

"I know why you always pick this booth, Matt."

I ignored my best friend, Jonah, and scanned the diner. I didn't see her, but that didn't mean she wasn't working today. She could be in the back.

I cracked my knuckles and tapped my foot impatiently against the worn linoleum floor. The Farmhouse Diner had been around for as long as I could remember. I'd sat at the long, curved counter with my feet dangling, and my seven-year-old self slurping up milkshakes while my dad flirted with the waitresses.

Back then, the walls were more of a cream colour instead of their current spoiled milk colour, the counter was spotless and chip free, and the booths hadn't yet shown the wear and tear they did now.

The food was good, but was it good enough to come back here every damn day for lunch? Hell, no. I'd had to increase my gym time by nearly half an hour just to mitigate the damage that eating the greasy food was doing to me. I wasn't a total gym rat like my friend Elijah, but I liked to keep the six-pack firm for the ladies.

Ladies? What ladies? You haven't been laid in over six months.

"Mattie!"

I turned to Jonah. "What?"

"I said, if you're going to force me to meet you here every damn time we have lunch together, then you're gonna have to start paying me gas money. The diner isn't exactly close to my office, ya douche."

"Oh please," I snorted. "It takes ten minutes to get everywhere in this place. It's one of the benefits of living in a small town."

I scanned the diner again. Shit, was she not here? She always worked Tuesday during the day.

"Maybe she isn't working today." Jonah echoed my thoughts.

"She always works Tuesday," I said. "Monday to Wednesday, she works the day shift, she's off Thursday, then Friday and Saturday she works evening shifts and off again on Sunday."

There was silence and I stopped scanning the diner long enough to glance at Jonah. The look on his face made dull heat burn in my cheeks. "What?"

"You're sounding a little stalkerish, dude," Jonah said.

"No, I'm not." My voice was defensive. "If I was a stalker, I'd know where she lived, how old she was, what her middle name was... shit like that."

"Whatever helps you sleep at night." Jonah studied the menu. "Hmm…do I want the greasy burger or the weirdly greasy chicken sandwich. So many decisions."

"The food is good here," I said. "Don't be a dick."

Jonah grinned at me. "Don't forget about Claire's birthday thing on Friday."

"Shit," I replied.

"You forgot."

"Sorry, man. I told Mia and Elijah I'd hang out with them, but I'll let them know I forgot about Claire's birthday and do something with them another night."

Jonah leaned forward. "Is it seriously not awkward between the three of you?"

"I told you it wasn't," I said. "We're friends."

"Okay, sure. But, let's not forget that Mia showed up to your place a few months ago wearing very little clothing in an attempt to seduce you. Then, when you turned her down, she started dating your good friend Elijah. And you're telling me that the three of you hang out like you're one big happy family without any weirdness at all."

I shrugged. "Maybe there was a little at the beginning, but not now. I'm honestly happy for Mia, you know? After you, she's my best friend. Elijah is a great guy and it's obvious that they love each other."

"You don't think that Elijah was a rebound for her after you told her you would only ever be friends?"

"No," I said. "I don't. I've worked with Mia for over three years and she might come across as quiet and a little on the shy side, but she knows what she wants. Maybe she thought she was in love with me, but the way she looks at Elijah? Man, she's never *once* looked at me like that."

"All right." Jonah closed the menu. "So, are you ever gonna ask Natalia out or what?"

"I did," I reminded him. "She turned me down flat."

"Yet," Jonah looked around the diner, "here we are."

I ignored him, my heart tripling in beat when the door leading into the kitchen swung open and Natalia walked out. Her blonde hair was in a ponytail, she wasn't wearing make-up, and that salmon-coloured uniform washed out her pale skin to the point that if I were on duty, I'd ask to check her vitals just to make sure she wasn't gonna pass out on me.

She looked a little tired and out of sorts and despite the sturdy, practical, and not at all sexy running shoes she wore, she limped the slightest bit.

"She looks tired today," Jonah said.

I glared at him. "Knock it off. She works a lot. It's hard being a single mother."

Jonah gave me a thoughtful look. "Jesus, you really do have it bad for her."

I didn't reply. I pulled at my t-shirt, smoothing it down, and rubbing a hand over my jaw. Fuck, I should have shaved today. Natalia seemed like the type of woman who liked clean-shaven men.

Her gaze landed on us and my stomach clenched

at the look that came over her face. One part annoyance, one part resignation, and one part do-not-fuck-with-me-today. She planted a tense smile on her face and walked toward our booth.

"Man, she looks pissed," Jonah said.

I wanted to argue, but there was no point. She *was* pissed.

Natalia Dixon, waitress, single mother, and the woman I'd fallen madly in love with, hated my guts.

"Hey, what can I get for you today?" Natalia's let's-just-get-this-over-with smile was firmly in place.

"Hi, Natalia, how are you today?" Jonah said.

Her smile warmed from frosty to warm. "Good, Jonah. You?"

"Good thanks. I'll take a water and the chef's salad, please."

"Sure." Her smile turned to arctic blast again when she faced me. "What can I get you?"

She never said my name. Not once. Until her, I'd never once thought about a woman saying my name before. I wanted her to say it, and not just when I was between those undoubtedly silky-smooth thighs of hers. Sure, hearing her moan my name would be unfuckingbelievable, but at this point, I just wanted her to say it in her regular voice.

"Hi, Natalia. You're looking lovely today."

Her smile spread thin and I could have kicked myself. I'd meant it to be an honest compliment, but she knew my reputation just like everyone else in this town did. She wouldn't take me seriously and I couldn't blame her for it.

I knew who Natalia was, both of us had grown up in the town and it was impossible to not at least have an idea of who a person was. But we didn't run in the same circles in high school. I'd been a bit of a nerd in high school, president of the damn chess club and shit like that, and Natalia was a cheerleader who dated the quarterback, Evan Fealan.

After graduation, Natalia had moved with Evan to Welling. Nearly four years later, she'd moved back home with a baby in her arms and no sign of Evan.

I'd changed a lot while she was gone. My former tall and gangly body had filled out and the old Andrews family charm hadn't skipped a generation. I'd spent my formative years watching my father charm his way into the pants of nearly every woman he met, and I'd found it easy enough to fall into the same pattern.

I'd heard through the small-town grapevine that Natalia had come home from work one day to find Evan in their bed with another woman and that she'd immediately packed up her things and their baby and moved back home. I knew she'd gotten a job at the diner, but I never ate there. It wasn't until almost six months ago, after a long shift and too hungry to drive any further, I'd pulled into the diner to grab a bite to eat.

One look at Natalia, at her dark brown eyes framed with impossibly long lashes and her slender but firm body, and that was it for me. I was a fucking goner.

I'd returned to the diner almost every day for

the next two weeks, being flirtatious and hitting on her repeatedly despite her obvious disinterest. I couldn't quite accept the concept that my usual charm wouldn't get me into her bed.

My arrogance made me believe that she found me as appealing as every other woman did – she just hid it better. So, even after two weeks of lukewarm response at best to my flirting, when I asked her out and she turned me down flat... well, you could have knocked me over with a fucking feather.

"Thank you. What would you like?" Natalia was giving me an impatient look.

You. Under me. Moaning my name. Cumming on my cock.

Sweat broke out on my forehead and my dick pushed against my jeans. I closed my menu and said, "Water to drink, please and I'll have the meatloaf and side salad. Thank you."

"Coming right up." She took our menus and I watched her firm ass sway in that godawful uniform as she walked to the counter.

"Well, if she doesn't spit in your food, count yourself lucky," Jonah said.

"Knock it off," I replied, still watching Natalia's ass. "She's not gonna spit in my food. I was nice to her and I didn't even flirt."

"It's impossible for you not to flirt," Jonah said.

I turned back to him. "I can't get her out of my head, Jonah."

He gave me a sympathetic look. "You should stop coming to the diner, Mattie. She's never gonna be into you and you're only torturing yourself."

"I can't," I said. "The thought of not seeing her…"

Jonah frowned a little. "Shit, Matt, you really are into her. Listen, don't take this the wrong way, but maybe what you need is to go to the club and find someone to take your mind off Natalia."

By "club", Jonah meant Sapphire. The Sapphire was a sex club in the city of Welling, about an hour from our small town. Both Jonah and I had gone to Sapphire numerous times in the past, me because I was looking to get laid with no commitment, and Jonah because he had certain tastes in the bedroom. Luckily for my best friend, his girlfriend, Claire, shared those same tastes.

"I haven't been to the club in over a year," I said. "Hell, I haven't had sex in seven months."

Jonah' jaw almost dropped to the table. "You're fucking kidding me."

"No," I said as my gaze returned to Natalia. "I'm not."

"Mattie, look at me."

I tore my gaze from Natalia and stared at Jonah. "What?"

"Are you in love with Natalia?"

I didn't reply and Jonah made a low groan. "Matt, what the hell, man?"

"What?" I gave him a defensive look. "You can't help who you love."

"Yeah, but… she's not into you. At all. In fact, she kind of hates you."

I winced and Jonah squeezed my shoulder. "Shit, sorry, that was a dick thing to say, but I hate the idea of you mooning after a woman who's never even gonna give you a chance."

"She might," I said. "If I can show her that I've changed."

"How are you gonna do that if she won't even talk to you?" Jonah asked.

"I'll figure it out," I said. "I have to."

৵ ৽

"Mattie, are you okay?" Mia gave me a worried look as I drove down the street.

"I'm fine," I said. "Stop worrying, Mia."

"You've been quiet all afternoon."

I shrugged. After I had lunch with Jonah, I'd gone to the gym for a quick workout. When Mia texted me to see if I wanted to have coffee, I'd quickly agreed and met her at Mugs Coffee shop on Main Street.

"You know you can tell me anything, right?" Mia said.

"I know. I'm fine, Mia. Maybe a little tired."

"Okay." She didn't believe me, but I was grateful when she didn't push any further. "You know, I could have called Elijah for a ride home. When he dropped me off, he said he could pick me up when we were done."

"I don't mind," I said.

"Elijah lives on the opposite side of town from you," she said.

I glanced at her before turning left down a side street. "You're happy living with Elijah, huh?"

A soft smile crossed her face. "Yeah. Really happy. He's a good man. I know it seems quick to move in with him, but with our work schedules, it was the easiest way for us to see each other. You know?"

"It's been almost eight months," I said. "That doesn't seem quick to me."

Mia laughed. "That's weird coming from you."

"What's that supposed to mean?" I replied.

"It means, you're the most commitment-phobic guy in town, Mattie. I know you've been totally crushing on Natalia lately, but still... the day you move in with a woman is the day they start handing out ice-skates in hell."

I didn't reply. Normally, Mia's gentle teasing wouldn't bother me in the least, hell, I'd be nodding and laughing along with her about it. But something inside me – something seismic in size - had shifted in the last six months, and now her teasing stung like a bitch.

Intuitive as always, Mia said, "Mattie? I've hurt your feelings, haven't I? I'm sorry."

"Nah, it's fine," I said as I stared out the windshield. "You don't have to apologize. I'm being...what the hell?"

I slammed on my brakes, making both of our seatbelts lock up.

"What's wrong?"

"Did you see that?"

"See what?" Mia scanned the empty street.

"There was a kid running down the sidewalk."

"I don't see anything," Mia said as I pulled over and parked. "Matt, the street is empty."

"She ran down that alley, I think..." Without waiting for Mia's reply, I cut the engine and slid out of my truck. I slammed the door shut and zipped up my jacket before jogging toward the alley. My boots crunched in the hard snow and I could see my breath.

Although the weather had warmed up some in the last day or so, it was still the middle of winter and it looked like the kid wasn't wearing a jacket. I turned right down the alley, scanning both sides as I slowly walked past the garbage and recycling bins.

"Hello?" I called. "Hey, kid? You around?"

A flash of pink caught my eye and I ran forward. A little girl, she couldn't have been more than two or three years old, was hiding behind the last garbage bin in the alley. She wore a pink t-shirt and a pair of jeans and her blonde hair was in two neat braids. Her cheeks and nose were bright red with cold and I could see her tiny body shaking.

"Hey, sweetheart." I squatted down, smiling at her when she took a step back. "What's your name, baby?"

She stared silently at me and I shuffled closer. "My name is Matt. What's your name?"

"Cold." Her thin arms wrapped around her shivering torso as tears dripped down her cheeks. "Cold, Matt."

"I know, baby." I stood and inched forward. When she didn't move away, I kneeled in front of her and quickly took off my jacket. I wrapped it around her tiny body before picking her up.

"Don't cry, sweetheart," I said. "It's okay. Where's your mama?"

"Mama's working," she said.

"Does she work around here?" I asked as I carried her back down the alley.

She shrugged before burying her cold face in

my neck. I rubbed her back through my jacket. I needed to get her into the truck and warmed up. "Don't go to sleep, baby."

"I not baby!" She lifted her head and gave me an indignant look. "I a big girl."

I smiled at her. She was far from big, in fact, she might have been the tiniest damn kid I'd ever seen. "Okay, sweetie. Stay awake for me, okay?"

"Otay," she said.

I wiped the tears from her cheeks before they could freeze to her skin. As far as I was concerned, her sassy attitude and trembling was a good sign. If she was hypothermic, she'd be sleepy and not shivering at all.

"What's your name, sweetheart?" I said again. "Can you tell me your –"

"Matt? Was there a… holy crap."

"Mia!" The little girl in my arms crowed.

I blinked at Mia as she joined us. "Do you know her?"

"Oh my God," Mia said. "Phoebe? Baby, what are you doing out here?"

"I not baby!" Phoebe said.

"I know," Mia said. She held out her arms and Phoebe shook her head.

"No, me stay with Matt." She pressed a kiss against my cheek before laying her head on my shoulder. "Cold, Matt."

"I know. We'll get you warmed up. Mia, how do you know her?"

Mia stared wide-eyed at me. "She's Natalia Dixon's daughter."

303

Chapter Two

Natalia

"That was delicious. Thank you, dear heart."

I smiled at Martha. "I'm glad you enjoyed it. Don't tell Cook Stanley this, but your pie has his beat by a mile."

"Oh, I know," Martha said with a laugh. "He'll never admit it, but he's been trying to get my apple pie recipe for *years*."

I grinned at her before taking her card and running it through the machine. She left me a sizeable tip for a cup of coffee and piece of pie, and I gave Mia's grandmother a grateful smile. "Thank you, Martha."

"Will you be coming to the knitting club this weekend?"

A couple of months ago, Mia had organized a knitting club. She had cajoled her grandmother into being our teacher and now, almost every week, we got together at Martha's house for - as Mia's best friend Isabelle liked to refer to it – a stitch and bitch.

"I think so. As long as you don't mind that I bring Phoebe with me."

"Of course not. I love having a little one around the house again. Reminds me of when Mia and Wyatt were young. I do love the little ones." Martha's smile held a hint of nostalgia. "Oh, did you hear that Maggie has opened up her own law firm?"

I nodded. "Yep, we had coffee the other day in her new office."

Maggie's new office was the spare room in Wyatt's house, but I was ridiculously excited for my friend. Trying to escape a crazed stalker, Maggie had moved to our small town about two months ago. We'd become friends when she started working at the diner, hiding both her past and the fact that she was a lawyer.

After Martha's grandson, local sheriff's deputy Wyatt Reynolds, helped put Maggie's stalker in prison, they'd started officially dating and she moved in with him. It didn't surprise me when a month later, she'd quit the diner and started up her own law firm.

"I'm so proud of her," Martha said. "She told me she already has two clients. I knew it wouldn't take long. Boris is completely useless and has been for the last decade."

By Boris, she meant Boris Galthwaite. Pushing at least seventy-five, he'd been the only lawyer in our small town for the last twenty-five years. Six months ago, I'd finally scraped up enough cash to make an appointment with him.

I was barely making ends meet and I'd desperately needed Phoebe's father to start paying child support again. I was crestfallen when, after finding out that Evan had moved out of state, Boris had advised me that seeking child support was a losing battle and not worth the bother.

But then Maggie had moved to town and now I was one of her two clients, and she was going after my kid's deadbeat father for child support with all the righteous fury of an avenging angel.

"Nat!" Rhonda, the owner of the diner was standing behind the counter. "Your shift is over, hon. Punch out and go home."

I smiled and nodded. Rhonda was a good boss, but she wasn't one for paying overtime, not even a couple minutes' worth.

"See you on Sunday," I said to Martha before heading to the back. Our staff room wasn't really a staff room at all, just a narrow hallway with small lockers bolted to the wall next to the shelf that held our time cards. I punched out, then opened my locker and moved my tips from my apron pocket to my wallet before hanging my apron in the locker. I had a small magnetic mirror on the inside of my locker, and I made a face when I saw my reflection.

I hadn't slept well last night, and my face was pale with dark circles under my eyes. Running late this morning, I didn't even have time to put on my usual light layer of makeup. Not that it mattered, there wasn't anyone I was trying to look good for.

There's Matt.

I scoffed out loud. Matt Andrews was a player and the last guy I would ever be attracted to.

Liar. You think he's hot. Admit it, girl.

Fine, maybe I did think he was hot and maybe I had spent more nights than I wanted to admit masturbating to the fantasy of having Matt's lean naked body in my bed, but it was nothing more than a fantasy.

If and when I decided it was time to find a guy, it would be someone who was sweet and genuine and reliable. Someone who liked kids and could be a dad to Phoebe.

Matt Andrews didn't fit the bill.

You don't know that for sure.

Like hell, I didn't. I knew Matt's reputation just like all the other ladies in our small town did. I'll admit, I'd been shocked the first time he came strolling into the diner and I realized who he was. The last time I'd seen him, he'd been thin, his dark hair cut shorter than it was now, and he was…well… a nerd who spent more time staring at a chess board than at women.

Now? Now, he was a bona fide hottie, his thin body filled out with a ridiculous amount of muscle, that dark hair perpetually in need of a haircut, and a flirtatious grin permanently in place.

He'd become a paramedic and maybe there was something innately attractive about a man who could literally save your life if needed, but I couldn't seem to rid myself of my attraction to him.

Which was stupid and pointless and frustrating as hell. Matt wasn't the settling down type and that's exactly what I was looking for. If I was even looking at all.

Girl, there's nothing wrong with having a bit of

fun. You're wound up tighter than a three-day clock. You need to let off a little steam and Matt Andrews is just the guy to help you do it.

I slipped into my jacket and slammed my locker shut. I wasn't interested in being another notch on Matt's bedpost.

Aren't you, though?

I wasn't. I couldn't be. My priority was Phoebe and keeping her warm, a roof over her head, and food in her belly. Being in Matt Andrews' bed might give me a momentary reprieve from my problems, but in the end, it wouldn't help me make enough money to keep my heat from being shut off.

I limped my way across the diner. Martha was still sitting at her table, texting on her cell phone and I gave her a brief wave as I headed toward the front door. I would pick up Phoebe from daycare, grab something cheap at the supermarket for dinner and go home. If I was really lucky, they hadn't actually shut my heat off yet, even though I was behind on the monthly payments again. I had the money to pay it on Friday, but –

"Nat?"

Mia had opened the front door of the diner, bringing in a swirl of cold air and I zipped up my jacket. "Hey, Mia. How are you?"

"Um, good." Mia's face was pale, and she was biting nervously at her bottom lip.

"What's wrong?" I asked.

"Are you finished work for the day?"

"Yeah. I was just leaving to pick up Phoebe from daycare. What's wrong? Is Elijah okay?"

"He's fine," Mia said. "It's, um, about Phoebe."

Fear splashed into my stomach like bitter acid. "Is she hurt?"

Mia wasn't wearing her paramedic uniform, but my immediate panic was making it hard to think straight. "Was there an accident at the daycare?"

"No. No, honey, she's fine. She's not hurt. We - we found her running down the street without a jacket."

"What?" The breath rushed out of me in a harsh exhale as I clutched at Mia's arm. "Where is she? Where's my daughter, Mia?"

"We have her. She's outside with -"

I pushed past Mia, ignoring the startled looks of the customers as I yanked open the door and ran outside.

My mouth bone-dry, my heart fluttering in my chest like a trapped bird, I stared wide-eyed for a moment at the man holding my daughter in his arms.

Matt Andrews.

Phoebe was bundled up in his jacket, with only her tiny head sticking out of it, and she kissed his cheek before grinning at me. "Hi, Mama!"

"Phoebe!" I ran toward them, skidding to a stop in the slippery snow, and tried to pull Phoebe from Matt's arms.

"Mama, no!" Phoebe's little arms poked out of his jacket and she wrapped them around Matt's thick neck, hanging on for dear life. "I stay with Mattie."

"Phoebe, Pheebs, come to Mama, right now," I said.

"No!" She scowled at me. "Mattie holding

me."

"Baby, don't -"

"I not baby!" Phoebe said.

I stared at her in silent shock. Phoebe was normally an easy-going kid, not one for temper tantrums, and until this moment, I was always her number one. While not shy, she preferred to be with me over anyone else, and without a dad in her life, she was often a little on the wary side around men.

Her clinginess to Matt was completely out of character for her and it made fresh fear flood my nervous system. Had she hit her head? Had she fallen on the ice and given herself a concussion?

"Phoebe, please come to me." My voice cracked.

"Phoebe, sweetheart, your mama wants to hold you," Matt said. He tried to hand her over and Phoebe wailed like a banshee and clung tighter to him, her little hands white against his tanned neck.

"No, Mama! Me stay with Matt!"

Desperate to be with my daughter, I did the only thing I could think of. I stepped forward, pressing my body against Matt's, and cupped the back of Phoebe's delicate skull. "Okay, honey. Okay."

Matt's free arm circled around my waist and I didn't object when he cupped my hip and held me tight. I pressed my forehead against Phoebe's and inhaled her sweet scent. "Oh, honey. Are you all right?"

"Yes." Phoebe kissed my nose and then giggled. "I went for a walk, Mama. It was too cold."

I wiggled my hand inside Matt's jacket and felt Phoebe's tiny body. She was toasty warm and some of my panic subsided a little. I stared up at Matt. "Is she -?"

"She's fine," Matt said. "She wasn't hypothermic, and she warmed up nice and fast in my truck."

"How did you find her?"

"Matt was driving me back to Elijah's place and he saw her running down the street." Mia had joined us.

I blinked back the tears that were threatening. "Thank you."

Matt nodded and it took everything in me not to lean against him and bury my face in his chest. My body was shaking and even though I knew Phoebe was okay, I couldn't stop touching her.

She made a face and pushed my hand away. "Mama, your hand is cold."

"Sorry, sweetpea. Honey, why did you leave daycare?"

Phoebe scowled. "Jenna is mean. She said I had to nap. I don't nap, Mama. I a big girl."

I didn't know whether to laugh or cry. Before I could do either, my cell phone rang. Still in the circle of Matt's arm, I fumbled it out of my purse and stared at the number.

"It's the daycare," I said. I wanted to be angry, hell, I needed to be angry, but all I could feel was a bone-deep weariness. I answered the phone with a curt, "Missing something, Jenna?"

As the owner of the daycare began to sputter and spit, I said, "Phoebe is with me. Luckily for you, she was found before she could freeze to death. I'm not interested in your excuses or your explanations. In fact, at this moment, I'm not interested in talking to you at all. I will call you tomorrow when I'm not on the verge of calling the police and reporting you for child endangerment."

I ended the call and shoved the phone back into my purse. Matt was rubbing my hip almost soothingly and I stared up at him when he said, "You should call the police, Natalia."

"Yeah, I will," I said. "I just – I need to be a bit calmer."

"Nat, you are amazingly calm considering everything that's happened," Mia said.

"Hey, everything okay?" Mia's boyfriend, Elijah, joined us, and Phoebe's eyes widened as she stared at his large body.

"Mama, big man."

"Yes," I said as Mia put her arm around Elijah's waist.

"Everything is good now. Thanks for coming to pick me up." Mia reached out and stroked Phoebe's soft cheek. "You be good for your mama, Phoebe. Okay?"

"Otay," Phoebe said. "Bye bye, Mia."

"Bye bye, Pheebs," Mia said. She squeezed my arm. "Do you need me to stay with you tonight?"

"No, we're okay. Thank you so much, Mia," I said.

"I didn't do anything," Mia said with a glance at Matt. "It was all Mattie."

"Hey, it's a party out here." Martha had walked out of the diner and Phoebe made a little squeal of happiness.

"Hi, Nana!"

"Hi, sugarplum. That's a mighty big jacket for a wee bit like you."

"It's Mattie's coat," Phoebe informed her. "I went for a walk and it was cold."

"You did?" Martha said.

She gave us all a questioning look and suddenly too tired and emotional to explain, I was grateful when Mia said, "Phoebe walked out of the daycare and they didn't notice. Matt and I were driving, and Matt saw her on the sidewalk."

"Oh, my goodness." Martha's normally cheerful face went somber. "Oh, sweetheart, you must have been so scared."

"I not scared," Phoebe said. "Just cold."

Martha's hand rubbed my back. "Are you okay, dearest?"

I nodded, my throat burning, and my lashes wet with unshed tears.

"Are you working tomorrow?" Martha asked.

I nodded again and she said, "Why don't you bring Phoebe to me tomorrow. I'll keep her for the day."

Now the tears did fall, and I sniffed loudly as Martha wiped the tears from my face in a no-nonsense manner. "Save that for later when the little one isn't watching. What time do you start at the diner?"

"Nine," I said.

"Perfect. I'll see you and Phoebe at eight-thirty then?"

"I... are you sure?" I whispered. I needed to

shut up. I couldn't take Phoebe back to the daycare, but I also couldn't miss a day of work. What Martha was offering was a lifeline and I'd be a fool to throw it back.

"Positive. Phoebe, my little sugarplum, you're gonna spend the day with Nana tomorrow. What do you think about that?"

"Can I have cookies?" Phoebe said.

Martha laughed. "You can have two cookies in the afternoon. Okay?"

"Otay," Phoebe said. She rested her head on Matt's shoulders. "I havin' two cookies, Mattie."

"I heard," he said.

"See you tomorrow," Martha said. "Mia and Elijah, will you walk me to my car?"

Mia nodded and Martha slipped her hand into the crook of Elijah's elbow.

The three of them walked away and I made myself smile at Phoebe. "Okay, sweetpea. Time to say goodbye to Mr. Andrews. He has to go home."

She pouted at me. "I want to stay with Mattie, Mama."

"You can see him again later," I said.

I realized I was still pressed up against Matt and dull heat infused my cheeks. I pushed away from him, his hand tightened for a moment on my hip before he released me, and I held my hands out to Phoebe. "C'mon, Pheebs. Mama's tired and we need to get home."

Her pout grew a little bigger, but she nodded. "Otay."

Matt shifted her in his arm. "I'll walk you to the car. We should keep her wrapped up until your car warms up."

"Right," I said. "That makes sense."

He followed me to my car, holding Phoebe while I slid behind the wheel, leaving the door ajar. I turned the key, groaning inwardly when the car made a few gasping wheezes of an attempt to start. It had been acting weird lately and I pumped the gas, hoping against hope that this wasn't the moment it chose to die completely.

It ignored my silent plea and refused to start.

Great.

The perfect cherry to my shit sundae.

"Do you know anything about cars?" I asked Matt.

He shook his head. "I can jump start a battery, change a tire, and change the oil. That's about it."

"Yeah, me too." I sighed. I wanted to cry, oh God how I wanted to cry, but I staved off the tears. Crying would only upset Phoebe. I climbed out of the car and slammed the door shut a little harder than necessary.

"Okay, I'm gonna call Maggie and see if she can give me and Phoebe a ride home. I'll take her into the diner, so you don't have to wait around."

"I'll give you a ride home," he said.

I shook my head. "You've already done enough for us today. I can't ask you to -"

"I don't mind. Phoebe, do you want to ride in my truck again?"

"Yes!" Phoebe cheered.

"All right. But," Matt smiled at her, "you need to go to your mama so I can get your car seat. Okay?"

Phoebe nodded and Matt handed her over to me. I held her tiny body, still wrapped in his jacket, in my arms and kissed her cheeks repeatedly as she giggled. "Your lips are cold, Mama."

I kissed her again and followed Matt as he carried her car seat to his truck.

Chapter Three

Matt

Natalia lived in one of the worst trailer parks in town. I tried not to let the disgust show on my face as I parked in front of her single-wide trailer. The siding was starting to peel away, most of the shingles on the roof were curling up, and I could see a long crack running the length of the big bay window.

"Thank you for the ride, Mr. Andrews," Natalia said. Her face was a dull shade of red and she wouldn't quite meet my eyes.

"I'll carry the car seat into the house," I said.

"No, no, you don't have to…"

I was already out of my truck and unbuckling Phoebe from the car seat. I put my jacket around her again. It was only a short walk to the trailer, but I didn't want her getting cold ever again. She gave me a big toothy grin before putting her arms around my neck and kissing my chin.

"Hi, Mattie."

"Hi, Phoebe."

"Pheebs, honey, come to Mama." Natalia was standing next to me and I breathed in her scent – a mixture of grease and stale diner food that was not sexy at all but still made me want to pick her up and carry her to the nearest bed.

"I want Mattie to carry me."

"I'm gonna carry your car seat, sweetheart," I said before handing her over to Natalia. "It's too heavy for your mama."

"Nu-uh," Phoebe said. "Mama is strong. Aren't you, Mama?"

"Sure, honey," Natalia said.

She didn't look strong at the moment. She looked tired and worn down and on the verge of tears. My inappropriate lust died and was replaced with the urge to comfort her. To hold her tight and assure her that everything would be fine and that Phoebe was okay.

Instead, I followed her toward the trailer, holding the car seat in one hand and keeping the other hand stretched out in front of me to break Natalia's fall if she slipped on the ice-covered sidewalk.

"Do you own or rent?" I asked as she unlocked the front door.

"Rent," she said.

I followed her into the trailer. It was shabby looking but spotlessly clean and Natalia gave me a nervous smile as I set the car seat down. "Okay, well, thank you again. I can't tell you how grateful -"

"Why can I see your breath?" I said.

Her face flushed and she held Phoebe a little tighter. "Oh, I, uh, keep the heat low during the day when we're not home to save money."

"Down, Mama," Phoebe said.

Natalia set her down and Phoebe threw off my jacket before scampering down the hallway and disappearing into a room.

I studied Natalia for a moment before walking toward the thermostat I could see on the wall. She immediately stepped in front of it, blocking it from my view, and I arched my eyebrow at her. "Let me see it, Natalia."

"You should probably go. It's getting late and I need to make Pheebs some dinner and give her a bath and -"

She made a little squeak when I put my hands around her narrow waist and lifted her out of the way. Neanderthal move on my part, but I didn't feel the least bit bad about it.

I stared at the thermostat. "The heat isn't turned down."

"Isn't it?" She said nervously. "Weird. Okay, well, thank you again. Bye now."

"Has your heat been turned off?" I said.

She didn't reply but her cheeks went from a dull red to fire engine red.

"Mama?" Phoebe was back and she was holding a doll in one hand. "It's cold in my room again. I don't like it."

"Phoebe?" I squatted in front of her and smiled at her. "What do you think about you and your mama having a sleepover at my house tonight? It's nice and warm and you can bring your toys. I'm making spaghetti for supper. Do you like spaghetti?"

"I love psghetti!" Phoebe shouted.

I glanced up at Natalia, expecting to see fire and anger in those dark brown eyes. Instead, they were swimming with tears, and she looked impossibly sad. I stood and resisting my urge to pull her into my arms, patted her shoulder awkwardly instead. "Pack up some clothes and stuff. I have a spare bedroom that you and Phoebe can stay in as long as you don't mind sharing a bed, and I'm not working tomorrow so I can drive you to work and Phoebe to Nana's. Okay?"

Her shoulders slumped and looking utterly defeated, she nodded. "Yeah, okay. Thank you."

"You're welcome." I squeezed her shoulder. "Everything will be all right, Natalia."

രു ഄ

"Mattie!" Phoebe came racing into the kitchen, wearing pajamas with little yellow ducks printed on them, her doll clutched under one arm, and her fine blonde hair wet and sticking to her skull. "Guess what?"

I closed the dishwasher and smiled at her. "What?"

"I pooped!" She gave me a look of glee before hugging my leg.

"Good job, Pheebs," I said.

"Thank you." She stood on my foot and grabbed my hand, leaning back and swaying back and forth. "I pooped and then I had a bath. Your bathtub is really big. Mama had a bath with me."

Sweat broke out on my forehead at the thought

of Natalia naked in my tub. The guest bathroom only had a shower, so I'd told Natalia to go ahead and bathe Phoebe in the master bathroom while I cleaned up after supper.

"Phoebe? Sweet pea, where are you?" Natalia stepped into the kitchen and I drank in the sight of her.

Her hair, the exact same shade as Phoebe's, was wet and coiled into a bun on top of her head. Her cheeks were flush with warmth and she was wearing a pair of blue leggings with a long grey t-shirt. My gaze dropped to her tits and I quickly looked away when Natalia crossed her arms over her chest.

I wanted to smack myself in the head for feeding her belief that I was nothing but a perverted playboy, but fuck, when I was around her, I could barely think straight.

"Phoebe, stop bothering Mr. Andrews, please," Natalia said.

Phoebe giggled. "His name is Mattie, Mama."

"His name is Mr. Andrews," Natalia replied.

"She can call me Mattie, I don't mind," I said. "She heard Mia call me Mattie and it's easier than Mr. Andrews, right?"

"You actually go by that?" Natalia said.

Weirdly, I could feel myself blushing. "Yeah, sometimes."

Still holding my hand in both of hers, Phoebe braced her feet on my shin and climbed up my leg.

"Phoebe," Natalia admonished. "He's not a jungle gym. Stop climbing him, honey."

"I don't mind," I said again as Phoebe giggled

and dropped back to the ground.

"I climbin' you," she said. She released my hand and danced in a circle, singing "jungle gym, jungle gym" under her breath.

"It's time for bed, honey." Natalia held out her hand and to my surprise, Phoebe whirled and grabbed my hand again.

"I want Mattie to read me the bedtime story, Mama."

Natalia shook her head. "No, honey. He's very busy and -"

"Mattie?" Phoebe gave me a look that would melt butter. "You read me my story?"

"Sure, sweetheart," I said before Natalia could protest again.

"Yay!" Phoebe jumped up and down before standing on both my feet. "Walk, Mattie."

I held her hands and walked toward the guest room, Phoebe giggling the entire way. I didn't have much experience with kids, but Phoebe was adorable, and I'd be lying if I said I didn't find her charming. Her happiness and delight over the littlest things made me want to do whatever it took to keep her happy.

"I'm so sorry," Natalia said behind me in a low voice. "She's not normally like this with strangers."

"It's fine," I said as I stepped into the bedroom. "I don't mind reading her a story."

"You have to lay on the bed with me, Mattie." Phoebe hopped off my feet and ran to the bed. "Boost me!"

I boosted her onto the bed, and she climbed under the covers. "Mama, I want Ariel tonight."

Natalia handed me a kid's book from the suitcase on the floor, and even though I didn't have children, I recognized the Disney version of *The Little Mermaid.*

"Lie down, Mattie." Phoebe patted the bed beside her, and I laid on my back next to her, grunting in surprise when Phoebe scooted close and rested her head on the pillow next to mine.

"No thumb sucking, honey," Natalia said gently.

Phoebe dropped her hand just as her thumb inched past her lips. "Sorry, Mama."

"It's okay, honey. You're doing a really good job."

Phoebe gave me an earnest look. "Only babies suck their thumbs. I not a baby, Mattie."

"Nope, you're a big girl," I said, and Phoebe gave me a happy smile.

"Read Ariel," she demanded as Natalia sat down on the side of the bed next to Phoebe. As I opened the book and turned to the first page, I couldn't help but reflect that as many times as I'd imagined Natalia in a bed with me, I'd never once imagined this particular scenario.

৵ ৶

I was sitting on the couch, staring sightlessly at a hockey game on the television when Natalia walked into the living room. She tugged self-consciously at her shirt before sinking into the chair next to the couch.

"Is she asleep?" I asked.

She nodded. "Yes. Thanks for reading her the story. I know this isn't how you usually spend your evenings."

"I had fun," I said.

"Right."

"No, really." I smiled at her, uncomfortably aware of how fucking good she smelled. "Phoebe is a great kid."

A soft smile crossed Natalia's face. "She is."

There was a moment of awkward silence and Natalia glanced at the television. "You like hockey, huh?"

"Yeah. My old man was a big fan. He got me into it."

"Did you play hockey?" She asked.

"No, I liked watching hockey, but I was never great at playing any sport. My dad enrolled me in a few after school sports teams, but I was more into reading and chess."

The corners of her mouth turned up. "Weren't you the president of the chess club in high school? You guys won like a regional championship or something in senior year, right?"

I clapped my hand over my chest in mock dismay. "Oh God, don't remind me of my former glory days. You weren't at the tournament because you were cool in high school, but when we won, the other guys in the club lifted me and our trophy up into the air like we'd won the Stanley Cup."

I was stupidly happy when she laughed. "Your dad must have been very proud."

"He was too busy trying to get into Mrs. Granson's pants to be proud."

"Mrs. Granson, our chemistry teacher?" Natalia gave me a look of shock.

"Yeah."

"But she and the librarian at the school…Mr. Granson. They were married, right?"

"That never stopped my dad." Even I could hear the bitterness in my voice. "They had a three-month affair in our senior year."

"I had no idea," Natalia said.

"No one did. My dad ended it when she started talking about leaving her husband."

"Wow… It… I can't believe it."

I shrugged. "My dad slept with half of our classmate's mothers. The ladies loved him."

"Like they love you?" Natalia said.

"I might be a manwhore like my old man, but I've never slept with a married woman." My tone was harsh, and I immediately felt guilty when Natalia winced. "Sorry," I mumbled.

"No, I'm sorry," she said. "That was a real shit thing to say to the guy who basically saved your kid's life and then gave you a warm place to stay for the night. I am sincerely sorry."

She gave me a hesitant smile. "Thank you again, by the way. Not just for saving Phoebe from freezing to death, but for giving up your spare room for the night, and for the delicious meal. My heat – I mean, I'm a little short on cash right now, but I'll be getting the heat turned back on when I get paid on Friday."

"You're welcome to stay with me for as long as you need."

She blushed. "No, I'm not … I mean, I wasn't trying to ask you to let us stay until Friday. I just wanted to… I'm not a bad mom, I swear."

I frowned and muted the television before

leaning forward. "I know you're not, Natalia. You're an amazing mom and it's obvious how much you love your kid. Getting your heat cut off doesn't make you a bad mom."

"Doesn't it?" She rubbed at her temples. "I know it's early, but it's been a really long day and I'm tired. If you don't mind, I think I'll head to bed."

"Of course," I said. "If you need anything in the night, just, uh…"

I trailed off into silence. Just what? My desire to get her into my bed and help her forget all her troubles by banging her until she couldn't think straight didn't exactly make me a gentleman. In fact, all it did was make me as big of a dog as my old man had been.

"Okay, well, good night." Natalia stood and gave me an awkward smile before hurrying out of the living room.

I groaned inwardly and sank into the cushions. Christ, I was a fucking idiot.

❧ ❦

I tossed and turned for over an hour before admitting defeat and getting out of bed. I was tired, but knowing that Natalia was in the room right next to mine? Sleep wasn't gonna happen anytime soon.

I eased out of my bedroom and moved silently past the spare room before heading down the stairs. I was barely off the stairs when I heard her. The sobs made my chest tighten and I immediately walked to the living room instead of the kitchen.

The moonlight shining through the window made it easy to see Natalia. She was sitting on the couch, rocking back and forth with her hands over her mouth to muffle her crying. The desolation and despair on her face made me rush forward and join her at the couch.

She made a startled gasp when I dropped onto the couch beside her. She swiped at the tears on her face. "S-s-sorry. Did I wake you?"

"No," I said. "Are you okay?"

I winced. God, could I be any dumber?

"Yeah I'm...." She burst into tears again and I couldn't fucking take it anymore. I pulled her into my arms and pressed her against my chest, rubbing her back as she sobbed like her heart was breaking.

"She-she-she almost died. My baby almost died and it's all my fault," she cried as she wrapped her arms around my waist.

"It isn't," I said immediately. "Honey, it's not your fault."

"It is," she replied. "I kn-new the daycare wasn't g-g-good, and I still took her there because I-I-I'm a terrible mother."

"You're not." I held her a little tighter. "You're not a bad mom, Nat. Don't say that."

She buried her hot face in my chest and sobbed harder. Not sure what else to do, I let her cry, holding her tightly and making sounds of comfort that probably didn't do jack shit.

After almost ten minutes, her crying was starting to slow down, and I snagged the box of tissues from the side table. She took a fistful and wiped her face before blowing her nose.

"I'm sorry," she whispered.

"It's okay. You're not a bad mom, Natalia."

She stared up at me, her vulnerability and her sorrow shining out of her like a beacon. "I am. I put Phoebe in a bad daycare, I can barely afford to feed her, I live in a shit trailer, and I can't even keep the goddamn heat on. It's supposed to get even colder for the next few days and I can't afford to turn the heat on until Friday. And that's only if my car doesn't cost an arm and a leg to fix, which it probably will because it's a piece of shit."

She balled her hand into a fist and punched her thigh twice. When she went in for a third time, I grabbed her hand and held it gently. "Don't do that, honey."

"I deserve it," she said. "I'm a shit mother who nearly got her kid killed. If it hadn't been for you, she would be…"

She was close to tears again and I cupped her face, tilting it up until she was looking at me, and leaning down until I could feel her warm breath on my lips.

"This," I gave her jaw a light but deliberate squeeze, "is not your fault, Natalia. Do you hear me? This is entirely the daycare's fault and you are not to blame yourself for that. They made the mistake, not you. They let her walk out of the daycare and into the cold without a jacket, not you. They didn't notice she was missing for nearly an hour, not you."

I squeezed her jaw again. "This is not your fault, honey."

"Then why do I feel like it is?" she whispered.

"Because you're an amazing mother who loves her daughter, and it's easy to blame yourself. But

I'm not going to let you do that. And as far as the heat thing goes – you and Phoebe are staying with me until you get the heat turned back on. If that's this Friday or a month from now, it doesn't matter. You're staying with me."

"I – we can't do that," she said. "I don't want to inconvenience you and -"

"You're not," I said. "The house is big enough for all of us, and with both of us working, we'll probably hardly ever see each other. You need your car fixed. Get it fixed first and then you can worry about getting the heat turned back on. Okay?"

She swallowed hard, the tears brimming in those gorgeous eyes. "Why are you being so nice?"

I swallowed down the hurt I felt at her words. It was my own fault that she believed I was a bad guy. Still, I couldn't help but try and defend myself a little.

"I'm not a bad guy," I said.

Embarrassment crossed her face, and my pulse hammered in my temples when she reached up and wrapped one soft hand around my forearm. She squeezed it gently. "I know you're not. I'm sorry. I'm tired and upset and not thinking straight, but I know you're a good guy, Matt."

There it was.

My name had left her perfect lips and it was like fucking music to my ears.

My hand tightened around her jaw when I realized she was staring at my mouth.

"Natalia." I meant to say it normally, but it came out as a moan. I could pinpoint the exact moment that the air between us changed, became charged with something I'd never dreamed possible… desire. Her lips parted and the tips of her fingers traced back and forth over my arm.

"Matt," she whispered.

"I should go." My voice was hoarse, the need in it evident.

Before I could pull away, Natalia leaned forward a bit and pressed her mouth against mine and I was in heaven.

Her soft lips brushed twice against mine and then I groaned and slid my arm around her waist. I yanked her into my lap, making her straddle me as I tangled my hands into her blonde hair and held her still. I angled my mouth over hers, pressing my tongue against the seam of her lips until they parted and she let me in.

My tongue tasted and teased her sweetness. Her lips were salty from dried tears and I could taste the mint from her toothpaste. I kissed her harder, deeper, anxious to show her that she was mine and always would be.

Her tongue touched mine delicately and I moaned into her mouth before dropping my hands to her hips and grinding my rock-hard dick against her pussy.

She gasped into my mouth, her back arching a little when I cupped one breast through her t-shirt. She wasn't wearing a bra and I pulled greedily at her nipple through the soft fabric. God, I wanted her so bad. Our kisses turned frantic and needy, our harsh breaths mixing and mingling as we kissed and kissed some more.

"I need you, Matt," she moaned against my

mouth before her hands pulled at the waistband of my sleep pants.

This was happening. Natalia wanted to fuck me, and I was more than willing to let her take what she needed from me.

Mattie, no. Don't do this.

I tried to ignore my inner voice as I kneaded Natalia's perfect breast and kissed her perfect mouth, but it wouldn't shut the hell up.

Don't, Mattie. She's vulnerable and upset and in the morning, she'll be full of regret. She'll walk out that door and you'll never see her again. Is that what you want?

She's doing this because she wants me, I argued. *She wants me.*

If you sleep with her tonight, you'll be exactly what she believes you are. A horny playboy who's only looking for sex.

That thought cooled my lust only a fraction, but it was enough for me to realize I couldn't sleep with Natalia. Not tonight.

I grabbed her hand when she tried to slip it into my pants and pulled my mouth from hers. She tried to kiss me again and I slid my other hand back into her hair and held her tight.

"Natalia, wait. We can't do this," I said.

"Sure, we can," she panted. She rubbed her pussy against my still-hard cock. "We need to do this."

"No, not tonight," I said.

She sat back and frowned at me. "You – you're turning me down? You sleep with everyone, Matt. But suddenly I'm not good enough for you?"

I winced and shook my head. "No, that isn't it. It's – you're upset and vulnerable and if I sleep with you right now, I'm taking advantage of you."

"No, you're not. I'm an adult and I know what I want. I need sex, I need to not think about – about…anything. Are you seriously turning down some no-strings-attached sex? Because I promise I won't get all weird on you in the morning. I know what you want from women, okay? I'm fine with it."

My erection had disappeared completely at her words. I deserved my reputation but listening to Natalia talk about it made me feel cheap and worthless. I lifted her off my lap before taking her hand and kissing her knuckles. "I know you think you want this tonight, but you don't, Natalia. You'll regret it in the morning."

"You don't know that. You don't know me at all." Frustration was written all over her face.

"I know you enough to know that a night of meaningless sex isn't what you want. Listen, if in a day or two you're feeling better and you want to-to maybe revisit what's happening, I'm absolutely open to that."

She sighed and pushed away from me before standing up. "Christ, I'm being rejected by Matt Andrews. Could this day get any worse?"

"Natalia, I'm not -"

She held her hand up. "No, don't… it's fine, really. I should go to bed. It's late. Good night, Matt."

I slumped against the couch, watching as she crossed the room and disappeared into the hallway.

Just fucking perfect. I had ruined any chance of ever being with the woman I loved.

Chapter Four

Natalia

"Nana!" Phoebe wiggled in Matt's arms and he set her down. She ran across the kitchen and wrapped her arms around Martha's legs. "Hi, Nana!"

"Hi, sweet girl." Martha stroked her fine blonde hair before smiling at me. "Feeling better today, dearest?"

I nodded and quickly handed over Phoebe's backpack. "This has an extra change of clothes just in case and some of her favourite toys. Thank you so much for looking after Phoebe today, Martha. I really appreciate it."

"Of course, Nat. You know I love having her here. In fact, I can take her for the next couple of weeks until you can find a new daycare."

I blinked back the sudden tears as a wave of relief washed over me. I took a deep breath. "Are you sure? Phoebe can be a handful sometimes."

"Of course, I am," Martha said. "It takes a

village to raise a child, right? Besides, little Pheebs here is going to be the perfect angel for me. Aren't you?"

"Angel," Phoebe sang before running back to Matt and hugging his legs. "You stay with me, Mattie?"

Before Matt could reply, I shook my head. "Matt has stuff to do today, sweetpea. You're gonna stay with Nana. You need to be a good girl for her, okay?"

"Otay, Mama." Phoebe was still clinging to Matt's legs. "Up, Mattie."

He picked her up and she patted his cheek affectionately. "I want you to stay with me."

"I can't stay but I'll see you tonight," he said.

"Otay. Gimme a kiss." She puckered her lips and Matt smiled a little before giving her a quick peck.

What the hell was going on with Phoebe? She always played strange with men. Before Matt, the only guy she'd gone near was Maggie's boyfriend Wyatt and even then, she'd only let him hold her for a few minutes. This weird and sudden attachment to Matt was the last thing I'd expected from her.

"Be good for Nana, Pheebs." Matt set her down and she danced away.

"Come give me a kiss goodbye, sweetpea," I said.

She skipped over to me and I knelt and hugged her tight before kissing her. "I love you so much, honey. Be a good girl and Mama will see you after work."

"Bye, Mama." Phoebe squirmed free and

returned to Martha. "Nana, I want a cookie."

Martha laughed and scooped her up. "You can have a cookie after lunch, dear heart. Now, how about we do some colouring?"

അ ഷ

"Can we talk about last night?"

I cringed inwardly as I unbuckled my seat belt. "I'd rather not."

Matt sighed and shut off his car. "Please?"

I glanced at my watch. "My shift starts in five minutes."

"I'll be quick."

I hesitated and then nodded. Phoebe had been an effective barrier to talking with Matt this morning and I'd spent the ride from Martha's to the diner on my cell phone with Jack's mechanic shop. If Lily, the receptionist and one of my knitting club friends, had thought it was weird that I'd dragged the conversation on about fixing my car for so long, she hadn't mentioned it. But I really did owe Matt an explanation and another apology. What I had done last night was beyond stupid and I was full of shame and regret.

More shame than regret.

I wanted to ignore my inner voice, but damn it, she was right. Being rejected by Matt Andrews, the guy who slept with every woman who showed even a whiff of interest in him, was a crushing blow to my ego.

Matt was staring silently at me and I gave him a faint smile. "I'm really sorry about last night. What I did was inexcusable, and I promise it won't happen again."

"You don't have to apologize," Matt said. "I didn't mind and -"

I winced. "You didn't mind... ugh, that's a roaring endorsement for my kissing skills, isn't it?"

"No, that isn't what I'm saying. Last night, you were upset and vulnerable and -"

"Please, you don't have to make excuses for rejecting me, okay? That just makes me feel worse." I yanked at the skirt of my horrid uniform. "I forgot that you flirt with every woman and I – I made a mistake in thinking that you were interested in me."

"I am interested in you," Matt said.

I laughed, the sound jagged and raw in the confined space of his truck. "Right, of course you are. I mean, who wouldn't want to bang a single mom who's flat broke, works in a diner for minimum wage and can't even put her kid in a decent daycare?"

I pulled at the collar of my uniform. "Tell me, is it the way the world's least sexy uniform shows off my muffin top, or the way it washes me out until I look like I'm the living dead that makes you want to bang -"

I made a muffled squeak when Matt leaned over, wrapped his hand around the back of my neck and pulled me forward until his lips met mine. His lips were warm and firm, and my entire body lit up with excitement when he brushed them repeatedly against mine.

Matt Andrews was, without a doubt, the best damn kisser in the world. Could I be blamed for kissing him back? For opening my mouth and inviting him in? For sliding closer until I could curl my hands into the collar of his jacket?

His tongue slicked across my bottom lip as his arm slid around my waist. He cupped my hip, kneading it gently as I pushed my tongue into his mouth. He sucked on it and I moaned loudly, my back arching.

Not caring that we were in the middle of the diner parking lot, not caring that anyone could see us, I tried to scoot closer, groaning with frustration when the arm rest thwarted my efforts.

Matt broke the kiss and leaned his forehead against mine, our breaths mingling as we both panted lightly.

"I want you," he said in a low voice. "You have no fucking idea how much I want you, Nat. I've been kicking myself all goddamn night and morning for rejecting you last night."

He pressed a gentle kiss against my mouth. "But after spending most of my life doing the wrong thing, just once I wanted to do the right thing."

I leaned back a little and stared at him. My mouth was tingling, and I touched my swollen lips before swallowing hard. What the hell was I doing? Kissing Matt, sleeping with Matt, was the last thing I should be doing. I had a broken car I probably couldn't afford to fix, a house with no heat, and no affordable daycare option. The last thing I needed was sex with the playboy of the whole damn town. I was using Matt as a distraction from my problems and that was a shit thing to do. I let go of his jacket and slid back in my seat until I was pressed against the door.

"I'm sorry."

He gave me a frustrated look. "Please stop apologizing."

I sighed and glanced at my watch. "I really need to go. I'm late for work."

"Yeah, okay." He ran his hand through his hair. "I'll pick you up after work."

"Oh, um, actually I have an appointment after work so if you're still okay with me and Phoebe staying another night with you, I'll just meet you at your place later."

"That's fine. How will you get to your appointment and what about Phoebe?"

"I'll take the bus to get Phoebe and to my appointment."

"No," he said. "I'll pick you up when your shift is over and drive you."

"I can't ask you to be my chauffer," I protested. "You're already helping me out so much and -"

"You're not asking, I'm offering," Matt said. "I'll see you at four thirty."

"Matt, I -"

"You're late for work," he said gently. "Go on, Natalia."

 తా తా

Matt parked in front of the mid-size bungalow and gave me a puzzled look. "You have an appointment with Wyatt?"

"Oh, uh, no. I have an appointment with Maggie. She's a lawyer and started her own practice. She has an office in the, um, house there."

"Okay."

To my surprise, he didn't pry about why I needed to see a lawyer. I was grateful he didn't. Today had been a long and tiring day. The diner was busy and the new girl that Rhonda hired to replace Maggie was slow to catch on. I'd tried not to lose my patience with her, but I'd barely slept a wink last night and I was exhausted.

To make matters worse, after having my car towed to Jack's shop, he'd called with an estimate for repairs. At nearly six hundred dollars, it would eat up every extra penny of my paycheque which meant no money to get my heat turned back on by this Friday. I would barely have enough left over to afford groceries for Phoebe.

Just thinking about food made my stomach growl. Money was so short that I routinely went a day or two without food so that Phoebe had enough.

You can't keep doing that, Nat.

No, I couldn't, but my only other option was to junk the car so that I could pay my heat bill and have enough money for food for both of us. But then I would have to rely on our small town's notoriously fickle public transportation system. I shuddered at the thought of having to get Phoebe up – who was definitely not a morning person – even earlier in the morning to get her to daycare on time.

You don't have daycare, remember?

New tension settled in my shoulders and neck and I rubbed at the base of my skull before plastering a smile on my face and turning to where Phoebe sat in her car seat behind me. "Ready to go see Maggie, sweet pea?"

Phoebe shook her head. "I want dinner, Mama.

I'm hungry."

"I know, honey. We won't be long and then I'll make you some dinner."

She pouted at me. "I stay with Mattie."

"No, Pheebs, you can't."

A big fat tear welled up and slid down her cheek and she turned to Matt. "Please, Mattie. I stay with you, otay?"

I sighed. "Phoebe, you can't -"

"Yes, baby," Matt said abruptly. "You can stay with me while your mama talks to Maggie."

"Yay!" Phoebe clapped her hands together, her crocodile tears forgotten. "I stay with Mattie, Mama!"

"Matt, I can't ask you to babysit while I -"

"Like I said this morning, you're not asking, I'm offering," he said. "I'll take Phoebe home and feed her leftover spaghetti for dinner. Text me when you're finished, and we'll come back and get you."

"I can take the bus."

"No," he said. "It's cold and you're not even wearing a winter jacket for God's sake. You'll freeze to death waiting for the bus."

He turned to smile at Phoebe. "You want spaghetti again for dinner, kiddo?"

"Yep," Phoebe said. She clutched her doll. "Bye, Mama."

I blinked at her. "Pheebs, are you sure you want to stay with Matt? Mama's gonna be a little bit and -"

"*Bye*, Mama," Phoebe said again before smiling at Matt. "Drive home now, Mattie."

A little grin played on Matt's stupidly perfect

lips and I wanted to roll my eyes but truthfully, it was kind of adorable how smitten Phoebe was with him.

I twisted in my seat and leaned over it to give Phoebe's smooth cheek a kiss. "Bye, sweetpea. Mama will see you soon."

"Yep." Phoebe was still smiling at Matt, but he was staring at my ass as I leaned over the seat. I blushed and opened the door before sliding out of the truck.

"You're sure?" I said one last time.

Matt nodded. "I am. Text me when you're ready to come home."

"Okay." I shut the door and limped my way up the sidewalk to Maggie and Wyatt's house as Matt drove away.

❧ ❧

"Wait, so you left Pheebs with Matt?" Maggie cut up some more cheese and laid it on the plate. My stomach growled and Maggie grinned before adding another handful of crackers to the plate already piled high with cheese and slices of pepperoni. "Grab the wine and the glasses, would you?"

"You think I shouldn't have?" I picked up the bottle of wine and the glasses and followed her toward her office at the back of the house.

"No, no, nothing like that. I mean, I don't know Matt very well, but Wyatt thinks he's a good guy. They play poker together once a month and I know he's worked out with him and Elijah a few times at the gym."

She sat down behind her desk watching as I

limped to the seat across from her and sank into it with a sigh.

"You're limping really badly tonight," she said with a frown.

"My plantar fasciitis is acting up. Why are you surprised that I left Phoebe with Matt?"

"Um, because you have that protective mama bear down to a science with her? Not that I think that's a bad thing, I just didn't see you leaving Phoebe with someone you hate."

"I don't hate him," I protested.

"Since when?" Maggie pushed the cheese and meat plate toward me. "You've hated Matt Andrews since I've known you."

I munched on some cheese and crackers as Maggie poured us both a glass of wine. "I think I might have been wrong about Matt."

"Oh, so he doesn't sleep with everything in a skirt?" She sipped at her wine before helping herself to some food.

"No, he does. But... I think he's actually a pretty good guy."

"Being a manwhore doesn't make him a bad guy," Maggie replied.

I winced, more shame curling into my belly. "I thought it did. God, I'm such a judgmental bitch, Maggie. I looked at Matt and saw some guy who banged as many women as he could and that was it. And in the last twenty-four hours, he saved my kid's life, let me stay with him free of charge and is being a chauffer and a babysitter. I seriously need an attitude adjustment, don't I?"

I had told Maggie everything that happened the

343

second I walked through her door. Well, almost everything. I'd left out the way I'd practically tried to jump Matt's bones last night.

Maggie shrugged before giving me a careful look. "Maybe, but - and yeah I'm being judgmental here too - maybe Matt's doing this for his own selfish reasons."

"What do you mean?" I ate another piece of cheese.

"I mean that Matt is obviously into you. He's flirted with you for months and hasn't gotten anywhere. Maybe he sees helping you as his chance to finally get into your bed."

"I tried to have sex with him last night and he rejected me."

I jumped up, wincing at the pain in my heels, when Maggie inhaled the cracker she was eating and began to cough and choke. I moved behind her and thumped her twice on the back with the heel of my hand. She dragged in a gasping breath.

"Better, thanks." She coughed again and then swallowed down some wine.

I limped back to my seat and took my own sip of wine as Maggie, her eyes watering, stared at me. "You tried to bang Matt?"

"Yeah. He said no."

"You're kidding me."

I looked away and pulled at the front of my uniform.

"Tell me exactly what happened," Maggie demanded.

"Not much to tell. Phoebe was asleep and I was sitting on the couch bawling my eyes out. Matt came downstairs and let me cry on his shoulder. Then I stuck my tongue down his throat until he said no and then I went back to my room more humiliated than I'd ever been in my entire life."

"Wait, you were crying and upset and then you started making out with him?"

I nodded. "He responded at first, but then he said he couldn't do this, that he would be taking advantage of me if he did."

"Oh my God," Maggie said.

"What?"

"That's about the sweetest damn thing I've ever heard."

"Yeah, well, it wasn't. It was humiliating."

Maggie poked at the cheese on her plate before taking a small bite of it and swallowing carefully. "Nat, he was super sweet. You have to see that, don't you?"

"No, all I see is being rejected by the guy who will sleep with anyone."

She threw a cracker at me and it pinged off my forehead. I glared at her and she shrugged. "You're being dumb."

"I'm not. I -"

"You are," she said. "I get it. You have had a truly terrifying and horrible twenty-four hours, but if you look past that, you'll see that what Matt did last night was sweet and kind, and exactly what he should have done."

I rubbed the cracker crumbs off my forehead. "Yeah, I am being dumb. I mean, I was kind of attracted to him even before all of this happened. I hated that I was, but I was. Only, now he's being super nice and kind and even though you're right in that he's only doing it to get into my pants… I really want to let him into my pants."

"So let him," Maggie said.

I gaped at her. "I can't. Maggie, he's not looking for a relationship and, besides, I'm not looking for one either. My priority right now is Phoebe and trying to figure out how I'm gonna keep her safe and warm and fed. I'm doing a terrible job at all three as it is."

"One – you're not. You're an amazing mother and you're doing the best you can do, and Phoebe knows how much you love her. Two – maybe a couple nights of amazing sex with Matt is *exactly* what you need."

"It isn't," I said.

"Don't be so hasty to decide that," Maggie said. "When was the last time you got laid?"

I chewed on my bottom lip. "When I was with Evan, so, I dunno… over two years."

"Okay, yeah, you definitely need to get laid."

"I'm not the type of girl to just sleep with a guy," I said.

"Neither was I. Then along came Wyatt," Maggie said.

"Yeah, but Wyatt loves you and wants you and that was obvious. Matt is only looking for a good time."

"So are you," she said. "You just told me that you don't want a relationship right now. But you're attracted to Matt and he's attracted to you, right?"

I cleared my throat. "We did, uh, kiss again this morning in his truck. And he made it clear that he wanted me despite what happened last night."

Maggie gave me a look of outrage. "You are seriously holding out on me, girl. Are there any other make out sessions I need to know about?"

"No," I said.

She gave me a suspicious look and despite my worry and my exhaustion, I laughed. "I promise. I've only kissed Matt twice now."

"All right, I'll believe you. Anyway, my point is – you're under nothing but stress and worry right now and you could use a fun distraction by the name of Matt Andrews."

"It's not a very nice thing to do to him," I said. "To use him like that makes me feel... icky."

"Because you're a nice girl. But even nice girls deserve fun with a bad boy, right? From what I've heard Matt Andrews is a pretty naughty guy. You can't tell me you don't want to find out how naughty."

"Maybe I'm curious," I admitted. "But I would just be using him."

"Like he's using you," Maggie said.

I sat back in my chair and sipped at my wine. Maggie had a point. I knew what Matt wanted from me and why shouldn't I take the same thing from him? No one would get hurt and it would be a nice stress reliever.

"Phoebe is what matters," I said. "Not me."

"No, you matter too," Maggie said. "Listen, I'm not a mom, but I know that you need to take care of yourself in order to take care of your kid. Maybe taking care of yourself means dusting off the old vagina for a night or two and getting yourself some of Matt's D."

She made a circle with her forefinger and thumb and poked her other finger in and out of the circle. "If you know what I'm saying."

"I know what you're saying," I said dryly. "I don't need the hand gestures."

Maggie laughed. "Honey, I think you need this. You said you were at Matt's house until Friday when you pay your heat bill, right? So that gives you tonight and tomorrow night to have a little fun. Once Pheebs is in bed, forget about your worries for a few hours and bang Matt until neither of you can see straight."

My growing lust for Matt circled down the drain at the reminder of my heat bill and just how much trouble I was in.

"I don't need to bang Matt, I already am fucked," I said morosely.

"Why's that?"

"Jack called me. My car is gonna cost six hundred bucks to repair. I can't afford that and turn my heat back on too. If I pay the car bill, I won't be able to get my heat turned on for like another two weeks."

"Actually," Maggie grinned at me and reached into the bottom drawer of the desk. She pulled out a file, my name was written neatly on the tab, and set it in front of her. "I think I can relieve some of your stress."

"What do you mean?"

She opened my file and handed me a cheque. "I got this in the mail this morning."

I stared blankly at the cheque and at Evan's

signature. "I – he paid child support?"

"Yep," Maggie said triumphantly. "He still owes you back payments for the last two years, but he's gonna pay them. His lawyer is dragging his heels on it, trying to pretend that Evan doesn't have that kind of cash lying around, but he'll have to pay it sooner or later. He'll probably do it in monthly instalments, rather than a lump sum, but if he doesn't start doing monthly payments for the payments he owes by next month, I'll have his wages garnished. But, for this month at least, you're getting what he should be paying monthly, and you'll receive this amount every month for certain."

"Oh my God," I whispered. "Maggie, I – I can't believe it. You're amazing."

She grinned at me. "Nope, just really good at going after deadbeat dads. Now, technically this payment is for next month, which is why the cheque is dated for Monday, but I'm sure Matt will be okay with you staying with him until then. On Monday, you deposit that bad boy and pay your car bill and turn your heat back on."

Tears were slipping down my cheeks and I stared at Maggie. "I can't thank you enough, Maggie."

"Just doing my job, honey." Maggie reached across the desk and squeezed my hand.

"If he keeps paying child support, I can actually put Phoebe in a better daycare," I said. "I could maybe even rent an apartment instead of that gross trailer. You've changed my life, Maggie. Do you know that?"

Maggie swallowed hard and I could see the gleam of tears in her eyes. "I'm glad I could help. Now, finish up your wine and your cheese and crackers and I'll give you a ride to Matt's place."

Chapter Five

Matt

For such a tiny little kid, Phoebe snored louder than a tractor. I squinted at my alarm clock, knowing exactly what or rather who, the tiny ball of warmth plastered against my back was. It was a little after one in the morning and I laid perfectly still, wondering what I should do.

After texting me that Maggie would give her a ride home, Natalia had returned to the house around seven. She'd immediately taken Phoebe upstairs to have a bath and I was a little weirded out by how happy it made me when Phoebe demanded I come upstairs and read her a bedtime story.

I'd read the story and then left them to finish their bedtime ritual alone. When after a half hour, Natalia still hadn't returned, I'd peeked into their room to find her fast asleep in the bed next to Phoebe. I'd shut the light off and returned downstairs, more than a little disappointed that I couldn't spend time with Natalia.

Phoebe made a loud snort behind me and I winced when she jabbed her elbow into my kidneys and then kicked me in the upper thigh. Christ, how did Natalia sleep with Phoebe in the bed with her?

She probably doesn't. She looked exhausted when she came home.

Yeah, she did, and while I knew that what she needed most was sleep, I was still disappointed that I'd spent the evening watching ESPN alone.

No, you're disappointed that you didn't get to fuck her. Admit it, dude. If she'd made any sort of move on you last night, you would have stopped pushing her away and fucked her.

I wanted to deny it but couldn't. I'd spent all day thinking about Natalia and that kiss in the truck. The way she tasted, her reaction to my kisses… if I didn't get her in my damn bed, I'd go crazy.

"Phoebe?" Natalia's soft voice made me tense in surprise. "Sweetpea, where are you?"

Before I could call out to her, I heard her walk into my bedroom. It was a clear night and I'd forgotten to pull the blinds before I went to bed. Moonlight was streaming in through the window and I heard Natalia make a little groan.

"Shit. Oh, sweetpea, what are you doing in here?"

She crept toward the bed and the mattress dipped when she sat down. Fuck me, Natalia was in my bed.

Keep it in your pants, dude. It's not like anything is going to happen.

Cool air drifted over my naked chest as Natalia carefully eased the quilt and sheet down.

Her hand slipped between my back and Phoebe and I tried not to shiver from her touch. The silence was suddenly broken by a loud 'braaap' that cut through the air.

"Um… that was not me," I said.

Natalia made a soft squeak of surprise and I turned over. "You know your kid looks sweet and innocent, but she farts like a damn sailor. That was… oh, oh my God."

I covered my nose as the smell hit me and waved the air in front of me. "Christ, that stinks."

I sat up, hoping the air would be a bit fresher at a higher elevation. Phoebe rolled to her back and her eyelids blinked open. She stared blearily at me before lifting her leg and farting again.

My eyes watered at the stench and I plugged my nose. "Oh my God, Phoebe, what did you eat?"

"Psghetti," she mumbled before patting the bed beside her. "Lie down, Mattie."

"Sweetpea, sit up," Natalia said.

Phoebe shook her head. "No. I farted, Mama."

"Yes, I know," Natalia said. "Do you need to use the bathroom?"

"Nope. I just fart." Phoebe lifted her leg a second time and let another one rip before giggling. "Smelly."

"I am so sorry," Natalia said as Phoebe rolled to her side and rested her head on my thigh. I was wearing sleep pants and her little hand stroked the material as she yawned. "Lie down, Mattie."

"Time to go back to our bed," Natalia said.

She reached for Phoebe and we both jerked in surprise when Phoebe made an ear-splitting scream and began to cry. "No, Mama! No! No! No!"

"Phoebe, stop," Natalia said.

"I stay with Mattie!" Phoebe screamed. Her little hands clenched around my pants when Natalia tried to pick her up and she kicked her feet and screamed again.

"Phoebe, enough," Natalia repeated.

"I wanna sleep with Mattie!" Phoebe shrieked.

I patted her back as she pointed her tear-stained face toward mine. "Please, Mattie. I stay with you, otay?"

"Okay," I said. "It's okay, sweetie. You can stay here."

She continued to cry, and I gave Natalia a helpless look. "Why is she so upset?"

Natalia looked like she was going to cry as well. "I don't know, she-she's never done this before or acted this way. Do you mind if I, um…"?

She pointed at my bed and I shook my head. She laid down beside Phoebe and rubbed her tiny back as she continued to cry. "It's okay, Pheebs. Tell Mama what's wrong."

"I wanna stay in Mattie's bed," Phoebe sobbed. "Please, Mama."

I laid down beside her and stroked her hair. "Shh, Phoebe, don't cry."

She wiggled up until she could rest her head on my ribcage. "Stay with you, otay?"

"Your mama will be lonely," I said. "You don't want her to be lonely in her bed, do you?"

Phoebe sat up and shook her head. "No. Mama can stay too."

Hell, yes.

Natalia rubbed her back. "No, sweetpea. Both of us are going back to our own bed. It's late and -"

"We not leaving," Phoebe said before grabbing the covers and pulling them up. She laid on her side and clung to my arm. "Go to sleep, Mama. Night, Mattie."

"Uh... good night, Phoebe."

I studied Nat in the moonlight. Despite how early she'd gone to bed, she looked tired and worn out.

"It's fine," I said. "It's a big bed. Just lie down and get some sleep, okay?"

"Letting her have her own way isn't good parenting," Natalia replied.

"Just for tonight. We're all tired, right? So, let's get some sleep and we'll figure out in the morning why she's being so..."

"Clingy to you?" Natalia said.

I nodded and Natalia covered her mouth as she yawned. "Yeah, okay. If you're sure you don't mind?"

"I don't." I reached down and patted Phoebe's back. "No more farting, kiddo."

Phoebe giggled. "I stinky."

"You sure are," I said.

"You positive you don't need to use the bathroom, honey?" Natalia said.

"I sure. Night, Mama."

"Night, sweetpea." Natalia laid down and gave me a tentative smile before closing her eyes.

I stared up at the ceiling, listening to both Natalia and Phoebe's breathing slow and deepen. Fifteen minutes later when Phoebe farted in her sleep before kicking me hard in the ribs, I covered my nose against the smell and realized that I'd never been happier.

రిల్ ఆ

"Wake up, Mattie."

I opened my eyes and squinted at Phoebe. She was standing next to the bed and she grinned at me. "I went pee in the toilet."

"Good job," I said before glancing at the clock. It was after eight and I had a moment of panic before I remembered Natalia was off today.

"Are you hungry?" I asked.

She nodded and checked behind me. Natalia was a quilt-covered lump on the far edge of the bed, and I sat up and swung my legs over the side of the bed. "C'mon, sweetheart, your mama can sleep in while I make you breakfast. Okay?"

"Otay," she said.

She took my hand and we walked out of the bedroom and down the stairs. I boosted her onto a kitchen chair and gave her a glass of juice. "Stay there for a second while I brush my teeth, okay?"

She nodded and pointed to my iPad. "Play *Peppa Pig*."

"Um, hold on." I didn't have a clue what or who *Peppa Pig* was, but I found a video quickly enough on YouTube. I left her sitting at the table watching the video and drinking her juice and headed back upstairs to my room.

I ignored my urge to climb back in beside the still sleeping Natalia – fuck, did it feel good to see her in my bed – and used the washroom and brushed my teeth before returning downstairs.

"What do you want to eat for breakfast, Pheebs?" I asked.

"Waffles."

"Um, how about pancakes?" I said.

"Otay." She didn't look up from the video as I grabbed the pancake mix from the cupboard. An hour later, pancakes had been eaten with enthusiasm and Phoebe was a sticky mess.

"How did you get syrup in your hair?" I asked as I cleaned her hands and face with the washcloth. I had brought her to the guest bathroom and set her on the vanity, and she giggled and kicked her feet.

"I don't know. Hey, Mattie?"

"Yeah?" I dabbed at her hair, trying unsuccessfully to get the syrup out.

"I love you. Do you love me?"

I froze, the washcloth pressed against her hair. "Um…"

"I love Mattie," she sang under her breath before hugging me.

I patted her back before setting the washcloth next to the sink. "I think you're gonna need a bath to get the syrup out of your hair, so we'll wait until your mama wakes up."

"Let's play dolls!" Phoebe tried to wiggle off the vanity and I grabbed her before she fell off.

"You can't jump off of there, sweetheart," I said as I put her down. "You're too little."

She grabbed my hand. "C'mon, Mattie."

I followed her to the guest room, sitting on the bed beside her when she grabbed three Barbies from her backpack and climbed onto the bed.

"Here," she said. "You be daddy doll."

I took the Ken doll as Phoebe picked up the Barbie. "This is the mama doll. Her name is Nat."

"What's the daddy doll's name?" I asked.

She shrugged. "I dunno."

I pointed to the third doll lying in her lap. "Is that Phoebe?"

She grinned and grabbed the doll by the hair, swinging it over her head in a big circle. "Yep! Pheebs Bo Beebs!"

I laughed. "Who calls you Pheebs Bo Beebs?"

"Nana does."

"That's cute," I said.

"I know I cute," she replied.

I laughed and she grinned at me. "Pheebs is the cutest and the smartest, that what Mama says."

"She's right," I said. "You're very smart."

"I know." She held the Phoebe doll and the Nat doll together and made them kiss. "Mama loves Phoebe."

"She sure does," I said.

She walked the Phoebe doll across the bed toward the Ken doll. "Daddy love Phoebe?"

"Yes," I said immediately even though I had no idea if Evan even had anything to do with Phoebe. She didn't act like he did, but she was only three. I glanced over my shoulder at the open doorway before saying, "Phoebe, do you see your daddy sometimes?"

She shook her head. "Nope. Mama says he lives far away."

"Phoebe?" Natalia came limping into the bedroom, dressed in her t-shirt and sleep shorts with her hair sticking up and pillow creases on her face.

God, she was hot even when she first woke up.

My gaze dropped to her tits. It was cool in the house and I could see the outline of her nipples against the soft cotton. I looked away in a hurry as Natalia sank onto the bed next to Phoebe. "Honey, you wake Mama up when you wake up. Remember?"

She gave me an apologetic look. "Did she wake you up?"

"It's fine," I said. "We had pancakes and watched some weird cartoon pig and then played. Right, Pheebs?"

"Yep," she said. She pointed at the Ken doll I still held. "That's daddy doll. His name is Mattie."

"Oh my God," Natalia breathed quietly.

Weirdly, I could feel my cheeks turning red as Natalia snatched the doll from me. "I'm sorry," she said. "Uh, Phoebe, it's bath time now, okay?"

"I want Matt to have a bath with me," Phoebe said.

"Nope." Natalia scooped her up and kissed her cheek. "You're so sticky, you're having bath time alone. The water will be more syrup than bath water."

Phoebe giggled and I cleared my throat. "Sorry. I didn't realize that she wasn't great with, uh, utensils."

Nat smiled at me and warmth infused my body. "No, no, it's fine. I didn't mean for it to come across like that. I so appreciate your help with her. Really. I haven't slept in like that in ages and it was a real treat. So, thank you."

"You're welcome," I said.

"Do you mind if we use your tub in the master bathroom again?" She asked as she stood and braced Phoebe on her hip.

"No, go ahead."

"Are you, uh, working today?" She asked.

I shook my head. "I don't go back until Saturday."

"Okay. Well, if you don't have plans tonight, I'd love to make you dinner to say thank you for everything you've done."

"I'd like that," I said.

"Good. Any food allergies?"

I shook my head. "Nope, I can eat anything and I'm not picky."

She smiled and moved slowly toward the door. "Perfect."

I frowned at the way she was limping. "Should you see a doctor? You limp a lot."

She shook her head. "No, my feet are a little sore from standing on them all day."

She kissed Phoebe's cheek and headed out of the bedroom. "C'mon syrup monster, let's get you cleaned up."

☙ ❧

"Again, again, again!" Phoebe screeched.

I threw her up in the air, grinning at her shriek of delight, before catching her.

After her bath, Phoebe had demanded I play with her again, and no amount of coaxing from Natalia to play with her instead would deter her. We'd played dolls for a while, then coloured, and after letting Phoebe climb all over me like a monkey, I was now throwing her up in the air repeatedly, much to her delight.

I knew that Natalia thought I was bored out of my skull, but I was actually having a great time. Phoebe was a sweet kid and she already had me wrapped around her baby finger and she knew it.

The doorbell rang as I tossed Phoebe up into the air again. Natalia had gone to the kitchen to get some water for us, and I caught Phoebe and settled her in the crook of my arm before heading toward the door.

"Who's that, Mattie?" She asked as slung her arm around my neck.

"I don't know, Pheebs." I opened the door and stared in surprise at Maggie. "Maggie? Uh, hi."

I didn't know Maggie all that well and had only seen her a couple of times, but Phoebe made another shriek of delight and held her arms out toward the slender brunette.

"Maggie!"

Maggie took her out of my arms and kissed her soft cheek before holding her close. "Hi, Pheebs. How's my girl doing?"

"I good," Phoebe said. "Where's Wy-hat?"

Maggie laughed. "Wyatt's at home."

"Maggie?" Natalia stuck her head into the hallway from the kitchen. "What are you doing here?"

"I came to see if Miss Pheeby-pie wanted to have a sleepover at her Aunt Maggie and Uncle Wyatt's house today."

"Yes!" Phoebe shouted. "I wanna sleep at Maggie's house, Mama!"

I glanced back at Natalia. Her face was flushed,

and she was avoiding my gaze as she gave Maggie a strained smile. "Can we talk in the kitchen for a minute, please, *Magnolia*?"

Maggie's grin widened. "Sure, *Natalia*."

She handed off Phoebe to me before smiling cheerfully at me. "We'll only be a second."

I stood in the hallway, holding Phoebe and not sure what the hell was going on as Maggie ducked into the kitchen.

"Hey, Mattie?"

"Yeah?" I glanced at Phoebe.

"I gotta pee."

"Okay. Do you need help?"

"No, I a big girl. I do it."

"All right. But call for me if you need help though, okay?" I set her down and she scampered down the hallway and disappeared into the half bath just beyond the kitchen. I waited for about half a damn second before I inched closer to the kitchen doorway and eavesdropped shamelessly.

"Maggie, what the hell are you doing?" Natalia's voice was low.

"Well, I was thinking about our conversation last night and I knew that you wouldn't do what I suggested, so I decided to help you out."

"I don't need help," Natalia said.

"No? So, you did what I suggested and banged Matt's brains out after Pheebs went to bed last night?"

"Keep your voice down," Natalia said, "and no, I didn't. I was worried Phoebe would wake up and hear us. Hell, she did wake up. I found her in Matt's bed at one this morning, and then she freaked out and made this huge scene about going back to her own bed. I was so tired, I gave in and the three of us slept in his bed."

"Okay, well, that's not exactly what I meant by joining Matt in his bed, but it's a start," Maggie said. "Girl, look, you need to get laid, but I totally get that you're a mom first, so I'm gonna make this easy on you. I'll take Phoebe home with me and keep her until you're finished work tomorrow night. In fact, I'll keep her until you're finished work on Saturday night. That way you won't have to pay that college kid to look after her like you usually do on the weekends. I'm saving you money and getting you laid. I'm like the best friend ever, right?"

"I can't ask you to take her during the week like this. You have to work."

"Oh please, I have two clients and neither of you are gonna need me today or tomorrow. Let me do this for you, Nat. You deserve a break. And I can't think of a better way for you to spend your break then in Matt's bed and under that smoking hot body of his. Forget about your troubles for a day and a half and give yourself a little treat in the form of – fingers crossed this is true – Matt's giant dick. All right?"

Say yes. Please say yes. My hands were tight fists, and my heart was beating so loud I could hardly hear Nat and Maggie.

"I've never been away from Phoebe for that long," Nat said.

"Well, if she's missing you too much, then I'll bring her back to you. Easy peasy. Plus, Wyatt and

I can bring her to the diner for dinner on Friday night and Saturday night so you can see each other. C'mon, Nat. You need this. It doesn't make you a bad mom to spend two days away from your kid."

There were a few moments of silence. The toilet flushed and I heard Phoebe singing to herself as she turned on the water in the sink.

"What if he rejects me again?" Natalia's voice was barely above a whisper.

I won't. Fuck, I promise I won't.

I wanted to run into the kitchen like an overeager teenager and shout the words at her.

"He won't," Maggie said firmly. "I worked at the diner, remember? I saw how he was when he came in to the diner. Matt wants you, honey."

I said a silent hallelujah and pledged right then and there to somehow, someday pay Maggie back for being my wingman.

"Mattie? Whatcha' doin'?" Phoebe had come out of the bathroom and my face burning with guilt, I backed up a step or two from the doorway.

I cleared my throat and walked toward her, saying loudly, "Just coming to check on you. Did you wash your hands?"

"Yes." Phoebe showed me her wet hands. "I couldn't reach the towel though."

"Phoebe?" Natalia came out of the kitchen and without looking at me, said, "Here, let's dry your hands off and then we'll pack up some clothes and toys for you to take to Maggie's house, okay?"

Relief swept through me and I leaned against the wall as Phoebe cheered excitedly. "Yay, I gonna ride in the police car!"

Maggie joined us in the hallway and laughed. "Sure, Pheebs. I'll ask Wyatt to take us for a ride in the police car."

"With the lights on," Phoebe demanded as Maggie followed her and Natalia down the hallway.

"Lights *and* siren," Maggie said with another soft laugh.

Chapter Six

Natalia

"Okay, Nat, you can do this." I smoothed down my hair and checked my makeup one last time in the bathroom mirror.

After Maggie left with Phoebe, I'd excused myself and went upstairs to take a long, hot shower. I had to admit that it was nice to shower without hurrying or without having Phoebe popping her head into the bathroom every two minutes.

I'd shaved my legs and armpits and applied lotion to my entire body before searching through the limited clothes I'd brought. I hadn't brought anything sexy to wear, but at least I'd brought my makeup with me. I'd dressed in my decidedly non-sexy jeans and t-shirt and did my hair and makeup.

I gave myself a final look in the mirror, sucking in my tummy a bit before smoothing my shirt. I thought I looked good, good enough to at least not have Matt reject me immediately when I asked him for a couple of days of no-strings-attached sex.

He wants you, Nat. You know he's not going to reject you. But are you sure this is what you want? You haven't slept with anyone else but Evan and is the town's playboy the guy you want to get back in the saddle with?

Yes, I decided, it was. Matt was perfect for what I wanted right now —a fun time with no commitment required. I'd been in a committed relationship with Evan and it hadn't stopped him from cheating on me. At least with Matt, I knew exactly where I stood. We would be just two people taking what we needed from each other without any emotions involved.

It was perfect.

I headed downstairs and poked my head into the kitchen. Matt wasn't in the kitchen and I moved toward the living room. My plan was to borrow his car to get some groceries for dinner and then, over dinner, I'd bring up the suggestion that maybe we could scratch each other's itch in a totally casual, just two people having a good time, way over the next couple of evenings.

The living room was empty, and I hesitated before climbing the stairs to Matt's bedroom. The door was partially open, and I knocked lightly before stepping into the room.

"Matt, are you…"

My voice died out into a whispery little moan when the bathroom door swung open and Matt stepped into the bedroom. He was drying his hair with a towel and he was naked.

No, not naked. But close enough.

A second towel was draped so low around his

hips that I could see his delectable v-line, the dark line of hair that arrowed down from his navel, and the small droplets of water that were trickling down his skin into the edge of the towel.

I studied his abdomen and chest with shameless eagerness. I drank in the granite-like muscles of his stomach, the light layer of hair that covered his upper chest, and the bulge of his biceps like I had never seen a man before in my life.

I hadn't... at least not like Matt. His body was utter perfection.

"Natalia?"

I lifted my gaze to Matt's face. "Your body is perfect. I was about to ask you if you wanted to have casual sex with me, no commitment required, but your body is perfect and mine is... not, and there's no way I'm getting naked around you, so, um, bye now."

My cheeks crimson, I turned for the door, internally screaming at the words that had come out of my mouth. I was an idiot.

"Nat, wait."

Matt had never called me by my nickname before and the foreignness of it made me stop in my tracks. My skin prickled with awareness when Matt moved directly behind me.

"Don't go," he said.

"I have to. Your body is too perfect. You don't have an ounce of body fat on your entire body, and I've got stretch marks and flabby parts and dimpled thighs."

Fuck, why couldn't I stop talking?

Matt made a low chuckle that sent shivers up

and down my spine. "It's not perfect."

"It is," I insisted.

"Turn around, Nat," he said.

I didn't want to. If I turned around, I'd be faced with his perfect hard body that I would never get a chance to touch or taste and it was depressing the hell out of me.

"Nat," he said in that deep, sexy-as-hell voice of his.

I sighed and turned, keeping my gaze trained on his face. He was grinning at me and I was certain that I looked like a damn tomato at this point.

"It's not perfect. Look, I have a scar here." He raised his arm and I stared at the thin line that ran along the underside of his bicep. "Another one right here."

He pointed to his ribs and despite my vow to not look any lower than his damn collarbone, I dropped my gaze. "I don't see a scar." My voice was embarrassingly high and breathy.

"It's right here." His warm hand took mine and he pressed my fingers against his ribs.

I sucked in a harsh breath as he skimmed my fingers back and forth over the small raised bump.

"Feel it?" His voice had gone a few octaves lower.

I wet my lips, my throat as dry as dust. "Y-yes."

"See, not perfect," he said.

"Matt, I… oh God."

I'd made the fatal error of glancing down and the way Matt's towel was tenting made my pussy wet in immediate response.

Matt leaned a little closer. He smelled so good, a combination of the fresh clean scent of his body wash and his own unique smell. I watched another trickle of water slide down his flat stomach, my urge to drop to my knees and lick it from his warm skin almost too powerful to resist.

"You do this to me, Nat," he said. "With one touch, you make me as hard as a fucking rock."

"I've had a kid," I said. "My body is -"

"Your body is perfect." Matt's arm slid around my waist and when he pulled me up against him, I couldn't resist rubbing against his erection. He groaned and cupped my ass, squeezing it with one hand while his other hand traced my collarbone. "You're beautiful and sexy and I want you very much, Natalia."

"I want you too," I whispered.

"Good." His mouth hovered over mine and with a low moan, I pressed my lips against his. His arm tightened around me, nearly crushing me against him as we explored each other's mouths with increasing urgency.

I stood on my tiptoes and pressed my breasts against his chest as he squeezed and kneaded my ass.

He kissed a blazing path down my throat, and I shuddered all over as I clung to him. When his hands tugged at the hem of my shirt, I raised my arms so he could pull it off. He dropped my shirt on the floor and stared appreciatively at my tits before tracing one big finger along the edge of my bra.

"Beautiful," he said.

"A push-up bra does wonders," I replied.

He gave me a scowl and I squeaked in surprise when he reached around behind me and unclipped my bra with a flick of his wrist. Before I could stop him, he had my bra off and on the floor with my shirt.

His big hands cupped my breasts and he rubbed his thumbs over my nipples. They beaded into hard points and I gasped when he gave them a gentle tug with his forefinger and thumb.

"Still beautiful," he said with a small grin.

"Thank you, I ... oh my god!"

Matt had picked me up and I clung to his shoulders as he carried me to the bed and dropped me on it. He stood beside the bed and unceremoniously tugged his towel off.

"Sweet mother of..." I licked my lips as I stared at his thick cock. There was a bead of precum at the slit and I was beyond tempted to sit up and lick it away. Before I could, Matt was leaning over me and unbuttoning my jeans.

"Hips up."

I lifted my hips and he pulled my jeans down, dragging my panties with them. Within seconds I was completely naked, and he was studying me with his hot gaze. I folded my arms across my belly, wishing I'd had the forethought to plan my seduction later when I could hide my imperfections with darkness and mood lighting.

"Don't do that, Nat." Matt stretched out beside me, his glorious cock rubbing against my thigh, and pulled my arms away from my stomach. "Everything about you is beautiful."

He bent and kissed me again, his tongue seeking mine out with gentle insistence. I was already addicted to Matt's kisses. The way he coaxed and teased was so different from what I expected from him.

His hand cupped my breast again and I arched into his touch. When he sucked on my nipple, I cried out and clutched at his head. How long had it been since I'd had someone's naked body against mine? Felt the warm touch of a rough hand? Too damn long.

Matt scattered kisses all across my upper body. He licked a slow path around each of my nipples, kissed and nipped the soft curve of my breasts and nuzzled the space between them.

I tensed when he moved down to my stomach, my hands automatically moving to hide and conceal. He took my wrists and held my hands at my side before kissing one of my stretch marks.

"You are gorgeous. Every mark, every freckle," his lips pressed against the freckle to the right of my navel, "I can't get enough of you, sweetheart."

I moaned loudly when he traced a path from my navel to the small patch of blonde hair just above my pussy. He kissed the curls before releasing my wrist and sliding his hand between my thighs. He pressed on my inner thigh until I spread them, and he smiled up at me.

"I've dreamed about eating your pussy for months, Nat."

"Months?" I gave him a startled look. "What do you... oh...oh fuck."

His tongue licked me from my wet hole to the

top of my suddenly throbbing clit, and I grabbed his head and ground my pussy against his mouth with shameless need.

He lifted his head, breaking my grip easily and smiled at me. "Did that feel good, sweetheart?"

"Yes," I moaned. "Please, Matt, don't stop."

"How long has it been since you've had this sweet pussy eaten?"

"A really long time," I gasped out. "Stop talking and keep licking."

His warm breath caressed me as he laughed and sent goosebumps popping up on my skin. He stroked my inner thigh with one big hand as I pulled hard on his hair, trying to guide his mouth back to my aching clit.

"You're going to cum on my mouth and then on my cock," he said.

"Yeah," I replied. "Yeah, that's a really good idea. Please, Matt, it's been so long."

He laughed and I cried out with pure need when he buried his face into my pussy and went to work. He used his mouth and tongue to work me into a frenzy, and my self-consciousness disappeared entirely under a crushing wave of lust.

When he slid one thick finger deep into my pussy and sucked on my clit, I was done. I screamed hoarsely, my body lurching upwards as my climax rushed through me. Lights exploded behind my tightly closed eyelids and I bucked and writhed against Matt's mouth as he continued to lick and suck.

I collapsed against the bed, the blood roaring past my eardrums and my heartbeat kicked up to a level I hadn't experienced since... well, never.

"I think I'm having a damn heart attack," I gasped out as Matt slid up to the top of the bed.

He chuckled and pressed a kiss against my shoulder as he cupped my breast. "Take a deep breath, sweetheart."

"Fuck, that was... oh my god." I stared blankly at him as I heaved air in and out of my lungs. "Where did you learn to do that?"

He grinned and pressed another kiss against my shoulder. "Are you ready to cum on my cock?"

"I - honestly, I don't know if I can," I said. "That was..." I made a weak little explosion motion with my hands as he sat up and grabbed a condom from the nightstand.

"I think you can," he said.

As he opened the condom, I reached out and traced my fingers along the thick length of his dick. He groaned, his body doing this all-over shuddering twitch that made me grin.

"Shit," he muttered.

"What?" I curled my fingers around his shaft and stroked him firmly.

"Ripped the condom." He tossed it carelessly on the floor and reached for another, hissing air out between his teeth when I rubbed my thumb over the head of his dick. "Fuck, Nat, stop distracting me."

"Is this distracting?" I said innocently as I squeezed and rubbed that delicious steel wrapped in velvet soft skin.

He groaned, his hips arching, before he ripped open the condom packaging with his teeth. His hand tugged mine away and I pouted at him. "No fair."

"Unless you want me cumming all over your hand, you'll give me a minute," he said.

I grinned, secretly delighted by his lack of control. "All right, I'll play nice."

I relaxed on my back, watching as he rolled the condom over his cock before turning toward me. "You good with me on top for our first time?"

I nodded and gave him a lazy smile before opening my legs. "Climb on, Doc."

He laughed and knelt between my legs. "I'm not a doctor."

"Close enough. Pretty sure you could give me mouth-to-mouth if I needed it."

He pressed his dick against my clit and rubbed lightly. I moaned and wiggled beneath him. "Too sensitive."

He slid the head down to my entrance and hovered there. "Sorry, sweetheart."

When he didn't move, I reached out and traced my hand over his flat stomach. "What are you waiting for?"

His face had turned serious and I stared up at him as he said, "Are you sure, Nat? Sure, this is what you want?"

"Yes," I said without hesitating. "This is exactly what I want, Mattie. Please."

He studied my face and then, with a gentleness and tenderness I wasn't expecting, slowly slid into me. He took his time, his gaze never leaving my face, as he thrust back and forth lightly. He was big and it'd been a long time for me, and I was both surprised and appreciated the patience and self-control he showed.

"Okay?" He asked when he was fully-sheathed.

I touched his face, feeling weirdly emotional over how sweet he was being, and nodded. "Yes, it feels so good, Mattie."

He moaned and leaned down to kiss me. "I love hearing my name on your lips, Nat."

I returned his kiss, tracing his lower lip with the tip of my tongue before sliding my arms around his waist. "Mattie, I want you."

He groaned again and braced himself on his hands above me. "I want you too, Nat."

He moved with slow, deep strokes. I rocked my hips against him, and we found our rhythm remarkably fast, our bodies moving together like this was our hundredth time together, rather than our first.

Mattie did this little rolling motion with his hips on every downward stroke that sent pleasure spiraling through my belly. When I reached between us and rubbed delicately at my clit, he moved a little faster.

"Do you mind?" I panted. "I can't always cum from sex alone."

"Sweetheart, you do whatever you want. Rub your sweet clit, play with your nipples, whatever it takes to make you cum on my cock," Matt said.

I hid my surprise from him. I'd assumed that Matt would be the type of guy who insisted that his woman came only from his touch or from fucking. Finding out he wasn't, only made me hotter for him.

"You're so sweet," I moaned.

He moved faster, the bed beginning to squeak

with the rhythm of our bodies.

"Rub your clit, sweetheart. Show me how you look when you're cumming on my cock."

I moaned again and rubbed my clit harder, pinching and tugging at it as Matt drove in and out of me with a hard and fast rhythm that made my toes curl into the bed. I held tight to his narrow waist with one hand and rubbed hard at my clit with the other.

When my orgasm rushed through me, he made a hoarse shout and drove in deep, the cords in his neck standing out as my pussy squeezed around him. He pumped in and out, his big body shuddering as he joined me in bliss.

He rolled off of me, lying on his back and staring blankly at the ceiling. I sat up and took the condom off of him, tying the end and tossing it into the trash can on the other side of the nightstand, before curling up next to him.

He put his arm around me and kissed my forehead as I smiled up at him. "You good?"

"So goddamn good," he said. "That was amazing, Nat."

"For me too," I said. "Thank you, Mattie."

He pulled me a little closer and kissed my forehead. "Sweetheart, it's me who should be thanking you. That was the best goddamn orgasm of my life."

ॐ ॐ

Matt

"Are you hungry?" I kissed Natalia's forehead, my hand tracing lazy circles on her hip as we laid in bed.

"A little, maybe." She tried to move back, and I held her closer, not willing or ready to let her go yet. "I should get dressed."

"Why?"

"My plan was to go to the grocery store to pick up some stuff to make you dinner tonight," she said.

I cupped her firm ass and gave it a squeeze. "I have a better idea. Why don't we stay right where we are, and I'll order in for dinner tonight?"

"I said I would cook you dinner."

"True. You could go for groceries, or you could stay in my bed and I'll eat your pussy again."

She laughed and pressed a kiss against my chest. "That's not even a choice. Screw going for groceries."

I made a dramatic sigh. "Thank God. If you had chosen grocery shopping over pussy eating, I would have had to become a monk out of shame."

She poked me in the side. "Oh please, you've had enough practice that it's practically impossible for you to be bad at sex."

Shame made me tense up. Until Nat, I'd never felt any regret over how many women I'd slept with, but knowing the way she felt about my sleeping around made me wish I had lived the life of a monk.

"Matt?" Natalia sat up and studied me carefully. "I'm so sorry, that was a hurtful thing to say."

"Nah, it's fine. I have a reputation for a reason." I smiled at her, but she shook her head.

"No, it isn't fine. I shouldn't have said it, and I feel terrible that I did. I'm judging you for the very thing that I'm now doing and that makes me a real toad."

"Hey, I deserve it. I do sleep around a lot." I wanted to tell her that I hadn't slept with anyone in over six months, wanted to somehow try and convince her that I was a changed man, but what good would that do? Natalia didn't want the new and improved Matt. She wanted the old Matt, the guy who didn't date or fall in love, the guy who was only looking for one thing.

As if she'd read my mind, Natalia said, "So, um, what we're doing here is a short-term thing, right?"

"Right."

"I mean, I know you're not into doing the relationship thing and I'm totally one hundred percent okay with that. I'm really, um, looking for…"

"Someone to scratch your itch?"

She flushed but nodded. "Yeah. I was thinking that maybe we could, uh, have some fun together until Phoebe comes back. Nothing serious, just two adults having fun together. You're good with that, right?"

"Sure. It's what I do best." Even I could hear the bitterness in my voice, and I plastered a smile on my face when Natalia studied me.

"Are you positive?" She chewed on her bottom lip. "I mean, it's okay if this was enough for you. I totally get it and I don't want to pressure you into doing something you don't want to do."

"Trust me," I said with an exaggerated wink. "I want to do you."

She giggled and the awkwardness passed.

"Good. Because I really want to do you multiple times."

"Speaking of," I rolled over and pinned her to the bed under my body, "I'm making it my personal mission to give you multiple orgasms. You good with that?"

"Hmm, let me think," she pressed her finger against her perfect lips and stared coyly at the ceiling, "I guess that'll work for me."

Chapter Seven

Natalia

I toweled off and studied my reflection in the steamy mirror. I looked different, I decided. Not so stressed and the dark circles under my eyes were gone. Of course, last night was the best night of sleep I'd had in months.

I wanted to pretend it was because of the child support payment – money was a huge stressor for me – but I knew it wasn't that. No, I was feeling so relaxed and slept so well because I'd spent the night in Matt Andrews bed.

I ran a comb through my wet hair and smoothed some lotion on. Sex with Matt was amazing, and I was already trying to plan how many more times I could bang him before I picked up Phoebe after my shift on Saturday.

I smiled a little and tightened the towel around my body before limping out of the master bath and back into Matt's bedroom. My feet were killing me and just the thought of standing on my feet for six hours later today was making them throb even more.

That's not the only thing that hurts.

I rubbed my inner thighs gingerly, my steps faltering when I realized the bed was empty. Before I could look for him, I heard the toilet flush in the guest bathroom down the hall. Matt wandered back into the bedroom, completely naked and with his hair sticking straight up.

He gave me a sleepy grin before climbing back into the bed and pulling the covers up. "Morning."

"Morning. Sorry, I should have used the guest bathroom to shower."

He shook his head. "It's fine. Use my shower anytime you like. It has better water pressure than the guest one anyway."

I smiled and limped toward the bed. "Compared to the crappy shower in the trailer, both of your showers are amazing. It's like trying to shower in a light mist at my place."

He sat up, frowning a little. "You're limping again. You need to go to the doctor."

I sat down on the other side of the bed, resting my back against the headboard and stretching my legs out in front of me. I tugged at the hem of my towel, tempted to climb on top of Matt and ride him to another body-shuddering orgasm. I reined in my libido and said, "It's fine. It's from standing on them all day in cheap shoes."

I made a little squeak of surprise when he scooched down the bed and grabbed my right foot.

"Matt, what are you...oh...oh God, oh...my...God."

I bit my bottom lip, my back arching as Matt rubbed my heel.

"Mmm, oh my God, Matt, that feels so good. You have no idea…"

He grinned at me and continued to rub my foot. "Tell me if it hurts."

"It hurts but in a good way," I said before moaning again. I leaned my head against the headboard and closed my eyes. Little moans and grunts of pleasure were spilling from my lips and I waved my left foot at him. "Do this one too."

He laughed and switched to my left foot, kneading and massaging with a gentle but firm touch to the bottom of my foot.

"Oh God," I moaned again, arching my back when he rubbed a particularly sensitive spot. "Yes, right there. Right there."

He rubbed and massaged both of my feet for the next ten minutes as I moaned and groaned and made happy little sounds of pleasure. I cracked open one eye when Matt cleared his throat and squeezed one foot gently.

"In case you're wondering," he said. "I am starting to realize that I need to up my game when it comes to fucking you. You moan louder and more often during a foot rub then during sex."

"Don't take it… oh God, yes, that's the spot… personally. I mean, sex with you is incredible, but this… this is… transcendent," I said.

He laughed and pressed a kiss against the bottom of my foot. "Is that better?"

"One thousand percent better. Thank you, Matt."

"You're welcome, honey. Anytime you need a foot rub, just ask."

I grinned at him as he stretched out on the bed next to me. "You're gonna regret…"

My mouth went dry and my mind went blank. Matt's dick was completely erect, and I stared hungrily at it as he reached down and pumped himself slowly. "Never thought giving a woman a foot rub would be such a turn-on."

I gave him a lazy smile, not protesting when he reached out and tugged on my towel. It slipped down to my waist and he stared at my tits, his hand stroking faster. I cupped my breasts, teasing my nipples with my fingers as he made a low groan.

"You're so beautiful, Nat," he said in a low voice.

"Thank you." I licked my lips, smiling when he studied my mouth, his eyes darkening with need.

I tugged the towel out from under me and dropped it over the side of the bed before turning and lying on my side with my head near his crotch. "Turn on your side, Matt."

He turned to face me, groaning under his breath when I propped my head up on my hand and wrapped my other hand around the base of his dick. I leaned forward and licked the head of his dick.

His entire body shuddered, and his big hand grasped my thigh. "Suck, honey."

I slid my mouth down over his dick, loving the taste of his salty precum as I sucked and licked his cock. His hips thrust forward, forcing more of his dick into my mouth. I hummed around him, my lips vibrating against his hard, hot flesh and he made another harsh groan.

He bent his head and kissed the top of my pussy before pushing up my top leg. I cried out around his thick cock when his soft tongue licked down my slit and probed at my wet hole.

His hand reached down and squeezed my breast before he pinched my nipple between his forefinger and thumb. My back arched and his warm breath tickled my pussy lips when he said, "Keep sucking, Nat."

I made a muffled sound of agreement and sucked on his cock as he licked and kissed my pussy. When his tongue brushed against my clit, I moaned again and pumped the base of his dick as I hollowed my cheeks and sucked hard.

His answering moan was muffled when he buried his face between my thighs and licked my clit repeatedly. More precum filled my mouth and I swallowed it eagerly before tracing the head of his cock with the tip of my tongue.

Matt sucked on my clit and I cried out before sucking hard and fast. I was on the verge of cumming and I thrust my mouth down over Matt's cock until the head hit the back of my throat.

He made a roar of pleasure and his cum shot down my throat just as my own orgasm washed over me. I ground my pussy against his face as the pleasure enveloped me in a cloud of pure ecstasy. I swallowed and swallowed again, loving the taste of Matt's cum. I released him, falling onto my back and licking the stray drops of cum from my lips as Matt collapsed on his back as well.

"Oh my God," he said. "That was…"

"Fast and furious and fucking fantastic," I mumbled.

He laughed and tugged on my ankle. "Come up here."

"Can't. Too weak…"

He tugged on my ankle again and I grumbled my displeasure but wiggled around on the bed until I was lying next to him with my head on his chest. He pulled the sheet and the quilt up around us and kissed my forehead. "Normally I'd apologize for cumming so fast, but…"

"It was perfect," I said.

"It really was. Thank you."

I giggled and slung my arm around his waist. "No, no, thank you… a foot rub and an orgasm? This is the best day of my life."

His low chuckle rumbled out of his chest and I gave his warm skin a kiss. "Don't judge my blow job skills by that one, okay? I was extremely distracted by your tongue in my pussy. I promise the next time I suck your dick, I'll be more… attentive."

He grinned and gave me a quick squeeze. "While I'm very happy to hear the words "next time I suck your dick", you really have nothing to worry about. It was incredible."

"Was it incredible because I swallowed?" I gave him a teasing grin. "I hear that nice girls always swallow."

"That might have bumped you from amazing to incredible," he replied with a cute grin. The grin faded a little and he cleared his throat. "I'm clean. I don't want you worrying or thinking that… I can show you my records."

I shook my head. "I trust you. I'm clean too but I'm not on the pill so condoms are a necessity. One accidental pregnancy is enough for me, thanks."

I rested my head on his chest again as Matt rubbed my back in slow circles. "So, Phoebe wasn't planned?"

"Nope. Evan didn't want me on the pill, he said it would make me fat and moody, so we used condoms."

"Seriously?"

"It's weird, right?" I sat up and wrapped the sheet around my body as Matt sat up as well. He grabbed a bottle of water from the nightstand and opened it before handing it to me. "Thanks." I drank and handed it back.

"Really weird." He took a few swallows of water. "No guy I know would rather use condoms just because his girlfriend might get moody from the pill."

"It was more the weight gain I think," I said. "Evan has a real thing about overweight people. They gross him out."

I stared at the water bottle in Matt's hand. "Joke was on him though. The condom broke and I got pregnant and gained weight."

"You're supposed to gain weight when you're pregnant," Matt said with a scowl.

"Oh, I know. I gained a normal amount during my pregnancy, but Evan wouldn't go near me as soon as I started showing. Then, after Phoebe was born, he insisted I lose the baby weight as quickly as possible. I'm lucky in that I have a pretty good metabolism, and I've always eaten healthy. I lost the extra weight fairly easily, but," I glanced down at my sheet-covered tummy, "the stretch marks were still there, and my flat stomach wasn't coming back."

"You're beautiful," Matt said, "exactly as you are."

"Thank you." I reached out and squeezed his hand. "That's a very nice thing to say."

"I mean it," he said. "Can I ask what happened between you and Evan?"

I gave him a wry look. "I'm sure you've heard."

"I've heard rumours."

"Well, the rumours are true. When Phoebe was three months old, I came home from our Mommy and Me group to find Evan in bed with one of the other accountants at his firm."

"Asshole," Matt said.

"Total asshole. And such a walking cliché. Do you know he actually listed off a bunch of reasons why it was my fault he cheated? I was too busy with Phoebe, I didn't take care of myself anymore, I didn't care about his needs, I made it all about Phoebe…"

I laughed a bit bitterly. "It's like he printed off a list off the internet of reasons why men cheat and just rattled them off."

"I'm sorry, you didn't deserve that."

"No, I didn't, but hey, at least I realized what a scumbag he was before marrying him, right?"

Matt nodded and I grabbed the water from him

and took another long drink. "Anyway, I packed up Phoebe and all of our clothes and personal stuff and came back home with my tail tucked between my legs. My parents wanted me to move to Iowa, they retired there shortly after I left with Evan, but I wanted to be here. I'd grown up here and I missed it, you know? Even though I knew it would be more difficult without my parents' support."

"I get it. It's why I never left. I love this town," Matt said.

"Me too," I said. "I wish I'd never left. I also wish that I hadn't let Evan talk me into not going to college right away."

"What did you want to take?"

"Early childhood education. I've always loved kids and I wanted to become a child development assistant, or something like that. But Evan wanted me to work to help support him while he got his accounting degree, and then I would go to college once he started working full time. But then I got pregnant with Phoebe. They have the course here at our local college, but it was too expensive. When Phoebe goes to school and I can save on childcare costs, I'll enroll then."

I smiled at him and he hesitated before saying, "Can I ask you something else?"

"Sure."

"Does Evan ever see Phoebe?"

"No, but not because I keep her from him. He never really had any interest in her, to be honest. When I moved back home, I told him I would be more than happy for him to visit her on the weekends. He said it was too far and he was too busy with work to drive here, so the first few months after I left, I drove to Welling every other Sunday so he could see her. But he started bailing on me, not showing up at the restaurant or he'd show up, hold Phoebe for five minutes and then leave. I couldn't really afford the gas money, so I stopped doing it."

"Does he pay child support?"

"He did until Phoebe was about a year old and then he left Welling and moved out of state and stopped paying."

"You're fucking kidding me." Matt's look of immediate outrage was actually kind of adorable.

"Nope. I tried a few times to get him to pay but he kept blowing me off and changing his number. I finally gave up. But then Maggie moved here, and she told me it was against the law for him to not pay and that she could force him to pay."

I handed the water back to him. "I hired Maggie – well, actually, she's doing it pro bono for me because she won't let me pay her even in instalments – and she went after Evan for child support."

"And?" Matt stared expectantly at me.

I grinned and drew my knees up, hugging them to my chest. "I got my first child support cheque on Wednesday. He still owes me back payments that Maggie said she'll get from him as well, but at least it's a start, right?"

"That's awesome," Matt said.

"It is. But, uh, the cheque is for next month which means I can't deposit it until Monday. Are you, um, okay with Phoebe and I staying with you until then? I'll pay the heating bill as soon as the cheque is deposited, and we'll be out of your hair by Monday night."

"That's fine," Matt said. "You and Phoebe can stay for as long as you like."

I smiled at him. "That's really nice of you, I know that Phoebe can be a bit much sometimes. Especially since she's taken such a liking to you."

"I like her. She's a good kid."

I nodded. "She really is. But that doesn't mean you want to play dolls with her or have her climbing you like a little monkey every time she sees you."

"I don't mind," he said. "Honestly."

I studied him for a few seconds before shaking my head. "You're not at all like I thought you would be, Matt Andrews."

He didn't reply and feeling vaguely like I'd insulted him, I said, "Thank you again for everything you've done."

"You're welcome."

I rubbed his hard thigh before wiggling my eyebrows at him. "Maybe I can repay you with a second, undistracted blow job…"

Instead of the enthusiastic 'yes' I was expecting, Matt's body stiffened, and he pushed my hand away from his thigh. "Are you sleeping with me as some sort of payment for helping you?"

"What? No, that isn't…"

"I know I don't have the greatest reputation in town, but I wouldn't expect a woman to fuck me just because I was trying to help her," he said.

"I know that," I said quickly. "Honestly, I do. I wasn't… I mean I slept with you because I want you."

"Do you?" He asked.

There was a weird thread of anxiety in his voice and I took his hand and squeezed it tight. "Yes. Very much. I've been attracted to you since the first day you strolled into that diner and started flirting with me."

He gave me a disbelieving look and I shrugged. "It's true. I know I turned you down when you asked me out and ignored your flirting, but trust me, it was very difficult to pretend to be immune to your charms."

He didn't reply and I squeezed his hand again. "I'm serious, Matt."

"Yeah, okay," he said.

There was a moment of awkward silence that I hurried to break. "So, I'm done work by nine tonight and Phoebe will still be with Maggie. Do you want to go to the late movie over at the Landmark Cinema? My treat."

"Oh, uh, I have plans tonight," he said.

My stomach clenched up into a tight fist, and I let go of his hand. "Right, of course."

"I can't really bail on the plans. You know my best friend Jonah? He comes into the diner a lot with me."

"Yes," I said.

"Anyway, it's his girlfriend Claire's birthday, and we made plans like two weeks ago to celebrate her birthday… I'm sorry."

"No, it's fine," I said hurriedly. "You don't have to apologize."

There was more awkward silence. I pasted a

smile on my face and said, "If you want to wake me up when you get home for, uh, sex, I wouldn't be mad or anything."

"It'll probably be pretty late," he said.

It might have been awhile since I'd tried to make plans with a guy, but I knew when I was being blown off. Defeated, I pasted another smile on my face. "Okay. Well, tell your friend I said happy birthday."

I leaned over and grabbed my towel from the floor before sliding out of the bed. I hurriedly wrapped it around me. "I'm gonna get dressed and make a sandwich for lunch before I go to work. Can I make you one?"

"No, thanks. I need to have a shower and then I have a few errands to run." Matt stared at the quilt as I headed for the door.

"All right. Um, have fun tonight. Bye."

"Bye, Natalia."

I scurried out of his room and into the guest room, shutting the door behind me before leaning against it. Stupidly, I was close to crying after being rejected by Matt, and I smacked myself on the upper thigh before whispering, "Stop it, you idiot. You did this to yourself. You asked him out on a goddamn date! What were you thinking? You told him yourself this was about sex only, so you can't be upset with him for not wanting anything but sex from you."

He doesn't even want that anymore.

I ignored my inner voice grimly. Matt was just pissed because I'd said some really stupid shit to him. I'd apologize again tomorrow and if I was lucky, he'd be up for another round or two of sex before I went to work.

Chapter Eight

Natalia

"Night, Nat."

"Night, Stanley. Have a good one, I'll see you tomorrow."

"Yep." Stanley covered his balding head with a bright red knit cap and walked down the stairs toward his car.

I checked the diner door one final time before trudging down the steps after him. For a minute, I was tempted to beg the brusque cook for a ride to Matt's house. It was dark and cold, and I'd missed the nine o'clock bus which meant I had to wait another forty-five minutes for the ten o'clock one.

I tugged my thin jacket around me a little tighter as Stanley climbed into his car and drove out of the parking lot without a second look at me.

My right heel throbbing, I limped across the parking lot. At least the bus stop was only a couple blocks away and I didn't have to go to Maggie's and get Phoebe first. It was freezing and I didn't relish the idea of dragging the poor kid to Matt's on the bus. I'd called and talked to Phoebe on the phone during my supper break and from the sounds of it, she wasn't missing me at all.

I smiled a little, remembering how excited she was when she'd told me about Wyatt and Maggie taking her to our local Chuckie Cheese tonight. I was so broke that taking Phoebe out and doing fun stuff with her was a rarity, and I hated that she was missing out on stuff that other kids got to do.

Not anymore. Now, with the child support from Evan, you'll get to do those fun things with her.

I bent my head against the cold wind and started down the sidewalk, thankful I had changed out of my uniform and into my jeans. They at least provided a little more warmth than the thin uniform. Headlights splashed across the road and I took a nervous step back, shifting my backpack on my shoulder, when the car stopped next to me.

The window rolled down and Mia stuck her head out. "Natalia! I'm so sorry we're late."

"Uh, late for what?" I looked past her to see Elijah sitting behind the wheel.

"Didn't Matt tell you? He asked me and Elijah to pick you up after work."

"What?" I gave her a blank look. "He did?"

"Yep. Hop in the back, it's freezing out."

I opened the back door and climbed in behind Mia. She turned in her seat and smiled at me. "Hey, have you ever actually met Elijah?"

"Not formally. Hi, Elijah, I'm Natalia."

"Nice to meet you," he said as he drove down the street.

"You as well. So, um, why did Matt ask you to pick me up?"

"Because your car is broken and it's freezing out and the bus system in this town sucks," Mia said. "But we were running a bit late because I had to stop at Nana's first. Anyway, how are you doing?"

"Good," I said. "I really appreciate the ride home. Thank you."

"Oh, it's no problem. It was on our way to Ren's anyway." Mia paused for a second before giving Elijah a look I didn't understand. "You should come out with us. Matt told us that Phoebe was with Maggie tonight. How often do you get a night out?"

"Not that often," I said. "But I don't want to horn in on your date night."

Mia giggled before squeezing Elijah's meaty arm. "We'd love it if you joined us. Right, babe?"

Elijah nodded. "The more the merrier."

I hesitated. I was tired and my feet hurt, and I was still upset about Matt rejecting me, but the thought of going to his house and sitting alone made me feel even more pathetic than being the third wheel on Mia and Elijah's date.

"Are you sure?" I said.

"Positive," Mia said.

"Then okay."

"Awesome!" Mia gave me a look of delight before twisting around to face the front. "We're gonna have so much fun."

⤳ ⤲

Matt

"Hey, if you don't want to be here, it's fine." Jonah nudged my shoulder before taking a drink of beer. "You showed up, said happy birthday and had a couple of drinks. You've met expectations."

I scowled at him. "Don't be a dick."

"I'm not," Jonah said. "I'm trying to get you out of here so you can get laid."

"Keep your voice down." I glanced at the others. Jonah's girlfriend Claire was talking animatedly to her best friend, a tiny redhead named Luna who worked at Mugs Coffee Shop on Main Street. On the other side of Luna was her boyfriend, the largest and quietest man in town, Asher Stokes.

"Listen, I know your time with Natalia is limited, so get out of here," Jonah said. "I told Claire all about you and your crush on Natalia, so she'll understand if you leave."

"You told Claire?"

"I tell Claire everything. I didn't think you'd mind. Do you?"

"No, not really," I said. "I just feel stupid for wanting someone that I can never have."

Jonah took a swig of beer. "Do you know for sure you can't have her? Have you tried sitting her down and telling her you want more?"

"She doesn't want that," I said. "She made it perfectly clear last night that all she wants is sex and that's only until Phoebe comes back."

"That blows. Sorry, buddy."

"Yeah." I checked my watch for about the hundredth time. "I fucked up with her this afternoon."

"How?" Jonah leaned in a little closer.

"I assumed that she was sleeping with me as payment for giving her a place to stay and… it was awkward as shit. She said she'd always been attracted to me, but I still acted like a pissed off kid having a temper tantrum. She asked if I wanted to go to a movie and I brushed her off and…I could see how embarrassed it made her. God, I was such a jackass to her."

"I'm sure you weren't that bad," Jonah said.

"She told me I could wake her up when I got home to have sex and I told her it would be too late."

Jonah winced. "I take it back, you are a jackass."

I muttered a curse before glancing at my watch again. "I asked Mia to pick her up from work after her shift. Her car won't be ready until Monday and she doesn't have money for a cab. I didn't want her waiting for the bus when it's so dark and cold outside."

"You should have picked her up yourself," Jonah said.

"I know."

"But you didn't."

"I know."

"Because you're a jackass."

"I *know*." I glared at Jonah who just laughed before looking around the bar.

"Listen," I said, "I'm gonna go. I need to talk to Nat, apologize to her."

"You definitely do," Jonah said, "but you don't

have to leave."

"What do you mean?"

Jonah pointed to where Mia, Elijah and - my heart kicked into overdrive - Natalia were walking toward us.

"Hey, guys!" Mia grinned at me as the three of them stopped at our table. "Fancy running into you here."

I gave her a what-the-hell-are-you-doing look that she ignored. Mia knew I would be at Ren's tonight celebrating Claire's birthday. She also knew about my crush on Natalia. About a month ago, after too many beers at this very bar, I had confessed my crush to both Mia and Elijah.

Now, I was sincerely regretting it as Mia gave me a wide grin. "How is everyone?"

"Good," Jonah said. "We're celebrating Claire's birthday."

"How lovely." Mia turned to Claire. "Happy Birthday, Claire."

"Thanks," Claire said.

Mia glanced at Elijah and Natalia. "The three of us decided we could use a drink as well. It's so crazy to run into you guys like this."

She gave Jonah a look that clearly said, "invite us to stay, you idiot".

"Why don't you join us," Jonah said with a small grin. "There's plenty of room."

"Are you sure?" Mia's look would have melted butter. "We wouldn't want to intrude."

"You're not." Claire pointed to the two empty chairs between me and Asher. "Have a seat."

"Thanks so much," Mia replied.

Natalia cleared her throat. "Um, there are only two chairs and I'm pretty tired, so I think I'll call it a night and -"

"Don't be silly." Luna jumped up and tugged on Asher's arm. "Sit in my seat, honey."

He moved over and she plopped herself down on his lap, slinging her arm around his thick neck and kissing his cheek. "You don't mind if I sit in your lap, do you?"

"You know I don't," he replied.

"There, three empty seats," Luna said. "Sit down, Natalia."

Before Natalia could sit next to them, Mia had practically shoved Elijah toward the empty chair. "Elijah, you sit next to Asher."

He sat down and Mia stole the chair next to him before patting the empty seat between us. "Here you go, Natalia."

"Thank you." She sat down and gave me a faint smile. "Hi, Matt."

"Hey," I said. "How was work?"

"Fine," she replied.

There was silence and then Jonah leaned around me and grinned at her. "Hey, Natalia. How are you?"

"Good, thanks. How are you?"

"I'm fantastic." Jonah nudged me in the ribs. "Introduce her to everyone, jackass."

I mumbled an apology to Nat before saying in a loud voice. "Everyone, this is Natalia. Natalia, this is everyone."

Jonah snorted his disgust as Luna waved at Natalia. "Hey, I'm Luna and this is Asher. You work at the diner, right?"

Nat nodded as Claire held up her wine glass and grinned at her. "I'm Claire, today is my birthday, and I've already had way too much to drink."

Natalia laughed. "It's nice to meet you, Claire. Happy Birthday."

"Thank you, Natalia." Claire tipped her glass to her before taking a sip.

As the others began to chat, I was uncomfortably aware of how quiet Nat was being and the way she avoided my gaze.

"Do you want a drink?" I asked.

She shook her head. "No, I can't stay too long."

"Why not?" I said. "When was the last time you had a night out?"

She shrugged and I leaned a little closer, hating the way it made her stiffen. "You deserve to have some fun in your life, Nat."

"I do have fun," she said. "Just because my idea of fun doesn't match yours, doesn't mean I live a boring life. Maybe I'm not big into going out drinking and partying, but I like spending time with my kid, okay?"

"I know that." I was more stung by her words than I wanted to admit it. "I like hanging out with Phoebe too, she's a great kid."

She didn't reply and I glanced around the table before standing up. "Come dance with me."

"What?"

I held out my hand and after a moment's hesitation, she stood and took my hand. I walked slowly to the dance floor, knowing her feet would be killing her, and took her into my arms. God, it felt so right to have her body against mine. We swayed to the music and I bent my head and inhaled the scent of her hair.

"Why are you sniffing me?"

"You smell good."

"I smell like stale French Fries and grease."

I grinned. "Yeah, you do."

She sighed, and I held her a little closer before pressing a kiss against her temple. "I'm sorry, Nat. I was a dickhead earlier."

"No, you weren't," she said. "I was. It seems like I'm always saying the wrong thing and making the worst assumptions about you and I hate myself for it. But I seem to keep on doing it."

"It's fine," I said. "I deserve my reputation."

She stared up at me. "Why do you do that?"

"Do what?"

"Constantly make excuses for my shitty behaviour toward you. I'm an adult and I need to own up to my mistakes. I've made a ton of mistakes about you and who you are as a person and I am truly sorry for it. There is nothing wrong with how you live your life, Matt."

I didn't reply and she reached up and cupped my face. "I mean that. You're a good guy. In fact, you might be one of the best guys I've ever met."

I wanted to kiss her. I wanted to tell her that I loved her and that she made me want to be a good guy, but it sounded cheesy and stupid in my head. And even though I knew she would never love me the way I loved her, I couldn't help but feel a flush of pride at her words.

"I mean that," she repeated. "You're amazing,

Matt Andrews."

"You're pretty amazing yourself."

She shook her head. "Not lately, but I promise to be better."

We danced in silence for a few minutes, before she said, "Thank you for asking Mia to give me a ride home after work. That was really nice of you."

"I should have done it myself," I said.

"No, you needed to be here at your friend's party." She gave me a quick look. "I'm not a crazy stalker, by the way."

"What do you mean?"

"I didn't know you were going to be here. Mia asked me if I wanted to go to the bar with them and I didn't want to sit home alone so I said yes. But if I'd known that you would be here, I would've said no."

"I'm glad you didn't know then," I replied.

She smiled a little. "I just want you to know that I got your message loud and clear earlier, and I promise I'm not going to..."

I frowned at her. "Not going to what?"

Her face flushed and she looked away. "Ask you for sex again."

Shit. I really had fucked up.

I tried to think of the right words to say, tried to decide how to convince her that my rejection had nothing to do with her and everything to do with me being a giant ass baby.

Aw, fuck it. The best way to tell her was to show her.

I stopped our gentle swaying and cupped her face before kissing her hard on the mouth. She

404

made a muffled sound of surprise when I slipped my tongue into her mouth and pressed her lower body up against mine. I was already hardening, just the taste of Nat's mouth made me horny as hell.

I pulled back and ignoring the amused looks of the dancers around us, I squeezed Nat's ass with my free hand and said, "This is the message I want you to hear, Nat."

I leaned down and put my mouth to her ear. "I was being an idiot earlier. I want you naked, in my bed, and moaning my name. Can you feel how much I want you?"

I pressed my dick against her, and she made a soft little moan that only I could hear.

"Can you, Nat?"

"Yes," she whispered.

"Good, then let's get the hell out of here and go home so I can get you naked and under me."

She licked her lips before giving me a sexy little grin. "Actually, I was thinking this time maybe I'd be on top of you. If you're good with that?"

"Sweetheart, I am one hundred fucking percent good with that."

Chapter Nine

Natalia

"Hey, beautiful."

I turned, a smile breaking out on my face when I saw Matt standing behind me. "Hi!"

I sounded like a giddy school girl, but I couldn't help it. The minute I saw him, I got all hopped up on hormones and lust.

Too bad you don't get to bang him anymore.

I ignored my inner voice, even though it was right. Maggie was bringing Phoebe to me after work and my two-day sex marathon with Matt was over.

Why? You can sleep with Matt after Phoebe goes to sleep. Why are you denying yourself what you want?

"How was your shift?" I asked.

"Good. Not that busy for a Saturday. I thought I'd stop by and bring you some leftovers for dinner." Matt held up a plastic container. "I made shrimp stir-fry for dinner. Do you like shrimp?"

"I love it," I said. "Thank you, that's so thoughtful of you. I'm actually about to take my dinner break, if you want to hang out with me?"

"Sure." Matt followed me to the staff booth. He sat down and I grabbed us both waters before easing into the booth across from him.

He frowned when I winced a little. "You okay?"

"Yeah. Sore thighs and..."

He gave me an adorably wicked grin. "Sore pussy?"

I blushed but nodded. "Yes."

"I'll kiss it better for you later tonight," he said.

"Oh, uh, Maggie and Wyatt are bringing Phoebe to the diner once my shift is done," I said.

His smile slipped for only a few seconds. "Right, of course. So, how's work been going?"

"Good. Well, tips aren't great tonight but..." I shrugged and opened the container of food. "This smells delicious."

"Cooking is only one of my many talents," Matt said.

I smiled at him. "You are very talented. Who taught you to cook?"

"My old man," Matt said.

"Your mom passed away when you were a kid, right?"

"Yes. Cancer."

"I'm sorry."

"Thanks. I don't remember her very well, to be honest. I was only five when she died. Anyway, it was just me and my Dad and he taught himself to cook and then taught me."

"It must have been difficult for you and your dad," I said.

His fingers tugged restlessly at the strings on his hoodie. "Harder on my dad, I think. He loved her a lot. Although, it didn't stop him from sleeping with half the ladies in town, married or not."

He laughed bitterly. "When I was a kid, I swore I wouldn't be like him. Swore that if I ever had a kid, I wouldn't parade a different woman in front of him every weekend like it was some sort of game I was winning. It's why I didn't date in high school, why I stuck to stuff like chess and the debate club because I knew high school girls weren't into that. But then my hormones got the best of me."

His smile was weary. "Next thing you know, I'm exactly like my old man."

"No," I reached across the table and squeezed his hand, "you aren't, Matt. You don't sleep with married women, and you're not exposing your kid to a different woman every weekend."

He stared at our fingers laced together. "I spent most of my childhood watching my father bring home different women every damn weekend. Some of them were nice to me, some of them ignored me, but none of them stuck around. I wanted a mom and all I got was a father who treated me like I was second place in his life. The women always came first. Always. I spent most of my weekends in front of the television, the volume turned as loud as it could go so that I wouldn't hear the woman in my father's bedroom."

I squeezed his hand again and blinked back the tears. The hurt and the loss in Matt's voice tore at my heart. "I'm so sorry, honey."

He cleared his throat roughly and refused to meet my gaze. "I'm not a parent, but I understand why you want to keep Phoebe from knowing we're together."

He finally raised his gaze to mine. "Honestly, I hate that I won't ever get to be with you again, but I love that you put your kid first."

Now the tears were slipping down my face and I pressed my lips together before whispering, "Matt, I -"

"Mama!"

Phoebe's happy shout made me wipe the tears away hurriedly as she barreled toward us. Maggie was walking behind her, and I smiled happily when Phoebe climbed into the booth beside me and hugged me hard.

I buried my face in her neck and inhaled deeply before kissing her face repeatedly. "Hi, Pheebs. I've missed you."

"Hi, Mama." Phoebe grinned at me before kissing me on the lips. "I love you."

"I love you too," I said before hugging her again.

Maggie slid into the booth beside us and smiled at Matt. "Hey, Matt."

"Hi, Maggie."

Phoebe's eyes widened and she twisted her head to stare in wide-eyed delight at Matt. "Mattie! Mama, it's Mattie!"

She squirmed out of my grip and slid under the table in the booth before popping back up on Matt's side. She climbed into the seat beside him and threw her chubby arms around his neck before kissing his cheek. "Hi, Mattie."

"Hi, Pheebs Bo Beebs," he said.

She squealed laughter before patting his face with her little hand. "You miss me, Mattie?"

"I did. Very much."

"Good." She climbed into his lap, resting the back of her head against his chest as she smiled at me. "I sittin' with Mattie, Mama."

"I see that." I popped a forkful of stir fry into my mouth as Maggie smiled at Phoebe.

"I know you're taking her home tonight, but Pheebs was starting to miss her mama, so I told her we'd come visit while you had dinner. Isn't that right, Pheeby-pie?"

"Yep," she said before looking up at Matt. "I ate all my dinner tonight."

"Good job, sweetheart." He smiled down at her and my chest squeezed tight. Sitting in the booth with Matt and having him look at my kid with so much affection, I could almost pretend that we were just a happy family having dinner together.

"Mama, I go home with you and Mattie tonight," Phoebe said.

"Well, yes, but not for a little while. You're going to go back to Aunt Maggie's first and then we'll pick you up from there and go home," I said.

"Nope," Phoebe shook her head before smiling at Matt, "I go home with Mattie."

"Not until later," I said. "You need to stay with Aunt Maggie for a little longer."

"I don't wanna," Phoebe said.

"Ooh, Pheebs, we were having so much fun

together." Maggie reached across and tickled her belly. Phoebe giggled and pushed her hand away.

"I know. But I go home with Mattie and Mama now."

"Mama isn't going home yet," I said. "I still have to work."

"Oh." Phoebe gave Matt a hopeful smile. "I go home with you, Mattie?"

"Sure," Matt said. "You and I will hang out until your mama is finished work."

"Matt, you don't have to do that," I said. "Maggie will keep her until I'm done work. Right, Mags?"

Maggie nodded. "I sure will. Phoebe, we can watch *Peppa Pig* and Uncle Wyatt will make us popcorn. What do you think?"

"No," Phoebe said stubbornly. "I stay with Mattie."

"I really don't mind." Matt smiled at me before kissing the top of Phoebe's head. "I've been jonesing for my *Peppa Pig* fix."

"Are you sure?" I said. "I work until nine."

"I'm positive. It's only two hours," Matt said.

"I know, but…"

"I'll take good care of her, Nat. I promise."

I smiled at him and not caring that Maggie was watching us, reached across and took his hand. "I know that. I'm not worried. But I don't want you to feel like you have to hang out with my kid."

"I don't." Matt squeezed my hand before smiling at Phoebe. "You're coming home with me, munchkin."

"Yay!" Phoebe drummed her feet against his

411

thighs before smiling at Maggie. "I love Mattie."

I nearly choked on my mouthful of stir fry. Maggie thumped me on the back and handed me my glass of water before smiling at Phoebe. "That's good, kiddo."

She smiled at Matt. "So, Pheebs' car seat is in my car, but her backpack is still at my place. Any chance you can stop and pick it up?"

"Sure. We'll come by after Nat's break is over and pick it up."

"Perfect. Well, I'll leave you guys to your family dinner. See you in a bit, Matt." Maggie slid out of the booth and walked away.

"Thank you, Matt. Really," I said.

He ruffled Phoebe's hair and smiled down at her. "I don't mind. I like spending time with her."

"That's 'cause I great," Phoebe said cheerfully.

Matt burst into laughter before bending and kissing the top of her head. "You sure are, kid."

જ ൸

"Hey, thank you for picking me up again," I said as I climbed into Matt's truck. I turned to smile at Phoebe who was strapped into her car seat in the back seat.

"Hi, Mama."

"Hi, sweetpea. Did you have fun with Matt?"

"Uh-huh." She yawned and stared out the window. "I up late."

As the street lights bathed Matt in dim light, I squinted at his neck. "What is that?"

"Tattoo."

"A tattoo?" I leaned in closer, the seatbelt cutting into my neck. "You got a Little Mermaid

412

tattoo on your neck?"

Phoebe giggled. "I got one too, Mama."

I turned and stared at her arm where a matching tattoo was plastered across her forearm. I laughed and turned back to Matt. "You let her put a temporary tattoo on you?"

"Tattoos," Matt said. "Don't be jealous of my new ladies, but I now have Belle, Princess Tiana, and Elsa tattoos on my chest."

I giggled again. "You know, if it wasn't so obvious before, it's completely obvious now."

"What?" He asked.

"Phoebe has you wrapped around her little finger."

He gave me an adorable smile that sent warmth rushing to my chest. "She does."

"Thank you," I said again in a low voice. "Phoebe really likes you and it's sweet of you to be so kind to her."

"I really like her too," he said. "I keep telling you, she's a great kid."

I smiled and didn't object when he took my hand and gave it a quick squeeze. I stared silently out the window as Phoebe sang softly to herself behind us. Matt would be a great dad. His patience with Phoebe, the way he so sweetly treated her... it made my chest ache. Phoebe deserved to have someone like Matt in her life and I was second-guessing my decision to hold off on dating until Phoebe was older. If I found the right guy, someone like Matt who genuinely enjoyed being with her, it would be good for Phoebe and for me.

Someone like Matt? Girl, Matt is perfect for

you and Phoebe. Get your damn head out of your ass.

Was he? He was certainly much different than I thought, but from what I'd heard, he'd never had a single serious relationship. The guy was in his mid-twenties and never had a serious girlfriend – that had warning bells written all over it.

People can change.

Yeah, they could. Not always for the better – Evan was proof of that.

"You okay?" Matt's voice was low.

"Yes." I made myself smile at him. "I'm good."

∂ ∾

I stared blankly at the ceiling before grabbing my cell phone and checking the time. It was quarter after eleven and I was wide awake. I studied Phoebe's sleeping body next to mine, smiling a little when she snored loudly.

Worried that I would try and jump Matt the minute Phoebe was asleep, I'd gone to bed when she did. I'd had a hot shower after she fell asleep and then climbed into bed. Matt had gone to his room only twenty minutes later and the faint creak of his bed as he'd climbed into it made me long to join him.

Would it be so bad to join him for a quickie? Phoebe was sleeping soundly, and I was confident she wouldn't wake up. Why shouldn't I crawl into Matt's bed for an hour or so? I'd spent the last two years taking care of Phoebe, worrying about money and bills and having enough food... why shouldn't I take a little time for myself? Why shouldn't I give myself one last round of sex with Matt? I deserved it, right?

Hell, yes, you do. But you know it's more than just scratching an itch now, right? You love him. You can deny it all you want, but you are head over heels for Matt Andrews.

My stomach made a funny little flip-flop and I pressed my hand against it. Admitting I was maybe in love with Matt, especially after only a few days, would make me a real weirdo. Sure, he made me laugh and he really seemed to enjoy Phoebe's company, and he was kind and generous, and the way he snorted a little whenever he laughed really hard was super adorable, but that wasn't love.

And, okay, maybe thinking about leaving him and returning to my stupid lonely trailer on Monday where I wouldn't see him every day made me sick to my stomach and hopelessly depressed, but that didn't mean I loved him.

I just liked him... a whole lot. A 'I can't even fathom being without you now' lot. That was normal and not at all weird. Right?

I threw back the covers and slid out of the bed, creeping silently out of our bedroom and down the hall to Matt's. His door was partially open and, before I could talk myself out of it, I slipped into his room and shut the door completely. I had taught Phoebe to knock on any closed door and wait for an answer before she opened it. If she did wake up, it would at least give me a few minutes to...

Stop banging Matt's brains out?

Crude, but yeah.

So wrapped up in my own head, I didn't hear

the soft groans coming from Matt's bed at first. Didn't notice the way the bed covers were tented or the rough motion of his hand under the sheet.

I stopped only a couple feet from the bed, my mouth going dry and my pussy going wet, as I watched Matt masturbate. His other arm was pressed over his eyes and I watched his wide chest rise and fall rapidly as another low groan fell from his perfect lips.

Fuck, watching Matt touch himself was way hotter than I ever imagined. Part of me wanted to stay right where I was and watch him bring himself to orgasm. Another part of me wanted to pull back those covers and replace his hand with my mouth.

Lust beat out the voyeurism, and I joined him at the bed, pulling back the covers as he made a harsh sound of surprise and half sat up. He stared blankly at me, one hand still wrapped around his dick. "Nat, what are you doing in here?"

"I couldn't sleep." I pressed a kiss below his navel, smiling at the way he moaned and twitched. "Looks like you can't either."

"Nat," he moaned when I licked his v-line, "please."

"I know I said we had to stop, but," I smiled up at him and trailed my fingers across his inner thighs, "would you mind terribly if I sucked your dick for a while?"

His hand was already wrapping in my hair, already tugging me toward that deliciously erect cock. "I don't mind."

"Are you sure?" I teased before licking the precum from the head of his cock. "You look like you know what you're doing with your hand."

He half-groaned, half-laughed. "Your mouth, Nat. Please."

I smiled smugly at the pleading sound of his voice before taking the head of his cock into my mouth. I sucked lightly and then traced the ridge with my tongue. His hands fisted in my hair, his hips jerking up as he made another low pleading sound.

I leaned back, ignoring the slight pain as my hair pulled and smiled up at him. "What were you thinking about while you touched yourself, Mattie?"

"You," he said. "Your tits, your pussy, your mouth... oh fuck, that feels so good."

I'd licked his cock while he answered me, and I licked it again before sitting up and stripping off my t-shirt and sleep shorts. I opened my legs and lazily rubbed my pussy as Matt watched.

"I'm so wet already, Mattie."

"Fuck me," he said hoarsely. "Fuck me right now, Nat."

"Soon," I said. Still rubbing my pussy, I leaned over him and took him into my mouth again. I bobbed my head up and down as Matt gathered my hair into a loose ponytail and watched me suck his cock.

"Oh fuck, yeah, just like that, sweetheart." His low moans of pleasure were turning me on more than my fingers rubbing my clit.

When his big body tensed and his cock swelled in my mouth, I pulled away, gasping for breath and licking my swollen lips.

"No, please, Nat," he whispered.

I smiled at him and showed him my wet fingers. "My pussy needs your cock."

He groaned again and made no objection when I reached into the nightstand and grabbed a condom. I unwrapped it and he helped me roll it over his cock, pushing my hands away when I moved too slow.

I giggled and patted his flat abdomen. "Someone's in a hurry."

"Ride me. Now." His voice was hard, and the change from his usual sweet tenderness sent an unexpected wave of lust through me.

Tossing aside my plan to tease and torment, I immediately straddled his hips, rising up a little so he could guide his cock to my waiting pussy. He pushed inside of me, the head breaching my entrance and making me moan happily.

His hard hands grabbed my hips, holding tight as I sank down onto his cock. When he was completely sheathed, he reached up and cupped my tits, squeezing and kneading them as I moved up and down.

"Faster," he demanded.

I braced my hands on his chest and thrust faster. The thick slide of his cock was pure pleasure and I leaned over him, brushing my mouth against his as his arms slid around me. He held me tight and fucked me with long, deep strokes. I ground my clit against his pubic bone, moaning and panting and begging him to move faster as he pressed kisses against my throat and upper chest.

"Yes," I whispered, "oh God, yes, right there, right..."

I threw my head back as my orgasm washed over me, clamping one hand over my mouth and only dimly aware of the way Matt buried his face into my throat to muffle his own cry of ecstasy. His big body shook beneath mine, his hips thrusting back and forth as we both panted harshly.

He pressed hot kisses against my throat, holding me still when I tried to slide off of him.

"Not yet," he whispered into my ear.

I relaxed against his big body, resting my head on his broad chest as he stroked my back with his warm hands. It felt so good to be in his arms. I was already feeling sleepier and I stifled a yawn as Matt kissed my temple.

"So good," I muttered.

"Hmm," he replied.

"Sorry I interrupted your personal time."

He laughed. "Sweetheart, feel free to join me in my bed whenever you want."

I kissed his chest and slid off of him. He tossed the condom in the wastebasket and I gave him a sweet smile when he turned to face me and put his arms around me again. "I really like being on top."

"I like it too," he said before kissing me.

I studied his face in the dim light. "Sorry I snuck into your bed in the middle of the night."

"I do not have a problem with it, Natalia."

I smiled a little. "I should go back to my own bed. If Phoebe wakes up, I don't want her seeing me in your bed."

A mask fell over his face and he nodded. "Yeah, okay."

"It's – it would confuse her, Matt."

"I know," he said. "It's fine."

Despite what I said, I didn't want to leave. I traced the princess tattoos that were plastered haphazardly on his upper chest. "I like your new tattoos."

He gave me a brief smile. "Thanks. You'd better go, Nat. It's getting late and I have to work in the morning."

"Yeah, okay." I hesitated before giving him a brief kiss on the mouth. "Thank you, Matt. Good night."

"Night."

I climbed out of bed and hurriedly dressed. I glanced at Matt. He had already turned on his side to face the wall and I ignored my urge to climb back into his bed. I was already giving him mixed messages by sneaking into his bed tonight, I didn't need to make it worse.

Chapter Ten

Matt

I toed off my boots and hung my jacket in the hallway. The house smelled delicious, like chicken stew and homemade biscuits, and I followed my nose to the kitchen. Natalia was sitting at the table, a glass of wine in one hand and a book in the other. I stared at her, feeling a wave of love that was overwhelming in its intensity.

She'd be leaving tomorrow, and things would change. The two of us living in the same town, but no longer lovers or even, I swallowed heavily, friends.

She glanced up, her smile warm and welcoming. "Hey, you're finally home."

"Yeah. Something smells really good."

"I made stew and biscuits for supper. I ate with Phoebe earlier, but I've got some warming on the stove for you."

"Thanks. Sorry I'm late."

"That's okay. Is it always this busy on a

Sunday?"

I shook my head. "No. There was a bad accident just outside of town near the end of our shift."

She studied me, a line appearing in the smooth skin between her eyes. "You okay?"

I nodded. "Is Phoebe still awake?"

She shook her head and a wave of depression washed over me. Even though it was after eight and Phoebe was usually in bed by seven-thirty at the latest, I had spent the entire ride home hoping that Phoebe would still be awake.

I made myself smile at Nat. "Okay, I'm gonna have a quick shower."

I left the kitchen before she could question me further. I stripped off my uniform and showered away the smell of blood and antiseptic and terror. Ten minutes later, dressed in a t-shirt and track pants, I still couldn't shake the lingering unease. I paused in front of the guest bedroom before slipping inside.

Phoebe was sleeping in the middle of the bed with her thumb in her mouth and her hair in her eyes. I sat down gingerly on the side of the bed before reaching out and brushing her hair away from her face. My hand was shaking, and I clenched it into a tight fist. I was being stupid, but I needed to see Phoebe, needed to make sure she was safe and happy and -

"Mattie?" Nat's soft voice caressed my splintered nerves as her soft hand caressed the back of my neck. "Honey, what's wrong?"

"Nothing," I said in a low voice. "I needed – I

mean – I wanted to see Phoebe."

Nat's hand squeezed my shoulder. "I can wake her up, if you'd like."

I shook my head and stood up. "No, that's okay. I -" my voice cracked, and I cleared my throat. "I'm gonna go eat."

I slipped out of the room and hurried down the stairs. I had zero appetite, but I had to get away from Nat for a few minutes. If she knew how much I cared not just about her, but about Phoebe, she'd run like a frightened deer. She didn't want a relationship with me, and I knew and understood why she didn't, but fuck if it didn't feel like there was a smoking crater where my heart used to be.

I grabbed a beer from the fridge, twisting off the cap and tossing it in the garbage before drinking nearly half of it. Nat came into the kitchen and, without speaking, she spooned out a bowl of stew and set it on the table.

"Eat, honey," she said.

I sat down, holding the spoon in my hand and staring at the stew. It smelled delicious, but my urge to eat was still somewhere south of never. Nat set a plate of biscuits next to the bowl.

"Thanks," I muttered.

When I didn't make any move to eat, she tapped on my shoulder. "Push your chair back."

I pushed it back and was numbly grateful when Nat sat down in my lap and put her arms around my shoulders. She hugged me hard and I buried my face in her throat as she kneaded the tense muscles in my neck.

I put my arms around her waist, breathing in her

scent and trying to forget the images burned into my head. After almost ten minutes, I raised my head and stared up at her. She cupped my face, stroking my cheekbone with her thumb. "Better?"

"Yeah. Sorry."

"Don't be. Do you want to talk about what happened?"

"The accident today, it was…" my voice was hoarse, "it was bad. Head on collision. The driver who caused it was drunk. Fucking wasted at four o'clock on a Sunday afternoon. He-he was dead when we got there, thrown from his vehicle, but we could smell the booze on him and there were open cans of beer all over his goddamn car and the road."

Nat kissed my temple and held me a little tighter as I stared up at her. "In the other car was a man and a-a little girl Phoebe's age."

She stiffened and now it was my turn to rub her back soothingly. "They're both okay. They both," I made a disbelieving laugh, "walked away with nothing more than a few scratches and bruises. It was a goddamn miracle, Nat. Their car was… they had to use the jaws of life to get them both out. The little girl sat in her car seat, not crying or panicking, just holding her teddy bear and staring at us with this look on her face, like…"

My voice cracked again, and I buried my face in Nat's throat for a second time. She rocked me back and forth, kissing the top of my head and making soothing sounds of comfort.

"I kept seeing Phoebe instead of her." My voice was as jagged as the broken glass at the accident scene. "I kept thinking what if that was Phoebe in the car, what if it had been her surrounded by chaos and blood? It terrified me, Nat."

"It's okay, honey." Her voice was a soothing balm.

"They're both fine. The little girl in the car – her name is Emily – is fine and Phoebe is fine, but I can't stop seeing it differently. It's why I needed to see Phoebe tonight. The entire drive home I kept seeing her in that mangled car and..."

"It's all right, honey." Nat pressed another kiss against the top of my head. I rested my cheek against her chest and listened to the steady beat of her heart. I had no idea how much time passed, but when Phoebe padded silently into the kitchen, I automatically dropped my arms from Nat's waist.

Instead of jumping off my lap, Nat smiled at Phoebe. "Come here, sweetpea."

"Why you sittin' on Mattie's lap, Mama?" Phoebe asked.

"Matt's sad, sweetpea. He needs a hug." Nat leaned down and lifted Phoebe into her lap.

Phoebe yawned before patting my cheek. "No sad, Mattie."

I put my arms around both of them and kissed Natalia's upper chest before kissing Phoebe's cheek. She smiled and yawned again before resting her forehead against my chest. "I love Mattie, Mama."

I stiffened, but Nat rubbed Phoebe's back. "That's good, sweetpea."

Phoebe lifted her head and gave me a sleepy look. "Mattie love Phoebe?"

"Yes," I said. "I love you, Phoebe."

She gave her mother a pleased look. "Mattie loves me."

Nat smiled at Phoebe. "I heard."

Phoebe rested her forehead against my chest again. I kissed the top of her delicate skull and held both of them a little tighter. I figured Phoebe was asleep again, but Nat made no move to return her to their bed.

"Mattie love Mama?" Phoebe's voice broke the silence.

"Yes." My voice was steady. "Mattie loves your mama."

Natalia's soft gasp was muffled by Phoebe's giggle. "Mattie loves Mama, Mattie loves Mama," she sang before lifting her head. "I gotta pee, Mama."

Nat tugged at my arm and I let go of them so she could slide from my lap. Holding Phoebe on her hip, she left the kitchen without a word. I stared at my stew for a few minutes before standing and walking upstairs to my bedroom.

I'd fucked up, but I didn't regret what I'd said. I loved Natalia and the weight of keeping that to myself was taking a toll. She didn't love me. In the morning she would take Phoebe and leave and I would be alone, but I wouldn't take back what I said, even if I could.

I stripped off my shirt and tossed it in the laundry hamper. Before I could take off my track pants, Natalia was standing in my room. She shut the door and stared silently at me.

"Is Phoebe…"

"Asleep again."

I stayed where I was next to the laundry hamper, not entirely sure what to say or do.

"Did you mean what you said?" Natalia asked.

"Yes. I love you, Nat. I've been in love with you for the last six months. I haven't slept with a woman since the day I walked into the diner and saw you for the first time. I go to the diner every day and eat greasy food because going twenty-four hours without seeing you is a nightmare."

Her cheeks were flushed, and she looked like she was on the verge of crying. Feeling terrible for upsetting her, but unable to stop the rush of words, I continued. "I've never had a serious relationship, I've never understood why people committed themselves to one person, but that changed when I met you. I don't know why, and I don't care. All I know is that I can't live without you. I want to know everything about you. I want you here in my home and in my bed for the rest of our lives. I love you and I love Phoebe, and I don't want to be without either of you. If you give me the chance to prove it to you, I will do everything in my power to be the best husband to you and the best father to Phoebe. I promise."

She didn't reply and I cursed inwardly. "You don't feel the same way, I know that, but I'm hoping you'll at least try dating me. Give me the chance to -"

"I feel the same way."

I blinked at her, certain I'd misheard her. "What did you say?"

She walked toward me and wrapped her arms around my waist. "I love you too."

"Bullshit," I said, and then winced.

She laughed and poked me in the chest. "Least romantic answer, ever, Matt Andrews."

"You – you don't love me," I said. "It's been a week, people don't fall in love in a week."

She shrugged. "I do."

"Why do you love me?"

Jesus, man, what the fuck? Shut your mouth!

"Oh, I don't know, maybe it's the way you are completely and totally gaga about my kid, maybe it's how you let us stay with you when we had no place else to go, or how you make me feel special and beautiful, or how you take care of me. Or maybe," her soft hands caressed my chest, "it's how easily you make me cum with that thick cock of yours."

My shock was starting to ease, and I studied her before giving her a smug smile. "I am really good in bed."

She laughed and cupped my face. "There's the Mattie I love."

"You seriously love me," I said.

"I seriously do. I know it's quick but, in my defense, I was actually stupidly attracted to you the whole time I was pretending you were the most annoying man in town. So, it's not that much of a stretch to go from 'I wanna repeatedly bang this hot guy' to 'I am in love with this guy who is not only hot, but is kind and funny and sweet and rubs my feet, and who loves both me and my kid'."

She traced the remnants of the princess tattoo that still clung to my chest, "Besides, in the fairy tales, the princess always falls in love with her prince after only a few days. Right?"

"I love you, Nat," I said.

"I love you too." She gave me a soft smile. "Now, what do you say we climb into your nice comfortable bed over there and bang like bunnies, Prince Charming?"

I picked her up and kissed her hard on the mouth. "Your wish is my command, princess."

ॐ ॐ

Natalia

"Wait... you and Phoebe have moved in permanently with Matt?" Maggie gave me a look of shock.

I sipped at my tea, raising my voice a little to be heard over the sounds of the others in Mugs coffee shop. For a Tuesday afternoon, it was weirdly busy. "Yes. I mean, I haven't moved everything over from the trailer yet, but I did give my landlord my notice. I have the place until the end of the month, but we're staying with Matt. After we're finished here, I'm taking Pheebs to the trailer to start packing."

"Mama?" Phoebe was sitting at the table beside me, her crayons and colouring book in front of her. "I want more hot chocolate."

I shook my head. "No can do, sweetpea. As it is, you probably won't nap at all. Too much sugar makes Pheebs a hyper pants."

"Hyper pants!" Phoebe hollered before grinning at Maggie. "I a hyper pants, Maggie."

Maggie smoothed Phoebe's hair. "Moving in together is a big step."

I nodded. "I know, but I love him, Mags. It's quick, but... we love each other, and I want to be with him. He's sweet and kind and he loves Phoebe and -"

"Hey," Maggie gave me a small smile, "I get it. I'm happy for you, Nat. Truly."

"Thanks." My cell phone rang, and I dug it out of my purse, frowning at the unfamiliar number. "Hello?"

"Natalia, it's Evan."

My mouth dropped open and I glanced at Phoebe. "Evan? Why are you calling me?"

"I'm in town for a while. We need to talk."

"You're in town? Now?"

Maggie was staring wide-eyed at me and I gave her my own look of shock.

"Yes. Can you meet me or not?" Evan's voice was impatient.

"Maybe," I said. "When?"

"Right now would be ideal," he replied. "I stopped at the diner and they said it was your day off, so I know you have time. Meet me at the Jade Cuisine in ten minutes."

Feeling off-kilter and sluggish, I put my phone on mute and stared at Maggie. "Evan's in town. He wants to meet right now."

"I'll come with you," Maggie said immediately.

"Actually," I glanced at Phoebe, "would you mind watching Phoebe while I meet him. I don't want her to see him, not just yet. You know?"

"Yeah. I'll stay here with Pheebs, but as your lawyer – do not agree to anything he asks, or sign anything he gives you. Okay?"

"I won't," I said. I unmuted my phone and stuck it back to my ear. "I'll see you in ten minutes, Evan."

"Good." He disconnected the call.

I threw my phone into my purse and touched Phoebe's face. "Sweetpea, Mama has to run a quick errand. You're going to stay here with Aunt Maggie, okay?"

"Otay," she said. She handed a crayon to Maggie. "You colour with me?"

"Sure." Maggie took the crayon before smiling reassuringly at me. "It'll be fine, Nat. You're not alone, you have Matt and you have me. Okay?"

"Okay," I said. I kissed Phoebe and hurried out of Mugs.

❧ ⚜

"Natalia. You're looking… tired." Evan stood when I approached him and pressed a brief kiss against my cheek.

The smell of his expensive cologne washed over me, and my stomach churned at the familiar smell. He studied me silently and I pulled self-consciously at my jacket. I'd bought it at the Goodwill last year and I knew it looked faded and cheap. Evan was dressed immaculately in dress slacks and a leather jacket that probably cost more than a month's rent for my trailer.

I cleared my throat and sat down at the table, not bothering to remove my jacket. A waiter appeared and poured me a glass of water.

"Are we ready to order?"

"I'll have the lunch special." Evan closed his menu with a snap. "Natalia?"

"Just water," I said. My stomach was still churning, and I had no appetite.

The server walked away, and I took a sip of water to ease my dry throat. "When did you get into town?"

"Last night." Evan took off his jacket and set it on the empty chair between us. "I'll get right to the point. I want to change our existing custody agreement. I want partial custody of Phoebe."

My entire body stiffened and my fingers clamped around the water glass. "What?"

"I want partial custody of Phoebe." He sat back in his chair and gave me a stiff smile. "She's my daughter too, Natalia."

"You've never wanted anything to do with her," I said. "Ever. And now suddenly, you think I'm going to allow you to have partial custody of her?"

"You're not going to *allow* me to do anything. I'm her father, I have a right to see my daughter."

"Yes, you do," I said. "I will be happy to arrange for you to have visitation with her. All you need to do is give me a week's notice and I'll make sure she's available for you to see when you're in town."

He shook his head. "I have a busy schedule and coming back to his piece-of-shit town once a month isn't happening. Phoebe will come to me."

I laughed in his face. "You can't be serious."

"I am," he said.

"She doesn't know you," I replied. "If you think I'm going to send my three-year-old child to a different state every month to be alone with a man she doesn't know, you're insane, Evan."

"It's my right," Evan snarled. "I'm paying child support every goddamn month, I wanna see the kid."

"So that's it," I said as awareness dawned. "You're pissed that you have to pay child support. You don't want to see or even care about Phoebe. You just want to punish me for forcing you to pay child support."

The way his body tensed, the deliberate way he tapped his fingers against his chin – his tell for when he was lying - told me I was right.

"Don't be ridiculous," he said. "I am her father and I have the right to see her. There's nothing else to say. Now," he reached down and grabbed a leather briefcase at his feet and set it on the on table, "these are papers I'll need you to sign. I've had my lawyer draw up the new custody agreement. It's marked where you should sign."

He pulled out a packet of papers and set them in front of me before dropping a pen on top of the paper. "Go ahead."

I brushed the pen away and picked up the documents. "I'll have my lawyer review them."

He sighed loudly. "Look, maybe your little hick town lawyer was able to get you child support, but this is something entirely different. My lawyer will chew her up and spit her out if required. Do you get that? Do us both a favour and sign the papers. Phoebe can start living with me part time next month. Once she starts going to school, we'll figure out a different arrangement, but for now, two weeks every month with me is reasonable."

I stood, locking my knees so he wouldn't see the

way my legs trembled, and shook my head. "No. This isn't happening, Evan."

"It is," Evan said. "You can't win."

"My lawyer will be in touch." I turned and walked out of the restaurant, keeping my shoulders back and my spine straight. My courage lasted until I was safely in my car. My body shaking wildly, I buried my face in my hands and sobbed.

る る

"Honey, it'll be okay. He's not going to win partial custody when he's never had anything to do with Phoebe." Matt gave me a worried look as I paced back and forth in his kitchen.

It was late, after eleven, but I couldn't sleep. I'd spent almost two hours with Phoebe after she fell asleep, just holding her and staring at her sweet face. The idea of not being with her, of not seeing her for two weeks at a time made me physically ill.

I pressed a hand against my stomach. "But what if he does? I can't go two weeks without seeing her, Matt."

"You won't." Matt stood and pulled me into his arms. He kissed me sweetly and rubbed my back. "He won't win, sweetheart. Maggie told you he wouldn't."

"She said that, but I could see that she was worried," I replied. "Judges award partial custody to fathers all the time."

"We won't let that happen."

"We'll have to go court," I said dully. "I know Evan and he's not gonna let this go until he gets what he wants. And what he wants is for me to suffer. Maggie is already saying that she'll do this for free, but I can't do that to her, Mattie. I can't. She's my friend but I can't take advantage of her like that. Except I don't know how I can pay her."

I rubbed at my temples. "Phoebe starts at the new daycare next week, but maybe I could ask Nana to babysit Phoebe in the evenings in exchange for me doing weekly housecleaning for her. Walmart is hiring part time right now. If I could get hired for evening shifts, then that would help me at least do a payment plan with Maggie or -"

"Sweetheart, stop." Matt's warm hands cupped my face.

I stared blankly at him as he pressed another kiss against my mouth before resting his forehead against mine. "You're not alone anymore. You and me," he kissed me again, "we're a team, Natalia. Right? We weather this storm together. Which means, I'll help cover the costs of Maggie's fees."

"What? No, I can't ask you to -"

"You're not asking, I'm offering." He gave me a lopsided grin. "Baby, I am crazy about you and your kid, and I will do whatever it takes to keep the both of you happy. We've got this. All right?"

Hot tears slipped down my cheeks and my lower lip trembled. Matt wiped the tears away with his thumbs. "Don't cry, sweetheart."

"I love you," I whispered. "I love you so damn much, Mattie."

"I love you too, sweetheart."

Chapter Eleven

Natalia

"Mama!"

"Hi, sweetpea." I zipped my jacket up over my uniform and weaved my way around the tables toward the front door. Matt was standing there with Phoebe in his arms and my heartbeat sped up. God, he was so handsome.

And sweet. And kind. And, also, amazing in bed.

Yeah, he was definitely all of that. Yesterday was one of the worst days of my life and Matt had been my rock. When we'd gone to bed, I'd been weirdly desperate for him and he hadn't made me feel stupid or awful for wanting to bang his brains out when I was so stressed about having my daughter taken away from me.

He'd given me exactly what I needed and wanted, and to my surprise, I'd managed to get a few hours of solid sleep last night. Considering how busy it'd been at the diner today, I'd needed the sleep.

"Matt picked me up from Nana's, Mama!" Phoebe sang out. "I love Mattie and he loves me!"

I made a little squeak of surprise when Matt pulled me into his embrace. He kissed me on the mouth as Phoebe giggled before poking him in the cheek. "You kissin' Mama, Mattie."

"I am, Pheebs Bo Beebs," he said with a grin.

I glanced around the diner. It was still full of people from the dinner rush and everyone was staring at us.

"Nat?" Matt squeezed me gently and I turned my attention back to him. "You okay?"

"Everyone's looking at us," I said.

"So what?" He gave me a careless grin that brought an answering one to my lips. "I want everyone to know how crazy I am about you."

"Crazy, crazy, crazy," Phoebe sang under her breath.

"You ready to go?" Matt took my hand.

"Yeah, let's go home."

Still holding Phoebe, Matt pushed open the door of the diner and led me outside. His truck was parked at the far end of the lot and he pulled Phoebe's hood up to cover her head before kissing her cheek.

"I need to keep my Pheebs warm, right?" He said.

"Yep," she said. "Mama, can we have hot dogs for dinner?"

"Not tonight, sweetpea," I said. "Tonight, we're having chicken and salad."

"I want hot dogs." Phoebe's mouth drew down

in a pout. "I want hot dogs and chips and a banana."

"Yes to the banana, no to the hot dog and chips," I said before turning to Matt. "How was your day at work, honey?"

"Slow. Mia and I spent most of the day cleaning and reorganizing our rig."

"Thank you for picking up Phoebe from Martha's house. I appreciate it."

"No problem."

I let go of his hand and reached behind him to squeeze his ass. "I'm planning on showing you just how much I appreciate it after the munchkin falls asleep."

"Sweet." He gave me a lecherous grin that made me laugh. "I'm more than -"

"Natalia?"

I stumbled to a stop, dropping my hand from Matt's ass as I slowly turned. Evan was standing behind us and I gave Matt a nervous look as he turned around too.

He grabbed my hand, holding it tightly as Evan approached us.

"What are you doing here, Evan?" I asked.

"I wanted to talk."

"Now isn't a good time," I said.

Evan ignored me, instead holding his hand out to Matt. "Evan Fealan."

Matt stared at his outstretched hand. "Matthew Andrews."

Evan blinked at him in surprise. "Matt Andrews? You've..." he looked him up and down, "changed since high school. Not exactly the nerdy chess kid anymore, are you?"

"Not exactly," Matt said. He shifted Phoebe in his arm. "If you'll excuse us, it's late and it's cold and we need to get Phoebe home."

"Home?" Evan turned toward me, raising one eyebrow. "You're living with Matt Andrews?"

"He makes me psghetti and I swim in his tub and I climb him like a jungle gym," Phoebe said.

Evan glanced at her and Phoebe gave him a large grin. "Hi, buddy. I Phoebe. Who are you?"

"Phoebe," I said hurriedly, "this is mama's friend Evan."

"Hi, Evan," Phoebe said. "I like your purse."

She stared at the leather bag Evan was carrying. Evan frowned at me before turning to Phoebe. "Phoebe, you don't call me Evan. I'm your father. You're to call me daddy."

I squeezed Matt's hand so hard that my knuckles went white. It wasn't that I didn't want Phoebe to know Evan was her father, I just hadn't expected her to find out this way.

"Nu-uh," Phoebe said. "You not my daddy. Mattie is my daddy." She kissed Matt's cheek. "Right, Mattie Daddy?"

Evan's face turned red. "Seriously, Natalia? You told our child that he's her father?"

I didn't reply and when Evan, his face turning even redder, stepped toward me, Matt dropped my hand and placed his hand on Evan's chest. "Don't."

Evan glared at him. "Get your hand off me."

Matt stared steadily at him and after a moment, Evan, his face nearly purple now, took a step back. Matt took my hand again as Phoebe slung her arm around his neck. "I pretty hungry, Mama."

"I know, sweetpea," I said. "We're going home now." I took a deep breath. "I'll call you tomorrow, Evan."

He stood silently and watched as we walked to Matt's truck. Matt buckled Phoebe in and then slid behind the wheel. By the time we drove out of the parking lot, Evan was back in his car and on his cell phone. I avoided looking at him as we drove past his car and onto the street.

"You okay?" Matt asked.

I nodded. "I think so." I glanced at Phoebe before lowering my voice. "I'm sorry. I'm not sure why Phoebe said you were her daddy, but I'll talk to her about it."

"If you don't want her calling me daddy, I get that, but just so you know, I'm perfectly fine with it," Matt replied.

I blinked at him. "You are?"

He nodded. "Yes."

"Matt, I…"

I reached for his hand and squeezed it hard as he smiled at me. "We're a family, Nat." He glanced in the rearview mirror and smiled at Phoebe. "You and me and Phoebe makes three."

"You and me and Phoebe makes three," Phoebe sang out. "Phoebe makes three. Phoebe makes three poops in the toilet."

She burst into giggles as Matt said, "Man, no one ever told me that kids liked talking about poop so much."

"I think that might be a Phoebe specialty," I said before squeezing his hand again. "Still want to be a part of this family?"

He smiled again. "Sweetheart, it's the only thing I want."

⮞ ⮜

"Yer man pickin' you up tonight?" Stanley shut off the lights to the diner before joining me at the front door.

"No, he's at home with Phoebe," I said.

Stanley snorted. "Never thought I'd see the day where Matt Andrews spent his Saturday night at home babysittin' a kid."

"People change." My voice was defensive, and Stanley regarded me silently for a moment.

"Yeah," he finally said. "I guess they do. Ya need a ride?"

I gave the gruff cook a surprised look. "Um, no, my car is fixed now. But, thanks."

"Sure. Set the alarm."

I set the alarm and we walked out of the diner. Stanley locked it and turned around, grunting in surprise. I turned and my stomach twisted when I saw Evan leaning against his rental car. I hadn't seen him since Wednesday night, and I hadn't heard from him either. I'd tried calling him the next day, but he'd ignored my calls and my texts. His lawyer wasn't returning Maggie's calls either.

I'd almost hoped that he'd given up, but I should have known better. Evan was stubborn. Even worse, he was pissed off. He put on a good show for people, but I knew the real him. Knew how vindictive and mean spirited he really was.

"What do you want, Evan?" I said.

"We need to talk."

"It's late and I'm tired. I've given you plenty of chances to talk since Thursday morning."

He glared at me. "I've been busy. My life doesn't revolve around you."

"Nor does mine revolve around you," I said. "You can't just keep showing up at my work place whenever you want to have a discussion."

"What? Are you mad because your dickhead boyfriend isn't here to defend you?"

"Watch your mouth, you little punk," Stanley growled at him. "You might think you're a big shot now with your expensive clothes and your three-hundred-dollar haircut, but I remember when you were a snot-nosed little kid. Keep talkin' to her that way, and I'll beat the shit out of you."

Stanley cracked his knuckles, and I choked back my nervous laughter as Evan backed up a couple of steps. Evan was four inches taller and outweighed the diner cook by at least thirty pounds, but he knew about Stanley's past as a championship boxer, just like I did.

"I need to talk to you for a few minutes," Evan said to me.

"Fine," I said. "Talk."

"Do you mind?" Evan stared at Stanley. "This is a private conversation."

"You want me to stick around, Nat?" Stanley cracked his knuckles again.

I impulsively stood on my tiptoes and kissed Stanley's grizzled cheek. "Nah, I'm good. Thank you, though."

Stanley eyed Evan again. "I'm gonna go sit in my car and I ain't leavin' until I see you get in your car and go."

"Whatever," Evan said.

Stanley nodded to me and walked to his car. When he slammed the door shut, Evan said, "Do you have the whole town fooled into thinking you're this fragile little doll?

"What do you want, Evan?" I said wearily. "You have five minutes and then I'm getting in my car and going home."

"I want you to break it off with Matt Andrews. Immediately."

I snorted laughter. "Do you seriously think you have the right to tell me who I can and cannot date? Get over yourself, Evan."

"I do when it affects my daughter."

"Matt is amazing with Phoebe," I said. "There isn't an issue."

"Bullshit. I've been here four days, Natalia, and the whole goddamn town is talking about you and Matt Andrews. You know why? Because he's the biggest man slut in town. According to my sources, he's banged three quarters of the women in this town. And now you're living with him and exposing our child to who the fuck knows what."

"Matt's past is exactly that," I said. "His past. People change, Evan."

"No, they don't," Evan said. "You think because you're spreading your legs for Matt right now, that he won't tire of you and go looking for something else? He will. Unless you do the same thing you did to me and try and trap him with a goddamn baby."

My mouth dropped open and I gave Evan a look

of disbelief. "The condom broke, you idiot. You were there when it happened, and if you had let me take the fucking pill like I wanted to, I wouldn't have gotten pregnant. But you know what? I'm glad I wasn't, because Phoebe is the best thing that's *ever* happened to me. You have no idea how amazing she is, how funny and sweet and smart she is because you don't care about her. You never have."

"That's bullshit. I've always -"

"No," I snapped, "don't you dare try and twist this reality. The truth is you had zero interest in Phoebe and that hasn't changed. You can go on and on about how you want to spend time with your daughter, but we both know this is nothing more than you being petty and vindictive. You're using Phoebe to punish me."

"You have no idea what you're talking about," Evan said. "If you don't break it off with Matt, I'll go for full custody, Natalia. Do not push me on this. I will not have that man around my daughter. He's a bad influence."

I laughed bitterly before yanking my car keys out of my purse. "You're just pissed because I dared to replace the great Evan Fealan with someone better."

"Better? He's a fucking chess nerd!" Evan snapped.

"And you're a washed up high-school quarterback," I said. "You're nothing. Your job doesn't matter, your money doesn't matter, your former glory days as a stupid high-school quarterback do not matter. *You* don't matter. Matt saves lives, Evan. He makes a difference in this world and he makes it a better place. You?" I gave him a look of scorn. "You just stink it up like rotting garbage."

"You bitch," Evan breathed.

"That's right, I am. You're warning me not to push you, but, Evan?" I took a few steps forward, stared into his angry face, and said in a quiet but deliberate voice, "You do *not* want to push me. Phoebe and Matt are the only things that matter to me and if you try and take either of them away from me, I'll destroy you."

"Now you're threatening me?" Evan said in disbelief. "This isn't going to help you when I take you to court for full custody."

I stepped back and gave him a soft smile. "Me? Threaten you? Why, who would believe that sweet little me would ever threaten anyone? Good bye, Evan."

"I have the right to see Phoebe," Evan snarled. "You can't keep her away from me."

I didn't respond, instead walking to my car and sliding behind the wheel. I waved at Stanley who gave me a nod, and I started my car, clicking my seat belt into place. I was weirdly calm, my hands weren't even trembling, and while it felt like there was a stone sitting in my belly, I could live with that.

Evan had already climbed into his car and driven away, and I took a deep breath before waving again at Stanley and driving home to Matt and Phoebe.

Chapter Twelve

Matt

"Hey," I put my arms around Nat's waist and nuzzled her neck, "the munchkin is asleep."

She leaned against me, her spine against my chest and her ass snug against my dick. "Thanks for reading her a story."

"You're welcome. Will you tell me what's wrong?"

Her body stiffened a little bit. "Nothing's wrong."

I kissed her temple. "We need to be honest with each other, sweetheart. I mean, I don't know jackshit about being in a relationship, but I know honesty is important."

She stared out the kitchen window into the darkness. "Evan was waiting for me at the diner when I finished work."

"Son of a bitch," I said, my arms tightening around her waist. "Did he do anything? Did he hurt you?"

"No, of course not," she said. "Evan is a shithead but he's not physically abusive or anything. Besides, Cook Stanley threatened to kick his ass if he did anything to me."

She turned and grinned at me. "Did you know that Stanley used to be a boxer?"

"What did he want?" I said.

She glanced away from me. "The usual bullshit. Don't worry about it, Mattie. I handled it."

I took her chin and tipped her face back to me. "Honesty, sweetheart, remember?"

"Gah. Fine, but don't freak out all right? Promise me you won't freak out, because I don't care what he said and I'm not worried."

"What did he say?" Bile was rising in my stomach like a flash flood.

"Some bullshit about how he thinks you're not good enough for us because of your past. He's just being a dickhead."

"Tell me exactly what he said"

"Mattie -"

"Tell me, Nat."

"He said that if I didn't break up with you, he would go for full custody of Phoebe. He thinks because of your, um, past, that you're a bad influence on Phoebe."

Stunned, I let go of her and took a couple steps back. Nat followed me, wrapping her arms around my waist and giving me an urgent look. "Matt, it's no big deal, okay? I basically told him to eff off and that I wasn't breaking up with you."

"No big deal?" The flood of bitter bile was in

the back of my throat now and I swallowed it down. "You could lose Phoebe because of me, and that's no big deal?"

"That isn't going to happen, honey," Nat said. "I talked to Maggie on the drive home and she said not to worry. That even if Evan takes this to court, she'll have tons of people she can ask to testify about your character."

"My character," I said through numb lips. "You know as well as I do what the people in this town think of me. Maggie's only been here for a couple of months, she doesn't have a goddamn idea what people say or think about me. But you do."

I pushed away from her and strode jerkily back and forth in the kitchen, tugging my hands restlessly through my hair. "If this goes to court, Evan's lawyer will have a dozen people on the stand giving the judge every goddamn detail of my whoring around for the last decade."

"So, we'll find fifty people to talk about how amazing you are. Mattie, you can't worry about this. You're not just you're past, okay? You're incredible and sweet, and I love you and so does Phoebe. Hell, if worst comes to worst, we'll have Phoebe talk to the judge. It's clear how much she loves you and how good you are for her. For God's sake, she calls you daddy and she's known you for less than a month."

I barely heard her. The moment she'd mentioned Phoebe talking to the judge, a numbness had stolen over me. "She's only a baby," I said. "I can't – I won't – let you use her to convince some judge that I'm a good guy. It's not her fault that

I'm not."

"Mattie, stop it!" Nat ran forward and clamped her hands around my face. "Listen to me. You are a good man and we love you. I am not afraid of what Evan may or may not do. All that matters to me is that you and me and Phoebe are together."

"Staying with me will make you lose Phoebe," I said. "You can't be willing to risk that."

"I am," she said calmly. "I am because I love you as much as I love Phoebe and I know," she gave me face a little shake, "it won't happen."

I pulled away from her. "You don't know that. I think – I think we should stop seeing each other."

"What?" Nat's face paled. "No, absolutely not."

"Nat, please," I said. "We need to think about what's best for Phoebe."

"What's best for Phoebe, is having you in our lives," she said. "I'm not going to let Evan tell me how to live my life, honey. I love you and I want to be with you."

"I love you too," I said, "but Phoebe is all that matters. I won't be the one who's responsible for you losing your daughter. If that happens, you'll – you'll hate me forever."

"It's not going to happen," she said.

"It might." My voice was bleak. "I'm gonna go."

"Go? Go where? This is your house, Mattie," Nat said.

"I'll find a place to stay. You and Phoebe stay here. Do not go back to that shit trailer, Natalia."

"Matt," she followed me down the hallway to

the bedroom, "you're acting crazy. Stop and take some deep breaths, okay? We're not breaking up over this. I'm not worried about -"

"I am," I said. "I won't be the guy who makes you lose your daughter. I won't Natalia. I can't even take that chance. I refuse to make you choose between me and Phoebe."

"Oh my God." She gave me a frustrated look. "Me deciding not to let Evan bully me into doing what he wants has nothing to do with you, Matt."

"It has *everything* to do with me," I snapped as I shoved some clothes and toiletries into my gym bag. "Please, Nat... I can't do this. I'm gonna leave. You can tell Evan that it's over between us."

"No," she said. "I won't."

"Yes." I glared at her and she shook her head stubbornly.

"No. Leave if you want, Matt. You're an adult and I can't stop you, but Phoebe and I aren't going anywhere." She grabbed my hand when I tried to walk past her out of the bedroom. "You and me and Phoebe makes three."

"Not anymore," I said. "I'm sorry, Nat."

I pulled my hand free and walked away.

రావ్ ఆర్

"You're a jackass, dude. I love you but you might as well have jackass tattooed right onto your forehead at this point."

"Jonah!" Claire had walked into the living room and she gave him a scolding look. "What the hell, man? That's not being a best friend."

She squeezed my shoulder and I gave her a faint smile. "Thank you, Claire. And thanks for letting me crash here last night."

"You're welcome, Mattie. You know you're welcome to stay with us for as long as you need."

"Nope, you're not," Jonah said. "You can stay here one more night and then you're going back to Natalia, you jackass."

"Jonah," Claire gave him a threatening look, "stop it."

"It's called tough love, Claire," Jonah said. He leaned forward and stared at me. "I've coddled him long enough, now it's time for the real shit."

"He's been here for like twelve hours," Claire said, "I think you can coddle him a little longer. His heart is broken."

"Yeah, because he's being an idiot. Listen, when I fucked things up with you, Matt came to this very house and told me to get my shit together. Didn't you?"

"Yeah," I said.

"So, get your shit together. You love Natalia and she loves you. That's all that matters."

"It isn't," I said. "Christ, Jonah, have you listened to anything I told you? She could lose Phoebe because of me. I won't let that happen."

"Natalia loves you and is willing to take that risk."

"I'm not," I said.

I stared moodily at the floor as Claire squeezed my shoulder again before saying, "Dinner will be ready in about twenty minutes."

"Thank you, but I'm not hungry."

"You haven't eaten all day, Mattie," she chastised gently. "You need to eat."

The doorbell rang and she kissed the top of my head. "Starving yourself isn't going to help."

She walked out of the room and Jonah gave me a grave look. "You need to be with Natalia, Mattie."

"I can't," I said hoarsely.

"You can." Jonah stood. "Also, don't hate me."

"Hate you? Why would I…"

My voice died out as Natalia walked into the living room. She smiled at Jonah and kissed his cheek. "Thanks, Jonah."

"You bet. Be sweet to my boy, Nat."

"I will." She waited until Jonah left before smiling at me. "Hey."

"How did you know I was here?" I said.

She hesitated. "I texted Mia who told me where you were and gave me Jonah's number. I texted him and asked if I could drop by and he said yes."

I grunted angrily. "Some friends they are."

Nat's phone dinged and she gave me an apologetic look before reading the screen. A wide grin crossed her face and she texted off a reply before sitting down on the couch beside me. "Don't be angry with them. They love you and are worried about you."

I didn't reply and she gave me a searching look. "You look tired, honey."

"I didn't sleep very much last night."

"Me either. I missed you. Phoebe misses you too. She asked for you as soon as she woke up."

"Stop it," I said. "Please, Nat, you're only making this break-up harder."

"You call it break-up, I call it you having a sleepover at your friend's house."

Despite my misery, my lips curled up in a smile. Nat gave me her sweet smile. "It's time for you to come home, honey."

"I can't," I said.

"You can." Her voice was calm, her look was loving. "We need you, Mattie."

"Evan isn't going to give up on this," I said. "If he knows that we're still together, he'll keep pushing and pushing until -"

"Actually," another grin crossed Nat's face when her phone dinged a second time, "I'm pretty sure Evan has changed his mind about getting custody of Phoebe. Come with me."

"Where are we going?" I took her hand when she offered it, relishing even that small contact.

"Outside for a minute." She snagged my coat from the hook in the hallway and handed it to me and I shoved my feet into boots. I followed her out onto the porch as a car pulled into Jonah's driveway.

"Is that Evan's rental car?"

"Yep," she said. "He texted me to find out where I was. I sent him Jonah's address."

"What? Why? He doesn't..." I squinted into the back seat. "Oh my God, is Phoebe with him?"

"She is." I couldn't understand why Natalia had a triumphant smile on her face. "I called Evan this morning and told him I thought it would be a good idea for him and Phoebe to spend some time alone together. He picked her up a couple of hours ago."

I watched in disbelief as Evan climbed out of

the car. He wasn't wearing a jacket and his designer t-shirt had a giant orange stain across the front. The crotch of his jeans was soaking wet and he pulled at them before yanking open the back door. He unbuckled Phoebe and pulled her out of the car, setting her on her feet.

"Mama!" Phoebe hollered. She took off in a dead run toward us and a surge of love so strong it took my breath away, went through me when she grinned at me.

"Hi, Mattie Daddy!"

She climbed the stairs, tripping on the top one, and I snagged her under the armpits before she could land on her face. I picked her up and held her tight. It'd been less than a day since I'd seen her, but I had missed her terribly.

"Hi, hi, hi!" Phoebe hollered at me. She had a ring of orange around her mouth and her small body was vibrating like a live wire. "Guess what, Mattie Daddy? Guess what?"

"What's that?" I said.

"I went to Chuckie Cheese's with Evan and I played a game and then I went in the ball pit, and then I had orange pop and psghetti, and then I dropped my drink in Evan's lap and then I threw up all my psghetti on him!"

She threw her head back and laughed hysterically before kicking her feet. "Put me down, put me down, put me down!"

I set her on her feet, watching in disbelief as she raced back and forth along Jonah's front porch. Phoebe had a lot of energy, but I'd never seen her so hyper and out of control. I glanced at Natalia who gave me a smug smile as Phoebe grabbed her hands.

"Swing me, Mama!" She screamed.

Natalia picked her up and swung her briefly before setting her back on her feet. Phoebe ran down the stairs past Evan who had wrestled her car seat out of the back seat and was marching grimly toward us.

"Evan! Let's make snow angels!" Phoebe screamed at him. She fell on her back into the snow in Jonah's front yard, waving her arms and legs back and forth in a frenetic motion. "Evan, Evan, Evan! Come make snow angels with me!"

"No," he barked before dropping the car seat at the foot of the stairs.

"Hey, Evan," Natalia said sweetly. "How did it go?"

"That – that *child* is out of control," Evan said. "She never stopped talking, she insisted I take her to that abomination of a restaurant and even after I told her to slow down eating her supper, she refused to listen."

He pointed to his wet crotch and his stained shirt. "She threw her drink on my lap on purpose."

"I doubt that," Natalia said. "She's only three, Evan. She gets a little clumsy sometimes."

"Snow angel, snow angel, snow angel!" Phoebe half sang, half screamed behind us. "I'm a snow angel, Mattie Daddy!"

"She threw up on me, Natalia!" Evan's face drew down in a moue of disgust. "She threw up on me and then she laughed about it. And she kept passing gas in the car, I had to roll down the windows the smell was so bad. You need to have her seen by a doctor."

"I'll take that under advisement," Natalia said. "Hey, you're here until Friday, right? Now that Phoebe is so comfortable with you, can you take her on Monday? Her daycare had an emergency and has to close for the day, and I have to work, so… it would be great if you could watch her. It'll give you a chance to really get to know your daughter."

Evan's face turned red and he shook his head. "No. I-I'm busy."

He glanced behind him at Phoebe who waved at him. "Evan! Snow angel!!"

"You'll have to find someone else to watch her," Evan said.

"Oh, sure, I totally understand. Mattie, you can watch her, right?" Nat said.

"Yes," I replied.

"Perfect. Evan, I'll keep my week free, you let me know what days you can take Phoebe and we'll go from there, okay?" Nat took my hand and squeezed it tight. "Oh, but I'm definitely going to need you to take her Thursday night. Matt and I have a double date with Jonah and Claire."

"I can't, I mean…"

"Pheebs, sweetpea? Do you want to hang out with Evan again on Thursday night?" Nat called.

"Yeah!" Phoebe shouted. "I hang out with Evan, Mama!"

Evan's face went from red to green and he backed toward his car. "I'll, um, be in touch about Thursday."

"Great! Talk to you soon," Nat said. "Pheebs,

come up here, please."

Phoebe stood and shook the snow from her body before barreling up the steps toward us. "Mattie Daddy, catch me!" She hollered before launching herself at me.

I caught her and she giggled hysterically before wiggling free and grabbing my hands. She climbed up my legs with her feet, leaning back and singing some kid's song I didn't know, as Evan got into his car. Nat waved at him as he drove away and then burst into laughter.

"Nat? What is happening?" I said as Phoebe hung off my hands and kicked her legs back and forth. "Why is Phoebe so... hyper?"

She grinned at me. "Before I sent her out with Evan, I may have given her some cookies, and then some ice cream, and then some chocolate, oh and a half dozen marshmallows, and then let her watch *Peppa Pig* instead of having an afternoon nap."

"I had cookies and ice cream, and then Evan gave me candy too," Phoebe said. "It was so good, Mattie Daddy."

I gaped at Natalia. "You hopped her up on sugar and no sleep and then sent her to Evan?"

"Sure did," Natalia said. "He needs to know how to handle Phoebe when she's hyper and sleep deprived. I was doing him a favour."

A grin broke out on my face, and Natalia cupped my face before standing on her tiptoes and kissing my mouth. "C'mon, handsome, let's go home."

৵ ৶

We crept out of Phoebe's room and I followed

Natalia down the hallway to our bedroom. It had taken four stories and three songs before Phoebe had finally fallen asleep. I collapsed on the bed as Natalia grabbed her cell phone from the nightstand.

"Holy shit," I said. "Your idea was brilliant, don't get me wrong, but I never want to try and put an over-tired, sugar-laden Phoebe to bed ever again."

She laughed and sat down beside me, resting her hand on my thigh. "Yeah, that was an epic sugar rush for the kid. But worth it."

She leaned over and kissed my forehead as I said, "Do you really think it'll scare Evan off from asking for custody? I mean, yeah, Phoebe was kind of hyper but -"

"It already has," she said.

"What?"

She gave me a gleeful look. "I just checked my texts. I had one from Maggie telling me that Evan's lawyer contacted her and he's withdrawing his petition for even partial custody. Apparently, Evan has had a change of heart about taking Phoebe away from her mother for such an extended period every month. I'm retaining sole custody of Phoebe and Evan will still pay monthly child support. He can have visitation as long as he provides prior notification that he'd like to see her, and he travels here."

"Holy shit," I said. "It worked. Your plan worked."

"Of course it did," she said. "I'm not just a pretty face, you know."

She leaned over me, her blonde hair falling like

a curtain around our faces. "What do you say we do a little celebrating?"

She trailed her fingers over my abdomen, and I cupped her face and pressed my mouth against hers. "I think that's a fine idea."

"Good. Get naked, Mr. Andrews."

I pressed a kiss against her mouth. "I love you, Natalia."

She smiled and traced my jaw with her fingers. "You and me and Phoebe makes three."

About the Author

Ramona Gray is a Canadian romance author. She currently lives in Alberta with her awesome husband and her mutant Chihuahua. She's addicted to home improvement shows, good coffee, and reading and writing about the steamier moments in life.

If you would like more information about Ramona, please visit her at:

www.ramonagray.ca

Books by Ramona Gray

Individual Books

The Escort
Saving Jax
The Assistant
One Night
Sharing Del

Other World Series

The Vampire's Kiss (Book One)
The Vampire's Love (Book Two)
The Shifter's Mate (Book Three)
Rescued By The Wolf (Book Four)
Claiming Quinn (Book Five)
Choosing Rose (Book Six)
Elena Unbound (Book Seven)

Undeniable Series

Undeniably His
Undeniably Hers
Undeniably Theirs

The Working Men Series

Made in the USA
Columbia, SC
19 January 2021

31242347R00254